The Shoemaker's Daughter

A NOVEL

HELEN MARTIN BLOCK

ISBN: 978-1-4834-1961-9 (sc)
ISBN: 978-1-4834-1960-2 (e)

Cover Design: Artist Miggs Burroughs
WWII Map: United States Army History Museum at West Point
Rose Handle Spoon Courtesy of Helen Martin Block
Leather Boot: Annette Gendler Photograph

Lulu Publishing Services rev. date: 08/11/2015

"Those who have a 'why' to live, can bear with almost any 'how'."

— Viktor E. Frankl, Man's Search for Meaning

DEDICATION

For my parents, Aaron and Gertrude Martin, survivors of the Second World War who rebuilt their lives, imparted optimism and strength, and openly shared their stories. They never forgot what being together meant during the darkest times.

ACKNOWLEDGEMENTS

Inspired and helped by many extraordinary people, I only mention a few. During the research phase, my Aunt Halina Hershkowitz, revealed details from her circumstances as a child survivor. Her insights helped to enliven my characters and settings. Suzanne Hoover, Professor from Sarah Lawrence has been my guide to the craft of writing. Jessica Bram, creator of the Westport Writers Workshop has helped me grow as a novelist. There I developed enduring friendships with colleagues, among them Lucy Hedrick, Penny Pearlman, Sally Luce, Teresa Peck, Laurie Stone, Joan Curran, and Susan Mleczko. It was a privilege to work with two fine authors, Julia Glass and Alice Mattison, at the Fine Arts Work Center in Provincetown. Sidney Kramer, who made his mark in the publishing industry, served as my agent and motivated me to find a publishing path. I am grateful to him for believing in this book. And to my dear husband Jeff – always encouraging, raising the bar and suggesting edits, often at his own peril yet often right. I thank and love you. To my son Gabriel, a willing listener and discerning reader, you are my gift.

THE SHOEMAKER'S DAUGHTER

May 1919 after two centuries of being partitioned, Poland was reunified as part of the Treaty of Versailles. In June of that year, along with the United States of America, Great Britain, Italy and Japan, Poland signed the Minority Treaty. This was the first international effort to establish and enforce minority rights. It assured the protection of all inhabitants' life and liberty without distinction of birth, nationality, language, race or religion.

In 1934, after signing the German-Polish Non-Aggression Pact, Poland agreed not to engage in anti-Nazi rhetoric. Shortly thereafter Germany's Chancellor Von Hindenburg died leaving Hitler as the sole leader. The advancement of German propaganda and the power of the Third Reich seeped its demonic hatred into the consciousness of European life. Nuremberg Laws instituted in Germany made it a capital offense to have intimate relations with Jews. Poland revoked the Minority Treaty it had signed in Paris and began repealing certain citizens' rights.

In the winter of 1935 the looming economic and social crisis gripping Europe intensified. Jozef Pilsudski was still the leader of Poland. He had been revered but controversial as a talented military man who brought Poland victories, treaties and status among their neighboring nations. His vision for building a successful, vibrant economic and military presence was pluralistic. Pilsudski called for the use of all the resources, especially its people, including the Jews. Within the year, Edward Smigly-Rydz succeeded him and embraced a different view. In enlightened places such as universities, he ordered Jews to be benched and segregated. Those who labored in Polish factories were dismissed. Then in 1936 the Primate of Poland, August Hlond, announced an official policy calling on all Poles to boycott Jews in business. As Poland's livelihood shrank, poverty and violence grew, and Hitler's aggression spelled certain war.

By 1939 the German Army was an advanced and powerful military machine.

Poland was invaded by Germany on September 1,1939. This surprise attack began the Second World War. The Polish army preparations were insufficient, making them incapable of dealing with the tactics of the German blitzkrieg. Poland had hoped their allies, England and France, would send immediate assistance but that never materialized.

This story begins in Nowy Targ, a small town in Poland's strategic Southern region located on Germany's eastern border. The region, rich in natural resources was ripe for lebensraum, the colonization of living space for the Germans and eventual control of all Poland. The Nazis began the enslavement of the Poles and many ethnic groups and planned the systematic annihilation of the Jews.

As the conflagration unfolds, we meet Aron Matuszyński, a Polish soldier, the gifted shoemaker by trade, whose fate would soon make him a prisoner of war. Imprisoned by the German Army, Aron must find a way to survive and save the woman he adores, the indomitable Gitel.

POLAND, 1939
CAMPAIGN IN POLAND, 1939

CONTENTS

CHAPTER ONE

1939 September

An armored panzer straddled a bank of the Dunajec River its long gun fixed on the smoldering field where he lay. Hollow soundlessness broken by muffled German commands crackled from a radio transmitter. Acrid smoke stung his nose and throat, and the few words he could decipher, staccato barks, sickened him with fear that he would be discovered not just as a Pole.

His face blackened by artillery explosives, Aron Matuszyński pressed against the wall of the trench and swept his eyes across an undulating plain. Black boots prodded bodies scattered like bloodied boulders shrouded in opaque dawn light. He slid back into the trench, a heaving chest and tortured moans what was left of his comrades-in-arms. To his relief he was intact. A patrol was nearing. *Tot* echoed across the field. He could tell the Germans were accounting for their dead. He braced against the crumbling wall working to control panic. He had to find a way to hide in his own body.

A German soldier thrust his bayonet at Aron. *"Gewehr,"* he said stabbing air at the rifles in the trench. This language, so close to Aron's, ignited every nerve. He fought against shifting his eyes at the rifle, alerting the enemy eyes piercing his own. Aron crawled over the bodies of men mired in battle swill and wrenched rifles from stiffening fingers. He pitched them over the trench wall and pulled out. The German soldier

1

kicked away the weapons and unsnapped his pistol from its holster. But he swerved from Aron. He cocked his head and aimed at the wounded Pole pleading from the trench. A sharp crack silenced him. Steel helmet shading the German's placid face, he shoved Aron into the line of passing prisoners of war.

The vision of the soldier's shattered skull, the cries of a man for whom he did nothing beat in counterpoint to triumphant German faces. Aron knew more than ever, he had to keep his wits and blend in among the captured. He had shared meager rations with the Poles of his company. They were united against the enemy. But as much as he had wanted to be accepted as a good soldier, he knew Jews were not considered true Poles. His Polish name could help keep his identity secret and he prayed that no one would recognize him other than as *Adam Matuszyński*, a true Pole.

During the cool September night before, the golden harvest wheat fields tranquil, Stuka bombers screamed over the foothills of Poland's towering Tatra Mountains, terrifying, leveling, maiming, and killing. In a surprise attack, German tanks had rumbled over the terrain clashing with the infantry that the Polish Army Krakow diverted from Katowice industrial zone. Skilled Polish gunners with antitank rifles stood up against the German offensive, inflicting numerous casualties. But the Poles' horse-drawn howitzers and compact tankettes were no match for the Germans' blitzkrieg apparatus attacking from both air and ground.

Bombs had ignited thatch-roofed houses, lighting the skies with fire spikes and turning night into hellish day. With no ammunition left, Aron sank into the hastily dug trench amid dying men. Quiet defeat fell over the battlefield and what remained of ravaged life. By dawn the German panzer corps took ownership of Nowy Targ, a town set by the banks of the Dunajec River where days before men had fished and lovers had strolled on shimmery moonlit nights.

Now Aron watched trucks unload an ant-like infiltration of Germans to fill the gaps of security left vulnerable by their heavy losses. A Pole he did not recognize tried to get his attention. Aron put a finger to his lips and nodded toward the fresh battalion swooping in. With rounds of shots, the Germans forced them into double lines, and loaded confiscated weapons into waiting trucks. Aron felt naked stripped of his rifle, the rucksack and the boots he had made his last possessions.

They marched due west on the scorched grassy plain, away from the river and its people, southwest Poland left defenseless. In the distance, scores of horses lay, rigor mortis transforming them into carousel horses discarded in a carnival of carnage. The same Pole he had not recognized fell in next to him. "Did you feel the ground move under you, too? A day ago, in the afternoon, I felt something. Now I see," the Pole said, struck by the terrible scene before them.

Aron was reluctant. The less he said, the better, but refusing to speak would appear suspicious. Pity for the wasted animals deepened his voice. "I felt the thunder under my feet."

"Do they still wear saddles? See riders? I can't make it out. Our cavalry has the biggest, strongest horses." The Pole marched straining to see.

Aron cupped a hand over eyes keen enough to qualify him as a sharp shooter for his company. "Yes, they wear saddles. No one's gotten to them yet. Maybe the riders were from the Krakowska Cavalry Brigade."

"The best in the world our cavalry," the Pole said, appraising the man in the sturdy boots.

The best cavalry Aron thought. But what could the bravest, most skilled horsemen in the world do against an enemy of iron? It occurred to him that some of the horses might have been bought from Nobleman Count Janad Dzianat, owner of the land where Gitel was raised. The Count bred horses and sold many to the cavalry. Aron's sweetheart, Gitel, had been a young girl when he had noticed her. She had become a woman of earthy beauty whose quick mind and energy drew him like a hummingbird to ruby nectar, his passion for her inseparable from survival. No matter she had refused his proposal months before, he knew how she felt. The heat and the attraction were mutual. He would pursue her, if he could find a way back. *I hope my Gitel is safe pounded through him as every reluctant step moved him further away.*

Driven mercilessly by the Germans, they marched all day, all night and into the next day. An indigo horizon loomed without end when they stopped along the Czech/German border. Filthy and hungry, his canteen empty, Aron dropped to the ground. Past midnight, the prisoners waited as Ukrainian captives distributed coarse dark bread.

"I am Ivan Grumlecki," whispered the soldier who had attached himself to Aron.

"Adam Matuszyński," Aron whispered back, his eyes on bayonets enforcing order in the dense night air.

"Ukrainians help them. That was no Polish they were talking." The Pole eyed the chosen ones from the Ukraine, Poland's long time enemy, with venom. "Where do you think the bastards are taking us?"

Several Germans neared, rifles fixed on the men hauling the sacks. Aron bent his head toward the Pole, almost as wary of the Ukrainians as he was of the Germans. "Grumlecki, you can be sure, no place good."

"My captain said there are rules for prisoners of war."

"Quiet down till they pass," Aron said. All this talk made him nervous, but if the Pole wanted to befriend him, it could provide cover. "They have plans."

The Ukrainians hauling the bread stopped. There were German shouts and warnings. Some prisoners pushed forward, hunger converting them into beasts ready to fight over tossed bread. "*Hund*," the Germans spat. Yet Aron understood his people were far beneath the respect Nazis had for dogs.

"What kind of plans?" Grumlecki persisted, tearing into the dry crust he grabbed as boots thudded by.

"The German devils always have plans. They signed a pact with our good friends, the Soviet Russians."

"Friends! What pact? I didn't hear about that." Grumlecki stuffed the rest of the coarse bread in his mouth, his eyes all but invisible, the stars hidden by foreboding clouds.

"They divided Poland between them. Both should go to hell." Aron shoved the last of his bread in the rucksack.

"Damn them. Poland is finally in one piece since the end of the last war. How do *you* know?" He picked crumbs from stubble on his cheeks and licked his fingers.

"I listened to my lieutenant." Aron tried not to reveal more. He had already said too much.

Suspicion tinged the Pole's voice. "Why are you around a lieutenant? You're plain infantry."

"He told me to check the ammunition. We were moving as reinforcement and got stuck at the river, like you."

The Polish soldier pushed closer. "What do you know about ammunition?"

Pole or not, he was asking too many questions. "I'm a sharp shooter," Aron said pursing his lips.

Grumlecki was silent for a moment. "Where are you from? Who are your people? Maybe I've heard about you."

Aron had to get the Pole off track, bring the conversation back to the politics. He was absorbed in politics. It was as natural as breathing. Aggravating as it was, he had always been intrigued, hovering around a radio where it was available, reading newspapers, making deductions that were not so obvious to others. His lieutenant *had* told him about the Nazi/Soviet Non-aggression pact signed weeks before Germany attacked Poland. Sworn enemies, they had promised not to attack one another and that Poland would be divided between them. Stalin agreed to supply Hitler with food and raw materials and Hitler, in return, would send the Soviets the best war machinery in the world. Fascists and Communists; evil partners Aron feared. It did not bode well for his people or Poland. He had argued with his oldest brother Meir, so sure of himself, his place in the world, a knack for business. With politics Aron was on equal footing, even better. But Meir had demeaned him. 'Shoemaker' he called him as if it wasn't enough Aron berated himself. The only shoemaker in the family. His brother ripped away his defenses the way Aron tore worn soles from broken shoes. He threw off the rising anger; how could he be thinking this now, here he admonished himself, dangers his family faced intensifying his own.

5

The Pole seemed to be studying him and Aron was forced to resume. "Those sons of bitches Ruskies stabbed us in the back again."

"Who trusts the Ruskies. I just want to go back to my wife. You know what I'm going to tell you?" the Pole said, raising his voice. His chin pointed at the ominous black overhead.

The prisoners, squeezed together in tight formation, shifted their hungry eyes to an impenetrable sky. The whine of airplanes sent up a joyous chorus from the Germans. A soldier pointed to the western sky and shouted through the deep- throated droning. His sparse words did not elude Aron. He understood enough of the dreaded German. Death was coming to them all, the stupid low Slavs. Soon.

Grumlecki spoke louder, compensating for the rolling thunder of the bombers fading eastward. "Matuszyński, if it wasn't for the God damn *Żyd,* we wouldn't be in this war."

Aron's jaw slackened. Had he misheard or had the Pole spewed that taunt? *Żyd.* A jab, a thrust to his heart, a sensation he had felt too many times, the unwelcome Jew, the outsider. The other. He breathed out the words, "Quiet down," trying to mask his fear.

"I hate the bastard Germans," the soldier seethed raising a fist, "but they know what to do with them. My priest says Jews make our troubles. Buy from your brothers he says. Poland for the Polish."

Aron turned away, hair raised on his arms. "Forget the politics. Yes, think about your good wife." *No matter where they take me, if the Pole discovers what I am I'll be finished. I have to separate myself if I get the chance.* He closed his eyes. Gitel's image filled him with longing, tenderness and a fierce desire to protect her no matter how hurtful their last time together had been. Aron was smitten with Gitel when she was a thirteen-year-old maiden and he a fifteen-year-old apprentice. They were little more than children and the memory of that first moment lessened his thirst and warmed him against the soaking rain.

* * * * *

As the sun rose on a mild March morning in 1927, Aron set out from the journeyman Lech's workshop ten hard kilometers from his hometown, Ksiaz Wielki. Lech, tight fisted with time and money had given Aron the day off as a reward. Aron had saved Lech from an upbraiding by a prosperous merchant. He took blame for unsatisfactory work on a pair of the man's shoes, and for the first time in the two years that he had lived and worked in Lech's inhospitable quarters Aron had received payment. Allowed to go home each Friday, returning Sunday afternoon to resume his toils, Aron felt fortunate. This would be a surprise for his family and by chance he would be there to celebrate a favorite festival, Purim.

An early spring dressed the trees and children began shedding thick clothing. Now less than a kilometer to go, his mind whirled with the joys of seeing his parents, his brothers and sister. He was curious about the pigeons living in the wood and mesh wire coop he had made. After spending time with his family, he filled his pockets with breadcrumbs, climbed the slatted attic steps and listened to them coo. Aron believed at least the smarter of the eight pigeons, one pair pure white, the others marbled brown and blue-grey would recognize the throaty throop throop he made when he held out his palm. His older brother Yankel was doing a good enough job collecting the droppings. The musty odor from a burlap sack under an eve signaled to Aron that Yankel would soon be trading the pigeon droppings to farmers for bits of their crop yield.

Late afternoon, the sun hung low on the grey church spire at the head of the market square. Farmers were packing the winter turnips, beans, potatoes and cabbage, foods remaining from the previous year's growing season, and would return the following Thursday, the customary market day. The revelers ready to celebrate replaced the wagons and some of the Poles stayed to watch. Children dressed in costumes made by a tailor father, a seamstress mother, an aunt or sister who was skilled with bits of colorful fabric filled the square. Two fiddlers, one dressed as Queen Esther and the other as villain Haman cavorted amongst the children. The musicians began to play and parents appeared wearing masks. They retold the story of how Queen Esther, a Jewess married to the King of Persia, was able to foil the grand vizier Haman's plans to purge the kingdom of her people.

Aron looked forward to this celebration. He marveled at the bravery of beautiful Queen Esther and he had special affection for Mordechai, the clever cousin of the Queen, who refused to bow down to the evil plotter, Haman. Aron was still too young to drink the plum brandy and slivovitz intoxicating the men. This was the one holiday that sanctioned drunkenness and he watched as the men became tipsy, their laughter louder. The square grew darker, the March night colder, and the gas street lanterns lit for this special occasion created the illusion of heat. But these musings in Aron's head abruptly stopped when he spotted a ring of girls spinning round and round in the middle of the square.

One girl danced care free, her body swaying to the rhythms of the fiddlers, her hands at her hips. Her steps followed the beat of the music with precision and energy and her face glistened in the glow of lamplight. She wore a hat fashioned into a crown and a cape defining what he imagined were shapely shoulders. Aron felt intoxicated. But he had not had one drop of the spirits. And so what was this? It was not as if he hadn't noticed girls or that he felt nothing when he saw a pretty one or one that had lovely eyes or a pleasant demeanor. He saw them glance at him as well. Why had he never noticed her before?

The musicians stopped playing. The young people were led to the synagogue at the end of the main street to shelter them from the chill. Tables were laid with triangular cookies and glasses of steaming tea. There was an assortment of cheeses, another traditional food to be eaten during the Purim festival. Aron joined his brother and seated himself so he could keep his eyes on the girl who entranced him. His brother Yankel, out of breath from dancing, grabbed a handful of cookies.

"Aron," Yankel said, "you're not eating. I didn't see you dancing. What's the matter with you?"

"I'm not hungry," Aron said.

"I've watched you staring at that girl, the whole night."

"I'm not staring. But who is she?"

"And I see her looking at you, now," Yankel said. "She's Wolf Herszkowicz' daughter."

"I didn't recognize her. If you know everything, what's her name," Aron said his heart beating faster.

"She's Gitel. And I think she's turning into the prettiest of his daughters. You see the cheeses on the tables? Her family makes it."

Aron took a piece of cheese and its flavor was to his liking. He looked at Yankel and told him he would see him later. He smoothed back his waves of brown hair and walked to the table where Gitel sat. She looked up at him and her alabaster cheekbones lifted into a smile.

"Do you remember me?" Aron said, sure his face had reddened.

"I'm not sure," she answered. "But I saw you sitting with Yankel and you look a little like him. I'm Gitel."

"Yes, Gitel, I'm Aron. Yankel and I are brothers. Can I sit here?" His eyes were on her face and his hands trembled when he sat next to her. He was not so close that they were touching, but he felt the intoxication again.

"I didn't see you dancing, Aron. You didn't like the music?"

"I liked the fiddlers very much…but I liked watching you more."

They sat not knowing what else to say.

"I have to go back to my apprenticeship on Sunday. Maybe the next time I come home, I'll see you some place, again," Aron said his voice cracking.

"Yes, Aron," she said, her eyes searching the deep blue ones staring into hers. "I would like to see you again."

* * * * *

Aron replayed the innocence of that moment. The next day would be here all too soon, what lay ahead unknown and terrifying. *If the Pole discovers what I am I'll be finished, I have to separate myself from him if I get a chance* reverberated. Yet calm enveloped Aron as if Gitel's spirit infused him with courage.

9

The chance came faster than Aron could have imagined. Assembled at dawn, a cold slanting downpour pricked the captives into unwanted reality. The Germans marched them steady northwest to avoid impassible mountain terrain and they sloshed through rushing Gorce Mountain rivulets. The rain slowed the pace and roiled the guards until their agitation rose. "*Schnell,'* the Germans demanded until their shots began. Wounded prisoners unable to keep pace fell beneath pounding feet. "They can't shoot all of us," a Pole screamed. He ran toward the muted hues of the forest canopy beckoning a hundred meters away. A dozen frenzied Polish soldiers followed, rifle shots cracking after them.

Aron stood immobile his eyes on a special armed unit that appeared out of hell. Machine guns fired rapid rattles of death and man after man dropped. Migrating crows resting in the bare trees escaped upwards, the grey sky specked black, their pleading caws for mercy unanswered.

The captain's *kubelwagen* raced to the front of the lines and veered to a splattering stop. A compact Nazi officer jumped from an open side panel of the small military truck. He raised an assured hand and grinned toward his machine gun contingency running back cradling their killing gear. The captain surveyed the downed bodies with field glasses and then turned toward the drenched captives before him. Bitterness and hatred marked the dirt streaked faces of the once fierce fighters.

"*Heil* Hitler," the gunners yelled, stiff arms saluting in exuberance. Their eyes shone from the fresh kill.

"*Heil* Hitler," the captain's arm answered. The eagle and swastika on his helmet appeared to grow with confidence as he ordered the lieutenant to his side. "Tell this bedraggled heap of garbage we will shoot the lot, if just one forgets." In excellent Polish, the lieutenant delivered this news and led the gunners away. The prisoners were shoved into their lines. Resignation resounded as they continued on the conquered Bohemian plain.

The sky began to clear, a blue puzzle behind fast moving clouds. Each kilometer brought them closer to what Aron had overheard was Bohumin, a railroad town near the German border. A train whistled in the distance.

It snaked through the blighted Silesian coal-mine fields thirsted for by the Germans since the 1920's. *Finally, Aron thought, the Nazis have it in their greedy hands ready to fuel the Wehrmancht.*

Behind the pack-horses and the officers in motorized vehicles were the guards. They marched the war prisoners past the massive railroad complex in Bohumin. Aron watched a long train of cattle cars grind to a stop in front of the ornate brick station building. A dozen *bahnshutz* in spotless navy police uniforms patrolled the platforms with dogs. The prisoners in the cattle cars pulled their arms from the slats.

Minutes later, Aron's group was in front of a huge compound surrounded by chain link fences, guard towers rising at each corner. They were funneled through coiled barbed wire gates. On one length of fence, prisoners enlarged open pit latrines. Others shoveled out the waste. The stench overpowered the rain-washed air. Line by line they were led to the latrines and then forced to stand at attention. The hum of voices fell silent the instant the captain spoke into a megaphone. He turned in all directions and signaled to the ready *bahnshutz*. They came forward with their dogs straining against taut leashes, eager for duty. The guards prodded the prisoners with bayonets and the *bahnshutz* handlers let the dogs nip the terrified prisoners' heels. Line formations led left or right to waiting empty cattle cars. Destinies were about to be decided.

Rechts. Linxt. Soldaten. Zug. Right. Left. Soldiers. Train. That was all Aron could decipher from the echoing megaphone. Always order and organization these German bastards practiced, Aron acknowledged with bitter respect. Would he be able to separate from the Pole who had revealed his animus? The consequences of the decision drove Aron's breaths in rapid, faltering puffs.

The mother tongue he spoke from childhood, Yiddish, rooted in the enemy's language was the only benefit Aron could imagine. Yet rather than comfort him, the understanding made him fear it would draw suspicion. He had heard the word *Judes.* German soldiers searched for them. He had watched the guards beat them and single them out to clean the latrines with their bare hands. He read it on the faces that also understood and he shrank further within his shivering body. Aron had chosen what for him was the shelter of being a Pole, and he dared not look at the Jews, lest his eyes betrayed sympathy for the ones Nazis deemed sub-human. His family raced to mind. *Gitel, he thought, without you, it is meaningless.* An overwhelming force screamed from every fiber. He had to live.

CHAPTER TWO

1914 December

Nestled among the vast forests and meadows of southern Poland lay the rural hamlet Giebultow. Stretches of gentle hills dotted with swaths of dense chestnuts, pines and maples enveloped the homes, sparsely clustered cottages sited as far as the eye could see. Queen Anne's lace and purple-headed clover hugged the roads in summer and thick pelts of snow bordered them in winter. It belied the reality that during the First World War their territory had been occupied by Russians, depriving Poles and Jews alike of food and safety. At the end of 1914, Gitel was born to Wolf and Hinda Herszkowicz, one of eight children, the daughter with the agile body, strong will, and ambition. The family lived in a one-room house with an attached small barn on farmland rented from the nobleman, Count Janad Dzianat. Owning land was a luxury most Jews could not afford and was often forbidden, so a tacit agreement between the Count and Gitel's father Wolf 'Giebultow', as he was known, rested on his family's ability to produce enough dairy products to trade for livelihood and pay tribute.

Gitel's father ruled the family with unwavering faith and ethics. A pious man he believed in a strict and good God, one to be feared. Powerfully built, he kept a full dark beard, well trimmed. Work was of paramount importance. His sons and daughters provided him with the labor necessary to keep the business, any interference with work or prayer rituals resulting in quick rebukes or worse. He expected complete obedience from his children. And almost always, he got it. Gitel admired her father's strength and fearless nature; she understood how hard it was for a Jew to survive rural life, to maintain respect and do business among Poles. He had to compete with and befriend those he encountered at market. With Jew or gentile, Wolf made it clear where he stood. Neither meek nor confrontational, Wolf 'Giebultow' was not a man with whom to trifle, and his daughter Gitel inherited this trait.

Gitel's desire to show her father her immense capacity for work was complicated by a fierce need to learn in school and experience the freedom of running through the fields. She was an inquisitive tomboy. And because her build was a softened version of Wolf's, he knew she was capable of hard work. He demanded far more from himself, carrying huge milk cans one under each arm, enormous bags of grain slung on a shoulder; a hundred kilo brick of cheese presented no challenge. When Gitel disobeyed, it was not to defy him but to be the girl she was. Quick with calculations for selling and buying, she dreamed of leaving Giebultow as the rhythm of the churner turned her mind from butter to other possibilities.

Hinda, Gitel's mother, was the perfect complement to her husband's uncomplicated approach to life. She had come from a family that valued learning; even the girls had been taught to read and write Polish. She was well versed in the ancient Hebrew prayer liturgy. After marrying Wolf her education helped ameliorate troubles between the children and their taskmaster father. She would gather her daughters when work was done and teach them by the glow of a kerosene lamp. The boys walked five kilometers to the nearest town, Ksiaz Wielki, and studied with the rabbi. Wolf saw more value in using his children to work the dairy but was forced to send them to Polish school by his wife. The threat of being fined by the local government was equally persuasive.

Gitel worked near her father, the round-tipped cheese knife slapping against the tin table top each time she marked a slice measured to the size of her hand. She finished cutting the slab into twenty smooth, pale even-sized bricks. Wolf watched from a corner of the dairy, the butter churn gripped between his legs, the paddle tempo swaying him in prayer trance. She scooped the fallen pale crumbs of the fragrant spring cheese from the grooved tin table then rolled them into a small speckled pot. This was for Mother. Sunday supper was always the noodles Hinda made that morning flavored with saved cheese shavings. Gitel finished her task, pouring buttermilk from a tall-necked can into various shaped bottles. Late morning sunshine called. Her almond braids bouncing, she ran into the house to help her mother.

"Mother, I produce more buttermilk in an hour than my older sisters can in three. They're interested in embroideries and hair brushing."

"You'd do well to observe their fine sewing skill." Hinda touched her daughter's hair. "I see you brush your hair more too, these days."

"When I finish my work I want to run outside, not sit at the table with embroidery." She touched her braids, the silken strands lingering between her fingers, a boy named Aron stirring her heart.

"You are a young lady, thirteen years old. You understand more each day. Don't you remember the lesson your father taught you last year?"

"Oh, I will never forget. And I'll never forgive him."

"You'll learn to forgive, Gitel. Our wounds heal."

"What he did to me, he wouldn't do to his precious dog, Bialek," Gitel said in the same tone she often heard from the man she had not yet forgiven.

* * * * *

It was on a fresh spring Saturday afternoon and her parents were taking their traditional Sabbath nap. The Giebultow woods, scented from rich red earth and young buds on greening apple trees, tugged at Gitel. Tender grass wet her bare feet as she pulled off thick stockings and worn shoes. She lifted her long dark skirt, freeing her legs and broke into a run when she saw Chaszka, her Polish schoolmate. Along Chaszka strode Stefan, a boy from a farm on the Count's land. They called out her Polish name, Guccia, and she dared to join them.

"Let's see who can climb the tallest one." Stefan pointed to a stand of leafed out maples. The three charged off, Gitel a close second to the long-legged boy. Choosing the tallest tree, he lifted a bare foot and shimmied his way to the first crook. He grinned and settled both legs kicking. Whooping, he beckoned the girls.

"Maybe we should just watch the big crazy cat scratch higher," Chaszka said, watching Gitel's face. "You better stay on the ground. If your father catches you, he'll give you a good one."

"Maybe," Gitel said, "but he'll have to climb up here to get me."

"Let him get me, too." Stefan pulled up to a higher limb.

"I'm going up." Gitel wound her skirt between her legs and jumped for a low branch. She braced her feet against the tree trunk. Her arms strong from beating dust out of rugs, churning butter, and carrying big bricks of cheese, made the climb easy. A quick glance down filled her with excitement. She stretched to reach higher. But the handiwork of woodpeckers made the maple tree trunk slippery with running sap. Gitel lost her grip.

"Stefan," she screamed, grasping at branches too thin to hold her. She slid, the twigs whipping her arms and legs until she gripped a thick lower branch with her legs to stop and ripped open her thigh. She looked down, heart pounding. Arms clasping the trunk, Gitel held on, wedged between webs of branches, three thick limbs from the ground.

"Guccia," Chaszka shrieked, "there's blood running down your leg. What are you going to do?"

Blood oozed from her thigh. Her skirt was ripped, her exposed legs covered with scratches. Her body began to tremble as waves of pain registered. Stefan slid down to Gitel and positioned himself below her. They inched to the ground.

"You got hurt bad," Stefan said with what sounded like admiration.

"You better get home." Chaszka stared at her bloodied friend.

"My father will let me have it if he sees me like this."

"Come home with me," Chaszka said. "We can clean you up there."

"I don't clean girls." Stefan could not help glancing at Gitel's bared legs. "Go to the stream, Guccia and wash up. Chaszka, your mother will tell everybody."

Circumstances prevented their taking pleasures in the small wonders along the brook path, springing frogs plopping into the water, lilies of the valley bending the last of their fragrant white cups. The girls did their best at the brook. Stefan looked away as Gitel pulled up the torn skirt past her thigh, exposing a deep gouge. She ripped two strips from her skirt and handed one to Chaszka. They busied themselves rinsing the cloth in the cool water, wiping the blood, repeating the efforts with little success.

"Is it better?" Stefan took a quick look.

"Yes, it's all healed," Chaszka snapped. "Why are boys so silly?" She wrung out the soaked skirt pieces and watched water rushing in reddened ribbons over rocks in the shallows.

"Leave him alone. Go home, Stefan, I'll be all right." Gitel was far from all right. With no further coaxing necessary, the boy ran from what would be trouble if he were spotted with the girls.

"Why did he have to climb so high?" Chaszka accused.

"It wasn't his fault. He's a boy, that's what boys do." Gitel pressed on her thigh, blood squeezing between her fingers. She swallowed hard and looked at her friend.

"So what does that make you, Guccia, a boy?"

"It makes me a girl who does what she likes."

"Guccia," Chaszka whispered. "How are we going to make it stop?"

"We need something long and strong to tie around." Gitel stared at her throbbing thigh. It reminded her of butchered meat and it sickened her. "Run back to the barn and grab cheesecloth. I saw my father tying a wound. My mother cut herself when she was pulling feathers from a hen she was making kosher. The knife slipped and cut her thumb deep."

"Kosher?" They were close friends from the same class, but most customs associated with Jews were alien to her Catholic friend.

"Never mind, Chaszka. Just hurry. Get cheesecloth to wrap my leg. A stack is on a shelf by the barn door," she commanded.

17

Chaszka whined with annoyance. "What if I get caught? What if someone sees me in there? What am I supposed to say?"

"It's our Sabbath. No one works today. Like you don't on Sunday. If anyone sees you, say your mother needs the cloths, but you were afraid to wake them. We trade with your family. Everyone knows you're not thieves."

"So kind of you, *Pinienka* Bleeder," Chaszka countered sarcastically.

"Hurry, please, I'm so cold."

Meadow grasses swished and parted until the girl disappeared from view. *So this is my payment for disobedience, Gitel thought. What if Father finds out? What could he do to me?* Shaken and chilled, she applied the makeshift compress, the fear of retribution from her father bringing shaming memories of the times he had belted her bare backside or hurtled scathing remarks, comparisons between her and her sisters who behaved like young ladies, while she was wild, untamed.

At last, she was relieved to see her friend running. Chaszka's flaxen braids swung side to side and as she got closer Gitel's eyes misted with gratefulness. Chaszka handed over the little bundle she was carrying. Gitel stared at her friend's face, smeared about the eyes.

"Here." She dropped to the grass. "This is what your sister gave me."

"She caught you," Gitel gasped, more frightened by the prospects of discovery than her own open flesh.

"Let's take care of your leg first. Eat the rest of the bread and cheese. I couldn't wait I was so starving. Did you make this cheese? It's good."

Gitel did not respond and began binding her leg with the cheesecloth. She fit the filmy cloths snug, one over the next, each hiding more bloodied mesh than the previous one. They worked accompanied by water lapping against the rocks; the sun falling on what Gitel knew was a Sabbath sky.

"What happened, Chaszka?"

"That white dog is in everybody's business," Chaszka muttered.

"Chaszka, how did you get caught?"

"I almost sneaked in the barn like you told me but Bialek started barking. He ran after me. I was sure he was going to bite. I got between the big milk cans and he growled and showed me his teeth. He wouldn't let me out and then I heard 'Who's in there?' 'It's me, Chaszka,' I yelled out."

"Who was it?" Fear and fury hardened Gitel's eyes.

"Your sister Faigle, always gentle, screamed at me. 'What are you doing? You know we have nothing for sale until tomorrow.' Then she must have felt sorry because her voice changed. She said silly girl stop crying."

Gitel's lips trembled. "Everyone will know."

"Your sister's the only one. She was on the lookout for you, Guccia. Bialek. That's why she found me. I hate that dog. She told me he'd stop growling if I put my hand out slow, for him to sniff."

"Bialek let you go?"

"We came out together. He had his tail between his legs, I was crying like some big baby."

"I could tell you were crying, Chaszka. I'm sorry." The girls looked at each other and the intensity of the moment brought anxious giggles.

"Then right away your sister says where is Guccia?"

"You didn't say, did you?" Gitel quavered.

"She's hurt. She needs cheesecloth. That's what I said. Bialek licked my tears. First he wants to eat me, then he's my big friend."

"Oh no." Gitel erupted in sobs of dread. She was trapped, a wounded creature who could think of nothing but escape. "I have to hide. Where will I to go?"

"I told her, Guccia doesn't want anybody to know. See? I came back alone. You know what I heard your sister say to that dog? 'Father is right, she is a little devil.' "

Gitel hobbled through the meadow, the sun low in the sky, insisting Chaszka take something home. Some butter, anything to show her thanks. But her friend skipped off, heading home, relieved of the burdens of the day. Bialek greeted Gitel with the joyous yips reserved for those under his protection. He pushed his nose beneath her skirt to inspect and ran about, his white tail waving with excitement until Gitel's mother came out of the house. Esther Faigle trailed behind. Gitel stood before them unable to utter a word, her clothing ripped, the pallor of her skin speaking pain and worry. Hinda led Gitel to the barn and sat her away from the dairy foods. She gasped when she pulled off the layers of cheesecloth from her daughter's leg, getting down to the torn flesh, a gouge so deep, she could almost see the thighbone. Gitel had paid little attention to the scratches covering her legs crusted with dried blood. They were the least of Hinda's worries. To Gitel's further embarrassment, her mother made her urinate onto a cloth to disinfect the wound. The thrill of climbing, the adventure with her friends, even her privacy was stripped away. Gitel was as exposed as the open, torn flesh.

All the while hanging over Gitel was what Father would do.

Her brothers came out to the barn as the first stars dotted the sky. By then the wounds were cleaned and she smiled at them and stood up. She pretended a limp. It hurt to put weight on the leg, and that was not pretend. Their mother told them to go inside and help Father light the *havdalah* candle, the ritual they observed at the end of every Sabbath to give thanks and bring in the weekday. She knew father would tell her no other of his daughters was so wild. None of the other girls ran with young Poles the way she did, shaming them. She was sure there would be a punishment. She followed her mother into the house, the promise of retribution stinging more than her leg pained.

"A doctor, maybe she needs a doctor," Wolf bellowed. The *havdalah* candle flickered on the table and shadows trembled in the room. Gitel's head fell on her chest where tender buds of breasts caused enough confusion. She was on the brink of young woman, battling a tomboy self that brought such grief.

"I don't know, Wolf," Hinda said. "It's very bad. Deep. God forbid she should become lame."

"Lame. If she's strong enough to climb trees with *goyim*," the coarse barb at non-Jews he hurled, "she's strong enough to heal. Lucky she didn't break it. You'll find out soon, Gitel." He glowered at her. "Tomorrow is a workday. What good are you going to be? Look at you. Smart in school, a stupid heifer here. You need more lessons at home? For you, school and playing are finished."

It struck hard. School almost over for the year, she begged her mother to plead the case to her father. At least let her finish five grades, only one more year. Children in the class, most of whom were Polish in rural Giebultow, would soon be released to help with farm work. She and her brother Mordche, just two years apart, sat in the same row. Gitel would no longer sit near him. She so fast with arithmetic always called on by the teacher to stand and answer when visitors came. She would no longer be with her friends. Gitel did not suffer from envy and could have cared less about many of the silly trinkets she accused her sisters of wanting, but severing her school life brought pangs of envy.

Her father had spoken. He would not be dissuaded.

Her love for school, that she would no longer be there was unbearable, and the mending wound gave her more time to think than she wanted. Summer months passed, hastening healing. She had no trouble walking and was running sooner than she let on, the scar a deep etched wound – a forever reminder. She was wary Father would catch her in some act that would not end well. And it was red apples hanging from the gnarled tree the Count allowed them to pick from, the browning leaves signaling the first frost that lit her father's wrath.

Drawn over the footbridge, she ran straight for the tree. Gitel jumped for the lowest branch and held on to pluck a perfect ripe apple.

"Come down, now." There was no escape. Wolf's arms were folded across the white work apron, his large feet planted with resolve.

She followed him into the house. Wolf removed a thick rope from the hook by the door. He grabbed Gitel by the arm and pulled her toward the bed. Hinda watched in silence, her eyes wide with apprehension. Wolf pushed Gitel to the floor, wound the rope around her leg and tied the other end to the bedpost. Unable to move more than a meter from the wall, Gitel's hand slid to her thigh. At least he had tied the rope to the other leg.

"Like a brainless heifer, this is where you'll sit until I set you free. If your head won't learn, maybe you'll learn the lesson through your ass."

He did not look at his wife or children as he closed the door. Wolf headed to the dairy where work waited.

No one said a word to her. Nor did Gitel want to speak. Her brothers and sisters looked away from the prisoner she had become, an outcast in her own home. The youngest, felt sorry and sat next to her until Father's footsteps. Bialek licked her hand settling himself down for the night, the place closest to his master's bed having been usurped by the interloper. She sat that way, refusing anything but sips of milk her mother insisted on. Like a heifer tethered, unable to relieve itself elsewhere, she too had no choice. The embarrassment drove tears of anger and a deep wedge between Gitel and her father.

At the end of the second day he untied Gitel and hung the rope back on the hook by the door. "I hope you learned a good lesson," her father told her, "something you won't forget."

No, she thought, the word forget burning. I will never forget.

CHAPTER THREE

1939 October

A rifle butt to his back snapped Aron into taking the chance. He had pieced together that the waiting cattle cars were going to Germany or Poland. The dubious Pole was in front of him. It had to be now.

"Listen,' he whispered to the Pole, "we have to go our separate ways. If they find out we're friends, that we know what's going on, they'll use it against us, get rid of us."

"You might be right," he said, searching Aron's eyes. "What can we do?"

"Leave it to me." Aron motioned with his hand for Grumlecki to stay in their line and said, half believing, "Someday we'll drink a vodka with a kilo kielbasa."

His heart thumped. He was pushed along as the two lines neared open cattle cars. Aron bumped to the opposite line. Food was the best trade he could offer when hunger was every man's constant gnawing companion. He slipped crusts of bread he had spared into the prisoner's hand now behind him. It succeeded. *Only one God knows if what I do is the right thing.* He stepped up into the huffing train car away from the Pole who he believed would betray him. *Deutschland.* Was he going mad? He had opted for of all places, Germany.

Two miserable days of no food or water, the prisoners pushed off the trains to relieve themselves and at the same time remove their dead, ended near Freiberg, Germany. The massive prisoner-of-war camp loomed beyond the train station. Along with hundreds, Aron marched to a stalag that promised bad times, if not termination. There were barracks, most in various stages of construction. Countless tents, scattered in clusters, held prisoners and many were unsheltered, a thin blanket and the bare ground their accommodations. He stood in a denuded field, guarded by a unit of Nazis who scrutinized with eyes that seemed to hear and smell what each prisoner might be.

Aron waited his turn. His eyes sought the white-tipped mountains with flourishing evergreen forest that overlooked Freiberg, a stunning contrast to the desolate raw ugliness of the stalag. His group neared the interrogation barracks and he inched forward to the open door. A faint odor of disinfectant heightened his senses.

Inside, late afternoon sunlight slanted through two windows along the whitewashed walls. Weary men in tattered uniforms stated name, age, and nationality and answered the inquisitor's questions.

He was next.

A round-faced Ukrainian translated for the German intelligence officer, a senior captain seated at a metal table. The captain in a pressed uniform on his stiff frame beat the typewriter keys as the Ukrainian interpreted. Between the two barracks windows, a security guard carried a machine gun and pounded the floor with his thick-soled boots. The guard's head veered from the double line of khaki uniforms in his charge to the growing number outside, amassed like fallen, yellowing leaves, their life force fading.

"Name and home country," in heavily accented Polish the Ukrainian interrogator demanded from Aron. A sudden visceral thought of Khmelnytsky who so long ago led the Ukrainian rebellion against the Poles and the ferocious Cossack pogroms against the Jews drenched Aron in cold sweat.

Giving his Polish surname would not draw attention. His deep-set blue eyes and wiry frame made him appear tall. His body clung to the khaki jacket and pants. He prayed these would not be stripped away. To be exposed so would reveal it all. Yes, that too. *Adam* rushed through his mind. *You are Adam, just a Pole.* He breathed in the scent of flesh wounds masked by disinfected air in the whitewashed room. His stomach churned. *Adam.* He mustered courage to his voice.

"Matuszyński, Adam, I am a Pole."

The German intelligence officer stood, the metal legs of his chair screeching against the concrete slab floor. He pointed to the back of the line and he spewed knife sharp words, "Stupid, shut your dirty mouths, *shweine.*" Pigs. Aron understood.

"You heard the captain, you pigs back there. Shut your stupid, dirty coward mouths," the Ukrainian translated.

Do not betray you understand anything. Be a blank, a Pole of no certain origins. Aron made his face reveal what reflected on the others, no more, no less, but macabre curiosity about what might unfold.

With a nod from the captain, the Ukrainian shoved his way past Aron. He approached the back of the line where the offending conversation had taken place. A beefy willing hand grabbed the Polish soldier and slapped his mouth.

"You shit Ukrainian." The Polish soldier spat a mouthful of blood. "You helped the Russians sell us to them. What did you get for it? You're here, aren't you?"

The captain's steely eyes shot toward his guard, motioning him to duty. The guard stepped past Aron, gun glinting from the light of the bare bulb dangling over his officer's typewriter. He stopped in front of the one who had spat. With a swift, practiced motion the guard thrust the butt of his machine gun into the soldier's side. The man slumped to his knees, his fists clenched.

Aron's eyes were on the guard, as the Ukrainian strutted across the concrete floor.

"Polack," the Ukrainian smirked at Aron, "where were you captured?"

The guard glared at Aron. *Steady,* he cautioned himself. Aron shifted his weight to slow his shaking knees. It was not the first time a German gun was pointed at him point blank. He had been shot at many times during battle and had returned the favor. *Where.* Where he was captured could put him in jeopardy. But the son of a bitch had called him a Polack. He was being taken for a *true* Pole. He released a slow breath and answered.

"Nowy Targ."

"Nowy Targ? Ask him how many dead." The captain interrupted, searching this prisoner's face. He knew that just a week ago, the German 22nd Panzer Corps had sustained a high number of casualties by the river near that town.

"How many dead?" The Ukrainian repeated his fleshy lips moistened with interest.

Aron understood the intelligence officer wanted an accurate German body count. He had no way of knowing why this German needed the information. Nor what would happen to him when he gave an answer. To be asked questions was to be vulnerable and to act as if one knew, could lead to more questions.

"My company was one hundred twenty men. It was night. Fighting finished. We were surrounded. Maybe a handful of my company was left next morning."

"Tell him to think harder," the captain said, swerving toward the guard.

The round-faced Ukrainian stepped closer to Aron. "You're still standing? Think harder, Polack. Maybe you'll be on the floor. Like your stupid countryman there," he grinned, waving to the end of the line with a beefy finger.

"I don't know," Aron said to the Ukrainian, avoiding eye contact with the intelligence officer "In the morning they walked us away from the river. Very fast. There were dead everywhere. Maybe hundreds. Many Poles and Germans, too many to count."

The captain stared at Aron. Officers were not taken to stalags. They were taken to *oflags*, *offizierslagers*, officer camps. He knew Poles had inflicted heavy casualties at the river. It was the officers that held interest, those who had information. He lowered his voice, "Who was your officer in charge?"

Aron waited for the Ukrainian to translate. It gave him an instant to weigh his answer. "Lieutenant Nowak was the commander," he said, his heart beating wildly.

"Was he taken alive, ask him." The officer, having gotten a name, made the Ukrainian press for what happened to Aron's commander. He needed intelligence to get out of this god-forsaken hole with its growing number of barbarians to house. There were coveted positions opening in work camps and talk of special camps, where one could make a reputation.

Aron shook his head and looked down. "He was dead on the field." But Aron had seen his lieutenant led away. The lieutenant had given him good treatment as a sharp shooter, shown him respect, knowing Aron was a Jew. The Pole, with whom he had parted, may have seen this officer led away. It was lucky he was not there to perhaps contradict him.

"*Tot.*" Good. Tell him to go," the captain said dismissing Aron.

Again Aron sat with arms overhead, hunger grabbing his sunken stomach. He had given false information. It was not in his nature to lie. Had he gotten away with it? Months before the woman that never left his mind, Gitel, had visited him in Sosnowiec, where he had established his *warschtadt*. In his shoemaker's workshop, she had listened when Aron gave a customer too much truth. Be a businessman. Tell them a week, maybe a few days and send them on their way, she teased. 'My word is my word' costs you customers.

He'd pretended annoyance, watching her finger fine leathers folded on his workbench already promised, her hand on a shapely hip, a flirtatious grin titillating him. So what if he took too long, obsessing over fit, taking precise measurements beyond what other shoemakers were willing to do, their time used on the next pair? Gitel looked with admiration at boots in the window stitched with perfection, the leather glistening. Aron's young

Polish helpers stared at his attractive girlfriend when she gave them *kliske*, the cheese dumplings she had made and carried from her small shop in Bedzin.

Her alabaster cheekbones raised in a smile, her melodious laugh stayed with Aron until exhaustion released him to dream on his cold dirt bed. His body was wrapped about her softness. She was safe in his arms. He had won Gitel. At last, she had become his adored wife. The years of waiting were over, the other man gone from her life. At least in his sweet reverie as he drifted in sleep. He dreamed it was early summer and the brook near her cottage flowed full of hidden mysteries. Gitel and he strolled hand in hand and it was a thrill merely to touch and breathe as one.

CHAPTER FOUR

1939 November

Five o'clock in the morning, the night watch was replaced with fresh guards. A good rest stoked their appetites to abuse the prisoners with renewed malice. Every morning after the roll call the guards pushed them to the latrines then slowed them down for the mess line. Prisoners anxious to move a step faster for the huge kettles to quiet hunger were beaten by the guards, dragged to the back of the lines and forced to stand and watch as the others received rations. A tall rheumy-eyed man, his uniform unrecognizable to Aron, handed him the same dark bread with a square of margarine. He filled Aron's metal cup with soup, bits of grizzle swimming atop tepid grey liquid. Aron gripped the cup in an unwashed hand and smiled to himself, imagining the soup his mother made when he was a boy, fragrant steam from her cooking pot curling up wisps of her raven hair.

Ukrainians were in front of him. They spoke unafraid of the guard who passed with his rifle slung over a shoulder. The Ukrainians complained about their plight over the weeks they had been in the stalag. From their fuller cheeks, Aron surmised they were getting other rations. He carried the soup back to an unfinished barracks that he and the other seventeen were assigned to build. His group, Poles, had been moved to the tents. There was no heat but it was better than the bare ground they had slept on, colder every night. Teams of the prisoners were assigned under German direction to build barracks rising to house what seemed to Aron tens of thousands being pushed into the same receiving yard he had sat in weeks before.

He returned from the latrine mid-afternoon grateful he did not have the ugly job of expanding waste trenches. Assigned to identified Jews or troublesome inmates, the stench from digging clung to them wherever they went. Aron passed the window of a barracks and there sat the same Ukrainians he had encountered that morning, hunched over in the position so familiar. They were repairing shoes, piles amassed near the open door of the makeshift cobbler workshop. The Commandant himself stood there, the insignia on his cap glinting rank and aura. In charge of Freiberg stalag, the striking man in a meticulous uniform seemed no stranger to having demands met.

"You call yourselves craftsmen." He motioned to the guard at his side. "Inform them this job is worth shit."

The guard shouted at the Ukrainian foreman, leader of the workshop team. Tapping tools ceased inside the barracks. The Ukrainian foreman stood at attention, willing his eyes from the Commandant's boots.

"Your repair work is fit for your ignorant countrymen. Either you correct this or you are going back to accommodations you found not to your taste," the Commandant said. "Tell the lazy bastards I will replace them." The Commandant turned away and pointed a gloved hand to the back of his boots. His voice pierced the prison yard, silencing the hammering and shoveling, a brief intermission of prison instruments and then, as if an invisible baton waved, the racket resumed.

Aron slipped forward, an unremarkable shadow, as the Commandant strode past the work crew. "Pardon me, *Herr* Commandant, I will make your boots like new." Aron pointed to the Commandant's boots and to himself. "They will be like new."

"He said he fixes boots. He will make yours, Commandant, like new," the guard translated.

"New boots." The Commandant laughed to his guard. "Tell him to get back to work."

His heart racing, Aron shook his head and pointed to the Commandant's uneven heels.

"Who is he to stop me? What insolence," he said arching his generous fair eyebrows. His guard batted Aron, a drab fly, out of their path.

"*Linxt.*" Aron pointed to the Commandant's left heel. "The left heel is the problem," he said. The brazen act was beyond anything Aron had ever done and he had used a German word. But *linxt* was repeated to the prisoners over and over wherever they marched. He had allowed himself to use it.

The Commandant looked at the heel, the one making his gait uncomfortable, the boot repaired by the inferior shoemakers in his charge.

"If you give me a chance, you will not be sorry." Aron was incredulous he was able to maintain outward composure, his voice seeming to come from another's mouth. "I am a true craftsman."

It was true, he was. Germans respected trades, real craftsmen, and made a point of selecting prisoners who had skills. They assigned them to maintain their growing occupation. It was an imperative to employ slave labor to support the expanding *Wehrmacht.*

"What is your name, prisoner?" The Commandant pointed at the gaunt man, the khaki cap on his head creased. This spark of discipline had captured the commander's attention.

"The Commandant asks your name," the guard repeated at once, staring at Aron.

Of course, Aron had understood what the Commandant requested. But he waited for the translation. "*Herr* Commandant," he said, "I am Adam Matuszyński."

And so it was that the Commandant walked back to his office quarters with Aron behind him. Aron removed the Commandant's boots and examined the task before him. He inspected the uneven heels, a chance to better his circumstance, perhaps within his grasp.

"Please, I will need tools, Herr Commandant," Aron said slicing the air with his hand in a cutting motion toward the heel.

The Commandant called in his lieutenant from the outer office. "Tell this prisoner to ask the incompetent oafs, the Ukrainians and Poles in his cellblock, for tools. That's his problem." His eyes fell on documents spread on his desk.

"*Danka, danka,* Herr Commandant, you will not be sorry," Aron said, backing out, the boots tight in his hands.

Aron walked back to his tent, thoughts whirling with excitement and dread. Luck, he said to himself. No one was in the tent. He bent down and hid the boots beneath the straw where he slept. *A mensch tracht un gut lacht.* Man plans and God laughs. The prophetic Yiddish phrase accompanied him as he returned to his work team. He picked up the hammer and drove nails into the wooden boards of the growing barracks.

A crescent moon rising, Aron left with the Commandant's boots. He coveted them like the precious sacred scrolls he had once held as the thirteen-year-old boy who leapt into manhood. He knocked and opened the door. There appeared to be at least one hundred Ukrainians in the new barracks. This was far better than what the Poles had, housed separately in tents. Conversation stopped. The bloody struggles between the Poles and Ukrainians, fueled by Russia's promise to cede land to both sides had opened old wounds. New violence fomented between them. Aron's eyes met the Ukrainian's in charge of the workshop. Both Slavs, their languages were different, yet similar enough to make themselves understood.

The Ukrainian foreman pointed. "What do you have there, that you grip like your baby?"

"Two babies," Aron said separating the pair the foreman knew so well. "I can make these babies much prettier. Who doesn't like pretty babies?"

"So what do you want, Polack?" The Ukrainian foreman snapped. He did not take his eyes from the Commandant's boots.

"The Commandant told me to find tools. There's no other place for me to go."

"Go to hell," said Alek, the skinny one by the window.

"I can tell you this, if you lend me tools, I will repay you many times over." Aron nodded at the foreman avoiding the man by the window.

The foreman snorted, "A rich Polack shoemaker. He'll pay me." He folded his arms over his belly snickering towards his compatriots.

"I'll repay you with my skill. I can show you how to remake a shoe so no one here could tell it was not from new leather. From the time I was a young boy I worked at our trade. You see these hands." He let the boots slide to the ground and showed his calluses, marks the labor of shoemaker had imprinted on his fingers and palms. As never before, he grabbed and embraced the skill he had loathed as the enslaved boy sold into low status.

"I know what that is." The foreman rubbed a finger over calluses on his own hands.

"My hands know secrets. I use new techniques to soften the leather, different stitching, stronger, elegant."

"What leather? These scraps are what we get," the foreman said. He threw a dry brown piece at Aron's feet. "Where do you think you are?"

"When they see what *we* can do, they'll find us leather," he said.

Aron picked up the boots. The foreman, his ten helpers, and Aron stood together, perhaps reflecting on more spoils and favors that could be garnered. Better food, cigarettes and items *verboten* to the prison population could be theirs.

"You recognize these," Aron said. His hand clasped the crooked left heel. "If we work together we'll have a chance to live better."

"Come to the workshop tomorrow," the Ukrainian foreman said striking a match to the stub of a cigarette he had horded. The sudden light illuminated the darkened barracks and showed his yellow teeth against unsmiling lips.

Brown parched leaves signaled the coming German winter. A November wind chased them about Aron's feet as he walked to the cobbler workshop, dawn fading into a new day. He held both boots under his arm, opened the door and for the first time in months felt warmth from a small ceramic stove in a windowless corner. The Ukrainian foreman motioned to him and Aron sat down on the workbench. He set the boots on the floor and noted each item on the small table meant to serve them all. There were files, a chisel, several hammers, knives, an awl and bits of sandpaper, several blocks of wood, assorted pieces of leather, a glue pot, and a pile of nails. A dented tin of black Dubutow Schmoll, a Polish shoe paste he favored in his own workshop at home, encouraged him.

"Can you find me just a little whiskey?" Aron said.

"Whiskey. We have a drunk. Are you crazy, you dumb Polack?" Alek said. He grabbed Aron's khaki shirt.

"Take it easy," Aron said. He stood his ground and the skinny Ukrainian let go of Aron's shirt. "I need some to soak pieces of leather. Just a little whiskey will help to soften the better pieces. The leather you have is useful only for heels, maybe soles."

"If I had whiskey," one of the Ukrainian helpers said licking his lips, "I wouldn't give it to you." He nodded toward the foreman and winked a smile at Aron.

At least one of them Aron thought, afraid to return the sentiment, *if not a friend, doesn't want to kill me.*

"Look," the foreman said, "I'll see what I can do to make a trade. If he's right it will help all of us."

"Good," Aron said. "I'll start with the heels on the boots and show you where the fault is in the repair."

He selected the best of the tools and laid them in order on the worktable, knife, file, hammer and small chisel. He picked up a knife and sharpened the blade along the smooth side of a file and did the same with the chisel. Then he gripped the left boot between his knees and wedged the knife in where the heel was attached. He picked up the small hammer and tapped down gently until the heel gave way, then inserted the chisel and tapped down hard; three sharp taps released the heel into his hand. He did the same with the other boot and placed the two heels next to each other on the worktable. "You see, this is the first problem," he said. "Unless the Commandant has one leg shorter than the other, one of the heels is too thick."

"Who fixed the boots?" asked the shoemaker who had smiled at Aron.

No one answered. It was clear it had been the foreman.

"Doesn't matter," Aron said. "The measuring is the most important. You can even have good technique, but if the measurement is not perfect, neither is the product."

"So go on," the foreman rubbed at his chin.

"Where the heel was attached to the boot," Aron said turning the left boot over, "you see it was not a clean job. Maybe small pieces from other repairs were left." Though Aron did not excuse the sloppy job, he glanced at the foreman giving him a possible out for his poor workmanship. The foreman relaxed his squat frame.

Aron filed the pads of the boots and made sure the surfaces where the heels would be attached were even. He selected pieces of leather for the heels and sliced the pieces to match. Next he cut the pieces to match the exact shapes of the heels and gripping each one, glued the pieces together. He glued the assembled heels back on the pads. There was no lasting jack, the cast iron piece he used at home to hold the boots securely upside down, so he held each boot between his knees as he refined the heels with the sharpened knife. He stroked the heels with the knife, careful not to take too much leather, but just enough to create a smooth, perfect line. Aron finished attaching the heels with four small nails, tapping with the little hammer to be sure the nail heads were unobtrusive. He opened the dented polish can. There was little left. But he combined it with a bit of wax used to strengthen twine for stitching. He warmed it between his fingers, making a thick tar-like paste and began working it into the tall boots, covering the heels first and working up to the shaft.

"The leather is thirsty," Aron said feeling their eyes upon him.

"Can you make a whole shoe?" one of the Ukrainians said, with almost imperceptible respect.

Aron nodded.

"You're good, Polack." The foreman shook his head.

"Adam," he said, assuming his Polish identity.

"Anton," the foreman answered with a first smile for Aron.

"Now the magic comes," Aron said. "We all know this trick. The polishing can take a long time. Slow. The longer the better." He took the only rag on the cluttered worktable. Squeezing it in his palms to soften it, he began buffing. First in tiny circles and then larger ones until the boots gleamed. "When a shoemaker sees his face looking back at him, he knows he's finished." He set the revived boots on the hard packed dirt floor.

"Like new, yes," Anton said. "You're good, Adam. Let me see if I can find whiskey."

Aron stepped out of the shoemakers' workshop and walked to the Commandant's headquarters, hugging the boots under his moist armpits. Nerves had worked him into a sweat as he repaired the boots, not from fear that his skill would fail him, though it had taken him over an hour, but rather from worry the Ukrainians would thwart his plan or ask questions about his training or family. A wrong word could put him in the ground with the earthworms his last companions.

He was stopped by a Nazi patrol their rifles willing to act with little provocation. Aron pulled the boots from under his arms as if they were shields. "Commandant," he said. The word parted the guards from his path and he continued to the headquarters. Aron smoothed his hair with blackened fingers, put his cap back on and waited by the closed office door to be summoned. His stomach kept him company, gurgling angry reminders hours before the next meager feeding.

"For *Herr* Commandant," Aron said as the door swung open. "His boots." He handed the boots to the lieutenant.

The Commandant took the boots into his hands and turned them from side to side, examining the heels. Aron waited, his mind darting between the chance of being caught and that of an uncanny piece of luck. He felt instantaneous joy when he saw the Nazi officer touch an epaulet refracting gold braid from the sheen on the shafts of the ebony boots.

"Tell him," the Commandant said, "he will personally see to my boots from now on." He took out a mark, lifting his chiseled chin at Aron. "Get my other boots. He pointed Aron to the corner where the other pair stood. "He has my permission to visit the canteen."

"*Danka, Herr* Commandant." Aron touched his heels together in automatic soldier response and answered in Polish peppered with the German, thank you, he dared to utter. "It will be an honor." He looked the Commandant in the eyes and took the money and the boots. Aron knew that a visit to the canteen alone was a miracle. White bread was all he could think of as he walked, white bread from the canteen to chase his ever-present hunger away. *Mazel.* Luck. *A mensch tracht un gut lacht.* Man plans and God laughs. He was afraid to even think about this turn of events, should it somehow be jinxed. So each elated step forward pushed him back to the summer of 1925, when he felt anything but lucky.

CHAPTER FIVE

1925 Shoemaker

Ksiaz Wielki, where Aron was born in 1912, was a small town in the state of Kielce. It served the needs of Prince Wielopolski as it had done for the magnates over the hundreds of years before. Queen Anna Jagiellon, last of her Polish dynasty, had bequeathed the land and castle to the Wielopolskis. The twenty-room castle, private chapels for the prince and princess, stables, barns, livestock buildings, and terraced gardens adorned the Hill of Mirow, high above the town. A graceful larch wood church was built for the peasants in the market-square. Ksiaz Wielki was accessible to the Warsaw-Krakow Highway, and businesses and trades developed as the Jewish population grew. World War I strained the economy. Poland was partitioned again. Poverty stirred the pot of religion and released rank vapors into the homes of Jews. While Prince Wielopolski remained adorned in grey linen and held his class rank, the peasants who worked the land and traded foodstuffs suffered.

The *schlachta,* nobles on the hill since Renaissance times, was as far away from Aron's family life as the full moon he gazed at with wonder. Perhaps it was his birth order, the fourth of six children or poverty and destiny that conspired against the thin, sensitive boy with the artistic hands. But in the summer of 1923, Ruchel and Mendel Matuszyñski made the decision to take their son out of school to begin his life as a shoemaker. Aron's brief childhood had ended.

He had been allowed to achieve only two grades in Polish school. The rest he had been taught in a *cheder,* the tiny room behind the rabbi's quarters, and that was for no more than a rudimentary five years. What was to happen to the pigeons he raised on the roof? Why was he torn from school against his will? Was there no other trade for which he was suited, Aron wondered? He was singled out for what among his people he knew was no honor. "We already have two tailors in the family, it is difficult enough for Father to bring enough food into the house and you worry about pigeons and school," his mother gave him to understand. The outcome for him was the low status trade of shoemaker. They placed him in the hands of one in town willing to begin Aron's training with the promise one meal a day would be included. That relieved some of the family's burden of providing food for Aron. Used to his mother's fastidious housekeeping, Aron was overwhelmed by the dirt and disorder of the shoemaker's home. But at least Aron was glad he had avoided being sent away and he could sleep at home. The Jewish shoemaker was neither skilled nor a good teacher and Aron's wan face spoke of the wife's cooking and generosity. After little progress his parents decided that Aron had to be apprenticed elsewhere.

The journeyman Lech, Aron's next teacher, was a taciturn young Pole. He was not a master shoemaker yet, but he was skilled enough to have begun his own business and supported himself. Lech lived in Zlota, ten kilometers east of Ksiaz Wielki. Aron hoped the town's name, sounding almost like the Polish currency, *zloty,* was a fine omen and envisioned his empty pockets would soon be filled.

Arriving there the last days of August, accompanied by his father, he stood on unfamiliar streets ringing with a cacophony of peddlers selling their wares, people bustling about involved in everyday affairs. Situated in a lowland valley even the city's air seemed to conspire against Aron. Embarrassed by his moist, deep-set eyes, he was unable to say more than, "Father, must I?"

"Aron," Mendel put a gentle hand on the boy's bony shoulder. "What am I to do? You'll see. Nothing is as bad as a person thinks it will be. We get used to things."

Twelve years old, a future for which he had no desire was before him. He was to stay with this stranger night and day, only to return home each week for the Sabbath. Aron already longed for home as his father's *kapota,* the long black coat, disappeared from view. His fate was sealed.

Lech lived in an alleyway in one small room crowded with a worktable bench, straw mattress bedding, a dusty pile of discarded practice shoes and another of customers' shoes waiting to be repaired. The tiny masonry stove in the corner opposite the window was used to burn coal for heat, only when their bones were near frozen, and never for cooking. A kerosene lamp was reserved for lengthening the workday until the boys in Lech's charge were ready to fall upon their straw pallets. Mid-day was the time the home smell of food found its way into the cramped room and stoked Aron's pangs of loneliness. He looked forward to seeing the young Polish girl whose pink lips sang a greeting, her yellow braid reaching her waist. When she delivered the pot of *kapusta,* the cabbage soup, for Lech and his two hungry apprentices, Lech would say to the boys, "What are you staring at? She's not here for you." But each admonition only amplified Aron's youthful ardor.

Lech valued his tools. He stood over the boys, Aron and the other apprenticed to him, not so much interested in their progress as to guard his tools. Lech's appreciation for his tools, his skill for disassembling shoes for repair, and his exacting cuts on leather to prevent waste were the lessons from which Aron most benefited. Summers, the outhouse odors behind Lech's room mingled with the open glue pot inside. Lech wanted the free labor that came with taking students. He was not averse to adding the job of cleaning the outhouse for the dozen users who passed by the narrow workshop window facing the alleyway, a task that otherwise fell to Lech. The first winter of Aron's apprenticeship was bitter and made more so by the twenty kilometers he walked each week. But at least the cold lessened the stink.

If a student was a quick learner, free labor was an advantage. While learning the trade a boy did everything Lech told him. He swept, he fetched water, cleaned the outhouse, stuffed new straw into the lice infested mattress in the summer. Lech saw how unhappy Aron was, torn from school and forced to take a trade for which he had antipathy. He was unsympathetic, never indulged the boy in any way and worked him hard.

"I see you can make perfect cuts in the leather," he said to Aron.

"Thank you, *Pan* Lech," Aron smiled. Yet no sentiment or smile was returned.

Quick to grasp, the rudiments of the trade, Aron possessed a sense of how to work the leather, turning it to show the grain in the most pleasing way. "Let me see how you did this," Lech said to Aron, hunched over a worn boot. Aron sat up, pleased with the attention, a shy laugh escaping from him. Lech, seeing the spark of this different approach and a diligence not common to the others in his charge, knew that Aron would serve him well. He began trusting Aron to do more work on customers' shoes even allowing him to take measurements and reaped the benefits while the boy received not one *grochen* in return.

Every Friday Lech released him with a grunt to go home. Aron worried he would not arrive before sundown, in time for *Kiddush* to begin the Sabbath. This was his day of rest, the holy moment when work was suspended. He wanted nothing more than to see the candles lit by his mother dressed in her white pressed blouse and hear his father's fine voice sing the prayers that blessed the wine and praised God's commandments. It was his most sacred and tangible link to the family and faith. The meal was less than sumptuous, the table modestly adorned, but the bond Aron felt was more urgent than ever. He dreaded the thought of a furious mother or his older brother Mier's derisions. But Aron made it, even if his young legs stretched in a sprint or he was pelted by rain or his boots were mired in slush. The family encircled him and he was one of them.

The first fall months became the drab expressions of days that would soon give way to the harsh Polish winter. Winter would bring opportunity for Aron's friends back home who had ice skates to enjoy the frozen tributary of the Vistula meandering the outskirts of his town. He could visualize the boys racing on the ice, their hands numbed with cold and their ears swollen translucent red. It did not matter that skates were old or homemade, the joy of gliding on the frozen river as a few passersby watched and marveled at their tricks made them impervious. These images of the boys filled his mind on a Friday walk home in December. His head down against the wind, hunger quickening his pace on the road, the crude thick-soled boots he wore hit something hidden in the leaves. Aron picked up a large curved piece of iron and tucked it under his arm. The shape reminded him of a skate blade. He guessed it was a piece that had come loose from a horse drawn sled. No matter what it was, the thought of ice skates, something he had never had, came to mind. How to make the one piece, into two pieces, was a problem. But how to get this done and get home on time was the other problem. Aron started to run with the treasure. There was only one place he might get help.

A Pole owned the forge. It was where wagon wheels were repaired, barrel hoops and horseshoes made, every type of metal work done. The one-story stone building, covered by a tin roof, stood alone at the end of the main street just where the town merged with the Warsaw-Krakow Highway. There was a steamy haze about the place. Whenever the sturdy tin door swung open, the clang of the metalwork and a blast of heat spilled out.

The blacksmith who owned the forge had enough work for two others in his employ. The Matuszyński family, especially Aron's successful brother, dealt with the owner *Pan* Slomynsk. Meir transported livestock to market that required large wagons. The numerous trips to surrounding towns meant he had to keep the wagons in good condition and his horses' shoes in excellent shape. Aron had run errands for his brother and so he knew the Pole. That afternoon the soon to be thirteen-year-old was there on his own business; to see what could be done with the treasure under his arm. As Aron approached, the blacksmith emerged along with a blast of heat. A thick leather apron covered enormous shoulders down to his boots and a cigarette danced between his lips. Everything about the coal-fired forge smoked.

"*Dzień dobry, Pan,*" Aron's eyes wide with hope and trepidation greeted the owner with the polite, sir.

"Adam," he said, "I see little of your brother, Meurik. Always with his team of horses in a hurry. Tell him he must see his old friend."

"Yes, I will tell him. But we see little of him ourselves," Aron said hoping his voice did not convey ill feelings for his self-consumed eldest brother Meir, known by all the Poles as Meurik, a prosperous man.

"I know you must be busy with important things, *Pan,*" Aron said. "But I found this fine piece of metal and I have an idea to make skates with it, if it can be cut in two."

"Show me this thing." The blacksmith reached out with a muscular hand, took a long drag, the ashes floating. Aron admired the way the man maneuvered the cigarette, the aroma pleasant. He handed the curved piece to the blacksmith. It seemed to Aron, the fascination with his treasure was not his alone.

"It has to be heated first. It's too small to break for what you have in mind. Take it in. Give it to my man to do, the scrawny one by the open flame holding the bellows. For your brother, I do this favor."

A favor, Aron thought and wondered if Meir would find a way to extract something from him, his less aggressive sibling the one apprenticed in Zlota unable to make one *grochen*. He would find a way, he thought, some way to make his brother more respectful. He had bested Meir during a recent discussion. Aron had said the name of their Polish Prime Minister, Wladyslaw Sikorski, before Meir could even utter it.

The blacksmith yelled orders. Aron walked into the forge. Sparks shot in indiscriminate patterns, a withering blast of heat stifled his breath. Watching this blackened creature made him think that at least being a shoemaker's apprentice was not *this* bad. He envisioned the man in this perpetual state and felt his hot misery. The helper grasped the piece in long tongs and heated the iron, opening and closing the bellows breathing into the flame, until the iron between the tongs glowed red. He dropped it on the anvil, waited for the piece to cool down just enough. With a whack of a blade, the blackened man split Aron's treasure in two. Again using tongs he thrust each piece into a tub of murky water. The pieces hissed and steamed. Aron watched, mesmerized by the outcome.

"Be careful with the sharp edge, boy," the blackened man said to Aron, the whites of his eyes and purple lips softening into a smile.

"Thank you, sir, I will," he replied. But it was exactly what he had hoped for, sharp edges. Aron hurried home in time to wash and get ready for Sabbath. His face glowed from the heat of the blacksmith shop and success. A son and a brother again, he shed the shoemaker shadow as his mother lit the match, covered her face with her hands and recited the prayers.

Aron stashed the pieces under the straw mattress he shared with his brothers. Over the weeks, in spare moments after the Sabbath, whenever demands were not being made of him, he took the metal pieces where no one could see and disappeared into creating. He sharpened the edge and smoothed the sides with a metal file. He attached the blades to wood salvaged from a wagon wheel. But he still needed leather laces and toe pieces to complete the skates. He knew where he could get the leather but was too shy to ask.

One winter morning, Lech saw Aron hanging back past time for him to go home. Aron stood, feeling the room become colder, Lech in no hurry to waste coal. He was afraid to ask Lech outright for leather scraps to complete the skates. Taking was out of the question. So there he stood by the workbench searching with his eyes the numerous items scattered on the table.

"Have you lost something?" Lech asked.

"No, *Pan* Lech." Aron stood unable to ask Lech for the leather scraps.

"What is it then? Are you afraid to go home to your mother?"

Color rising to his ears, he pointed to the table. "I will work extra time. I need small pieces of leather for skates I am making."

"Here, take these." Lech gathered up a few brown and black scraps.

"I need one thin piece for laces, too."

Lech handed him two narrow strips that had been shaved from soles. He grinned, "You have two feet, no? Tell your mother to send you back earlier Sunday morning."

Aron ran most of the way, excited by the prospects of finishing the skates. The dreariness of the day, the dried glue on his fingers, the growling in his belly were all forgotten as he envisioned himself gliding on the ice wearing skates he had made.

The skates were simple, functional and embodied Aron's commitment to using an aesthetic, inborn. Though he lamented what he lacked, an unschooled mind neglected by fate, he saw that his labor could yield value. This was the first piece of work that made him feel accomplished and it brought him respect among the few Polish boys with whom he skated. They admired how the skates slipped so easily onto Aron's boots and how well he maneuvered on the ice.

"Adam, you're good with those skates you made. Who showed you to make them? That one in Zlota?" asked the oldest of the boys.

"No, not him. He is only interested in the pretty girl who brings him *kapusta*. I just knew how." *But,* he thought, *my mother would say I should use my golden hands on smarter things.* "Let's go boys! Who'll skate across the river first?" They all sped away in their motley garb, aiming to beat Aron on his fast skates, made with his own hands. They could not beat him.

It was his becoming a Bar Mitzvah that trouble began with his mother. Ruchel spun her tight frame around on the chair. "How long will you be such a child while your older brothers make a fine living? I know how much time you spend with the Poles. Instead of concerning yourself with your craft, and becoming a man, you skate. You worry more about the care of the pigeons. Who has such ideas?"

"My dear mother," Aron said, "I work long hours. I skate only on Sunday in winter when the boys come from church and then I run back to Lech."

"Church. A Jewish boy does not have time for such foolishness. What do you get from running on the ice with the *goyim?* You will have nothing but trouble. You hear me? I'll throw out those worthless skates."

Ruchel turned away. She continued darning socks, working the needle with long nimble fingers. "Instead of spending time with the rabbi you race around on ice."

"Mother, I won't do it anymore. I know I will be a Bar Mitzvah in the spring. I already read the prayers with the men in our synagogue." Aron stood beside her. How much he wanted to say he hated becoming a shoemaker, how he envied her approval of Meir. He needed approval because he thought so little of himself. But he dared not say such things to his mother or anyone. He knew that nothing was easy for her and he looked down at his boots and saw them for what they were, old, crude and part of the poverty in which they were caught.

"I'll make sure you don't!"

They were alone in the house. His father had left at dawn with butchered veal to sell at market. The pigeons cooed from the roof. Their melodies usually soothing seemed to stoke Ruchel's fury. She walked over to the straw bedding where Aron slept, bent down and pulled out the skates. Dangling them by the laces she took the hammer from a wooden box by the hearth. She threw the skates on the dirt floor and smashed and smashed, each hit of the hammer crushing Aron's tender childish dream. Dented iron remained. He never skated again.

* * * * *

For several months in comparison to many others in the stalag, Aron had it good. In fact, he had never had so much bread, white bread at that, all the potatoes he could eat, a piece of *wurst,* spiced German sausage on occasion, something he had never tasted in all the years of his life. He even had cigarettes to trade. Aron crossed the blue iced yard on his way to the shoemakers' workshop past the swinging bodies of young Polish soldiers hung two days before. The khaki tattered uniforms swung empty of life, twisting and twirling in the January squall. "No stealing will be tolerated." the loud speaker blasted from the tower. Nazi henchmen pointed at the latest lesson as prisoners trudged to their assigned jobs.

The Polish men could not have been more than eighteen when they had been conscripted. They may have thought of their maneuvers as vacations, play-acting war, target practice, learning skills for survival and sizing up who would be a friend. The life of a soldier may have been a respite from the hard labor they did to make a living. The two were caught with bread stuffed under their flimsy jackets. Poor boys. Aron had trained with boys like these. They reminded him of the men from his trench, their fingers hardened around antiquated rifles.

Aron had sent bread to his parents, bought with marks the officers gave him from repairs. He was allowed to do so by convention rules and he lived by rules the Germans enforced, changed, ignored or perverted. Aron had never stolen bread. Yet now, he would worry. He agonized over his family, where Gitel could be, the charade he played. There was no room for error. Death hung in the yard to prove it.

Again he would have to listen to the favored Ukrainians gloat over news from the front and watch them, and the Poles jeer at the Jews in their midst, beaten until their brittle bones cracked. They were thrown into the worst tents to starve and freeze. A week before in the yard, a prisoner had confronted Aron. *"Du bist ah yid,"* the furtive voice had hissed. *You are a Jew.* Aron had stared ahead and walked away from the man whose feet were wrapped in rags. He pretended he had not understood, the same way he had pretended not to understand the Nazis and kept his identity from the brutalized and the segregated as he did from everyone in the stalag.

Near the workshop, the snow swirled and fashioned into Lech, the journeyman's image. *As a young shoemaker, Lech was my taskmaster, and I his slave. Here, in a true prison from where I may never leave alive, being a shoemaker, what I hated, protects me. What I thought was cruel then is a whisper in the wind compared to the screams in the storm I may face.* Letting out a slow breath, he said a prayer to give him strength, the ancient Hebrew almost escaping his lips.

Aron clapped fingers over his mouth, about to open the workshop door. It was Alek, the one who detested him. "A Jew," Aron heard him say in a joyous voice. "I found out what he is, the filthy Jew shoemaker. We have that shit, just where we want him."

Aron's hand dropped from the door. *They've caught me. I'm found out.* Sweat pricked his spine. *Oh, Gitel my sweet girl.* He closed his eyes. *Nothing has been easy for you, for us. Our road has been filled with hardships, but this may be my end.*

CHAPTER SIX

1925 Gitel's Way

The road from Giebultow twisted and turned as Gitel became a comely country maiden. She had never been allowed to return to school, not to even finish the paltry five grades offered in the tiny hamlet. She was more determined when her older sisters married and the burdens of their work fell upon her. The enmity with her father drove her need to escape.

"Dear God," her aunt gasped, "this is you, Gitel? Look at you. A frightened, lost colt with a bedraggled coat. Who came with you, Gitel?"

"*Tanta*, just me. I came alone."

"Alone? You came alone to Lodz?"

Gitel looked down at the knotted fringe her shoe had discovered. Unaccustomed to carpets, her aunt's city apartment was a dazzling vision of furnishings she had never seen.

"Your mother and I were not raised to make such business. Does my sister know what you have done? Where you are?"

Gitel sought the floor again. Perhaps it would open up and swallow her away from her aunt's horrified questions.

"Is this what young ladies do today? From where did this idea come to your head?" Gitel listened to her aunt mutter. "And how did you get here? May God forgive me, maybe not having children is a blessing after all."

"Please, *Tanta*," Gitel begged. "Please don't make me go back." Now safe, tears wet the brave face she had worn for days on the run.

"Who's sending you anywhere? Go and wash. And you will eat something. I have water in my house, not like your poor mother who drags water from a hole in the ground."

"We all help our dear mother," Gitel said, turning to face her aunt before following the woman's reprimanding finger toward the washroom.

"While you eat, you'll tell me how you found me. Not once were you in Lodz. How you had the sense." Gitel's aunt rushed to the cupboard.

She ate the marbled bread and pickled fish her aunt placed in front of her on a porcelain plate that was smooth, stark white. The milk was good, Gitel thought, but not as fine as what she was used to. At least in Giebultow something was more to her liking.

"You look better already, Gitel. With a clean face you are a pretty young woman. How old are you, you should have long years in front of you. So…I'm waiting."

"Fifteen." Her eyes admired a small table with a lamp. Its base portrayed a shepherd, the staff reminding her of a farmer who kept his sheep from straying over the bridge and into the brook by her house in Giebultow.

"Fifteen it's not unheard of to get married. But tell me how you found me. It's seventy-five kilometers from that *dorf*, the stuck-away hamlet where you live."

"I walked to the train that goes from Meichow to Sosnowiec."

"Walked? Strong like your father."

Gitel, often compared to the man from whom she had just escaped, shook her head. "I like to walk, *Tanta*. There is so much to see."

"Young legs can see. But from Sosnowiec how did you get to me?" The woman sat forward.

"I caught rides in wagons."

"You rode with strangers? From our people?"

"Polish farmers gave me places in their wagons. They were very kind."

"Kind. You know what, Gitel? You had *mazel*. That's all. More luck than anything else."

"Mother says *mazel* is better than beauty, being smart or having gold and that it comes from God."

"And how many days did you have this luck? Where did you sleep? Maybe it's better I shouldn't know."

"It took me only three days and two nights," Gitel said, a smile lifting her sculpted alabaster cheekbones, her green eyes opened wide. "One barn I slept in had a beautiful brown horse."

"Only three days." The woman shook her head afraid, to absorb more. "You'll finish this story. Tomorrow is another day. My niece sleeps with horses."

Finding her way, using her own devices was not lost on Gitel. She felt grown up, but realized she could not remain in Lodz. The second day, Gitel's aunt had another visitor. Wolf had tracked his daughter. What the punishment would be this time, Gitel had no idea. Extra work she could endure. Her father only said one thing to her. "This I do for your mother. I'm not going to bring you home next time. If you leave again, don't come back."

After he told her this, neither said a word.

Gitel had plenty time to think on the way home, bouncing on the bench next to her father, who coaxed his mare along until they stopped to feed and water the animal. As difficult as it was, she had found her way to Lodz. She had been frightened. But it had not stopped her. Gitel had discovered a well of courage.

* * * * *

And then she was nineteen and winter was master. Snowdrifts piled high against windows, the thatched roof invisible beneath a white crust. Gitel and Deborah, her youngest sister, sat close at the table their heads almost touching, voices blending in excited murmuring.

"They have secrets," Hinda said, her metal spoon skimming the bubbling iron pot of bulgur flavored with bits of veal. Winter weekdays she baked bread before the sun lit the room, the oven providing heat, its coals glowing orange. Rising in tin pans covered with white cloths, sat three loaves she had kneaded from coarse rye. Now afternoon, they were ready to serve *mitug,* the main midday meal.

The comment hung in the room, Hinda's daughters conversing an instant too long before her husband opened the door. He stamped his tall fur-lined boots. The last bits of snow melted on the compacted dirt floor. Wolf stood, broad shoulders shedding the thick wool overcoat. He grabbed the skullcap from atop the cupboard, a quick replacement for the snow dusted brimmed cap. Watching his grown daughters in idle chatter, he washed his hands in a bucket.

"Wolf Giebultow's daughters talk while their mother works."

Gitel started, "Father." The tone made Deborah nudge her sister's knee.

"Father," Deborah said, standing, "we are ready to eat. We were waiting for you and our brothers."

"And what does my daughter, Gitel, have to say?" Wolf said, watching her set his plate before him. He smoothed the last flakes of melting snow from his dark full beard.

"I say first we eat, before the food gets cold," Hinda said, drawing her shawl closer. "Where are my sons?"

"I hear them, I hear," Wolf said. The blessing over the food continued to move his lips.

Gitel cleared away her father's plate. She felt her thickened fingers as she thought of the years of making cheeses, carrying big tubs from the dairy to the general store in front of their two rooms. *I know what I have here. Maybe what it will always be. Eight years old and he called me to help in the dairy the moment I came from school. Not everyone had to work so hard. But he feels this in me, as it is in him. What my life could be with music, and business and maybe with educated people who bend their minds, not their backs.*

52

Wolf pushed back the chair, his eyes closed. The after-meal blessing moved his lips with fervor. A thought took root in Gitel. *I am going to Bedzin. I'll have a store. I will stand with the women in the Big Synagogue. Mother taught me to read from her siddur. I read just as fast as some of my brothers. There is a Kino. Just like the movie house in Sosnowiec where I saw Molly Picon last year with Aron. He tells me I could be an actress. Aron. Why can't I stop thinking about you? My head spins with thoughts I should not have when you put your arms around me. And then my head pulls me in another direction. What is my father going to do, tie me to his bed like he did when I was twelve or drag me back from my aunt in Lodz? I'm not the girl of fifteen. I'm a nineteen-year-old woman. If I have to, I'll run in the middle of the night.*

"Father," Gitel said when her father's eyes opened. "I need to talk over something with you."

"Gitel," her mother said, "Father has to see the *porets*. There is trouble. The Count is busy and the days are shorter."

"Your business will wait, Gitel," Wolf said. He reached for his coat and black cap.

"You see yourself what's happening with the milk I buy from him. Where is he selling it? And what's going on in this world? Without milk how am I going to make a living? Cheese from snow!"

"Mother," Gitel said when her father had left, "you know where I want to go. Deborah wants to come with me. I'm not blind. I see what's happening here. We'll have a better chance to make a living. It's in my blood to sell. I'm alive when I'm with people."

"Young women alone in a big city. Unmarried young women. What will the family think of such things? Your oldest brother was already in my arms when I was your age. Gitel, your father will not let you do this." Hinda smoothed the apron and hung it on a hook by the coal stove.

"Mother, my dear mother. What do I have here? Aron has gone to Sosnowiec."

"You encouraged him to go," Deborah said, cupping breadcrumbs she swept from the table into a delicate hand.

"That's where he can make a living," Gitel said. "I care for him, very much."

"But you turned him away, when he asked you last year," Deborah said, her voice wistful.

"Is a shoemaker the only man in the world? It wasn't the right time," Gitel said louder than she had intended, ashamed she had lost her temper.

Devorah looked at the curtains she had sewn framing the windows crackled with frost. She turned to her mother. "Gitel has Aron. Even if his parents are poor, they are good people. Father had nothing against him. Who is there for me? I'm not pretty like Gitel."

Hinda stood silent between the two daughters she was losing control of.

"I'm not going to talk about Aron. And you are pretty enough," Gitel said, brushing back a blonde curl that had escaped from Deborah's embroidered headscarf.

"Please, don't be cross with me," Deborah said, her eyes avoiding her mother's.

Hinda took her *siddur* from the cupboard and placed it on the table. The leather-bound book opened to a page without the guidance of her hands. She had taught all her daughters to read the sacred words. This moment she sought something for herself.

"With or without Father's blessings I have to leave, Mother," Gitel said. "What will you say to my father?"

Hinda grew up in Lodz, a big city pulsing with Jewish culture. Gitel knew there was a place in her mother's mind that was still connected to a different world. Glimpses of it had impressed her when she had run away to her aunt. She watched her mother close the *siddur,* stroking its cover like a well-loved elderly parent.

"Bedzin has places for us to live. I've been there many times with father when we've sold our products. We'll start with a small store. I'm not afraid to work and I won't be alone. Deborah and I will be together."

"Afraid to work," Hinda said shaking her head. "You have too much of your father in you, Gitel, you don't know when to stop. Since you were a little girl you listened with respect, but many times did what you wanted.

You are a grown woman with your own understanding. What I think. It will be useless to bother your father with this. You'll anger him and make it worse for all of us."

It never left Gitel's thoughts. She waited until the brook nearby the house churned over moss-covered rocks, burbling, the season bringing new life. When Gitel looked out of the barn the wood footbridge connecting their side of the brook to the dirt road summoned. *Soon I will walk over the narrow wood bridge and not look back.*

Secrets are hard to keep. And though Gitel had heeded her mother's warning not to say anything to anger her father, Wolf confronted her. "You want to leave your mother, your father, the family, and go." Wolf tossed an empty milk can into the wagon by the barn. The mare stood with a large hoof relaxed, aware her master had no intention of leaving. "I haven't given you a house to live in? The name Herszkowicz means nothing to you? The Count respects these hands. A paper you never needed, you could figure faster in your head than your brothers when you were a young girl. Instead of gaining sense, are you losing it?"

Gitel stared at him. She calculated each word. "Father, my older sisters and brothers have left."

"They are married with their own families," Wolf said. "You are not. And you will stay here where you belong."

"I try to do everything you ask of me, Father."

"Then you will obey me and stay where you belong. You will act like what God made you, a woman." He turned to the house to see if Hinda was watching. She was the gentle one with the children, the tall, intelligent woman who made his life more bearable and barely complained.

Gitel stood straight and quiet, the broad shoulders she had inherited from her father unbending.

"No words," Wolf said. He went into the barn to retrieve the other milk cans. "You will stay here, Gitel. If you try more of your tricks, you will pay a price."

The next morning, stars visible over the sleeping countryside, Wolf and Mordche loaded the wagon with dairy products and made

55

the twenty-kilometer trip to Sosnowiec as they did each Thursday. Late morning, they were in the market square filled with wagons, produce, dry goods, squawking hens in crates and wares of all kinds. The barter lasted till dusk, after which Wolf and his son bedded down for the night at his sister's house, the benefactor each week of a good brick of cheese and a bottle of buttermilk.

Gitel had lain awake and waited until she heard the sound of the horse's steps echoing away. Her father and brother Mordche on their way, there was no better time. Gitel did not know what her father had meant when he warned she would pay a price. By nature superstitious, she found it troubling, but not troubling enough to stand in her way.

"Deborah," she whispered, shaking her sleeping sister's arm, "you have to get up now before Mother stirs."

"Stop," Deborah murmured half asleep and pushed Gitel's hand away.

"Hush," Gitel said, shaking her sister's arm again. "Do what I say. I'm leaving and if you want to come, you have to get up. Now."

Gitel had already put her dress and the few things she owned in a satchel. It sat in the barn behind the barrels of setting cheeses. Now she helped Deborah assemble hers.

"You've awakened Mother," Gitel whispered. "Does the whole house need to know?"

Hinda sat up in the bed, empty of Wolf. "You're leaving," she said, eyes making out the dark forms of her daughters, fingers covering her mouth.

Gitel stepped around to her bed. "Mother, please don't get up. We'll be gone in moments."

Hinda rose and went to the cupboard. She sliced bread, wrapped it in a cloth then placed it in her speckled enamel pot. She wound another cloth around several utensils and handed them to her daughters. "A poor dowry for my dear daughters," she whispered. "Go in health and I wish to see you return in health."

"Come, Deborah," Gitel said. They hugged their mother and left in darkness reading thoughts in each other's liquid eyes, then turned in fate's direction.

Friday, before day began, the two men returned to their wagon, fed and watered the mare. Mordche carried sacks on his back, items they had traded to replenish their grocery. He covered the sacks with the oiled tarp to protect their things from eyes that did not always have the best intentions. By afternoon, when Wolf and Mordche returned to Giebultow, men, mostly Poles, waited for cigarettes, salt, sugar, tea, tins of sardines. They knew the Herszkowicz family closed early on Friday and that Wolf made no exceptions. But this Sabbath evening he had two empty chairs at the table. His sons knew enough to observe and listen. Anger made Wolf's eyes black as the scarce coal waiting to be relit again after the Sabbath. "You see how a father is disobeyed," he began. "My night of peace is broken and the day that follows will be broken. How many days like this will there be? Hinda, this I didn't expect. A rich man I'm not. But a fool I'm not either and when a father tells a daughter to stay, she must. Two decent daughters I have left. Esther Faigle and Balcha. The others have no names."

Hinda remained silent. It was her way. She watched the candle flames she had lit at sundown. She was caught in a world she knew was turning too fast to understand. Even if somewhere in the past she had lived a different life, a city life, it had ended long ago. She had made the choice to be with Wolf. This had become her life. And now she looked at him, as she had for thirty years. His face open to his only master, it revealed prayers for his daughters in a world stirring with events perilous to be a Jew.

CHAPTER SEVEN

1934 A New Life

Bedzin captured Gitel. Tall buildings four and five stories displayed signs with perfect Polish lettering, the kind she remembered from her schoolbooks. A sign hung from an awning in curled Yiddish script, decorated with a fat-bellied baker, the braided breads floated above his head. The sisters laughed, jostling back and forth between the streets and wood sidewalks. Packed trolley cars clanged with urban dwellers. The stores brimmed with books, furnishings, clothing, food, religious articles and things they could not identify. Strollers ambled arm in arm and aromas permeated the air with city spice. She and Deborah lingered in front of a shop window displaying a suit, the jacket rich maroon, the skirt only inches below the mannequin's knee. Their reflections were in stark contrast. Gitel made up her mind that with hard work and with a little *mazel,* she might shed some of her sturdy things, and wear a soft and stylish suit that hugged her waist. If she did well, she and Aron would have an easier life together. He had proposed. Gitel wanted Aron but also wanted her own success. This part of Gitel that drove her to make her own way, Aron understood. She also knew he was disappointed and would not give up.

For a week the sisters lived with Cousin Riesel with the dense brown wig. At first she threw pitying looks at the young women whose regional accents marked them. But the industry of the country cousins overshadowed what they lacked in sophistication. Gitel and Deborah felt Riesel's hospitality wane daily. It hurried the search to find the place on one of the poorest of Bedzin's narrow streets. What it did not offer in space, it was close to the main market. Gitel valued the bustle and traffic a short distance from her *vinkl*, tiny hidden corner. She figured the two of them could live there. They were used to sharing. If the eight of them had fit into two rooms, she and Devorah could make do. Gitel had learned as a small, strong girl, she would manage. She could endure.

On the second day, as the sisters scoured the grime from walls and the ancient oven, a distinguished dark haired man, mature in Gitel's eye, old in Deborah's, appeared. Gitel was shining the only window they had, when she heard his voice.

"A young lady who works so hard," he said. "A pleasure to see and rare among Bedzin's young women. I am Dovid, Dovid Weintraub."

Gitel's heart quickened, drawn to the man with a silken voice. He sounded educated. *Could he the kind of man she fantasized about then pushed from her mind? How did she dare think these things?*

"I am Gitel Herszkowicz." Her face felt warm and she knew it was more than exertion.

"Miss Herszkowicz, you are new here, yes? This is yours?" He pointed to the door ajar, the room in full display.

"It's ours. My sister, she's inside. Deborah, come out." Gitel was struck; a schoolgirl found daydreaming who needed help finding her place in a primer.

Deborah stepped from the room so small it would have been impossible not to have heard and let the broom relax at her side. She looked at Gitel's face, her sister's green eyes lit. "So you already have a customer," she said turning to the man whose features matched the voice, the hands revealing infrequent use for labor.

"Well, it depends on what you have for sale. A man needs far less than a woman."

"Even men have to eat," Gitel said, recovering enough to feel at least one foot on the ground.

"We do." He exhaled the words to Gitel. "This must be your charming sister, Deborah Herszkowicz. Unless there are more of you hidden in there."

"We have nothing to hide. Mr. Weintraub, is it? See for yourself."

"Deborah," Gitel said, "I'm sure Mr. Weintraub only meant it as a joke."

"Please call me Dovid. I'm not such an old man." He pretended to stroke his hand through a long beard, though his was trimmed.

"Well, Mr. Weintraub," Deborah said, turning to the business of sweeping, "we hope you come back to us soon. Gitel is famous for cheese making and cooking. She can tell you how much her boyfriend likes whatever she makes."

"Deborah," Gitel said, "I'm sure Dovid can make up his own mind."

"So, I'll have to come back, yes, Gitel? If your cooking has as much flavor as you do, I wouldn't be surprised if you have many suitors."

"By next week you won't recognize our place," said Gitel.

Dovid crossed the street and Gitel stepped into the room to line shelves with strips from an old oilcloth hoping the distinguished man with the short dark beard would return. She watched Devorah step on a chair to scrub clean the pockmarked back wall where they slept. Gitel hung two of Deborah's embroidered towels across the window as curtains.

Deborah glanced down at her. "This is how you show your loyalty to Aron? I know what that man is after and it's not your soup. And the way you looked at him. I've never seen a sillier look on you face."

"I don't know what you're talking about, Deborah. The way you're acting is how to chase away customers." It was only hunger she told herself. That's what she felt. But she knew better. This was not a hunger satisfied with food.

"Dovid, Dovid, Dovid." Deborah walked around sniffing the air, removing imaginary gloves. "I wonder what he does for a living. If we never see him again I won't cry a tear." Deborah wrinkled her nose and began unwrapping the last of their Cousin Riesel's leaden noodle *kugel.*

By the following week their *vinkl* had changed. Used to the dirt floor from home, the old patched wood beneath their country shoes told them they were becoming city ladies. Work began at sunrise and ended when the kerosene lamp was lit late at night, using more than the smallest amounts of fuel beyond their means. But summer was here, the days longer and best of all Father had agreed to bring products to sell in Bedzin. The Count had told Wolf the head of Poland's Church, Primate Hlond, had directed Poles to stop doing business with Jews. There was pressure on the Count. He had cut the amount of milk he sold to the Herszkowicz family again. "A black year," Father had told Mordche, "1936 is going to be a black year." Their Polish customers in Giebultow dwindled month by month. And since they still brought products to market in Sosnowiec, he agreed with Mordche an outlet in Bedzin could benefit the whole family. Mordche hoped this would lead to peace between father and daughter.

On the same day as the week before, Dovid Weintraub stopped at Gitel's door open to the tumult of street life. Sleeves to her elbows, an apron wrapped about her hips, she rolled out dough and cut it with practiced control, a stack of small squares accumulating on the table.

"I've never seen such industry," Dovid said stepping inside. "What are you making?"

"Oh, you'll see when I'm finished." Gitel's face was warm again. They were alone, Deborah gone to bring apple cake, a present of thanks to their bewigged cousin. As she cut the dough sheet Dovid's eyes following her supple milk white arms. "I wondered if we'd see you again this Thursday."

"I pass always this way to teach the sons of very fine families." Dovid lowered his voice and spread his hands on the edge of the table. He leaned so close, his dark suit jacket brushed her arm. "Maybe on a Sabbath we could go for a walk, Gitel?"

Gitel's heart fluttered. She drew her exposed arm away. The image of Aron's hands, the long strong fingers in contrast to Dovid's, made her hesitate. But she answered yes.

The sisters grateful for Sabbath their only day of rest walked home arm in arm following the service in their *shteibel,* one of the numerous single room congregations they had found soon after arriving. On the way home Gitel talked about the grandeur of Bedzin's Big Synagogue and convinced her sister they should experience praying there. Soon Gitel's quick pace brought them back to the Peasant Gate, the entry to the enclave where the Jews lived. A few trees there had found a way to seed roots in cracks along cramped streets. They adorned the fortunate buildings on the breezy May afternoon.

As was customary they sat down for *mitug*, the main meal. Deborah watched her sister who appeared to be dreaming rather than eating, her usual good appetite at bay. "The pot cheese is turning. I know we have no choice but to eat what can't be sold. Is that why you're not finishing what's on your plate, Gitel?"

"No. I like it sour with a little bite," Gitel said.

"Reminds me of Dovid."

Gitel shook her head and ran her fingers over small cuts. She had worked too fast with the knife to keep up with demand. They had begun using their little dining table to serve her specialties as well as to sell them. The idea had brought more business and pleased her customers. "I'm meeting Dovid for a walk," Gitel said. "It's not as beautiful as our woods but the forest is not far. Come along. Maybe you'll stop missing Mother so much. Why don't you like him?"

"Because I like you so much. And I know Aron is ten times the man."

"Dovid is educated. He takes students from fine families. He has ideas. But his father can't spare money now for him to start a business."

"Spare him money? He has plenty time on his hands from what I see," Deborah said, rolling her eyes. "Last week you expected help with the policeman who bothers us with threats and fines, where was Dovid? He told you he knows about a lawyer. Knows rich families in Bedzin. You went to the police station again to find the name of a judge, and Dovid forgot to meet you."

"A person can forget."

"Gitel, a person can seem one thing and be another."

Gitel passed through the Peasant Gate for the second time that day and here it opened to the wider streets packed with families in finery. She smiled back at a few people who had become customers, marveled at how fast she was establishing a reputation. She paused at the Big Synagogue, the stained glass windows reminders of where the wealthy and learned sat and prayed. Perhaps she and Deborah could squeeze into the back of its upper balcony where the women sat. Neither would have a hard time with the prayers. They could *daven* with the best of them even if they would not be dressed fancy. No, she'd wait until they saved enough. By Rosh Hashanah, the New Year holiday, if they were lucky with sales and the restaurant continued to attract, they would have pretty suits made. If not by the best tailor, then a decent one with whom Gitel could *hondle.*

Up the hill, close to the synagogue remained the ruin of the Polish castle, a giant of stone and turrets on the bank of Przemsza River, the dark water a mirror of what lie ahead. The woods fresh and green were on the edge of what was becoming her city, Bedzin. She wore her navy blue dress with little pearl buttons straight up to a white collar, the one she had begged her mother to have a seamstress sew years before. But it could not hide her figure nor could the skirt swinging below her shapely calves help but reveal a young woman born to work, dance and run with limitless energy. Her hair was rolled into two loose braids and her lips stained with a luxury she had allowed herself, a tube of lipstick the color of ripe wild strawberries ready to be picked by the end of July.

There he was leaning against a shade tree, blooms of purple lilies bordering the path. Dovid's face exuded what Gitel believed, was the light of intelligence, hidden beneath the shorter beard worn by modern religious men. As she strode toward him she imagined he was one of the fortunate, one who had studied beyond mere basics, reserved for those with time, money and often both. It separated the peasants from the educated, rich from poor. The times she walked by Bedzin Gymnasia, the high school for young men and young women, she remembered the dream she had been denied. Everything cut short. Education, more than wealth carried *kovid.* Maybe enough money could buy respect too, yet

63

her mother and father spoke in hushed tones of those who studied Torah. They walked closer to the divine; they were listened to and revered.

"You look more beautiful each time," Dovid whispered. They walked into the woods. He pulled Gitel close and before she could object, kissed her hard. She pulled away but held the feeling of Dovid's lips pressed to hers. The kiss awakened her body to desire and confusion.

"You look surprised, unsure. I couldn't help myself. I like you. Very much. You're not like the others, Gitel. That's what I felt the moment I first saw you."

"Let's walk," Gitel said. She needed to ground her mind and body with movement. Was she different? She was walking with a man she did not know well. Kissing in the woods. She knew Aron well before they kissed. Then weren't they still children when he told her she held his heart? But what she felt was real and it was not only passion. She cared for Aron, the gentle, sweet shoemaker who was always full of news about what interested him, the world and its mysteries. She had to think. Did educated men have other ways with young women? Was she backward from country life? The lure of what she perceived strung her along.

She touched her lips as they walked through the ferns unfurling on the forest floor. Dovid stopped and took her hand, her face shadowed by the sun beginning to descend. "I'm sorry I could not come the other day, to the police station. My father asked me for a favor. How could I refuse? Gitel, from what you've done in such a short time, you can take care of yourself."

"Don't worry." She sensed he stumbled over his words.

"Worry, no. When I'm with you, I don't worry." He kissed her again, pushing a leg between hers. Gitel pulled away, her senses alarmed.

"Deborah will be looking out for me."

"Your sister doesn't like me," he said. He lifted his black felt hat for the coming early evening breeze.

"Deborah misses our mother. We look out for each other." She laced her fingers behind her back and set the pace.

"Are you in a hurry? There is a place we can sit not far from where you live, have a tea. I don't carry money on the Sabbath, but the owner extends me credit. Tell me, Gitel, the business goes well?"

How was she to answer this question? Business is what lit her from within. The fact that she was taking chances and struggling fed her courage and made her want it all the more. Aron knew this and read in her what was impenetrable. But what disturbed Aron most about himself, his reticence and lack of education, drove her toward Dovid.

"Maybe the café is not right. I know somewhere else to talk about private things." Gitel searched his face and wondered what was behind the beard. Why on earth should this even occur to her? Was she looking to find fault with him or were Deborah's warnings playing through her mind? "It's private enough at the place you first mentioned, Dovid. What do you want to know about our business? We're not from the Bedzin *negidestes*, your city women with fortunes."

"Gitel, when I say alone, I mean a place we can be together, do you understand?" He took her hand and brought it to his lips.

"Dovid, I'm not worldly like the women you must know, but I think I understand." She slipped her hand from his.

"No, you have the wrong impression. I'm interested in your business because I think of the future. A woman like you, who can help a man whose life is wrapped in the joys of study, is a pearl."

Was this a prelude to some kind of proposal? If he was serious, what had led to it? She was not raised to be frivolous and disloyal. Aron came roaring into her heart and still this unresolved need within her refused to listen. An educated man with students from wealthy families wanted her. She was overwhelmed. Gitel said, "I only like going around in circles, when I dance."

Dovid gripped her hand. "Gitel, I know you like me. What would be so wrong if I took you to a friend's house? He was my study partner at the most important yeshiva in Bedzin. I want you. The way you move, the way your eyes flash at customers, how our lips meet and you shiver. I want you to be mine."

He took Gitel's arm and they left the leafy coolness of the woods and the overpowering scent of lush lilacs blooms. They passed the ruins of the castle. Dovid raced down the hill to the bustle of the late Sabbath strollers. His words tantalized and flattered yet this urgency forced hesitancy to her steps. They turned onto Prodovana, a street Dovid explained was famous for the milliners who drew business from the *negidestes,* wealthy women for whom there could never be enough ornate hats. The street sliced in half by shadows of a late day sun, she followed him into a squat building. Dovid tapped on the door of an apartment and when there was no answer, he knocked again. No one came to the door. But instead of leaving, he turned the handle and entered.

Gitel peered at a darkening room with two tables, a dozen disordered chairs and stacks of books. She was perplexed. When Dovid had said a friend's she believed it must be a man who lived with his parents or a married couple he knew. Something felt wrong. Voices came from other apartments, a baby cried and she heard muffled singing with a familiar melody. "I don't think anyone is home. We should come back another time," she said.

"Gitel, what you don't understand is this is an opportunity." He pulled her inside and shut the door.

"Dovid, is this a schoolroom? Do you have a lesson planned for me?"

He grinned. "No lessons, Gitel, I just want to have you for myself. This is where my friend and I tutor the children of the rich if you have to know."

Gitel faced the door. "I don't like this, Dovid. You have the wrong idea about me. You tell me one thing, then the story changes. I want to leave now."

"It's a friend's apartment. I told you the truth." Dovid's eyes penetrated hers. He pulled her away from the door, grabbed her arm and smothered her mouth with his lips.

Gitel broke his grip and turned to the door. She put her hand on the knob but he was right behind her. He shoved his weight into Gitel and pulled up her dress. The doorknob jammed into her belly and he tore at her undergarments. He thrust against her again and again. She threw her elbows back as hard as she could and caught Dovid's chest. He gasped. Gitel whirled around and faced him. Her hair flew undone, her eyes were wild and frightened.

Dovid burst out laughing and fell to his knees. "I told you," he said and caught his breath. "I never met anyone else like you." He reached up for her hand. "Nothing happened, Gitel."

She turned away, smoothed down the dark blue skirt of the dress and with shaking fingers fixed her hair. "I'm going home."

Dovid got to his feet. "When you calm down, I'll talk serious with you. You told me how your father admires the learned? It's time for me to talk dowries. I'm a scholar, what you always wanted. And with your help I'll be a businessman too. You're mine now, Gitel."

Gitel stepped around him, opened the door and left. For an instant she listened to heated words between a man and woman from somewhere in the building. She sped down the dark corridor and stood on the teeming street. *I'm not sure what that was. But I am sure, I am not his. No one can find out what happened here. Not my sister, no one, ever. And trust that man again? What would Aron think if he found out? I am ashamed.*

CHAPTER EIGHT

1938 Policeman

The policeman smacked his stick against the door and smirked at the faces watching from the windows. Inside, Gitel mimicked the policeman smoothing his mustache and motioned Deborah back. Gitel opened the door, a bowl of steaming grouts in her arms. "Deborah, our policeman is here," she said aware the neighbors listened for each word. "It's so early the birds sleep."

"*Pani* Herszkowicz, you can joke. It's never too early for me. You owe the *zlotys* from the weeks before. You'll owe every week. Clear? Doing business in Bedzin, it's not free. You people think you have special privileges here? It's over."

"I went to the police station about the *kara* and no one would explain about this tax or the fine you threaten us with. Who was asking money from me, of course, I said nothing. Just to understand."

"*Pani* Herszkowicz, you ask the wrong people." He pulled on the mustache curling about his stiff lips. The stone blue eyes scanned the alley. Neighbors peering through their windows disappeared.

"I asked business people at the market, too. Experienced ones. They had nothing to tell me."

"Who are these people? Maybe they need a visit, too."

Gitel looked up and down the Rybna Alley and shook her head, a broad smile the only thing she gave.

"Nothing to tell? Think I'll disappear? You don't know me."

"I don't jump to every tune."

"Jews will jump to the Endecja Party tune, *Pani* Herskowicz. Isn't it too bad your Jew-loving Pilsudski is dead?" He touched his cap then turned to stare in the window. Gitel stepped in front of it. He had made lewd remarks to her sister. How dare he leer at Deborah and say Jew girls want what Poles have. It revolted Gitel when the word *want* had slipped off his tongue like a wriggling worm. It was all she could do not to slap his face.

"You chase away my business and ask for money. Should I shake it from my sleeve?" She pushed a lock of auburn hair into her scarf.

"I'm a patient man. Shake it from where you like." He put up his patrol stick as if to block the door.

Gitel stepped around him, heart thumping. "I'm a patient woman. You'll excuse me, officer, I have work to do." Inside she mouthed to Deborah, he should burn in hell.

The policeman did not relent. "Stop showing fear," Gitel told her sister. "He's a mad dog." She knew they had to get rid of him. Not that trying to bribe him hadn't crossed Gitel's mind. But he enjoyed harassing them too much and she sensed it would be of no avail. He was hurting their business. She learned from merchants that no such fine was asked of them. If there was such a law, the others had been exempted. Perhaps being a young woman made her vulnerable. Yet there were many women who sold up and down the streets. This Pole was being emboldened by something.

Gitel said nothing about Dovid, but Deborah noticed he had not stopped by and that something was amiss with her sister. Gitel blamed her behavior on the worries over the policeman and the looming last resort, pleading their case before a judge. Deborah begged Gitel to see Aron in Sosnowiec and get his advice. But she understood what Deborah was really after and though she was desperate to see Aron, she feared he would detect there was more than one problem in Bedzin.

She rode the crowded tram to Sosnowiec. With nothing to keep her mind on work, Gitel dwelled on the warning from her father. *You will pay a price.* Was this her price? Had Dovid tried to rape her? She had led him on, allowed him to put her in the position. The word was ugly. Rape. Something that happened to women dragged into the woods by hoodlums. She had been told stories about the Cossacks who defiled women and scarred them for the rest of their lives. Gitel had prayed at the *shteibel,* her eyes filled with tears. She peeked over the divider that separated the men from the women and searched the faces of the men. They appeared earnest, absorbed in prayer and she knew some of them were well educated with families and wives. Why had Dovid chosen her? She had drawn a man whose motives were dishonorable. She was a young woman who had been chaste when her body had asked for more, her strong desires tempered with reason. She and Aron had been on the verge, when they fell into each other's arms, lost in desire. They had pledged to wait.

Now Gitel stood in front of the shoemaker's cooperative on Targova Street, the suit she had worked hard to afford woven with shame. She opened the door and Aron jumped to his feet. His eyes devoured her. His young Polish helpers stitched shoes and pretended not to watch as Aron swept Gitel from her feet. Unable to contain adoration, he stroked her cheek and whispered how much he had missed feeling her next to him. She put her head on his shoulder. Soothed by genuine ardor there was momentary relief from humiliation. But Aron's face flushed with pride deepened her remorse all the more.

In the evening Aron and Gitel walked to the *kino* to see 'The Dybbuk.' Completed only the year before, it had been filmed in a Polish *shtetl,* like the small town of their youths. They sat in red velvet seats, their bodies touching, surrounded by the hushed theatergoers. Hypnotic piano filled the darkened theater. Then the screen lowered to unveil Leahele, a young woman betrothed to the rich man her father has chosen while her true love, a mystic scholar, withers away and dies heartbroken. Leahele runs to the cemetery and falls on the grave of her beloved. She begs forgiveness.

She cries and pleads at the grave of her dead mother to intervene, to stop the ill-fated marriage. But nothing Leahele prays for helps. After the wedding, Leahele becomes possessed by the *dybbuk*. The devil has entered her soul and she reels between the spirit of the earnest scholar and the flesh of a man she was forced to marry. Leahele loses her grip on sanity. The evil *dybbuk* cannot be exorcised from her poor tormented soul. She succumbs to madness and finally to death.

Cymbals shivered and the last note of the piano faded. Gitel sat chilled, as if the *dybbuk* gripped her with its icy fingers. She slipped her arm in Aron's and squeezed his hand, hers stiff and cold. "Why do you take it so serious? It's only a movie," Aron whispered. He tried to change the mood and told her how lovely she was. "In the suit you had made, Gitel you're prettier than the actress." Gitel smiled without joy. Aron drew her close and lifted her chin. "Next time, I'll come to you."

"It would make me happy," she said. But her eyes told another story.

"Something is wrong, Gitel. I know you too well." Her pain was his and he sensed a dark presence.

"It must be the movie, Aron."

"Gitel, tell me the truth. I feel it's more than that."

"I'm worried. I hope I can find a way to stop the policeman from ruining our business. He mentioned the Endecja Party. You know about these things."

"The Endecja party is with the Nazis. Their leader Dmowski waited until his enemy, our friend, Pilsudski died. Dmowski is Poland's Hitler. Do I need to say more?"

Gitel stared ahead. "I'm going to a judge. I don't know what else to do."

"It may be the only way, Gitel. If you get a decent Polish judge, maybe you'll have a chance. This Endecja Party is gaining control. They want to shut down our businesses and crush us."

"Aron, I've been fighting for months. I wasn't afraid. Until now. Will I be able to do anything?"

"You will, Gitel, my darling," Aron said. "I believe in you. You'll find a way."

That night Gitel slept at her aunt's apartment. She awakened in the dark room sweat soaked, her supple muscles stiff until light crept in. Gitel went back to Bedzin unable to shake off her shame and guilt.

* * * * *

A cold November gust quickened Gitel's pace as she neared the tall brick government building. She had no choice but to face alone what rested on her young broad shoulders. She asked the clerk at the front desk when she could see a judge.

"You need to engage a lawyer to be seen by a judge. Don't you know this?" the clerk said addressing her like a dumb child.

"Of course I knew," she said, but she did not. "I have no money to engage anyone." Her voice tremulous, Gitel explained her case. She looked directly at him. "I understood that Poland was a country with a reputation of rights for all people, even as poor as me."

The clerk left. Chuckling upon his return, he asked her to follow.

Gitel faced a clean-shaven man with a white starched collar she sized up as old as her father. He motioned her to come forward and stand before his desk. "I am a magistrate, Judge Szymborski. So you know about Polish rights." He looked at Gitel suppressing a smile.

"I don't know much about rights, *Panie* Judge Szymborski. I think I know right from wrong."

"You believe a policeman has wronged you, *Pani* Herszkowicz, is it? You appear quite young. Where is this business of yours?"

The judge lifted a pen, dipped it in the ink well. "And how are you wronged?" She stood straight and with her earnest country demeanor began. "Your honor Judge Szymborski, I live not far from the Peasant Gate. I came to Bedzin with my sister to make an honest living. We have a tiny store and we live there. I have no complaints. I cook and bake. People say everything I make and serve is good. My sister sews fine embroidery on towels and ladies items. This policeman comes and tells me I must pay him a tax and the *kara,*. Every week he comes and threatens to close us down if I don't pay him. When he passes he scares away customers."

"You are a Jewess?" the magistrate said, his eyes acknowledging what he had surmised from where she lived and her name.

"Yes, *Panie,* I am," Gitel said with surety.

"So have you applied for a license? Are you aware small merchants will have to pass a test or be taxed? Is this what the officer means? Maybe you are confused, *Pani* Herszkowicz."

"No. Your honor, this I did not know. I'm sorry. The policeman said nothing about a test. He wants five *zlotys* every week from me, a tax for doing business and the *kara,* a fine for not paying the tax. Your honor, how can I give what I don't have. And how will I be able do business? He marches before our store swinging his stick, calling us bad names, almost every day for many months."

"This policeman, he has no right to disturb you, if what you say is true. But at the same time you will need to take a test for a license. All small merchants will he required to do so. The rules in Poland are changing, you understand? If you don't pass the test, you will be taxed."

Gitel wanted to know if this test was for all Polish merchants or just for Jews. She was quite sure she knew the answer and it would not be in her interest to ask. "Your honor, I am not bad at figuring in my head, I write and read, but I am not well educated. May I please ask how much the tax would be if I did not pass the test?"

"This I cannot say. Before I make my decision, one last thing. You never mentioned the name of the policeman."

"*Panie,* his name is Molecki."

"Molecki." The judge's brows lifted and he nodded with recognition. "I will write a judgment. The policeman will not bother you. My clerk will tell you when to come for the test."

"Judge Szymborski, thank you for your help. Your letter, *Panie,* do I show it to Policeman Molecki and he will not come back to bother us?"

"*Pani* Herszkowicz, he will not disrupt your business. This I can assure you. You may go." Gitel felt light and free. No matter what this test would mean, for now she had beaten her tormentor. She waited for the clerk to bring the promised judgment. *The test, how will I ever pass a test with my four grades in school? Well, at least I am good in arithmetic.* Gitel folded the sheaf of paper and slipped it in her leather bag, a present from Dovid, its stitches coarse, machine made. She thought about Aron's artistic, fine leatherwork. He said he believed in her. *Well I believe in you, Aron.* Gitel raised her collar against the wind and ran down the steps.

On the way back she passed the Bedzin Gymnasia and stared up at the school windows. Students sat in their high back chairs, heads trained on the teacher. It reminded her of how she had once sat. Her hand went to her thigh where the wound had healed and the scar had toughened her, a lesson never to be forgotten. Strong and tough. The words lifted her for what might lie ahead. There was good news and she was anxious to get back to work. She had defended herself and this gave her more strength then a plate full of her noodles and sour cream, though her stomach said otherwise.

Gitel showed Deborah the judge's fine handwritten document and the young woman choked back tears. "I hope we never have trouble with that policeman again."

"But there's more to do now. I have to find out about a test." Gitel got up and fed the stove a few coals.

"I didn't want to tell you, Dovid was here. I don't trust him, Gitel. You like him, I don't."

"Deborah, I know what I have to do." Gitel tied an apron around her waist and was lost in what she knew best, work. "Maybe I don't trust him as much as you think."

Late in the afternoon Dovid appeared. She had not seen him since the evening when he had shown the disturbing side of himself. They went out for a walk and he took her arm with proprietary resolve. She moved his hand away and faced him. "Dovid, let's just be friends. You said you know important people. Can I believe this?"

"Gitel, for what you accomplished today and you're *still* upset? I lost control. This will not happen again."

Gitel could not stop the revulsion shooting from her eyes.

"Gitel, you're angry over that? I have news for you. A famous lawyer in Bedzin is the uncle of one of my students. He's fighting the Polish courts over testing and taxing our merchants."

"I need to see this lawyer."

Dovid looked away. "I spoke to your father about a dowry."

Gitel stared at him. The man's brazen act and now this. "You spoke to my father?"

"Of course. I met him in Sosnowiec. Your father is a plain-speaking man. The times are hard and there is little money for a dowry."

Gitel crossed her arms and scrutinized the face that revealed his mercenary intension. She was incensed. The man in front of her was unscrupulous. The harm he may have done her and that it jeopardized her life with Aron required she remain calm. "Dovid you think that you have shamed me so that now you can do whatever you'd like with me. Do you think the rich parents of the children you teach would like to learn that you tried to force yourself on me?"

"You would never tell anyone such a thing, Gitel. To suggest it would hurt you more than me," Dovid said with his silken voice.

"Dovid, you don't know what I would, or would not say."

He let out a long, slow breath. "I'll arrange for you to see the lawyer. You'll change your mind about me."

Gitel did not reply. Her mind was on the lawyer. She had gotten what she needed.

The lawyer lived on Modrezejowski. Gitel knocked on the door and thought it must be a mistake. A dingy paint peeled exterior was not what she had envisioned for someone who was a famous lawyer. A short man in a fine tailored suit and skullcap atop thinning blonde hair came to the door. Yes, he was the lawyer and he knew of her needs. He led Gitel into a room, its velvet curtains and Persian rugs in shades of reds and purples in sharp contrast to the outside. There were bookshelves filled from floor to ceiling. He bid her to take off her coat and showed her to a large chair. She recognized it was stuffed with fine goose down. Gitel was in a world into which she had never stepped. She had plucked down from uncooperative fat-bottomed geese and she estimated to stuff a chair that size would have taken a small hill of airy white down. He looked at Gitel's hands as if reading her mind and asked her to tell something of herself and family. She was a girl with a dream, she said, that dreams were not enough for she was willing to do whatever she must, to achieve it. He listened and nodded his head. What she had experienced was an ordeal, worrisome for Jewish merchants he explained. A smile came to his lips when Gitel told about a victory, her judgment.

"Miss Herszkowicz, the year you came to my city, yours now, 1936, the Primate of Poland, August Hlond accused the Jews of being usurers, traders and frauds and directed Poland's religious leaders to institute a boycott of their businesses." He paused and put his graceful hands together. The ugly accusations against her people were stirring. "I have a good friend," she said. "He told me he read about this in the newspapers."

The lawyer stood. Gitel rose. "You have a wise friend if he helps you learn what we face. Do not worry this moment. My petition before the Bedzin County Magistrate has been accepted. For now the test for our small merchants is delayed." He held the coat she had worn through many seasons and she slipped it on. She was almost as tall as this learned man who made a slight bow, the kind she had observed gentlemen give well dressed ladies on fashionable streets. "You are a brave and clever young woman in any case," he said opening the door. "What is inside a human being to my experience is not often a match to the exterior."

What he meant by these last words filled Gitel with questions. She crossed the street. A glance at the façade conjured the image of Dovid. She had judged his outside, what he appeared to be. For him, she thought, it turned out to be the opposite. There were things within her that had to be examined. What had led her to the unsavory experience with Dovid? She was late. Gitel hurried to the market. There would be a poor selection from which to choose and she would be forced to *hondle* harder with the very merchants for whom this learned lawyer had won a victory.

CHAPTER NINE

1939 Falling Apart

Aron was nineteen when Gitel became more than his clever, pretty girlfriend. She had not said a word about how she had run away to her aunt in Lodz. The bravado of a fifteen-year-old had sparked the determination of a young woman who wanted more. But he had noticed. The pull of his opposite pole, a force of nature forever to be obeyed, both attracted him and made him wary. Now, seven years later, it was time.

Conscripted into the Polish Army, Aron had trained on maneuvers and had not been with Gitel for months. He was bursting to tell of the commendations awarded him for rifle skills, surprise her with the news he was doing well enough to propose, even if war was on everyone's lips. Sunday morning his two helpers in church allowed Aron a few hours away from the *warschtadt*. He pumped his legs against a stiff wind sweeping past horses thudding on the hard-pack road. A faded blue bus cloaked him in noxious fog. It blasted its horn at pack bearing peddlers clogging the road.

His ears pink beneath a woolen cap, he angled through the narrow streets to Gitel's *vinkl* wedged among shops in Bedzin ghetto. Aron jumped off the bicycle, excitement beating his heart, removed the leather laces and shook his pant legs free. He knocked and recognized the energetic footsteps. The pungent sweet aroma of *yushkie,* potato soup, enhanced the hunger for the woman opening the door.

He stood, unsure how to begin his mission. "Gitel, you look so well." Her eyes wide with surprise, she smiled and led him inside."

He scanned the room, remade. An earthen crock held cheeses and butter. Jars of pickled red beets sat on a shelf his eyes stopping at canned plums suspended in sugary syrup.

"I see you like my plums," she said color rising to her cheeks, fingers reaching for his hands.

"I like every bit of you." He drew her close but Gitel pulled away. It was a dance, a reaction she could not help, sensing governance over her being. She relented arms falling, off balance, unsure of what she wanted. He slipped off the kerchief, stroking silken waves, melting the resistance, and felt her lips lingering on his.

She stepped back, arm's length and assessed. "You're thinner."

"I need a wife."

Gitel linked arms and sat him at the table. "First, skinny bones, I need to feed you."

"I could live from the sun and your love, it would be enough," he said.

He followed her deft movements, eyes on the shapely legs. She set down a bowl of potato soup and sat knees pressed against his. He breathed in its warmth and began spooning.

Gitel watched him satisfied she could please him this way. Care for him. She had been smitten for what she felt was almost her whole life. He was handsome with sensitive bearing and forthrightness. His keen mind surprised her. How did he know so much when he barely had education and thought so little of himself? It bothered her and they often argued about his reticence. You're the only one they made become a shoemaker she'd ask and then was sorry. Having hit his bottomless pit of self-denigration she'd follow with what a fine craftsman he was. It rarely ended well for she knew it was not such an honor to be a shoemaker. Yet his work was exceptional.

She felt a chill, Aron's eyes penetrating through a wall of trust she had breached.

"Gitel, is it over?"

"I told him it was over," she said. "After everything, you still want me?"

"Yes." His chest heaved as if in pain. He blurted, "When I found out I wanted to tear him apart."

Gitel shook her head. She had been silent, swallowing her pride, afraid if she accused Dovid of trying to force himself on her, *she* would be seen a diminished woman. All along he had betrayed her, dared to inquire about a dowry without her knowledge. She shook her head. "Maybe if we weren't alone," she said, "he wouldn't have tried. Maybe it was not all his fault."

Aron pushed away from the table. "Maybe that's true," he said unable to look up.

"I never really cared for him, Aron. It was my silly dream about the educated, thinking this would shine on me. It doesn't matter what he said."

Aron gulped for air, the word educated drowning him in recrimination. "Oh Gitel, my strong, smart girl. He only wears the hat of a Hasid. He has the heart of a cheat."

Gitel shrugged her shoulders, the pragmatic, easy nature he admired infuriating him more. He wanted to hold her, forgive her, forgive himself, and it stoked his anger. She understood what stirred his tender heart. He knew the same of her. Another reason he adored her. There was no pretense. All lay bare from when they were mere children.

They stared in silence.

"I made a mistake. And you? You had Surele. The dark little raisin, a father with money for a big dowry."

"You leave Surele out of this. There never would have been a Surele if not for a Dovid. I'm a man. I never made promises. What would you have me do, sit alone day and night?" He beat his long fingers against the yellow checkered oilcloth. "I'm willing to forget some things," he said his voice a soft breath.

Gitel pale, the sun retreating from the window, brushed away tears. "Then why can't you forget what gnaws in your guts? Why do you think it?"

"Why do you need to work night and day? You don't have your own pack of troubles? We are what we are."

She let out a measured sigh, her lips coming together in almost a smile. "I don't know what to do myself," her face a question, eyes downcast on work-worn hands. "Here I have something. Leave Bedzin?"

Aron stormed out of the shop. *Money,* he thought. The streets were filled with people rushing to buy and sell and make a living as best they could, calling to friends hanging out of windows in shabby buildings lining the narrow streets with the smells of savory cabbages, old books, and the masses. 'Begin the Begine' played from a radio somewhere, the mellow tones bathing him in memories. He was drawn to this woman for whom there was no rational way to explain his need nor want, its pull natural and mysterious as the ancient moon over earth's waters.

He stepped in, planting his limbs uncensored, elegant, his eyes searching her face. "Gitel, I'll try to change. With you maybe I will. One thing that won't change is how I long for you. Maybe I won't be a wealthy man. But I can make a living. The boys in my *schumacherie* like me and we work together hard. Last month I sold nine pairs of shoes. Can you imagine? We have so much work in 1939, a time like this."

"I could trade for leather." She said, then stopped, a free bird afraid it might be caged. "But Aron, the war."

"Gitel, they are calling for maneuvers again."

She reached for his hand. "What if I have a baby? How could we ..."

"You've given me the answer, Gitel. If you're not ready now, you will never be ready. Your father still comes here to trade? You can tell him yourself what you did to me. He knows who is an honorable man."

"Aron, don't go away like this."

"How should I go away! With my tail between my legs?"

"I care for you, only you."

"Not enough, Gitel. When you wake up, it may be too late." He stared at her framed by the doorway and threw his leg over the bicycle frame. She grabbed his jacket sleeve. But he wrenched free, and pushed down hard on the pedal. Anger propelled him away.

What have I done, throbbed at her temples. Why hadn't she been able to explain better? But then that part of her, the control spoke. *I've worked hard. Won my own battles against their rules. Always rules. My father's rules. I'm almost a twenty-three year old woman.* Gitel peered at all that surrounded her. It felt empty. *I have hurt Aron, my beloved. How could I have been so naive? The war. Oh, my God. I pray we will be together.*

Aron peddled, the dream of having Gitel for his wife unfulfilled. In months he could be holding a rifle, an outsider in the Polish Army, surrounded by enemies. Worst of all, Gitel had broken his heart.

CHAPTER TEN

1940 Discovered

Aron stood by the barracks door as if paralyzed, his protective mask disintegrated, the ruse ended. They were gloating. Where was he to go? Nowhere. If he ran from the stalag, the guards would shoot him on sight.

"That's right. One of his own across the courtyard told me," Alek said. "He says to me, you know what that shoemaker is? I recognize him. He's a Jew. That shit! I smelled it from the beginning. What are you going to do?"

"What am I going to do?" The foreman lowered his voice. "This news is going to the Commandant with me. Do you hear? All of you. Your damn mouths are shut. I tell him."

Aron opened the door. "*Dzień dobry*," the words razors in his throat. He dropped to his workbench and lifted a broken shoe. His heart raced and he held the shoe tight in a feeble attempt to control the trembling. Their smiles of triumph and contempt bore into his shoulders.

"*Dzień dobry*," the foreman answered, mocking. "Yes, it is a good morning. We started with good news. Did you hear?"

Nothing, he would say nothing. *What will be will be. What is going to happen to me only heaven knows.* An iced stillness took him over.

"I smell *Żyd*. What do you say to this, Matuszyński?" Alek's eyes flashed with victory.

Laughter erupted. And the snorting of foraging pigs. Aron reddened, sweat on his forehead, his eyes on the foreman's face.

"Do you smell something, Matuszyński?" The foreman twisted his mouth in disgust.

"It's what I am," Aron said.

"Maybe we need proof," the foreman snickered at Aron. He stood. The others followed.

"Get up." Alek pointed at Aron. "They say the Jew dick is even uglier than the Jew face."

Aron had felt the man's venom from the first moment. He looked away from the tormentor and stood, arms hanging, prey bound for slaughter.

"Say it," the foreman shouted. "Say what you are."

"I'm a Jew." There was nothing left to say.

"You'll get yours, you filth," Alek said through clenched teeth. "Let him keep his little Jew dick by the shit in his pants."

"Get to work. I'm going to the Commandant. Keep our prize safe till I get back." The foreman stepped out into the swirling snow, the sweet heat of triumph enlivening his steps.

Late afternoon Aron was taken from the workshop to the Commandant's office. Was he not the same man valued for his skill? The Germans had come to respect him as a *meister,* a master craftsman. In this office he had found the courage to tell the Commandant he could repair his boots like no other shoemaker in his *stalag.* What exceptional qualities could he speak of now? The Commandant wore the boots Aron had remade, polished to mirror sheen. He towered over Aron, the medals flashed on his grey uniform and the eagle affixed to his cap was ready to devour a Jew. Aron's heart pulsed through the worn khaki jacket.

"You admitted what you are. This is all we need to know." He shoved aside the Geneva Convention Manual on his desk. "The lieutenant will instruct you."

Aron prayed for his life.

His boots crackled as they met the frozen ground, a speck to be eradicated. What had god made him that he was so loathed? He passed the shoemakers waiting for rations and overheard words carried on a gust of wind.

"Why should they send him home? Why Matuszyński? Always he has luck."

"Luck, eh, you dumb ass?" the foreman said. "The Commandant's lieutenant told me they're shipping out the whole lot of them. His luck is over. They'll work the Jews till they drop."

"But the Germans are sending him home and we rot here." Alek said.

"Are you stupid? Home to meet his death. I hear they have something good for us." The foreman's yellow teeth chattered in the January freeze. "The Nazis are sending us to be helpers in a special camp called Auschwitz."

The next day Aron was marched to the Freiberg Rail Station. He could not understand why he had not been killed the moment he was found out and feared he would be shot along with the other Jews, his body left to rot in the woods. But the Nazi guards concentrated on fitting their boots into the tramped down snow to avoid the high white drifts.

Aron had stuffed bread and a few cigarettes he had hoarded over the months in a pouch he had fashioned from workshop scraps. Under his boot linings he had smoothed twenty marks, spared from visits to the canteen. The guards ended the march on the train platform dense with passengers wrapped in layers of clothing carrying valises and packages. A fierce wind whipped their faces, most of them ethnic Germans fulfilling the *Lebensraum* imperative to live in places emptied of Jews and Poles who were being shipped to labor camps, displaced further east or murdered.

A whistle pierced the countryside quiet and the wheels of a train rattled down the track until it slowed to a stop. The crowd on the platform disappeared into dense warm steam. Behind the throng waited the prisoners and the Nazi guards. The passengers filed up the metal steps and the guards shoved the seventy prisoners into the cars. They backed away when all their charges were on board and stood with rifles ready until the train pulled out of the station. It creaked over the iced tracks, gaining speed. No one paid attention to Aron, wedged between chord-bound boxes and valises. He began to breath with the hypnotic rhythm of the rocking train. *What am I? What am I?* What kind of prisoner was he? Could this be a blessing or would he be butchered taking his next breath.

In the crush on the platform he was separated from most of the unfortunates and avoided making eye contact with the ones in his car. *Mazel,* he thought to himself. A passenger wiped condensation from a window and Aron caught glimpses of snow-bowed trees, the silhouettes filling him with the wonder nature offered so opposite the plans of men. Yet Ksiaz Wielki danced in his heart. Anxious to see Gitel he did not know if she was still in Bedzin or if she was even alive, a horrid thought he banished.

The train moved for hours at a steady pace and rocked Aron into a reverie he used to regain equilibrium…he runs with Gitel through the Count's meadow, the sun pouring its warmth over them. She speeds ahead, her hair flowing wild and free. He catches Gitel and feels her playful resistance. They tumble into golden hay and he kisses Gitel, her lips sweet. She opens her eyes and they tell him he is everything, for all time. And Aron hopes.

The train stopped in Munich, Stuttgart and Nuremberg and more Germans boarded ready to take their new *rightful* places. Aron disembarked to relieve himself and walked several cars away, wary of being recognized, watchful of the Jews who had also separated from the group when their opportunities arose. Aron acted as a lone traveler and pushed to settle by a door. Though it was colder, he would be close to the stairs should there be a reason to escape.

He listened to German conversations and gleaned more than he wanted to hear. Their admiration for Hitler turned his empty stomach. Their references to the *kreig,* how well the Nazis' war advanced, disheartened him. Warsaw had been bombed into total destruction, the Luftwaffe on its way to wipe Poland away for good. He felt a surge of loyalty and remorse for the men he had left in the trench. The Poles were fanatics about their sovereignty and he believed they would go underground. He snapped back to what was immediate. What remained of his uniform could draw attention but Germans so far from Poland seemed unconcerned with a worn-out drab khaki coat. He had stuffed his cap into his jacket and worked to strike a relaxed unmilitary pose. Aron picked at food he had hoarded, careful to conserve for what lay ahead and was relieved to have a water source, snow. But any sense of calm was over once he recognized the name of a Silesian border town. They had crossed into embattled Poland.

The train bucked and strained on the tracks, the wheels buried in four feet of snow groaned to a halt. The conductors cursed the Polish blizzard, ran through the cars, and shouted for men to get off the train. Aron followed the volunteers. There were few shovels and some men jumped back into the cars. The wind pelted them with stinging snow and crusted over the tracks. A crew of about fifty dragged to the front of the cars, where a wall of frozen slush built around the locomotive apron.

The thought that he had a chance to disappear, perhaps to flee east and escape, came and went as Aron slipped his khaki cap on. Where could he go in such a storm and what would be his chances? He kicked loose ice on the wheels and helped clear hundreds of meters of track before the locomotive could push forward. The frozen men dragged back to the cars. Aron's ears were the color of beet soup, his hands prickled with needles. For the short time he worked there was camaraderie. He was a disciplined member of a group joined in a single purpose, a soldier. He had once again worked with his enemies, all of it temporary. He slipped the frozen cap away as the train gained momentum. Aron was back in its power, in its peril.

Several days later, supplies gathered along the route for the *Wehrmacht*, the trip was over. The sun cast a purple veil over Krakow as Aron reached his closest point home. Leery, he walked from the station among disembarked passengers until they disbursed. Where was he to find a place for the night, how was he to make the last fifty kilometers to Ksiaz Wielki without getting caught? Krakow was in chaos, the streets littered and barricaded, yet it had not been bombed. The coming night suited him and he slinked in the shadows past the elegant buildings that had enchanted him the first time he had ridden his bicycle to Krakow. Aron spied an armband with the yellow Star of David on the arm of a man. The man hurried in the direction of ancient Kazimerz, the Jewish quarter. The sight of it hit the core of Aron's being with fear and loathing for his enemy. They were being singled out. He would soon be made to do the same, he thought, if he made it home alive. He put his head down and moved silently along an alleyway. He had no identification. In his Polish uniform, the last thing he wanted was to be stopped by a German soldier. But wearing that uniform and being identified by a Pole could be an advantage.

A Polish woman wrapped in a blanket approached and he was careful not to startle her. Shivering, blowing into his hands, in muffled tones, Aron let her into his world of secret bravery. He told her he had escaped from a prison camp for Polish soldiers, that he killed a Nazi and stole his money. He pointed to his uniform and made clear he had to disguise it or he would be caught. The woman listened to his story, her eyes already cold with grief. She crossed herself. "In Bochnia, not far from here, you heard of it, known in all of Poland for our salt? My brothers were shot in December. December 18. Fifty-six good Poles they murdered on the same day. Jews, too." She spat and wiped her mouth.

Aron nodded. He was exposed. He needed to camouflage. The person he had stopped would be unsympathetic, no matter what he wore, if she knew.

"You heard of these *Einsatzgruppen*?" she said. "Killers. Nazi killers trained to murder us."

"Yes," he said but of *Einsatzgruppen* he not yet heard. He looked at the woman's blanket. It was why he had stopped her and he had to make his move. "If I'm spotted," Aron said, "there will be one less soldier left to defend Poland. Would you sell me your blanket?"

The sight of a German mark unfolding in his palm as a trade for her worn blanket made her gasp. She peeled off the blanket, stuffed the wet mark deep into her coat pocket and crossed to the other side of the alley. Aron threw the blanket around his shoulders, her body warmth welcome and passed an empty storefront. An image reflected from the window, the face round compared to its usual spare cheeks, even after little food and hard travel. He had never looked better. Who would believe it, he thought. The man in an old blanket with the best story he might ever tell, winked back. Aron was pleased his uniform coat was hidden and he had more protection from February. *A mensch tracht un gut lacht.* Man plans and God laughs. The words brought a quick smile to his lips and he gave thanks.

Now less than fifty kilometers from home after nine hundred kilometers across Germany into Poland, the last stretch loomed endless. The city in darkness, Aron walked north on the Warsaw-Krakow Highway until he found a shed and sneaked inside for the night. At first light he was back on the road and licked from his fingers, the last of the crumbs he had conserved. Wary of every sound, he heard a horse clomping behind him. Instead of passing, the wagon slowed and Aron faced a horse snorting.

"You're a soldier, no? I know one of our uniforms when I see it." The man driving the wagon stared at Aron's coat sleeves poking from the blanket.

Unable to deny the obvious Aron tightened the blanket about his shoulders and looked up at the man on the wagon seat.

"You are right, *Pan,*" he said. "I escaped from a stalag in Germany."

He gave Aron an approving look. "Maybe you came across my son? My boy is Piotr Tomislaw. We're from Bochnia." The man seemed older in an instant, his brow pressed into deep furrows.

Aron had passed Bochnia, the same town the woman had told him of where the massacre had been. "Where was he fighting?"

"He is with the 2nd Warsaw infantry." The man sighed. "I know about Warsaw. We hope he is alive. Our last son. The youngest was killed when the Germans slaughtered many in my town. His mother cries day and night."

"I'm sorry, no. The stalag holds thousand and thousands of our men. I hope your son will soon return."

"Yes, we hope. Get in. I take this load of salt from the mine to Sosnowiec. What's your name?"

"Matuszyński." It was a pure Polish name and it had served him well. He could say nothing of his workshop in Sosnowiec. "Thank you, *Pan* that will put me closer to my home town, Miechow."

"I pray someone helps my Piotr. Brave soldiers need our help. One day the Germans will suffer for what they do to our land, our people."

Aron lifted himself into the wagon. Our land our people echoed in his ears. To what people, to what land did he belong? The man signaled the mare. She dug her shoes into the packed snow and pulled. They rode in silence. Aron was grateful and wanted to talk to the Pole, but knew it would not be wise. In the afternoon, the horse slowed and stopped. So close to Sosnowiec, he could run into any number of people. He jumped off the wagon and pulled the blanket up to shield his face.

"Take this, soldier." The man unwrapped a cloth and handed Aron a cabbage roll, the scent of meat released.

Aron swallowed his hunger and reached under his coat. He pulled out the leather pouch he had made in the stalag. "I wish your son luck. You're a kind man, sir. It's all I have to thank you."

"Very nice," the man said, "something for my wife. You have a talent with leather."

"No, I have no idea about leather," Aron said, "a friend made it for me, long ago." He watched the mare kick up snow, confident she would soon be rid of her burden and eat her straw.

With fifteen kilometers to go Aron took off, more akin to flying than walking. He had traveled many times from Sosnowiec to Ksiaz Wielki. Though the rolling fields were covered white, winter could not disguise broken chimneys, destroyed houses and toppled barns. He saw the dislodged on the road pulling wood carts with their salvage. It gave Aron a small taste of what the war had brought to his home area during the six months since the Germans struck. What his own people might be facing, and Gitel, never left his anxious mind. The closer he got, the more he worried about what he would find.

CHAPTER ELEVEN

1940 Invasions

W hile Aron was being unmasked in the stalag, Nazis had swept through his town. Thick chains thwacked on the tires as their truck had rolled in and halted in the square. Two *Schutzstaffel*, Waffen SS dispatched to ensure compliance, slid from the cab of the truck. The huge frame of the leader of the operation, Sturmmann Private First Class Prinz, cast a pernicious shadow. He sniffed the air, offended by *untermenschen,* the less than human inhabitants in his sight.

In 1935, Prinz had the great honor of listening to the German mastermind of the SS, Heinrich Himmler. At first glance, *Reichsfuhrer* Himmler, a short nearsighted Bavarian with a nonathletic build disappointed Sturmmann Prinz. But soon he was struck with Himmler's belief in Aryan superiority. His hatred of Jews and the ruthless measures he condoned to purify the German race showed Prinz that he was under the master of Hitler's terror. Himmler's rhetoric won his allegiance forever.

SS Prinz threw his massive shoulders back with national pride. He had not yet risen above rank of private, and though it was true 1940 was only beginning, he needed to advance. He was willing to use all of his talents. When he gave the order, a tarp lifted from the back of the truck and five black uniforms slithered onto the fresh snow. Unlucky Poles, young and old, Jews, children, everyone in the square were the first to absorb blows from their swinging truncheons. The SS lined up the beaten unfortunates in front of the church. The town folk hidden in their houses were dragged out to assemble; some unable to think clear enough to grab a coat against January.

Hubner the Volksdeutche, whose mother tongue was German, stood in the square and watched in awe. The language unspoken in his town at last throbbed with familiarity. He spoke up when SS Prinz asked if any of the louts standing in front of him understood a proper language. In that moment, Hubner the Volksdeutche volunteered his services and elevated himself above the conquered. Prinz had found his perfect man.

Hubner's work began with an immediate translation. Two of the SS stroked thick ropes slung from their shoulders and SS Prinz instructed Hubner to say those who did not comply would be hanged with rocks tied to their feet to insure a slow, painful death. With sincere uplifted tones Hubner told the assembled their travels were restricted, enforced labor would begin in the morning, living arrangements would be altered to accommodate the worthy ethnic Germans arriving without notice, and all schools were closed. Trade with Jews was over under penalty of being sent to a labor camp. He finished, his voice betraying a sense of relief the duty was done. There was a hint of nostalgia for the people he had lived with in harmony if not great affection, and he kept his eyes from faces he knew belonged to those lower than the Poles.

Next afternoon SS Prinz watched as Hubner delivered the next edict. Every Jew, from infant upwards was gathered in front of the church. The list of names in Hubner's hand had been hurriedly compiled by a newly appointed group; the Judenrat. Eight Jews were chosen to organize the community and cooperate with the will of the Nazis, their ingenious organization and intimidation tactics almost impossible to resist. In exchange for protection and favors Judenrat members, a few well off, a few duplicitous, a few with empathy, agreed to enforce the restrictions and take on tasks of choosing which Jews would be selected for labor camps first.

The Judenrat leaders stood at Hubner's elbows, their faces confident facades, hearts deluded by self-interest and fears, believing they could help. In a canvas bag once stuffed with Hubner's brushes, paints, rags and tools of his trade were enough yellow stars for the two hundred and seventy-five Jewish families who would be under his once paint-stained thumbs. They were the same people he had lived among for twenty years and had made a living painting their homes and stores. The Jews shivered while his voice soared. It was evident the man had practiced German all the years with his wife and children in the privacy of his home and he flaunted his Polish with a German cadence he had once hidden.

A day later he waved a yellow star. By the end of the week each Jew twelve years and older would be responsible for buying one. The curfew was eight o'clock. He, Hubner, had the authority to punish anyone seen on the street without the yellow star affixed to his armband. And death was not out of the question, did they understand? In the biting cold sunshine, they nodded, and when Chaim Abromczyck let out a loud sigh, Hubner took his first present from the Nazis, a luger from its holster, and whacked the bridge of the tailor's nose. "You are lucky today, Abromczyck," he said in his new voice. "The blood drips only from your nose. It is your house I take to be my own. Your family will move in with one of your good Jew friends." He smiled and snapped the pistol into the holster. The Jews were dismissed and by then the shadow from the church spire, the fine wood structure built by the Nobles Wielopolski, which had stood in the square since 1733, darkened the day.

* * * * * *

The February night Aron hid in the shed, less than a day from reaching home, Polish hooligans attacked his family. Breaking glass and screams shattered what little peace the Matuszyński family had. It brought them one step closer to the ugly events to unfold. The family tried to protect themselves from the flying glass and rocks crashing through the windows. Ruchel, Aron's mother, and Pescel, his sister, stifled screams, their ice hands over their mouths as an ax hit the door. Mendel, Aron's elderly father and his young brother were powerless against the four liquored haters wielding axes. The hoodlums screamed vile epithets and pissed against the split door.

"Next time we burn you into hell."

"Like rats, we'll smoke you out. *Parshawa Żyd*, dirty Jews," a voice taunted. They promised they would return to finish the job. Then disappeared into the night.

Howling wind blew snowdrifts through the shattered windows and blanketed white the glass littered floor. The family shivered for hours, and lay so until clouded breaths were visible in sunlight streaming through what were once windows. Bones numb, the water in the bucket capped with ice the little apartment in shambles, they saw what had befallen them and huddled grateful they were alive.

This was Aron's welcome home. He had dreamed of the warmth of his family and found them in misery. From one hell into another he had stepped. A few scratches were nothing, his father assured him. The family stood together, their arms entwined, breathing as one. "It's you we were so afraid for, in a prison held by our biggest enemies." Aron pushed his anger down, his heart throbbing with pity for the anguish his family had bore, overshadowing the months of his ordeals.

But it rose against the vicious hoodlums when he saw his mother Ruchel standing in a ruined room, the place she had done everything for them, her hands busy mending, and caring for the little that belonged to them. Here, he had grown from young boy, with all the hardships the family endured. He had never seen a thing out of place, a cup or a utensil neglected. Who were these Poles he wondered that had so much hate against people that scratched a living and met their obligations, never asking for anything, no matter how arduous their lives. Hadn't his mother always found a way to give a few *grochen* to even the less fortunate Jew or Pole?

"Aron, don't get excited. It won't help." Mendel shoved broken glass off a chair and sank down. Our own *Kristallnacht*. You were the first to tell us about Hitler."

"This is what you've come home to. From a Nazi prison to maybe worse," Itchele said.

"You didn't want to believe that it would come here." Aron said. He pitied his haggard father unable to protect his wife and daughter or Itchele, his son, just old enough to scrape whiskers from his chin. What he would have done pricked at Aron's conscience.

He helped his mother pick up broken plates, one of her hands wound in a blood stained cloth. His sister Pescel was wrapped in silence, a mane of blonde ringlets tangled about her shoulders. The horror of the night rendered her luminous skin, death-like, her sensuous lips bloodless. Pescel swept the dirt floor with a disbelieving, detached gaze. "In less than a year and a half you see what's happened," Aron said to Pescel, trying to draw her into the conversation, into what warmth the family could offer. "November 1938, stormtroopers smashed store windows and stole whatever they wanted. They burned synagogues to the ground all over Germany. They murdered without stop. And where are the thousands of men they dragged off? They threw them into concentration camps. That was the beginning."

"So where should we go?" Mendel said. "The Nazis are among us now. Our police, even if they were still here, would do nothing for us." He blew into his hands, reviving his old fingers, and shook his head at Aron. "You put on so much weight when I first saw you, I thought you were swollen with disease."

They all laughed. "Now we see how you could send bread." Itchele patted his stomach, what there was of it. He smiled and nodded at Aron, the word 'Gitel' formed on his lips, and he watched Aron's eyes light with relief and happiness.

Aron grabbed Itchele and hugged him. "You're becoming a man, brother."

Mendel winked knowingly at his sons. "Don't think your mother and me didn't thank you over and over for what you sent. It saved us, Aron."

"There is work to be done." Ruchel stepped over to Aron, her silver candlesticks cradled in her arm. She examined Aron's face, unaccustomed to its roundness and cupped her hand for an instant beneath his chin. "With all our other *tsuris,* this trouble has to befalls us. But you have come home." Aron lifted her hand to his lips.

"Itchele and I will find something to block the windows, Mother," Aron said.

"Take your father with you. Mendel, go with your sons. Just look out for the hoodlums. They promised to kill us. I believe them."

"Pescel, start a fire in the oven with the broken wood from the windows. We'll have tea and I'll find something for us to eat when you come back. Let's get to work. What women can do, men have no idea," she said to her only daughter, Pescel, whose beauty had brought no luck to herself or the family.

"I have plenty idea," Mendel said, his heart filled with devotion to his wife of many years.

For Aron, coming home and stepping into the family's frightening reality was still a gift. The Commandant released him to death yet he had eluded the dark ones' powers, had by chance and his wits returned. His desire for Gitel had fueled and strengthened him, his dream of her by his side never waning. Strewn with joy and heartbreak he had not given up destiny's path and was more determined than ever.

CHAPTER TWELVE

1940 A Winter Proposal

Aron and Mendel went to the blacksmith shop in hopes of finding materials to secure the smashed windows and door. "Love burns inside of you," Mendel said. "That is why you don't feel the cold. I am an old man and mine is a little cooler." Aron gripped his father's hand, no words needed. The blacksmith Slomynsk was the same Pole who long ago had enabled Aron to fashion the ice skates. He listened to Aron and Mendel tell about the attack, his face impassive. The man agreed to help but was anxious to be rid of the Jews standing by his forge. He spared an old board once laid down for his workmen to keep the heat from melting their shoes. The Pole less stout, his height diminished by the years still lifted the thick splintered board as if it were a twig and handed it to Aron. Mendel extended a hand to the Pole he had known his entire life. He gestured to Aron who promised to make repairs on the blacksmith's boots as soon as he got hold of leather.

"Now go to your woman," Mendel said when the board lay on the frozen ground beneath the black holes, once windows. "Itchele told you last night when your face begged and you were too ashamed to ask about Gitel in the middle of our *tsuris*. She is safe for now with her parents. I heard she and her sister ran home with just the clothes on their backs as the Nazis closed off Bedzin ghetto. They shoved hundreds inside the Big Synagogue then burned it to the ground."

"Father," Aron said, "I've seen too much death."

Mendel rocked back and forth a prayer for the dead moving his lips. "My son, when your eyes and heart are filled with her, Gitel will tell you of her ordeal." He put his hand on his son's arm and nodded toward Giebultow.

A frozen band of white, the road meandered to Giebultow. The adjacent brook shone translucent. Capped with ice, the hills and homes yet protected in the remote hamlet, took a last gasp before the stranglehold. Aron crossed the footbridge and there it was, the way he remembered, from when he was a journeyman pursuing his maiden.

"It's you!" Deborah said, the first of the Herszkowicz' to see him. She stared at Aron her face set in an astonished smile. "Gitel," she yelled, "take your hands off that churner and come out. You have a handsome visitor." Deborah disappeared into the dairy, squeaking commands, turned about in confusion and ran out.

"You've forgotten my name, Deborah?" Aron winked.

"Oh, Aron," she laughed. "You look so ... good. When did you come back from the army?"

"Yesterday, Father barely recognized me. He thought I was swollen and on my deathbed." Aron's eyes were on the barn.

Gitel stepped out. Aron had not seen her in many months. The outline of her body and the green sweater draped over her shoulders flooded him with youthful times. She exuded warmth as she came closer and he perceived hints of something new. Her chestnut hair hung in a loose single braid and accentuated the sensuous side she often chose not to reveal. A quick look of desire held his gaze. Her striking alabaster cheeks rose in a shy smile and mirrored the strength and beauty she held within.

"Deborah is correct, Aron. You look well." Gitel had longed for this moment and now stood unsure to even hope.

"I'm going to tell mother who is here. Everyone." Deborah beamed and Gitel nudged her sister toward the house.

Aron faced Gitel. "You gave me reasons to fight for my life. I came back to you."

His words made her pause. And she dropped her head, her voice barely audible. "Aron, I never stopped thinking about you. What happened between the two of us. I couldn't rest. I prayed you would be safe, just to see you again."

Aron reached out his hand. Gitel pressed his hand to her heart. "Are you cold? Should we go inside?" *I was so foolish, can he still want me* spun within as she led into the dairy barn, the scent of sweet cream enveloping them.

"I've never felt more warm." He brought her to him. "Do you know what you mean to me, Gitel? You were my heart the whole time I was in the stalag. I need you." He touched his lips to hers, a gentle searching look on his face.

Gitel tasted his warmth. "I've missed you. Everything about you." She turned away. "I didn't think you'd still want me."

Aron stroked Gitel's shoulder and when she turned to him he pulled her close. "I'm going to talk plain. The story of what happened to me while I was in the army, it's not why I came." She reached her arms around him. They stood together, wanting to be a couple.

"Our time is unsure. What I've seen, Gitel." His young face revealed lines of suffering. He took her hand again. Time had changed the girl fingers he raised to his lips.

"Yes, my hands have stories," Gitel said.

"In Ksiaz Wielki, friends disappear, a relative is dragged away. I know one thing. I want you. Only you. I know what I am. And I've known about your wishes. There's no more time for dreams. I promise you, I will work for you and give you whatever these hands can make. I am not so bad."

Gitel's eyes filled. "Oh, Aron, I wish I had been able to make you understand how good you are. How strong and smart. I heard you cared for your parents. Even when you were a prisoner you sent them bread. You are my dream."

Aron lowered his eyes. "I had enough. The thought of us kept me alive. At times you were my food, my water. Be my wife. Will you?" He reached for her this time unafraid to let his passion go and her body did not resist. They stood together embracing, unable to separate for a long while.

"Yes, Aron, I want only you. It is time we were married."

CHAPTER THIRTEEN

1940 March

Time.

The decision to marry was optimistic and problematic. Purim, only weeks away was the same festival when years ago Aron's and Gitel's hearts had stirred. As the spring thaw loosened the frozen earth and March winds awakened sleeping creatures, they chose, Shushan Purim, March 25th 1940, and on the Jewish calendar secretly kept, the 15th day of the month Adar in the year 5700. The heat burns, call it love Wolf and Mendel said after they gave their blessings. But then wondered if their children knew love alone was not enough. Where were Aron and Gitel going to live? Would Aron be allowed to work? Aron not taking his eyes from the woman he adored told their fathers they were not children, a fact supported by his twenty-six and Gitel's twenty-four years. Aron had retrieved his tools from the abandoned workshop in Sosnowiec. His Polish helper had promised to return them if Aron survived combat and he had honored the promise. Who knew, Aron pondered, carrying the heavy bag of tools, similar to the ones that had saved him in the stalag, if he would have to make this deal again. Gitel negotiated to rent the attic apartment from the baker and his wife on the future of her soon to be husband's shoemaker skill.

While Aron searched for leather, Gitel prepared food at her sister Balcha's house, where the wedding would be. The rabbi, afraid to take the risk, sent the *ketubah* and accepted two braided breads as payment for the marital contract. The rhythm of life once led in Ksiaz Wielki was compromised but a few yards of Balcha's muslin from her shuttered dry-goods store persuaded the bathhouse matron in charge of the *mikvah* to ready it for Gitel. The *mikvah* ritual was now rarely allowed and the women no longer refreshed the monthly cycle of relations with their husbands. For Gitel, it was not only her duty as a bride. She needed to cleanse her soul.

On her wedding morning Gitel was ready to bathe scrupulously clean and undergo the matron's required inspection. She walked to the bathhouse alone and entered the blue tiled room. For the first time, she stepped down into the small pool and immersed her milk white body. Gitel did not know what to expect but was filled with awe as the water washed over her. She was ready to purify for her beloved. Her eyes spilled salty tears and merged with the warm rainwater about her nakedness. The terrible guilt of being disgraced by the man in Bedzin, nearly fouled against her will, began to drain from her and flow into the *mikvah* water. Gitel begged forgiveness from God. She was ready to become a married woman.

Now Monday afternoon, the last day of the festival, one by one the handful of friends and family ducked through Balcha's door aware the yellow stars they bore could exact a price for sharing happiness. Mordche and Yankel stretched a white prayer shawl over the bride and groom's heads to serve as the *chuppah* wedding canopy. Gitel dressed in her tailored brown suit stood by Aron, her face hidden beneath a white lace veil. When Aron smashed the glass beneath his foot, it was with joy and vigor he had never felt. He lifted Gitel's veil and their lips met to seal their lives as one.

Mazel tov, mazel tov, the words echoed in soft unison.

Mendel uncorked what he believed was the last of his homemade bottles of *slivovitz*. "On Shushan Purim," he said his old eyes moistened, "the jovial mood must be unlocked to open our minds to the One."

"*L'chaim,*" they said, their glasses with just enough spirit to toast the bride and groom and swallow the rest with a secret prayer. To life, long life.

For the wedding meal they savored each bite of Gitel's *pitcha*, the garlicky concoction covered with a layer of diced egg to complement the brandy and the bread soaked with the juices of glutinous aspic. Gitel refused to abandon the idea of dancing. Though there were no musicians, she clapped her palms, reddening them like her flushed face and pulled her sisters up, thumping one foot behind the other. Aron grabbed Gitel, his wife, and they danced the polka, twirling with enough energy to make the floorboards sing. Hinda's eyes reached each loved face and nodded it was time. Out of breath they encircled the couple and joined hands. They had almost forgotten themselves. Yet it was impossible. Purim or not, the Haman of their day, Hitler's hatreds permeated everywhere, everything. Staying together too long was on each mind and the golden liquid shared to celebrate was not enough to dull the truth. *Mazel tov*, one by one each whispered and left hoping to avoid Hubner patrolling with the luger in his belt. Or perhaps someone lurked and was willing to sell them for a few zlotys or a small sack of potatoes.

Their two days of honeymoon were spent in Giebultow, the bride and groom bundled in a goose down cover, the trousseau from Gitel's family beyond what they expected. They reveled in its luxury, the billowy down encased in damask. Aron hummed, *Shein veh de lavunah*, you are as beautiful as the moon, its brightness shining over the countryside. The repressed heat simmering for years ignited as his hands and words caressed Gitel. She wanted to please him and learn to feel free. As free as when she danced and spoke her mind and took her risks. A whole woman.

"It took a war and my capture to catch you," Aron teased rolling on top of her, his lips brushing her neck, his body tense with anticipation.

"You'll never escape from me," Gitel said. She wrapped her strong arms around his bare shoulders. The smooth lean muscles beneath her fingers responded to her touch and she felt her body ask for pleasure.

The sweet days over, they walked back to Ksiaz Wielki and entered, the attic room of the bakery on Dembrowska, man and wife. They had borrowed money from Dr. Yoblonski to furnish with a bed, a table, and a little bureau. The most important items were Aron's workbench and array of tools. He needed help to buy leather but begged Gitel not to overwork because by May she was already pregnant. But Gitel was Gitel and knew what she had to do. "I don't care," she told Aron, "if Hubner sees me or not, I'm going to find leather. But first I have to deliver our blessed news."

CHAPTER FOURTEEN

A Blessing

G itel left before the women filled their buckets at the town well, the streets still dark. She raced to Giebultow, new daylight filtering through the trees. At the brook she bent to sip chill water from her palms and splashed her face and arms. She breathed the air scented with meadow grasses, the cows anxious to graze and sun themselves after a winter of straw rations. Gitel waved to a Polish farmer she knew since childhood. He turned away.

She crossed the wood bridge over the brook and only a short distance ahead was her parents' thatched roof house. *How did we all live in that house and produce so much in the small barn? At the same time I know it was because we had to.* Their circumstances had required it. Wolf's favorite dog Bialek was long gone, but he still kept a dog to guard against marauders scouring the countryside and warn against Nazis who had begun raiding storerooms, confiscating food, animals and any goods to which as victors they felt entitled. The bitch yipped with excited barks. As Gitel approached, the dog's black tail whipped the air. Two remaining chickens scattered and clucked with annoyance.

"Yes, yes," she said, patting the dog's back, "you know me. Leave the poor chickens in peace."

Gitel's father rushed out of the dairy barn. *"Da bude!"* Wolf shouted at the dog in Polish, directing her to crawl at once into her doghouse. "So you remember where you were born." He nodded at his daughter, reached out as if he wanted to touch her then dropped his hand.

"Father," Gitel said, "Aron and I talk about you, Mother and the family everyday. That the time passed and we did not see each other for weeks is a sign of how hard it is to live a normal life."

"A normal life," Wolf said, "who lives a normal life? The Count is not even living a normal life. Last week he rode down on his big white horse. He likes it better than his oldest son, and he told your mother and me we should leave for a safer place. Where is it safe, I asked. To this he had no answer. If it comes to giving us shelter you can be sure he will save his own hide and we Jews be dammed. I'm not going anywhere. Come to the house. From the way you look, Aron is not feeding you."

"Father, we have enough," Gitel protested. She took a closer look. Behind the graying dark beard, his once robust face had grown thinner. Her father had never said a word to her about the man from Bedzin who had tried to extract a dowry from him. Her father had kept this confidence and protected her honor.

Gitel missed her sisters and brothers, especially Mordche. They were alike. Not in appearance, but in spirit. They possessed exceptional strength and were both driven by unlimited desire to work, do business. Just like their father, Wolf. She longed to see Deborah and share stories about Bedzin, though Gitel was not one to talk about how they had heard the cries from inside the burning Big Synagogue and smelled the dark smoke rise over the town. She had terrible dreams about the last scream fading and how she and Devorah threw on their best clothes, ripped off the yellow stars and walked out of the ghetto. Her decision had saved them. Wolf said it was by God's grace.

Gitel was feeling queasy. Her mother would greet her with more than warmth, with food. She followed Wolf into the house. Hinda jumped up from the table. "Mother," Gitel said as they embraced, "my dear mother, I've missed you. Are you managing still?"

"We do whatever possible to get by, Gitel, every one of us is under hardship. But you, what is happening to you?" Hinda eyed her daughter.

"Gitel, is it possible…?" She stopped and busied by the iron cook stove not wanting to alarm Wolf who stared at his daughter with a worried frown. "Wolf," Hinda turned to her husband, "maybe the cheese I set a few days ago is ready in the form."

"My wife, when women start to talk, men must go. I understand. I'll have a look. Speak with your daughter. Maybe you can find out why she looks like a skinny herring soaked in brine too long." He raised his thick eyebrows at Gitel before closing the door.

"Mother, I'm pregnant."

"Gitel," Hinda shook her head, her eyes wide. "*Mazel tov*. As soon as I took a look at you, I suspected."

Hinda's face sagged and Gitel read her concern *my daughter, you were born as the First World War began and now you repeat this hardship.* She took a plate from the cupboard, sliced bread, peeled a hardboiled egg and sliced it in half. Such a luxury was necessary for her pregnant daughter. Eggs, small packages sometimes carried life. Her daughter's package would be growing and she made a silent prayer, added a few coals to the oven and put the kettle to boil. "Gitel, please eat. Your father will come in later and we'll eat together. I forbid you to wait. Who knows better how strong you are, but a woman who is going to be a mother is a changed person. Remember you carry your child. Now is the easy part, my dear daughter." Hinda sat, her fingers smoothing the cloth on the table, unable to keep still. Gitel, mindful that her parents, her sister and brothers would not eat their fill, ate just enough to quell her nausea.

"Where are Deborah and my brothers?" She brought the plate to her mother.

"You couldn't finish the little I gave? Deborah is helping Esther Faigle with the children." Hinda drew up her frail frame. "Your youngest brother is with Mordche. I begged them not to go. Is an armful of cabbages worth it? The Nazis march everywhere. If they catch them they could be sent to work camp or who knows where. They shoot to kill." Hinda's hands dropped to her lap.

Gitel sat in silence, soft whining of the kettle between them. "Mother, while the day is long I have to try and find leather."

"There's no use to talk to you or Mordche. Take the eggs to Aron. I'll wrap a piece of cheese for you," Hinda placed the items into a small basket.

Gitel hugged her and laughed. "Mother, thank you. Do you feel my fat belly? When Aron makes a few *zlotys* with his next pair of boots, we'll repay you."

She traversed the rolling hills but soon felt vibrations beneath her feet. A low cloud of dust rose in the distance and the thudding intensified. Gitel tightened the green sweater about her thickening waist. Two horsemen slowed to a cantor and stopped. Gitel was relieved she recognized Count Janad Dzianat. Owner of the vast estate Kolo Palacu overlooking Giebultow, he lived there with two sons and his mother, his wife the young Countess having died in childbirth. The stone manor house, stables of horses, piggeries and dairy barns required the labor of many peasants. When he sped his favored steed across the high plateau sweeping across his ancestral home the peasants glimpsed their master and were reminded of his power.

Count Dzianat sat upright on the Arabian its high tail a white plume. His maroon linen riding coat fit snug and his face was rosy from the pleasures of riding. The fair untamed mustache adorned full lips and his cheeks were unaffected by deprivation gripping the less fortunate. Count Dzianat relished and believed he deserved comforts befitting the *schlachta*, the nobles and he still exuded the good spirit of his class.

"*Prosze Pani, dzień dobry,* please, madam, good day." The Count spoke first, the courtly manners delivered with the practiced pride and grace of a Polish noble.

Gitel answered without hesitation, "*Prosze Panie, dzień dobry,*" and added, "*Hrabia* Dzianat," his Polish title of Count. She nodded to the young man next to him. He leaned forward in a slight bow, forced out of duty. The imperious son, unlike his father, avoided Gitel's eyes. He rested his hands on the tooled horn of the saddle and sat motionless atop a grey dappled gelding glistening from the heat of the ride.

"*Prosze Pani,* our young *Hrabia* Lejyk," the Count said his gloved palm open toward his son. "Have you seen anything unusual, strangers on your way? We look for thieves culling sheep from what is left of my herd. My peasants are clever enough to leave no evidence, but these brazen ones spill a trail of blood. Of course, it may be the enemy as well."

"I have seen no one," Gitel said. If it is the peasants, she thought, who could blame the hungry like us stealing from you?

"What is your business here?" Lejyk said in a flat voice, an inquisitor willing to illicit information through any means he deemed necessary. He glared at what was bound around Gitel's sleeve.

"I was visiting my father, Wolf Herszkowicz." Gitel addressed the Count then looked into Lejyk's narrowing dark eyes.

"Ah, *Pani* Herszkowicz, forgive, my son. You understand we are anxious to catch these thieves even my dogs have been unable to track," the Count said. "The pressure to protect what is rightfully ours is becoming distasteful."

"I am no longer a Herszkowicz," Gitel said. "Adam Matuszynski, a good shoemaker and I were married several months ago.

"My congratulations to your husband, *Pani* Matuszyñska." The Count glanced at his son having reiterated the necessary gentility toward the working class, lessons he had learned as a young *schlachta* and hoped to pass on to this resistant oldest son.

"Isn't he the lucky one," Lejyk said, a smirk on his lips, the smooth youthful brow unaffected, war or no war. His horse shook its head and sidestepped close to Gitel, the mane separating into silver strands in the brilliant sun. The young noble did nothing to rein in the horse. Gitel stood her ground. *Give him one pig and he thinks he's a prince* she thought restraining a look of dislike.

"Do you remember, Lejyk," the Count said, flicking his riding crop toward his son's gelding, "when this young lady's father brought a daughter up to the house for a wedding?"

"No, Father, I do not."

"I do." Gitel turned toward the haughty voice.

"Father, we have business," Lejyk said, holding his rising anger in check. His father was not one to tolerate insolence.

The Count signaled his horse with a gentle tap to its arched neck and swung down. Lejyk had no choice but to follow. The three stood together. "So you remember. I rode down to your father and insisted he bring the entire procession to me." The Count breathed in wild flower sweetened air, all which belonged to him, keeper of the natural bequeathed bounty.

"My parents were surprised you asked them to do such a thing." Gitel was sorry she had admitted this fact, but it was too late.

"I was intrigued by your customs and how could they refuse? The peasants from all around followed your people up. When was it, ten years ago?"

"Yes, *Panie Hrabia* Dzianat." She nodded her head, the auburn braids not so different from those her mother had fixed the morning of Esther Faigle's wedding, a summer day in 1930. She had helped her mother prepare the food and remembered how her sister was as nervous as a hen that watches her first brood peck from their white shells.

"A fiddler and a clarinetist led the bride and groom up our hill." The Count inclined his gloved hand. "Your people raised a blue wedding canopy over their heads and a priest made the ceremony."

"We call him Rabbi, the one who makes the ceremony." And it brought thoughts that for her wedding this same rabbi had been too afraid to come nor did she have a proper *chuppah,* the color of sky open to the heavens.

The Count laughed, his well-fed hips in concert. "My mother, the Countess passed out a candy to every child who crowded about. They each kissed her hand. She's one for all the old fuss, our queen!"

Lejyk stood aloof, impassive, not a glimmer of remembrance registering. He hit the riding crop against his boots, surveying the undulating green hills. His face betrayed the lust to possess.

"That was the only time any of us saw your house, *Panie* Count Dzianet." Gitel's mind ran between worlds, colliding. Her ceremony before God had been hidden. Her world was shrinking.

They mounted their horses with the grace of noblemen born to ride. "Ah, my house. These days I have much to worry over," the Count said, his face wistful, the confidence of his bearing threatened by ominous change. "They take away my peasants. So who will care for our needs? There are rumors they will confiscate my land to resettle the German barbarians. Here where my ancestors rode against invaders sabers drawn, upon horses sired by our own hand. Perhaps we will have run to my beloved wife's family in Bucharest."

Gitel's eyes locked with Lejyk's. The smoldering black eyes revealed his mother's Romanian lineage. The young man's jaw clenched with disgust for a father who bared his soul to a peasant.

"Even Prince Wielopolski of Ksiaz Wielki, complains his rights are compromised. Is my country to be torn apart again, crippled, our gentility destroyed? My beautiful Poland, what is to become of her honor?"

The Count nodded to Gitel and with one quick motion they took off, the white stallion leading, his mane flowing with blue, yellow and red ribbons, the colors of his master's coat of arms receding into the past.

CHAPTER FIFTEEN

Who Is Friend

Dust settled. Gitel's eyes sharpened and fell on a patch of mushrooms poking forth, fluted ivory heads. She picked the mushrooms, shook rich brown earth off each stem and inhaled their woodsy scent. *How lucky* she thought as she filled the basket. Perhaps she could trade mushrooms and the eggs for what Aron needed most. Gitel carried a few zlotys and would for as long as she was able. No, she would never wait for a man to place money into an outstretched palm. Hadn't she braved starting her own business, worked like a demon to make a living? She hadn't made a fortune but enough to spare for her and Deborah to buy stylish suits and hats that complemented good figures and turned heads on Sabbath strolls. Enough to drop a little money each week in the box where she and her sister prayed, enough to share profits from the dairy products with her father.

It was many days since she had anything to sell or barter. Maybe the mushrooms were a good omen. Ahead close by the wagon path was a farmhouse she knew well. Gitel wondered what kind of reception she would receive. There was no sign of the owners, Chaszka's parents, her best school friend growing up, Polish neighbors with whom she and her family had lived in harmony. Perhaps they had leather or knew someone who did. Now a chill separated her people from the Poles. Unspoken by some, acrimony seething from others. Who could she trust? Perhaps no one.

Gitel shook off the thoughts. She would think of what they needed for now and nothing more. But her friend's mother might sense she was pregnant. Why risk anyone knowing she was more vulnerable? That the monster Hubner valued Aron's work as shoemaker meant he had to produce. To stay a step ahead meant she must try wherever there was opportunity. One way or another Gitel had to help her husband and prepare for the baby.

Chaszka's mother came to the door as she approached. Gitel lifted the basket to her waist. "*Pani* Bukowska, I hope you're well."

"Yes, Gitel, you visit your parents? I haven't seen you for a long time." The woman's eyes searched the wagon path. "I see my Chaszka less. And like all mothers in these times, I worry. Her two boys grow, the older almost four. You girls were good friends."

"I see Chaszka sometimes. I live in Ksiaz now too. Her big one runs next to her, the little one she holds in her arms."

"You married the shoemaker, Chaszka told me. I wish you luck."

"And to you. We all need it." Gitel paused to the ticking of a clock. She reached into the basket and held out a few mushrooms as the woman's eyes followed her arm, hesitating on the yellow star. "You see we country girls always find things. Please *Pane*, have some for a nice soup."

Pani Bukowska took a handful of mushrooms from the basket and brought them to her face, relishing their delicate scent. She looked at the meadow popped with clover. A goat pulled off purple flower heads, another on its hind legs, reached for tender leaves on a low tree branch. The woman shook her head. "It all appears the same this moment. Look at them," she said, "how busy. My oldest goat, the white one, was there when you and Chaszka ran in the fields. You see how her wild, young one tries to climb?" She smiled and Gitel remembered her own climbing days.

"And now I'm a married woman who needs to buy leather for her husband."

Pani Bukowska's eyes betrayed fear. Perhaps it was the warnings not to trade with Jews. Gitel not knowing what else to say reached into her pocket and touched the folded *zlotys*, as if to reassure herself. The woman followed Gitel's hand, a hint of interest on her face. "My husband promised Dr. Yoblonski he would make him boots. Adam is the doctor's favorite shoemaker."

"Oh, Dr. Yoblonski? He helped Chaszka with her second when the poor thing had the whooping cough. A good man."

Gitel sensed a chance. "If you are worried the doctor will know where the leather came from, it would be only our business. I promise you, *Pani* Bukowska, I'm Wolf Giebeltow's daughter, and you know what our word means."

"Come in. Who knows which enemy watches?"

Gitel stepped in and waited by the door as *Pani* Bukowska disappeared to the back. All the years they had been friends she had never been in Chaszka's farmhouse. Gitel's eyes swept the tidy room and stopped at a carved wood clock her friend had spoken of with pride. *Smaller than I had envisioned but then Chaszka was a little girl when she had told me of the treasure, her grandmother's big ticking clock.*

Pani Bukowska returned with two skins of brown tanned leather. It was more than Gitel expected and she knew the woman would want a good price. Her pocket held nine *zlotys*.

"What do you think, Gitel?" *Pani* Bukowska turned over each piece to show how supple. "My husband traded with a tanner near Sosnowiec."

"They are nice pieces. Yet small for boots." Gitel knew Aron would be able to use these for the shafts. The rest of the boot he might have to piece together from another lot. But even to her amateur touch it was fine leather. He would be pleased. "Will you take seven *zlotys*?"

Pani Bukowska smiled. "Chaszka told me you were a tough girl. No, I can't let these go for so little. Five *zlotys* each."

"Eight for both and my husband will fix a pair of old shoes and make them new."

She left the room again and returned with her husband's church shoes. "If the doctor is your husband's customer, then we have a deal."

Gitel gave the woman the money and pushed the old shoes as far into her basket as she could, careful not to crush the eggs from her mother. She folded the leather pieces and tucked them into her blouse.

"You look pregnant with the leather filling out your blouse," *Pani* Bukowska giggled as Gitel stepped out of the house.

"Yes," Gitel nodded. "Thank you, thank you, *Pani*. My husband will be happy to see I'm pregnant with leather."

"Remember, not a word to anyone." The woman's eyes had lost their friendship. Fear said goodbye.

Gitel walked along the Krakow Warsaw Highway, the road running north and south connecting Ksiaz Wielki to other towns. She was glad most of the way from Giebultow had been off this main road. She stopped. There it was, a light flutter, a faint sensation, the first she had felt. And then another. A wave of sudden realization, she placed her hand on her abdomen seeking this separate life. But the tiny flutter was gone. *I know you are there now. You are alive. Ours.*

She had leather. The basket swinging from her arm was filled with fragrant good things from the earth. What her mother had given her, the eggs, signified more than a gift of food. Could a man understand such a thing? Would she share this with Aron? It was between mother and daughter. Her mother had conveyed the meaning of pregnancy at her time of great worry; how war had taken joy and replaced it with angst. And yet she, Gitel had been the one chosen to be born as the First World War tore Europe open. Her mother had endured, protected, saved her. Would she be able to do the same? And her father, imagine how powerful, how he must have taken upon himself to find a way to feed his young family amid privation and pogroms. She and her mother had a new bond. Gitel not only loved and respected the woman; she had discovered more of her mother's spirit and divine parallels embodied in the precious eggs.

CHAPTER SIXTEEN

A Husband Warns

Hubner was on a rampage. Starting with the Jews, he took away their homes. The inhabitants he deported to work camps. As he had decreed Abromoczyck's house would be his, the man, his wife and four children were sent to Belzac. From that house Hubner planned *lebensraum* for the ethnic Germans streaming across Poland's western border to rid the town of its undesirables. Food was scarce and the ban on trade between Poles and Jews built hostility, hunger and panic. It was just as the Nazis planned.

Gitel's pregnancy was a constant concern. Never daunted by hard work, worry about it did not occupy her. She was strong and agile in her third month and exuded a guarded glow. While able to conceal her condition she would be in the better position to outwit those who would find her compromised if they knew. Whenever she went to see her parents, Gitel brought home a cabbage, beets or a few potatoes. She made pots of beet *borscht* soup and *kapusta*, a favored Polish cabbage soup on the clay stove in the attic room, the aromas bubbling from her pots masking the glues, waxes and polish on Aron's workbench. There was no table covered with the yellow checkered cloth like the one in her Bedzin store but she carried a pot filled with steaming soup down to the street and ladled it into whatever container a customer held; a small pot, an earthen jar, the sweet smells coaxing a few *grochen*.

115

Aron was pleased Gitel was able to barter but argued with her about safety and his shrinking ability to control their lives. Hauling water from the well before the sun gave light was no guarantee Hubner would not spot him and assign a menial task that kept him from his trade. Gitel was defiant in her optimism while he struggled with news from Lodz, Czestochowa and Warsaw where starvation rations, lack of sanitation, crowding so bad that typhus outbreaks piled diseased bodies in the streets. There were reports Poles were being displaced east by the hundreds of thousands and countless Jews were being sent to concentration camps or murdered on the spot.

Aron and Gitel had no choice but to find ways to better their chances to survive. Yet he was consumed with worry when she walked to nearby towns to find materials. Maybe she would be questioned or detained, snatched away or worse. "Stay in Ksiaz Wielki," Aron said. "Stop running from town to town. Forget about leather."

"So who is going to buy it for us, the man in the moon?" Gitel asked.

"You are a smart one," Aron said. "Who cares about leather if something happens to you?"

"What's going to happen if you have nothing to make shoes with? What are you going to use to make boots, your mother's tablecloth? If you send away a customer he goes elsewhere.

"They like my craftsmanship." Aron stood ready to bar the door.

"I know you still have a few orders. You can't make the shoes, buy the leather, and do it all. I'm strong. No one can see I'm pregnant. While I can I must help."

Gitel washed the floor, a damp rag under her foot, and moved the chairs and table. She fixed the white rectangular cloth embroidered by Deborah covering the bureau. She rubbed the candlesticks she used each Friday night before Aron made the Kiddush, the blessing that welcomed the day of rest and their intimate moments as husband and wife.

Then she readied herself to leave. Aron stared as she put on her green sweater against the morning chill. She was right. There did not seem to be a hint. It was still a secret. Only the family knew.

"People have more to worry about than counting my months. I left you potatoes and a glass of beet borscht for your meal." She walked over to his workbench and cupped her hands about his face. "Don't forget to eat."

He moved her hands to his mouth and kissed the palms. "When a husband asks a wife not to go somewhere," Aron frowned, "she should listen to him."

CHAPTER SEVENTEEN

Encounters Good and Bad

A drizzle fell on the morose faces on Dembrowska, the main street, a place to be avoided. Perhaps she should go back to the apartment and grab her hat to protect from the rain. But then Aron would make more of a fuss. There would be an argument. No, she would go on. She reasoned if any locals had skins to trade they might choose not to travel on such a day.

Yes, it was an ideal day to buy leather. Zlotys they had saved were hidden inside a seam of her skirt hem. The pocket held some *grochen*.

Her usual stride, purposeful was somehow more graceful. Though Gitel's body did not betray many changes, the knowledge that it soon would, made her mission surge with energy to stay beyond the reach of enemies. She was at the end of Dembrowska, passing food and yard goods stores once owned by Jews, now in the hands of Poles, when she spotted Mendel Matuszyński walking toward her.

"Father-in-law, Mendel," Gitel said with respect and affection for the man she had known most of her life. "How is your health?"

"My kind daughter," Mendel said, "first, I must know where you go in the rain. Here, take this." Mendel held out the long handle of a black umbrella. "You see how Ruchel, my dear wife, cares for this old thing. Not a bit of dust even on the frame. She is a woman who never rests. Even the rabbi's wife marvels at her skills. She embroiders everything within her sight, I am surprised she has not embroidered me," Mendel added with a wink.

"I hope to buy materials for Aron," she said. "Please keep your umbrella. I don't mind getting a bit wet."

"I wish you better luck. There was nothing for me to buy, not even the tripe. With the heavy fines on *shochets*, they won't let us slaughter kosher. If an animal is available the Nazis steal it. Look out well for the Poles. They point us out for a handful of beans. So, you turn down an old man's offer?" he added with a shy smile.

Gitel took the umbrella from his hand and gazed at her father-in-law. For a man of eighty-two he stood straight, a slender body belying his age. A long grey beard lay neat about his face, a face that knew worry and poverty.

"Go along," he said, clicking his heels like a gentleman. "I will not melt in the rain like sugar. Ruchel tells me I am not that sweet."

But she knew better. He was gentle and good and very sweet.

Gitel watched her father-in-law walk toward his alleyway. When he turned, she resumed a fast pace. The umbrella was coming in handy already; shielded from the rain, her face was hidden. She walked south on the Warsaw Krakow Highway and peeked from under the umbrella at the trees that held their May buds closed. Soon they would burst with pink and white blooms. She felt kinship with the countryside.

Gitel wore the new boots Aron had made for her, simple, sturdy and elegant. He had taken hours just to fit her good-sized feet. And though she had argued to make her feet look more stylish, to cut them smaller, Aron knew better. She planned to show them off as the workmanship of the shoemaker for whom she was buying leather. The well-shined brown boots were caking with mud but her feet were dry and comfortable. She slipped off the armband. *That's right,* she said to herself, *Jude.* Her heart pounded with both the thrill of disobedience and the fear of being found out.

* * * * *

119

Aron held the boots that belonged to a penniless peddler, Hanek the Hunchback. The day before Gitel had seen the misshapen pauper in front of the bakery and had run down the stairs with a pan of bread soaked in broth and watched him suck the mixture into his toothless mouth. Aron read her eyes when she came up with the empty pan and the boots. How could we turn away this unfortunate almost barefoot standing in the rain? There was always someone worse off, it seemed. He stared out of the attic window. Raindrops plinked from the uneven roof slates and he imagined Hanek was either hidden under someone's steps or standing tucked beneath their overhang, his feet mired in mud. Or perhaps he was not phased by it all, pestering the few going about their business with the pack of mismatched oddities slung on his back, imploring, "Who will buy from an old peddler?"

Aron stood, held what barely resembled boots, and stretched. Hours of sitting hunched strained his back. The shoemaker posture exacerbated the *whys* of his destiny intertwined with angst grinding away belief. Had he been predestined for a life of perpetual burden, like the hunchback? Instead of scraping a living hauling junk from town to town, his family name forgotten, forever referred to as Hanek the Hunchback, would he always carry the stigma of shoemaker? He was a young boy the first time he had stared at Hanek and been moved by the deformity. Aron remembered his father had told him some hunchbacks are invisible to the human eye, but we all carry a hunchback. No one can see his own.

The peddler's crooked feet repulsed Aron, but at the same time he felt pity for the man and put aside another job. The boots repaired numerous times needed soles and heels. The peddler would want to trade for the repair. Aron hoped Gitel would be there and pick something she would want. She was better at *hondling* and liked the back and forth game. Not that he was unable to *hondle*. He negotiated with many a customer.

He wiped off the mud-caked boots. His mother Ruchel, immaculate, ingrained habits in him, in all her children. Her hair, shiny black as a crow's feathers, made him smile as he emulated quick strokes whisking the crusty pieces with the brush and little shovel Gitel used to remove coal ashes from the stove. He ripped off what remained of a heel with a curved tool, his small crowbar. Aron picked the last pair of stubby wood heels from salvage and began filing them down to fit the peddler's boots. He cut a stiff scrap of leather in half and shaved the pieces with a short knife, repeatedly sharpening it on a stone. He nodded to himself, recalling how he had demonstrated his techniques to the Ukrainian and Polish shoemakers on the Commandant's boot. By the grace of heaven he now had the opportunity to make a small payment of thanks. What he could spare would only serve as half soles but the pieces covered almost the entire bottom of the peddler's boots and he stretched his talent to make a seamless fit. *Not bad* he thought as he applied glue and clamped each boot. Then he placed a few tacks between his lips ready to nail the heels. Finishing, he set the boots upside down on the iron last to dry. No, he would not use any of the precious polish he had left in the round tin. Hanek the Hunchback would have to make do. What was left of the polish Aron would conserve for the doctor's choice boots.

Gitel walked several kilometers and spotted a place in the distance that looked well cared for. She had passed the house many times by wagon on business with her father but this time she left the road and began walking up the path. It was well marked with dog prints but no dog barked. As she approached, a woman opened the door and stood in the shadow of a darkened room. Dressed in black, she wore a matching headscarf knotted beneath her chin making it difficult for Gitel to tell how old a woman.

"*Dzień dobry*," Gitel said.

"*Dzień dobry*," the woman said. "I don't recognize you. I was just at the window to see about my sons. You look for someone?"

"No, *Pani*. I need to buy leather."

"We have no leather. My husband, killed not long ago, left me with two sons almost grown," she said. "To the army they want to go, too. What army, I ask, when they know the Germans overrun us. Then who will I have? Don't bother searching here. We have no leather to sell."

"I am sorry about your husband. Please, *Pani,*" Gitel said softly to the woman, "Maybe your sons know where I can buy it. I am willing to give a good price. Look at these. My husband is a real craftsman at making boots, shoes. He made these."

The woman looked at Gitel's boots. She moved closer, her eyes running over Gitel as if judging a prize sow. "My sons have gone to a neighbor who has troubles with a horse. They took the dog too. I asked them to leave the old dog, my husband's, but they don't listen to their own mother. Now, with the war no one knows from one second to the next who will come. They bother us with their filthy ways, always trying to buy food." She stared at Gitel's face. "You're not a Jew, are you?"

Gitel shook her head, twisting her mouth with disgust at such a suggestion. "*Pani,* the wife of a man who makes boots like this could not be a Jew."

"What is your name and where are you from? It can't be far. You are on foot. And in the rain."

Gitel was still holding the umbrella. She folded it to divert the woman's attention, at the same time stepping under the overhang by the door. In a white cloth she had tied around her wrist was an egg and potato. It would be hours before she would have a meal with Aron. Perhaps she should offer the woman some of it. No, she decided to take another tact. Placating a stranger with food might appear anxious.

"*Pani,*' she said, "my mother would be disappointed in me. I have lost my manners. I am from Swiecie where my dear parents and their parents have long lived. My family is Wisniewski. Now I take my husband's name. My mother warned me he was a tyrant. As talented with his hands, is how mean he is with his fists."

"How is it that your husband is not in the army?" the woman said.

"A good question, *Pani.* The enemy sent our brave men back. He came home from the army even meaner than before. My shoulders are blue and black from him." Gitel sighed. "I pray the leathers in this region are as fine as its people."

Dog barks grew louder. As she finished her tale, Gitel turned and it ran straight for her growling and lunging at the cloth tied around her wrist. Gitel smacked the dog with the umbrella. It ran back yelping to the tall young man approaching.

"My older son, Janek," the woman said with admiration in her eyes for this handsome offspring.

"I hope you will not hit me too," he chided Gitel. "I see you are a fighter."

"She came from Swiecie to buy leather. I told her we have none," the woman said.

"Mamusha, for enough *zlotys*, I will find her leather. But you will have to stay the night," Janek said, eying Gitel. "Your town is too far from here."

"No one is staying the night. I'm not providing for another mouth. She's married. Be on your way," she said to Gitel. "Go."

"Go inside, old woman," he said no longer with the endearment 'Mamusha.' His mother did not move.

"Tell me, who made the boots to fit those pretty ankles?" He stepped closer and Gitel smelled sweat laced with that of an animal.

"Perhaps your kind mother is right. I have overstayed my welcome." Gitel backed away from the door, her mind alarmed, her body pulsing with warning. The muscular Pole's eyes flashed salacious intent.

"How many zlotys are you carrying and where are you hiding them? There?" He reached out and flicked a finger at the cloth dangling from Gitel's wrist. "Somewhere else maybe?"

Gitel reached her free hand in the pocket, what she was about to say interrupted by the sound of a distant gunshot. Her chest tightened. Was it another of her people caught, would she be next? But for the moment the focus was no longer on her. Another shot blasted, echoing.

"That's our rifle." Janek turned toward his mother. "Gregor just shot the horse. I told that stupid dreamer the horse was almost dead, to just leave it. But he has to play the angel. He couldn't even do that with one shot. And now we'll have the Nazis snooping around again. He knows the bastards have disarmed us."

"Gregor will be back soon, Janek," the woman said. "I don't want trouble with this girl and her business." She lowered her voice and pointed at Gitel. "Go now if you know what's good for you."

Janek spat at Gitel's boot. "Get off of my land," he sneered. "I see you have nothing for me."

"Yes," said Gitel, stepping toward the path opening her umbrella. "I must start back." She walked away as fast as she dared, her legs trembling. The mangy dog started after her, snapping at her heels, but she knew the dog was a better enemy to confront than the young man who may have tried to grab her money or do far worse. "Get away, you dirty cur," she hissed and smacked it with her father-in-law's black umbrella.

Gitel was back on the road, her heart beat slowing, a hand over her softening belly. She was grateful no worse had occurred, but she had no leather either. This was a story she would not be anxious to tell Aron. If that man Janek had stuck his hand in her blouse he would have found a surprise. When Gitel was more than a kilometer away, she stepped behind a stand of trees and stuffed the armband into her undergarments. *This is where it will be from now on, except when I'm wearing it. And how long will I still pass as one of them? How long until I come across someone who recognizes me?*

Rain ended, the midday sun warmed Gitel's upturned face. Her favorite, white lilies-of-the-valley sat in the fields bordering the road. She would travel no further than a few more kilometers. If no leather was to be had then so be it. It would not be the first time she was unsuccessful. But she would to be more careful. Doctor Yoblonski, a respected Pole, was taking a risk to order from her husband. Aron had the good skins she had bought days before from Chaszka's mother. Perhaps if she found something else Aron could use, she would not come home empty handed. The idea renewed her courage.

A fork lay ahead. West was familiar. It was also the direction of Bedzin. She had never taken the east fork and maybe it would be safer, less chance she'd be recognized. Was she brazen to try again? She had gotten away. Scaredy cats hid and got nothing.

But now her stomach reminded her she had not eaten for hours and she stopped by a stand of trees to unravel the cloth with the egg and boiled potato. She bit into the potato and it reminded her of Aron. How exacting he was. "Don't over boil the potatoes," he'd say. "You're always in such a hurry and don't allow the potatoes to cook slow, so they fall apart."

"Listen," Gitel would say, "if you're such a good cook, then you make the potatoes."

"My mother Ruchel, she cooks a perfect potato!"

"Fine, then go home to your mother and eat her potatoes."

"You'll learn to go slower."

"You'll learn to go faster."

Faster, slower, Aron had not given up on her. Everything was going fast, who would have predicted that in months she could be rocking a baby? She would not think of that, it was unlucky to plan such things before they happened. Aron had known about her affair with the man in Bedzin and still wanted her. While another man may have looked upon her as damaged goods, turned away, he forgave. She closed her eyes, grateful. Lost in thought, she savored the egg. There was another the side. Nothing was perfect enough for Aron. These ways of his, obsessing over each small detail. Even if it motivated him to work with high standards, it impeded output. Perfectionism she did not understand permeated his existence and heightened their conflicts. If he lost his temper easily she was the opposite. She folded the cloth with bits and pieces for later, stuffed it into the pocket with the few *grochen*, and chided herself for daydreaming even if it was only for moments. How dare she lose sight of where she was; what she was. She had just been confronted by danger. Gitel jumped up and took a long breath of fresh washed air.

A wagon was approaching. The driver paid her no mind, the horse kicking up mud clumps as it trotted past. Gitel felt relief her appearance drew no attention. Young wheat and barley plants lay low, beaten by the rain. Rows of early potato plants sprouted in fields on both sides of the road. Gitel avoided deeper ruts and with the sun behind, her face reflected in the reddish puddle mirrors. She worked up stray hairs into her braids and shook off the splatters from her skirt.

In the field ahead a man in patched trousers came into view. He swung a scythe at dried bent corn stalks and seemed to search for anything forgotten from the last harvest. A dry ground up ear of corn could feed a chicken, the stalks a treat for a cow. The severe food shortages required that nothing be overlooked. He looked up, tucked the scythe under his arm and started toward Gitel. He removed his cap. "*Dzień dobry.*" His face creased into a smile and he made a slight bow. "It's become a nice day. You must know people on my road. So few come this way."

"*Pan, dzień dobry,*" Gitel said. "It would be pleasant to know people here, but I know no one. I am helping my husband, a poor shoemaker. He has no leather left. I don't know what we'll do if he can't work."

"No, *Pani*. Whatever my wife and I had has been sold, not that we had leather. Her family gave us nice things before the country started having tough times. Her father was a prosperous grain dealer. My fields here were rich with grains for him. Now they lie fallow, our house with the few things we need to survive." He pushed his graying hair under the cap and slipped it back on.

"Perhaps there is a neighbor who may be able to help me,' Gitel said.

"Do you have *zlotys, Pani*?" he asked.

Gitel considered before answering. She wanted to give the impression she had money without acting braggadocios. Unable to strike a deal was one thing, losing money to a stranger through imprudent action was another. She had no idea of his intentions, but there was a sadness and honesty she discerned. He appeared to be a Pole who suffered, his life squeezed from him. She decided to take a chance. "*Pan*, I have *zlotys* enough to buy. If not leather, perhaps you have good hard wood my husband could use to fabricate lasts or heels."

"Wait here," he said. "Let me see what I can find." The man walked away toward a weathered good-sized hut. He disappeared between pieces of dingy wash, frayed, limp laundry strung on an abandoned clothesline and into the barn behind. A black and white cow grazed in the field near the barn a ways from where she had already picked clean the fresh growth. Gitel pushed her lips together and made the kissing sound she used to summon cows that grazed in the fields of Giebultow. The cow looked up, flicked her ears and started toward her. While the cow swayed back and forth on her haunches, Gitel removed a few *zlotys* from the hem of her skirt in a move she hoped prepared her to deal.

The bell around the cow's neck clanged with a languorous rhythm. As she approached Gitel watched the pendulous udders. She was tempted to milk the cow and squirt the warm creamy liquid directly into her mouth, but was afraid the man would catch her stealing. "Come," Gitel said to the cow. The cow rubbed her head against a fence post. She looked at Gitel with her huge brown eyes as if pleading to be relieved of her heavy burden. "I wish I could help both of us," Gitel said patting the cow's ears.

With the rain gone flies had reappeared to torment the cow. She flicked her ears chasing the pests, but they returned. "Every living thing has a problem," she said. "You have flies and we have Germans and Poles." Gitel reached up as one of the flies came back to bother the cow and in one swift motion caught it in her palm. It buzzed angrily in Gitel's fist and when she released it, the fly took off to freedom. "I wish our tormentors were so easily choked off," she shared with the animal. The cow walked away and resumed foraging. Gitel stood on the drying road, a warm breeze reviving the matted field and waited for the man to return. Moments later she watched him carrying things wrapped in a blanket.

"You are lucky," the man said, opening the blanket to show intricately carved chair legs and two dry leather seat bottoms. "My wife once had fancy things, furniture you don't see but in rich homes. Her mother sent fine things, wood chairs, carved heavy ones made from oak my wife cannot now even lift. She is in bed most of the time. Our house is the way a house looks without a woman. Poverty and bad health are partners here. I hold on to what has become of our life." He shook his head as if resurrecting a vision. "If your husband is skilled he can make many sturdy heels from this wood, maybe soles from the seats."

Gitel picked up each piece, weighing it in her hand as the man spoke. She brushed away the dust on the chair bottoms feeling with her finger for damage. Oak was exceptional and Aron would be able to make excellent heels, maybe even lasts. Not wanting to give away her position she said, "*Pan*, the wood is strong but fancy or not the carving makes waste. There will be little left from the pieces to make lasts."

"*Pani*," he said, "I ask eight *zlotys* for this fine wood. I know about shoemakers, if he's smart, he'll use the chair bottoms for soles, old leather or not. If you want the lot good, if not I'll carry it to my barn."

"*Pan*," Gitel said, putting on a disappointed face, "my husband will be very angry with me if I pay so much for broken chair pieces and leather older than his wife. Let me offer you four *zlotys*. It's a good price."

"Give me six *zlotys*. Where are you from?"

"Swiecie is my home town," Gitel lied again never imagining this town would soon become a place of horror.

"Then you have far to walk. For the blanket give me fifty *grochen*. How will you carry them, inside that old umbrella?"

"I'll give you the fifty *grochen* and we make the deal. This way we both get a fair price and I'll be able to carry the broken pieces." Had she relented too soon? She compared the encounter to what she had experienced hours before. Here was someone willing to help. That she was a Jew may have changed it all did not matter. Truth was danger.

"You are a good business woman," he said, nodding at Gitel, reading the green eyes that emanated intelligence, compassion, and something that eluded him.

"And you, *Pan*, are a fair man. I am sad for your wife. Now I must start back. It's a long way home."

Gitel removed the money she had prepared from her skirt pocket and handed him the agreed amount. Neither knew the other's name. She turned in the direction of Ksiaz Wielki. Aron would be disappointed but what she carried over her shoulder would be useful. She hoped Dr. Yoblonski sat with Aron for a fitting.

* * * * *

Aron heard lumbering footsteps and was disappointed. They did not belong to the doctor. He opened the door and there she stood, the grain dealer's wife whose husband served on the Judenrat. Some shoes brought to him were preposterous and this woman stood in a pair two sizes smaller than her feet. "You see, Matuszyński," she said, pointing, "my feet are swollen. And my ankles? Only our enemies should feel such pain."

"Where did you have these made?" Aron stifled a smile. "Maybe the shoemaker measured wrong."

The woman sank on the chair next to his workbench and positioned her right foot forward. "I sat in his filthy house so he could measure and this is the result," she sniffed, looking around Aron's sparse room.

"Did you go for fittings?" He examined the shoddy workmanship as she turned her feet from side to side giving the full impact.

"Fittings," she said adjusting her ample bottom, "what fittings? He told me to come back the next week and all would be perfect. If this is perfect than I am Queen Esther."

Aron recognized the workmanship. As a young shoemaker, before he went out on his own, he had sat next to Tobias, both of them toiling over the shoes they were given to fix. Tobias ripped out the old stitches not caring about damage to the leather and used rapid uneven stitches to finish the jobs. Aron did the opposite. It was apparent from the beginning who was an artist and who was not. Aron received criticisms for being too slow and their discussions of partnership ended. But those uneven stitches were like a signature.

"My dear woman," Aron said, "I'm a shoemaker, not a magician. I cannot make a shorter shoe into a longer one. But I have a suggestion. If you leave them, I can turn them into open pumps. If your toes stick out a touch you'll have room for your feet to breathe. At least you'll walk in more comfort. If not, give the shoes to a daughter."

"I will talk this over with my husband. He told me to go back to the bum. It was my feet the shoemaker said, it wasn't his fault they grew fatter and there was nothing he could do. He had a nerve. Now that shoemaker has disappeared. You can imagine where they dragged him off to."

Aron stood. He felt for the man. Bad or good shoemaker, he did not deserve to be enslaved in a camp. But the woman hung over the chair and made no move to get up. "Where is your wife? She runs around and doesn't have time to feed you? Look at you, skinny like a stick."

"My wife helps a friend," he said, guarding Gitel against prying. Aron feared the woman's connection to the Judenrat.

She smoothed her skirt as if brushing off his comment. "Listen, there is another reason I came. I'm going to talk plain, Matuszyński. You could help out. If you give a little information about where some of the young men are keeping themselves, things will get better for you. Hubner has work quotas you know. You'll get more work from the Germans."

"Of course," he said his lips smiling, the hand reaching to help the woman up empty of friendship. She rose with a smug face and Aron showed her to the door.

"If you want to be a fool than nobody can help you."

He watched her sway down the narrow steps, the hefty body an anomaly, each thud bulging her ankles out of the shoes. Aron did not believe she would return and though he needed the work, it was not a project he was anxious to pursue. The room was darkening and his wife was not there. This woman of his, would she ever learn? What if one of the hooligans caught her? She knew there was a curfew and if Hubner was in a bad mood or SS Prinz was lurking about anything could happen.

He checked his watch. It was seven. By eight o'clock curfew, the numbers on the watch would no longer be visible. There was nothing left of what Gitel had reminded him to eat. His wife seemed able to make something out of thin air. He sliced a piece of the bread Gitel had baked and chewed with relish, marveling at how good a plain piece of bread could taste. *I am so hungry I could eat the rest of the bread but then what would Gitel have?* He covered the bread with the cloth, got up to glance through the attic window and sat back down at the workbench hoping his wife would soon be home.

Gitel slipped on the yellow star. *Yes, I do what I must as much as I hate this on my arm. They can kiss my rear end.* Aron would not appreciate her saying such a thing, not so ladylike, but she knew it was what he felt too. He'd be worried about her. The sun was low. She broke into a fast walk. Soon the Wielpolski's castle would be on the rise. It made her think of the encounter with the Count and his son. She had shared her feelings with Aron about the Count. Maybe, just maybe, if a desperate time came, they could get help. She realized it was but a wishful thought and pushed it out of her mind, a mind attuned to pragmatism.

The road dipped, the castle disappeared from view and Gitel was on Dembroska again. Two Poles passed her on the almost dark street eying what she carried. Her muscles weary from shouldering the load tensed and her heart quickened. At least she was not far away from pushing the door open to the bakery.

CHAPTER EIGHTEEN

Gitel Comes Back

Aron read *tehillim* by the dim light of the kerosene lamp and concentrated on something other than worry. The beauty of the psalms, each word he read aloud, calmed his fragile nerves.

"How long, O LORD? Will you forget me forever? How long will you hide your face from me? How long must I bear pain in my soul, and have sorrow in my heart all day long? How long shall my enemy be exalted over me?"

His glue-stained fingers turned the pages and though he lacked formal education he knew what moved him. The psalms, the only poetry he had ever known, misted his eyes.

His heart open, he heard footsteps and rushed to the door. He still wore the leatherwork apron and touched the *yarmulke* on his head in reverence for the psalms. The hallway was unlit. Now light from the attic room cast jagged shadows on the walls and made the eyes that strained to see hollow and distant.

"Gitel." The word lanced his worries.

"Aron, am I happy to hear you." She stopped to catch her breath.

He rushed down the steps. "And me, you," he called.

Aron took the bundle and encircled her in his arm. They leaned into one another.

"Gitel, you know how to make a man *meshugge*. Isn't it crazy for you to go out and take such risks?"

"Everything is a risk." He followed, gripping the hand she extended behind her. The next moment they entered the apartment. "With you here this is a home. When you're gone it's just a place to work." Aron dropped the bundle on the floor and stepped toward her. "You are the most beautiful woman." He took her in his arms and stroked her hair. Then took her sweater off and his work apron. He inhaled her scent. "You are like damp spring air. Let me help with your boots."

They stared, their faces reflecting joy.

He brought the washbasin and a rag with the morning wash up water and felt the blisters on her palms. "Gitel," he whispered.

"I told you I would take care of my boots." She pulled her hands away.

"Finish that later. It's past eight o'clock. When was the last time you ate? If you have no mercy on yourself, can you think of the baby?"

"You're right," she said, "bread."

"What's in the old blanket? What are the people like in the countryside? Did you have problems?"

"People are people," she said.

"So you had plenty *tsuris,*" Aron said running a hand through thick waves of hair. He slipped off his *yarmulke.*"

"Are you afraid someone is looking that you have to take it off?"

"No matter how hard you try, I'm never going to be a Hasid. Tell me what happened and where you went."

"There's time for stories. First, I'll take care of us."

She went to the cupboard and removed the cloth from the last of the bread. From a jar she drizzled a bit of chicken fat on the slices and arranged them on a plate. She unrolled a paper wrapper and picked off the last of briny herring. "Here," she said, bringing the meal to the table. She poured what was left of the water into short thick glasses, set up the plates and sat down in her stocking feet, too tired to retrieve slippers. Aron came over and watched as she ate. "Do you need an invitation to your own table?" she said. "Your plate is empty."

"I want you to eat. I ate."

"I can see how your belly hangs over your pants," she giggled. "You found nothing else, just bread, am I right?"

"You know how we men are, helpless without a woman. You eat, Gitel. Your face tells what kind of day you had." He walked over to the bundle and unknotted the blanket revealing the chair legs and the seat bottoms.

"Look at him. Curious, like a cat. I'm sorry, Aron. No leather. I was afraid to go near the towns with tanneries. Too many people and *them*."

"The pieces are good." He nodded with approval, assessing with an expert eye. "Did they throw in that old umbrella as part of the bargain?" Aron thought of Hanek the Hunchback, the umbrella not unlike what he may have drawn from his pack as they had *hondled* earlier that day.

Gitel smiled. "Don't you recognize your father's umbrella? The dear man saw me this morning when I was leaving in the rain and made me take it along."

When he saw she had finished and was putting things in order he said, "You'll tell me more in the morning. It's time you rest. Let's get into bed."

"I know you, Aron. When I lie down next to you it won't be to rest."

"No more talk."

He took Gitel's hand and led her to the bed. "Get undressed. I'll turn off the lamp. We have to save precious kerosene."

They undressed in the dark. Her treasure, the down cover floated over their bodies, shielding them from the night chill. In bed Aron, sure of his hands, drew Gitel to him and spoke with caresses. She felt his heart racing against her breasts and from his breaths how aroused he was. She often submitted when his passion was greater than hers, but there were times when she needed him as well and this night she released herself. He felt her body heat and her moist thighs. When he entered Gitel, she made sounds of approval and dropped her arms to the bed in surrender. Aron moved in her with pleasure, brushing his lips against her neck and silken shoulders. She moved with him and when he released inside she knew she had never known this uncontrolled desire. As her heart calmed, Aron wrapped himself around her and slept. Was it the pregnancy she wondered as the down tented her into sleep? Her passion for Aron was growing.

Birds played staccato melodies in the morning. Aron slipped out before Gitel stirred. He wanted her to rest. Her level of energy and ability to work were out of the norm. From girlhood she had been a force to reckon with, a wild colt that had received enough blows to cooperate but not to break. In the street were Polish men with whom he once chatted. They avoided each other and Aron continued to the wellhead. The trees were alive with fresh growth from yesterday's rain. Overnight tiny leaves had connected into green lace against golden light of the new day. He lingered a moment. *A beautiful world filled with ugliness.* He pumped the water, filled the buckets and started back.

Days before, Hubner had grabbed him for a work detail to clean apartments emptied of Jews to be replaced by Volksdeutche ready to spread their wings. Afterwards he marched Aron and two tailors to his house, the one that was once Abromczyck's. They repaired confiscated shoes, jackets, coats, pants, and dresses, items worn by families they had known. Late at night, Hubner released them. Gitel's only words to Aron were, "Sit down and eat." She was pale with worry and knew he had not been allowed even a swallow of water.

Glad to be off the street with filled buckets, he knew each day was less sure than the previous. He had to find a way to become invisible. How long would it be until he was taken permanently? When he opened the door Gitel wiped off the chair legs and had assembled something for a breakfast. "It's like magic," Aron said.

"After this, the magic is over," she said scooping a morsel on the plate, her eyes enticing Aron to eat the rest. "What were you reading last night before I got home?"

"Don't get too excited. I'm not turning into a scholar you'll have to support as I idle away time. I know you and your secret desires for the religious types."

"Never mind,' she said. "A simple question turns into an accusation."

"This is the kind of husband you married. Not a scholar. But maybe I'll be able to put a bit of food on our table."

135

He brought over the measurement workbook and showed her the orders he had taken from the doctor and a Judenrat member. He had come with the same proposition Aron had gotten from the overbearing wife of the grain dealer. But the man had insisted his shoes be repaired.

"You would have more customers than time in the day to satisfy them. Even now you have work."

"There would be more work under the complete thumb of the Judenrat. Their protection and business with Hubner, is it worth it, Gitel? With the baby coming, am I making a mistake not to give them what they want? Am I too much of a hothead."

CHAPTER NINETEEN

1941 Birth

Unlike ordinary labor, which she had never turned from or feared it was the labor of having the baby that in the last days haunted Gitel. Her body covered in a clammy film, she pled with Aron not to go down to the street. The week before he had been taken to shovel snow, carry coal to the Nazis' headquarters and then marched to a mill twenty kilometers away to empty the last of the grain. The Pole who owned the mill was shot dead. Aron and the others carried sacks of grain on their backs returning to Ksiaz Wielki unsure they would set eyes on their loved ones again.

The child was coming. He had to go down and do his best to get coal for the frigid attic room. Before Aron could slip away, he was spotted and taken to scrape horse stalls. The horses chewed straw and sipped water through soft fleshy lips. Aron's remained parched. Then he was forced to clean the out houses of the new burghers who complained about the backward lack of plumbing they suffered. Ten hours later, unable to have gotten even a handful of coal, he was released. He found Gitel sitting in the dark, her breaths rushing out of control. Aron lit the kerosene lamp and lowered it to a flicker.

Gitel gripped his hands and moaned. "Aron, get Balcha." She stifled a scream and tried to stand but fell back to the chair. Her water broke and the gushing warmth turned into laughter.

"So this is a comedy?" His mind in confusion, he tried to calm himself and his wife.

Aron ran to get Gitel's sister, many houses from the bakery, Gitel alone. The thought of losing her made him oblivious to the curfew jeopardizing his life. Balcha was asleep but assured him her sister would do what all other women were able to do. She put together a few things, he unsure what, his head and heart galloping in opposite directions. Aron took his sister-in-law's arm and steered her down the iced blackness.

The baker's wife heard commotion and ran up to her tenants in the attic. Now the two women, both mothers, hovered about issuing orders. A weak orange flame flickered in the kerosene lamp. It illuminated Gitel's glistening face, belying the chill in the unheated room. Balcha and the baker's wife moved Gitel to the bed to calm her down. But terrible pains ripped through her and she told Aron he had to fetch the doctor. Aron ran down to the street again. He was no longer aware of the winter cold or that it was two o'clock in the morning, the first of February 1941.

He woke Dr. Yoblonski, who grumbled about the time as Aron, wild-eyed and desperate, begged. The doctor asked what progress Gitel had made toward birth as he readied, letting Aron know he should refuse to do this *verboten* thing. The doctor threw on his coat. They peeked from his doorway and stepped onto the deserted street.

Dr. Yoblonski hurried Aron to fetch more water from the well and turned to what was about to unfold. The baker's wife he dismissed asking her to send up coal if possible for the idle cook stove, the room barely warmer than the winter night. He examined Gitel and while she stared at him, her apprehensive eyes absorbed the news it was going to be a breech birth. The circumstances required Gitel's full attention and help he explained. He was concerned about the cord, which in breech births could choke off the baby's breath when strong labor started. From the few he had attended over the years, Dr. Yoblonski knew there would be little time to deal with such a problem once the birth began. There would be no way to ease the pain. They had no whiskey. The doctor looked over at his favorite shoemaker, pallid and scared. "Go to the stairs for some air, Adam," he said.

Labor became intense and the doctor guided Gitel to squat on the sheet Balcha threw on the floor. She tried hard to stifle screams, but the pain intensified and she let loose a shriek before her sister could quiet it with strips of towel she had made ready to muffle cries. Shivering with effort Gitel bore down. She forced out the tiny feet. The doctor waited and encouraged as a baby began to emerge. Minutes later, with Gitel's last strength and the doctor's strong grip, a girl child's head fell forward into his blood smeared waiting hands.

The sun was rising as Aron crept up the stairs, startled by the sounds of a different cry. He opened the door, his eyes craters of worry for Gitel. The child was wailing and he trembled from relief. He felt a sudden stranger in his own home. Balcha, her *shaitel* hair in disarray, followed Dr. Yoblonski as he reassembled implements. She offered the exhausted man what she saw on Gitel's table; boiled potatoes in their skins, the meal untouched. The doctor smiled toward his patient white and spent, the infant at her breast. He nodded his thanks and waved away the food.

"You're a lucky man. She's strong, brave, your wife. This kind of thing does not always end well. Your daughter, you heard her, a boss already." He smiled his approval.

This was the first he knew. His child was a girl. "Dr. Yoblonski," Aron started, but covered his face, hiding tears. "Please, please let me pay you."

"Bring me the good *slivovitz* your father makes, Adam. You gave me more than a fair price. He glanced at the boots he wore, the cut and simplicity Aron's signature.

"I'll see what I can find for you, doctor," Aron said.

Her skin translucent pale, Gitel called to Dr. Yoblonski. But her voice was too weak to be heard as she mouthed, "I'll help."

He patted her shoulder. "Rest, you have time for this."

"You heard the doctor," Aron said with a loving warning to his wife. "Rest."

"My mother has the Easter on her mind in the middle of winter. She bothers me for plums for the pudding. Even with the war, this is what the old lady thinks. See what you can do. Plums for her and *slivovitz* for me. It would be very nice." The doctor glanced at his completed work then climbed down the narrow steps. He checked the street already lit with morning, pulled up his collar and walked very fast from the committed crime, helping Jews.

Balcha shook her head. "My sister was right. Something was different. Who else but Gitel would have a daughter ripping forth, feet first?" She slipped out and left them, a family.

Aron sat and watched Gitel, asleep, the child wrapped snug beside her. *A girl,* he said to himself. A daughter. And then the thought of what it meant for a father to have a son, a firstborn son, crowded out the relief that it was over, that Gitel and the child had made it through the difficult birth. This thought that he would have preferred a boy made him feel that even here he had failed. What kind of man was he to think this? But was it not the dream of every Jewish father to be blessed by sons, many sons? His eyes moved from the sleeping child and again to Gitel. He would say nothing of this to her. Not admit he was disappointed. But Gitel would know. She read everything written on his face, sensed his thoughts. Wasn't that why he could not live without her? He tiptoed near them, his wife and this tiny *beshefinish,* creation, with the few golden wisps of hair floating on her perfect head.

Several weeks later two Judenrat members of Hubner's handpicked Jews came to warn the couple they had put themselves and their neighbors in danger. Aron's eyes bulging, he lowered his voice to a menacing rasp. "What should I do, kill her so she doesn't cry?" Gitel calmed him down and the baby began to wail. Not that she hadn't wanted to tell them their daughter, Devoire Ita, is a good baby. She felt like telling them a baby has to cry and she doesn't very much, except now because of you two smug, sour busybodies. She refrained. It would stoke her husband's anger. When the two left, Gitel rocked the child and she quieted. "If I take the baby to my parents sometimes, care for her there, help out a little in the dairy, what would be so bad?" she put forth to Aron.

CHAPTER TWENTY

Plums and Brandy

D evoire Ita bounced in her arms. Gitel passed the last tailor shop on the street and glimpsed through the window of the cramped apartment. Aron's best friend rocked over a sewing machine. Her face softened when she got to the rustic stone synagogue. She hummed to the baby, the same waltz tune Aron had sung last night when he took her in his arms and twirled her round and round, she accusing him of acting *meshugge,* he replying yes, he was crazy for her. The synagogue door was no longer ajar nor was there low murmuring from men draped in white prayer shawls, swaying like ripe stalks of winter wheat.

The purpose of the visit quickened her steps. Maybe her in-laws had *slivovitz* or the plums set from long ago. She and Aron could repay the doctor with what he asked. The armband she wore assured no one on the street would offer to sell her potatoes, dried beans, flour, any items to trade so common in the past. The Poles willing to trade were fearful of reprisal from watchful eyes ready to implicate them in *verboten* behavior with pariahs. She passed the nice wood frame houses that once belonged to Jews or Poles, now inhabited by the occupiers. With frequency, the dispossessed Jews were moved to ghettos in Krakow, Lodz, Czestochowa, and Bedzin, where they vied for morsels of food, twenty and more jammed into a room without sanitation and from there transported to labor camps. Many Poles were moved east, interned in labor camps, their

141

intelligencia obliterated. The Germans were interested in the Poles as a slave population, a subjugated, uneducated, nationless people, ready to serve them. As for the Jews, a plan of action was under way that would impress the lowest sadists.

Gitel turned the corner to an alleyway and a few steps further she stopped at the weather-beaten building where in two little rooms Aron, his brothers and his sister Pescel had been raised. The windows were still boarded from the attack the night before Aron had returned from the prisoner-of-war camp. Already this morning sweep marks from her mother-in-law's hard twig broom were scratched into the dirt walkway.

Before Gitel knocked Ruchel was at the door. "Gitel, come in, come in. Let me see this beautiful child, maybe you'll have something to eat." She reached for her granddaughter in the practiced way of a woman who had raised many of her own.

"Mother-in-law Ruchel, please, don't trouble yourself with feeding us. We ate. I brought you a few beets."

What Mendel was able to provide even in better days was paltry and Ruchel took the few beets from her daughter-in-law with a shy grateful smile. She waited as Gitel's eyes adjusted to light stealing through the nailed boards. "This is a world upside down." She ran and got a spoon to put into the hand of her granddaughter and the baby brought it to her pink lips.

Aron's sister clapped her hands and smiled at the child. Pescel shared her father's nature. Among the Matuszyńskis and their good looks, she was exceptional, with sensuous curves and dazzling blonde ringlets drawing eyes wherever she stood. "Are you holding up with the baby?" she said reaching to touch the child's fingertips.

"Whatever we can, we do. You see how she grows." Gitel stopped to search for the right words but it was her way to speak her mind. "We can't forget our debt to the doctor. I hope you'll be able to help us."

With the air of a woman in charge, Ruchel went to the coal stove. On top sat an enamel water kettle. It gleamed, as did everything. Gitel's eyes moved around the room and into the tiny adjacent alcove and she listened to her father-in-law chanting the morning-prayer service. Mendel swayed rhythmically, a phylactery on his forehead, his left arm bound by the leather strap. He motioned to his wife he was almost done, nodded to Gitel and kissing the fringe of his *tallit* walked back to complete the prayers. His voice was melodic and strong and Gitel imagined her own father would be done with prayers by now, her mother hanging out a few pieces of laundry she had scrubbed in a tall pail.

Ruchel made tea from dried apple peels and set the steaming glasses before Gitel and her daughter. There was no sugar, another of the many luxuries beyond their means. "Mendel," she called to her husband, "shall I make tea for you?"

Mendel came in, the neat white beard framing his face. He rolled down his left sleeve covering the marks on his forearm from the leather prayer strap. "I thank you, my wife, but I must leave. Sit with our Gitel and talk. Gitel, it's a joy to see you and our newest, let her grow and be well."

A trace of disappointment on his daughter-in-law's face forced his voice to rise with optimism. "Maybe today there'll be a farmer at the market willing to sell to an old man."

"I see," Ruchel said. "Mendel, I'll put together something for you." She rolled pieces of turnip into a stiff white cloth.

"If I am fortunate, I'll bring a calf to the *shochet* for slaughter. Put in a good word for me," he said stepping outside, pointing to a cloudless blue sky as Ruchel pressed the tiny bundle into his other hand. Saving face for this elderly man was on all of their minds.

Gitel told her mother-in-law about what Dr. Yoblonski had asked after the birth. Ruchel listened as she mended Mendel's sock, the baby's eyes following the quick needle pricks. Ruchel shook her head. She waved the mended sock, her eyes narrowed unable to hide the antipathy. "Dried plums. *Slivovitz.* You and Aron know we have not worked the orchards for years."

"I don't know where to turn," Gitel said.

"The doctor and his mother are fine people and I would like to help. But the Count no longer deals with us and not just my family, none of our people," Ruchel said. "We have not rented his orchards for years. Yes, once it was a different story, there was ample supply. Now what is left? Nothing. Mendel made his living every summer this way since we were married more than thirty years ago. Each spring after Passover, we moved everything we needed, pots, bowls, bedding, foodstuff, and the few clothes for our backs. The boys and Mendel made our lean-tos out of branches, cut what they needed from the trees, and in a wink we had our house for the summer. How he and the boys made a roof that did not leak when it rained, I can't explain. There we lived, watching the orchards, caring for the fruits on the trees. Mendel's sons from his first wife, may she rest in peace, were a big help. Nice boys, and the daughter was a fine girl to me, respectful. I raised them before our children were born. They were like my own. God forgive me, kinder than one of my own sons. I cooked for them all, washed clothes in the brook."

Ruchel stopped talking. The wagon wheels that creaked by agitated her fingers.

"Mother," Pescel said, "they're moving another family out. I can feel it."

"Everything comes to an end." Ruchel covered her eyes, avoiding the boarded windows.

"Mother-in-law Ruchel," Gitel said. "Tell me how it was. I want Devoire Ita to hear. Whatever she understands, I want her to know where she comes from and how things used to be."

"In those days we had a free life. Maybe not so free. We had plenty *tsuris* but we spent our days together, with or without problems. The Count's caretaker, with him we made the arrangement to rent the orchards. He knew Mendel. He was a good Polack. It's an old story. No one could own land and we were in no position, to even buy a patch of ground. We made the best of it and found a way to scratch out a living."

"Aron told me he was free and happy in the orchards. I think his love for nature's things began there, when he was a young boy," Gitel said.

"Was it beautiful?" She lifted her blouse and gave the child her breast. Devoire Ita's eyes closing with contentment.

"The fields were filled with flowers and the fragrance of the delicate blooms on the plum trees was better than any perfume," Ruchel said taking a deep breath as if the scent lingered about her. "In the evenings my handsome sons entertained us. Yankel, his dark blue eyes flashing, told stories, sang, and danced, and the moon and stars gave us light. In the morning as Mendel and the boys said their prayers under the open sky we were surrounded by God's creations. The birds sang with them as they made the blessings for our new day, for the fruit on the trees, for the bread I made to eat."

Gitel's eyes moistened with thoughts of her own family and how sweet life had been during holidays, how intertwined Aron's world and hers had been from the time they were children, their riches coming not from the paltry material world but from the heart of what it meant to join together the bonds of faith and the delights of simplicity. She moved her sleeping child to the arms of Aron's mother and hoped the woman would be there to hold the child as she grew. Ruchel cradled her and smiled at her daughter-in-law, this independent woman, her son's life partner.

"Late summer when it was ready our boys climbed the trees to shake the fruit loose. They yelled and jumped as the plums plopped to the ground. We brought back thousands of plums in bushels by wagon. Mendel and the boys sold them fresh just after Rosh Hashanah. Later in the fall we dried them. Mendel brought the harvest to the market for our customers. Everyone bought, Jews, the Poles. We sold most of it and kept what we needed for ourselves. The summers ran away so fast. Even with all the hardships, I know how sweet life was then. Those were our happy times, a bitter life in their place now. Where will I find dried plums for the lady now?"

"Mother-in-law Ruchel, please think. If we can pay the doctor what he asks, in secret he'll send Aron customers and we will help you and ourselves.'"

Ruchel stood to take away the glasses on the tablecloth, which she had hemmed with pale blue cross-stitches. As worn as it was, she cared for it and the little she possessed.

"Mendel used to make jars of *slivovitz* brandy with the fresh plums. The Poles waited for his strong brandy. If I could find a jar of *slivovitz*, maybe on the bottom of the jar there remain plums, if they haven't fallen apart," Ruchel added. "Uh, the *goyim* liked Mendel's *slivovitz*. And Mendel liked it too."

"Could there still be something left?" Gitel said.

"We'll look in the cellar," Ruchel said. "It's cold and dark and who knows what runs around, maybe rats. Let Pescel hold the child."

"I'm less afraid of the four-legged rats than some of the two-legged ones I meet," Gitel said, handing Devoire Ita to Pescel, who began a fine game of banging spoons, a new fascination for her precocious niece.

"Come, the child is in good hands," Ruchel said. She wrapped herself in a brown shawl, touched the *mezuzah* on the doorframe, a sign of respect for her faith, and led Gitel to the back of the house.

Gitel prodded open the cellar door with a hard push. The women climbed down the uneven rungs warped by time. A repugnant odor did not discourage Ruchel and Gitel from exploring the cellar, its low ceiling covered with webs. As their eyes adjusted they brushed filaments attaching to their faces and clothing.

"Those hoodlums who broke up my home should smell from their heads like it does down here," Ruchel whispered.

They groped their way to a corner near what was once a window, now also without glass. Ruchel stopped, careful not to step on shards scattered on the uneven dirt floor. "I see the hooligans did not forget the glass here either," she said. "What is this?"

Gitel looked to where Ruchel pointed. There stood a large jar, thick with dust and slivers of glass on the lid.

"Please, God in heaven," Gitel said, "let this be some kind of help." Taking a closer look she nodded to her mother-in-law.

Ruchel's face held a quizzical expression. "Either he knew and has been hiding the jar or forgot about it. I will talk to Mendel tonight," Ruchel said. "Let's take a look at the plums at the bottom of the jar."

"The jar still has a couple whole ones," Gitel said a smile of thanks lifting her lovely cheeks.

"Will this be enough and would the lady use plums that can make you drunk from one whiff?" Ruchel laughed.

"That's a good question." She put the jar down in the same spot. "I will leave it to you, mother-in-law, Ruchel."

"Mendel will come to you tomorrow, Gitel. Tell Aron we will help him pay his debt. Always he worries what everyone thinks. A husband can keep such secrets from a wife? I'll let Mendel discover this for himself." She gave her daughter-in-law a knowing look as they climbed the steep steps and emerged into the light of midmorning.

* * * * *

Early spring Gitel began taking Devoire Ita to Giebultow as much as she dared. She sped through the forest and would stay with her family until late afternoon. Gitel helped her father in the dairy and shared the growing child with her adoring grandmother, Hinda. It gave Aron time to work and lessened tension from the Judenrat. This mild summer day had gone well but on the way back, a German soldier stopped Gitel. She stood stunned as he explained in German, laced with poor Polish that he searched for Jews smuggling food. She had never seen him before and with the armband covered by the baby she cradled he mistook her for a Pole. She feared for herself but for the baby she was petrified. Would he search her, find the cabbage and turnips she had hidden in the child's blanket and do who knew what?

Pointing at the bundle in her arms, he asked had she anything to show him. She shrugged her shoulders as if she understood nothing. A smiling, ignorant proud mother, she willed her hand not to tremble and opened the blanket to reveal Devoire Ita. The baby's hazel eyes peered out with curiosity, copper wisps of curls waving in the breeze. Gitel knew the child could not speak yet, but what if she could and had blurted out a Yiddish word? Gitel's temples throbbed and sweat ran from her armpits. Her hair, covered by a drab peasant scarf, and her perfect white skin emboldened her to smile. This expression frozen on her lips, she prayed her face displayed guileless ignorance. As a Pole there was no guarantee she would not be detained or molested, but discovered as a Jew with food on her person she and the baby could be murdered in the middle of the sunny field, without question. The German smiled at the beautiful child and she returned his smile. Gitel held Devoire Ita so tight the child began to cry. The soldier waved them on.

It was the final time Gitel went to her parents until the decision loomed. What were they going to do? Stay and be taken away by the Nazis or find another way? It pressed ever harder, the time to decide about to end.

CHAPTER TWENTY-ONE

Joy Midst Terror

The name of Aron's and Gitel's grandmothers were bestowed upon the child - Devoire 'little bee' and Ita 'home-ruler'. The name was a perfect fit for the child Dr. Yoblonski said entered feet-first like a little boss. Aron insisted the gold wisps growing into strawberry curls and the eyes pools of shining light were attributable to his grandmother. Gitel said, "Fine, let it be your way."

Aron's workbench held endless fascinations and Devoire Ita soon crawled and pulled up against his legs. She waved curious fingers above her reach while Gitel boiled white dishcloths converted into diapers, a pungent mix with the glues and wax polishes. Aron sat her on his lap and sang *uuf in pripichik, brent a fireelle,* the Yiddish words *on the hearth a little fire burns,* bringing moments of happiness in a world with flaming depravity.

Devoire Ita accepted Gitel's early training to use a metal potty, coal to boil diapers almost impossible to get even if they could have afforded it. She taught the child to swish her hands in the bucket of water by the oven and to feed herself with the tiny rose-handled silver spoon from the trade with Hanek the Hunchback. Whenever Aron left the apartment Devoire Ita heard Gitel's appeals to be careful, the Germans will catch you. So by her eighteenth month she tugged on Aron's pants before he opened the door, shaking her curls, "No, *tatteh,* the Germans will catch you." He lifted her with pride and sorrow and brushed her velvet cheek before she wriggled down to find something new to explore. He'd open the attic door and ask a higher power *please don't let this be the last time.*

Summer of 1942 the first story of Belzec sent shocks through the town. On Hubner's orders the Judenrat had to single out more young men for the Plazow work camp and then for Belzec. A baker's son escaped from Belzec.

"The women. First they took them," he sputtered a tortured grimace on his lips. "They brought them back with shaved heads." The neighbors looked at the young man as if he had lost his sanity. "Have you ever seen women without hair, shamed, their eyes naked?" He told of hundreds and hundreds of men and women who were put into a building never to come out.

It was too fantastic to believe. The Judenrat denied any such thing could have happened. How could he have gotten back, two hundred kilometers with the Nazis everywhere? He must have hidden and tells this fantastic story, they accused. They insisted Belzec was like Plazow work camp near Krakow, for able-bodied workers. But the young man repeated his story with a whimper. "I saw with my own eyes. No men, no women came out. Where did they go?"

"The boy is in his wrong mind and you better put this ridiculous story out of your heads. Make sure the rest do," Hubner warned the Judenrat. "You are lucky no *aktion* has been forced upon you." Then he stepped up his demands. The Judenrat had to increase quota with promises that if young men went willingly, their parents would be safe. Hubner extorted anything parents still possessed to buy a reprieve for a son, his promises soon broken.

Aron met the young man at the well early one morning. He knew what terror could do. The smell of death and the plaintive last moans of life were part of Aron now. He had crawled over the dead. Aron searched the young man's face. He wanted to say something but the boy stared ahead and slipped into the house that used to belong to his parents. He hid among empty sacks in the cellar where flour was once stored to make aromatic breads, rolls and butter cakes. His mother and father had been sent to Belzec with him.

Hot summer winds wilted hopes. Rumors about the round up to empty every house of Jews passed back and forth between Aron and Gitel's families. Hubner dropped hints the liquidation was imminent. The last Friday of July his lust for killing erupted. As if a silent clock struck, families stood to light the candles and avert the darkness of the sun's absence. Diminished stubs of wax that served as Sabbath candles illuminated the faces of mothers, fathers and children, many not yet old enough to understand. It was at this moment that Hubner and two helpers waved revolvers, kicked open doors, dragged the terrified families out and herded them to the cemetery. Sixteen people, six adults, the rest children, shivered on the balmy night, stars one by one blinking overhead. Fathers begged Hubner, the Volkesdeutche elevated by the Nazis, to spare the children. Two mothers with little ones' heads buried in their shoulders were the first to fall. Shrieks and prayers extinguished as bullets hit the rest with ugly pops.

The next morning volunteers from the burial society viewed the bodies lying among the headstones etched with reminders that Jews had lived in Ksiaz Wielki for over a century. Because it was Sabbath they had to wait until sundown to begin the rituals. They carried the bodies to the nearby mortuary and cleansed them. With no time or materials to build simple caskets the bodies were wrapped in plain white shrouds. Fear, kept friends and relatives away. Two from the Judenrat and two from the burial society dug shallow graves all day Sunday until the last of the sixteen murdered was buried. The killers mocked and walked free with impunity. How convenient they had made it, they laughed, for the bodies to have already been in the cemetery and still the stupid Jews had made it harder for themselves. The vacant apartments would soon be filled in this tiny town of the General Government, the Polish territory designed for administration and resettlement by the Nazis.

Late autumn gold and pale brown touched the countryside. But Aron sat lost, empty. *The seasons have come and gone my whole life. Its beauty has filled me with awe. Now, I am blind to it. I'm without them.* The knowledge rocked him on his workbench. *My dear parents. Gone. My sister. My young brother. Gone.* The night before, in the dark of the new October moon the SS had come for Mendel and Ruchel, Pescel and Itchele. They were among another ten removed. Their few neighbors kept silent, afraid they were next. The news had not reached Aron until morning. Yankel threw open the door stiff and lifeless as the broom in his hand, the one their mother had held for the last time and left the circular scratches on the dirt floor as she had done so many times before.

Their shoulders shook with misery. "What harm did they do anyone?" Aron rasped. "Eighty-three years old. Last week, I saw him help a pregnant Polish girl. He carried a bucket of water for her. Is there a heaven or only hell?" Aron's words dripped with hatred. He tasted bile.

They knew there was little time left for any of them.

"Aron there is always hope. Maybe we'll see your dear parents again," Gitel said. "Your beautiful sister." They spoke in Polish so the child could not understand the hushed words. But Devoire Ita watched her father weep, his mouth an embittered slash of pain. Would his child see her grandmother or grandfather again, two old people for whom work was unlikely? The young man's account of the Belzec concentration camp became a ghost in their midst.

At surreptitious meetings Aron's and Gitel's families debated about how to avoid capture. Was there a way to hide? Where could they go? Who would shelter them?

Disaster seeped into every room of Ksiaz Wielki, Judenrat members were suffering the same fates. Gitel insisted she had to go to Giebultow, the terrible news she could not shake from the loss of Aron's family driving her to chance it. Devoire Ita's legs hugged her waist and she paced the five kilometers in a run, her senses on guard, searching in every direction.

There he was, Wolf, by the dairy room, beaming at her child. Devoire Ita jumped onto his open broad chest, bouncing under his graying beard. He snorted, pretending to devour her clapping hands. She giggled, free here from warnings to hush. Devoire Ita pulled his beard and Wolf whined, a smitten pup.

"You like playing with Zaide Wolf," she said. Gitel took her child from the man she could not remember playing with. "Father, how are you doing? We have to make decisions."

Wolf followed her inside. They sat at the table words stuck like splintered bones in their throats. Suddenly, the door burst open. Hinda gasped. Gitel pulled Deborah Ita close, her body ready to leap. Mordche rushed in, an unwieldy sack tugging at his shoulder.

Wolf slammed his hand on the table. "This is how you open a door? You made your mother white. We didn't expect you till night."

Devoire Ita started to wail. "It's your Uncle Mordche, child." Stroking her back, Gitel shot a look at her father. Mordche let the sack thud to the floor. He withdrew turnips and potatoes with a magician's flourish.

"All for you," he winked at the child. "Wait till you see what else," nodding at his father to make peace. He pulled out a black lump and spun it on the table.

"Coal." Wolf whistled capturing Devoire Ita's attention.

"I walked to Miechow and took it right from the tracks when the bastards were busy with unloading a train. I'm not the first with that idea but we'll be able to make a decent trade. Gitel, your mind is on your face."

"Mordche you took that risk? They'll get you. Strong and young, their noses sniff out men like you."

"I take risks? What about you?"

Gitel shielded her brimming eyes. The child pried away her fingers as if it was a game. "I speak Polish so she won't understand though she's picking it up. They've taken Mendel, Ruchel, Pescel and Itchele."

"Oh my God, what are we going to do?" Hinda said in her refined Lodz accent, the one Polish peasants who came to trade liked to hear. She held her arms out to the little girl, a grandmother who understood how empty of this joy Ruchel was now. Her pained sigh brought them all to tears.

"There's no stopping them. Have you and Yankel found somewhere for us?" She asked Mordche. Her brother's eyes told Gitel he shared her pain. She flashed back with hers the urgency of what had to be done.

"I'm not going anywhere." Wolf walked to the door. "There is nothing I can do for my dear Mendel and Ruchel but pray. Pescel, oh. I told you last time I will volunteer. I hear if a man like me goes, the family may be spared. Is there not a God who comes to us in the darkest times and shows his might?"

"Father, you've heard what they say is happening in Belzec," Gitel said. "Who knows where they'll send you?" She watched her mother and Devoire Ita count the potatoes on the table. If only the world would allow for these small pleasures. Aron was without his mother now. Gitel treasured even more the conversation she had shared about war and pregnancy. Between a mother and a daughter. She felt bottomless love for this woman's wisdom and tenderness and the losses stung all the more.

"I say we run as soon as we organize," Mordche said. "Take as much food as we can, what's on our backs, and whatever we have to protect us from the coming winter. Anything of value to trade, the silver candlesticks, any jewelry left." Mordche dragged the sack to the door.

Hinda stood. Her granddaughter's tiny hand grasped her long skirt. "Who has anything left, Mordche? The Poles refuse to trade and the only way to get food has been to almost give away our valuables."

"This is not ending so fast. Aron learned the Russians are pressing from the East, Father," Gitel said.

Wolf pushed his chair back. "The Russians, a pox on them. They're worse than the Poles. You see these ten fingers? Look around. I did this. Yours too, Hinda my wife. This is what we know, this is what I'm going to use, what I always did."

"Wolf," Hinda begged. "Be reasonable. We have to listen to our children."

"Father," Mordche pled. "The Koniecny family on Count Dzianat's land is giving us a place for seventeen people, eighteen with Devoire Ita. They're fine, good people. The arrangement is in the hayloft, over the huge grain barn. The man takes a chance with his life. His sons will help and the daughter and wife don't know. He wants five hundred *zlotys*. Meir is putting it up."

The clock swung its little pendulum. The soft tick seemed to grow faster. Wolf stood and gripped the table, his flashing dark eyes sealing faces with unspoken affection. "Seventeen," escaped through his steel lips. He took the child in his arms, kissed her cheek and left.

A day later Hinda awoke in the bed she shared with her husband. Wolf was gone.

CHAPTER TWENTY-TWO

1942 The Hiding

One week before the November 7, *aktion* would take place, Hinda, Deborah, and her young brother were the first to sneak onto the Koniecny homestead. Yankel's wife and their two sons were next. Each small group assembled and left their homes in the middle of the night hoping the new moon would provide cover. Bundles under their arms, hearts racing the families crept through the open meadows, into the woods and made their way to the barn.

Aron and Gitel stared at the bed, the chest and Devoire Ita's crib sturdy on its rockers, everything empty of purpose. Nothing could be sold or even given away. To do so would reveal too much. Again, Aron had made the deal to store his tools with the Polish shoemaker in Sosnowiec. Should Aron never return, all of it would belong to the Pole. They did not dare thank their landlords, the baker and his wife or say farewell to their eldest, fifteen year old Halina who had lavished affection on her young neighbor, Devoire Ita.

They stared at the room for the last time dusk softening the emptiness. Aron and Gitel touched the *mezuzah* on the doorframe, bringing fingers to their lips. "Me," Devoire Ita pointed. Gitel lifted the child and let her play, mimicking the world of Jews into which she had been born.

There was room for little where they were hiding, not that they had much of value to take. Aron had ninety zlotys in his pocket from toiling on shoes and boots. They packed the foods Gitel had bartered, then cooked and readied for this moment.

For five apples she traded the blouse that matched the brown suit she had tailored in Bedzin. She wore the suit now, the last fine thing she had saved for during happier days as the owner of her store. The cherished down cover was wrapped around two pots, two knives, two spoons, a pillow to be used as the child's bed and the fedora of green felt which, when pulled over Gitel's auburn hair, remade her eyes into hooded emeralds. For the child she took the coat Ruchel had sewn, boots Aron made with room to grow and the rosebud silver spoon. Devoire Ita held her sawdust doll the plaster lips ever smiling.

Bundles ready they waited until shadows consumed the room and night released them. "We're going to the Zaide Wolf," the child announced. Why else would they take so much but to visit Giebultow, her grandparents in the countryside where she could talk loud and laugh? "Yes," Gitel told her. "What a smart girl you are." There could be no explanation for a child not yet two about hiding from death.

Devoire Ita was asleep on Gitel's shoulder when Aron led the way down the stairs. The street deserted, Gitel went first and walked as fast as she could past the houses. When they were out of sight Aron followed with the bundles on his back. Once they reached the shelter of the woods they felt more assured they would not be spotted, only relieved when the Koniecny hay barn was before them.

The last ones to creep, the moon beginning to wax and no longer a reliable friend, were Mordche and Yankel. Carrying a sack of bread, their pockets filled with tins of sardines, they climbed up the ladder and yanked it up to the hayloft. It was crowded, seventeen squeezed together under the rafters of the barn. They stared at one another each family group settled into what was now their space. For how long no one knew. Gitel peeled off her armband along with the others. The five children, eight to twelve years, scrambled to see who could collect the most yellow stars. "Children are children," Hinda whispered and hugged her grandchildren as their mothers watched with sorrowful eyes, reprimanding them for making too much noise with their shoeless feet.

They worked out systems to cope with their place of straw without sanitation, water, heat or means of cooking. The men were in charge of dragging cans of waste to dump into the woods, carrying up several buckets of water a day, keeping sentry and the ever more pressing task of finding food. Aron was most adept at keeping watch, his heightened senses and soldier training serving as danger detectors. The women were keepers of the food and its distribution. They were soothers for the children who suffered the elimination of what it was to be a child. The illusions this was just temporary, that their spirits would carry them through with the help of the One, had to be believed.

In the middle of December at dusk, after a month of hiding, just as they began to ease from the numbing silence of the day there was rustling from the hay right below them. Aron thrust his fist into the air, the agreed upon danger signal. Now everyone knew someone was in the barn. They froze. Parents gripped their children. Gitel frantic to control the youngest clamped a firm hand over Devoire Ita's mouth. Each exhaled trembling breaths and waited, sure they had been found. There was silence and then quiet footsteps. Whoever it was, had left the barn. Their thumping hearts began to slow.

Hours later after intense whispering and bickering over what to do, Yankel climbed down, shoved his arms deep into the hay and felt around. He found a package and ran up the ladder with it.

The family groups shuffled to get close. They watched Yankel unwrap the package, the size of a large brick, and as if from a single mouth, there was a gasp. It was money. Lots of money. "Take it back down," they mouthed almost in unison. "We would be crazy not to," Balcha whispered hoarse with belligerence. They all agreed, their eyes wide with panic, the sun beginning to rise, thankful the children were asleep. Yankel climbed down and shoved the package deep into the hay where he had found it.

What to do was argued for days. If they took the money whoever hid it would search and find them. If they did not take the money it was only a matter of time before they would have no way to buy food and sweeten their chances. Life was chance and this was luck. Luck? Bad luck was what it was, a chance to be discovered Hinda advised. Was it worth being killed?

In the end they agreed. There was no choice. Late at night Yankel shimmied down and retrieved the package. They watched as he held up brown and grey Bank Polski bills, his eyes gleaming so, they almost lit the rafters. Meir grinned and helped Mordche count the fortune. Most were *dwa zloty*, two bill denominations, some ten, and a few were twenty. They laid out the *zlotys* in small stacks. There were five hundred *zlotys*.

Each creak they heard after that was the hider returning to claim the fortune, and they would pay with their lives. Aron suspected it was stolen from the Count. The Koniecny family rented land from the Count. He was sure it was none of them, honorable people. But in the meantime, whoever had hidden it had not come back. So far, they had gained a way to buy food.

The difficulty of having a very young child hidden was apparent from the first day. Yet, the faces she made and the impetuous questions she asked lent a spirit of lightness. The same time she brought them pleasure, the danger of drawing attention when any sound during the day could lead to discovery pressed on each conscience and built tensions. Devoire Ita was with Gitel and Aron most but squeezed in between all of them. She favored her Grandmother Hinda and when the game of being quiet reached its limit she looked from face to face and raised the question, "Where is Zaide Wolf?"

Hinda whispered to the child, "He's coming." Wishing it was so. "The longer we can stay quiet like a little kitten, the faster he will come to us."

"Where is the little kitten?" she squealed and mewed drawing looks of anger, a sharp hush and a push from an aunt. Devoire Ita sobbed. Gitel grabbed her, squashing the child beneath her to muffle the cries. Aron whispered words entreating her to stop and she did. There was quiet in the hayloft. Quiet, until Devoire Ita remembered she was a child.

Aron and Gitel avoided the heated whispers and tried to shield her. Winter brought biting cold and chilled the families' safety, humanity and patience. Keeping a child in the hayloft that could not be stilled might be the end of them all. A decision had to be made.

CHAPTER TWENTY-THREE

1942 Her Friend

Gitel left the hayloft on an early April morning, frosty air breaking into cool spring. She had to find a place for their daughter. With twenty *zlotys* in her pocket she slipped through dew covered woods. A drab scarf hid her face, the brown suit jacket hung loose about her body. She reached the edge of town and peeked from behind trees at the dark streets, deserted and devoid of life. Gitel ran behind the house where her Polish friend Chaszka lived. She crouched unsure of how she would say the words she had gone over and over in her head. Gitel heard stirring and hoped it would not be long before Chaszka's husband left to fetch water. As sparrows began to chatter, the door opened and heavy footsteps made their way toward the wellhead. Gitel dashed to the front of the house and knocked.

"We have nothing here," Chaszka said from behind the door. "Go away."

"Chaszka, it's Guccia. Please, please let me in."

Chaszka cracked the door open. A young boy hugged her neck. "What are you doing here?" She looked at Gitel, an apparition. Her eyes disbelieving she said, "I thought you were …gone. All your people have been taken away."

Gitel looked from side to side searching the street, her eyes imploring. Chaszka opened the door a bit wider and pulled her friend inside. "Where were you?"

"I can't tell you, Chaszka." She pushed the scarf back freeing auburn braids and smiled at the child lifting his head. "He looks like you, the same sweet face."

"Guccia, my husband will be back soon. Maybe he speaks with someone, but soon. What if anyone saw you?" She let the boy down and gave him a nudge. "Go to your big brother."

"I'm going to speak plain. You know I have a girl. You've seen the child. She's just twenty months. Chaszka, people say she's very smart. My husband, Adam, sees the world in her. Where we are is impossible to keep her. I need your help."

Chaszka shook her head and backed away. "What can I do? Guccia, you know the troubles we have here every day. Somehow my husband has been able to keep a little food on the table but for how long? The Nazis stomp around. They do whatever they want."

"There is nothing in the world more precious to me. I would give my life for her. But who we are, that wouldn't even save her. With you, she'll have a chance. Chaszka, remember how you always told me you want a girl? If you take her in and I don't live, you'll have a girl. A beautiful girl." Gitel reached out her hand to the Polish woman she had known her entire life.

"What if I have trouble from him? Sometimes he's not so easy, my husband. And what if someone notices and tells?"

Gitel took the zlotys from her pocket and squeezed them into her friend's hand. "It's all I have. You'll say with the war you were afraid to show you had another one. She's fair with eyes like your boy."

"Both have my eyes. What will I tell the boys?"

"Tell them the stork brought her. Remember how we believed? And when we'd see storks on a roof it was proof?" The two women laughed. Chazska's boys came running, the older chasing the younger.

"Stop," Chaszka said. "Say good morning to your, *ciotka*. Your auntie used to run around crazy like you." She grabbed the older child and hugged him as if she might never see the boy again.

162

"Yes," Gitel said, a grateful smile beaming from her eyes. "I'm your auntie from far away." The boys satisfied with this, ran back to chasing. "I'll bring food for Devoire Ita. In Polish we call her Lotti, little gold one, for her hair." Gitel's voice stayed strong for the most important sale of her life. "I'll bring you whatever I can. You are the only one I trust. I saw your mother not so long ago."

"She told me, Guccia. I don't know. You are asking me to take such a risk."

"Yes. I am. I'm a mother like you." Gitel stopped, fighting to keep composure, her voice quavering. "Chaszka, she is a small wonder. My heart aches from thinking I won't be able to hold her and feed her. Please. Give my Lotti a chance."

"He's coming, Guccia, I hear him. Go now." Chaszka opened the door and as Gitel slipped behind the house her friend whispered, "Bring her."

The following night, Gitel made the same trip this time carrying the child wrapped in the coat and a tiny bundle under the other arm. Again she crouched behind the house and woke Devoire Ita, the sun glowing behind the child. Gitel told her how lucky she was because she was going to meet new brothers and her other mommy. The child's eyes widened, trying to comprehend her mother, whose smiles and hugs and soft warnings to be quiet were quickly followed by the slice of bread and butter put into her waiting hands. Gitel watched her chew, combed her hair, feeling each ringlet slip through her fingers.

"I want you to be a very good girl," she murmured. Listen to what your new mommy says. And your new brothers will be happy to have someone else to play with. You'll be able to talk loud and sing." The child made a loud squeak and Gitel nodded but put her fingers over her daughter's lips sticky with butter and brown crumbs.

When will I see her again never left Gitel. What she spared from her own meager portions and from Aron's occupied the part of her left empty. Gitel helped the women dole out food and she looked covetously at the shrunken portion allotted, her child no longer in her lap. There were no arguments over the food, but Gitel sensed as the found money ran out desperate fights would flare. She and Aron worried if the child was getting her equal share of food, if she was treated like family or shunned, an unwelcome guest who had overstayed. The couple had no place to go, no privacy, endless days of shifting from one leg to the other, whispering or gesturing with hands, and the awareness their senses were heightening into those of wary prey animals. The only relief Aron and Gitel had was when they lay down in their straw corner everything shrunken from the absence of the child, only the heat of their bodies and sweet stirrings for each other pulsing with life.

Aron longed to touch his child, hear the voice that had sung with him but Gitel counseled against it. The possibility of an encounter with Chaszka's husband was dangerous and men were easier targets. She promised she would remind Devoire Ita of the songs they sang, remembering how Aron accompanied the child with his deep tones as the girl repeated the words, so proud to please her father.

The last Thursday of June, Gitel climbed down the ladder, each rung freeing her, each rung placing her in jeopardy. A slinking shadow, she passed the large dairy barn on the road as she had done each time before but noticed the storeroom door ajar. She crept closer and listened. When it was apparent the room was empty she slipped inside adjusting her eyes to familiar sights.

Though it was huge in comparison to the operation her family had, a block of ice in a corner caught her attention. There was a good size slab of butter sitting on top and her mouth watered, the pale yellow color and sweet scent pulling her. She kept her eyes on the door as her mind flooded with how much butter she could shave without it being noticed. What if she was caught? Her father's face came before her with an admonition and then, with a knowing nod, disappeared. She was doing this for her child and realized she was capable of anything. Her temples beat with excitement and peril. She removed one of the round-bladed knives at a wood table, sliced pieces from either side of the butter, ran her fingers along the blade licking off the remains from her finger and replaced the knife. Once outside the door her heart was at her throat and she ran to the woods. *I don't feel sorry.* She ripped several large leaves from a skunk cabbage and wrapped them around the butter. She laughed to herself *I'm a good thief now* and darted among the trees.

Each time Gitel appeared it unnerved Chaszka. There was always the moment of tension. Gitel was afraid someone would spot her at the door. She feared her friend would be found a Jew sympathizer. She knew the Polish woman was terrified a neighbor would find out about the child and report her. Gitel no longer had to wait until Chaszka's husband left, but she preferred he was not there. The time before he had asked if she knew there were signs tacked to doors and trees warning Poles they and their families would be shot for harboring Jews.

Gitel knocked, her face concealed by the scarf. "It's me."

Chaszka opened the door and Gitel sidestepped in, chest heaving.

"Wait, I'll wake her." Chaszka disappeared into the back where they slept.

Gitel put the leaf package on the table. She took the child from Chaszka, the tangled hair resting on her breast. "Wake up my sleepy girl," she whispered, "Devoire Ita, I mean Lotti, I have something for you." Gitel's voice roused the child and she clutched at her mother's jacket shaking her head awake. She carried her daughter to the table, removed from her pocket pieces of bread she had saved from the food allotments and placed them next to the leaf-covered package. "Chaszka, look what I brought for you." Gitel peeled back the leaves to reveal thin pale yellow slices. Chaszka saw what Gitel was doing, brought over a knife and stepped to the back where her boys slept.

This time when Gitel spoke, Devoire Ita sat up and stared at her mother. Gitel pressed her lips to her child's forehead. "Mm, I have nice butter for your bread this morning. Tell me, are you eating like a good girl?" She began spreading the butter, the broad leaf beneath a green wilted plate.

Gitel spoke in Polish. The child poked at the leaf but answered in Yiddish. "The other mommy doesn't put butter so thick on my bread like you." She picked up the bread and licked at the butter, a kitten's pink tongue tunneling through delicious rich cream. "It's from the Zaide Wolf?"

"Show me how nicely you speak Polish now, Lotti. Yes, a present from your Zaide." Maybe it was Gitel thought as she made the lie, maybe a present from someone watching over us.

Chaszka came back, this time holding the hand of each boy. They sat at the table and Chaszka did the same for her boys, using Gitel's present on good-sized pieces of bread for their morning meal. The children ate and Gitel's friend signaled that her husband was away and she could stay a little longer this time. "Yes, Father will be back tomorrow, isn't that so children?"

But it was clear to Gitel from Devoire's pale face that the father who would be back tomorrow brought no smiles like those on the boys' faces while they scooped the butter onto their fingers, relishing its richness. Gitel took her daughter to the bucket after they ate and stood, her heart aching as the child washed her hands the way she had been taught, the boys running over to splash. It was getting late but she lingered, dressing her daughter in stained clothes she wanted to scrub, noticing how Devoire Ita pulled up her own stockings. Gitel detangled curls, thicker and longer, each pull bringing an objection from the child more interested in being petted on her mother's lap.

"Where is my *tatteh*?" Devoire Ita asked mixing Polish and Yiddish. She put her small hand on her mother's cheek.

"Your *tatteh* asked we should sing your best song," Gitel said without answering the question. She had promised Aron they would sing but she made a game of just humming the melody and avoided the words. The nearness of the child brought feelings of fragility. An intense longing washed over Gitel. She told her daughter goodbye in Polish, as she dared not use Yiddish but in her mind were the words *mah lachtyk kind*, my child of light.

CHAPTER TWENTY-FOUR

A Calf

That night as the group huddled under the rafters Mordche, Aron and Yankel whispered with such heat their voices spiked into audible fury. "Over the prospect of slaughtering a calf," Hinda warned, "you'll bring an enemy to us. Stop now. Quiet down." But Yankel argued they needed the meat. The sardine tins were long gone. Scarcity and competition with Poles for food depleted the found money faster than was sustainable. There was barely enough bread to keep them from starving, the children always hungry, the adults worse off. "While we have any money left," Yankel wheedled, "we buy a calf."

Aron scowled at his impetuous brother. How on earth would they butcher and cook the meat? What of the smells that might alert enemies? Yankel had ready answers. "And what of the Koniecny family harboring us?" Aron, red in the face, threw at Yankel. "Do you have one thought about putting them in jeopardy? You are a lunatic," Aron mouthed shaking his head.

"If I am, it's because lice eat me and hunger kills me. Look at us," Yankel hissed. "We are becoming a pack of hunted skeletons." Hands on his matted shock of hair, he slid back to his wife and took the bread portion she placed in his hand. Yankel swallowed his hunger and slipped the crusts into the hands of his children. The following night, to no one's surprise he brought a calf onto the property.

Aron guided the logistics of when would be safest to make a fire, warning day or night presented danger. He would help but never be part of such an enterprise again. They could be tracked and caught by the smells of cooking because it was common knowledge there were partisans living in the vast forests. Both Polish partisans and Jews hid so from the Nazis. They all worried the Polish Underground Resistance, at times known to be hostile could find and kill them. Aron reminded them the hatreds Poles had against the Jews could not be underestimated even if the AK, Armia Krajowa were brave fighters and was striking back hard against the German enemy. And back and forth it went with prayers from Hinda. "May God shield you from all our enemies," she pled softly, the *siddur's* worn leather cover held to her heart.

When the reds and pinks of sunset became purple of night, Aron, Yankel and Mordche sneaked off to the woods, a kilometer from the hiding place, the calf not so happy to be prodded and pulled by a rope around her neck. Yankel teased his brother over the treatment of the animal, whose frightened brown eyes and shudders made Aron pat her haunches, the calf's smooth tan hide like silk under his palm. "And besides," Yankel accused, "you want a piece of her cooked flesh as much as any of us."

"It's what our father had to do most of his life," Aron told his brother. "Part of a cow, or a butchered calf he sold in order to make a living. That was our life." Aron felt the calf calming but he knew she had been taken from her mother and that somewhere in the countryside a distressed cow lowed. "If you can still remember how many times we were witness to a good *shochet*, a decent Jew would never use his sharp blade in the act of slaughter unless the animal was calm." The vision of his gentle father Mendel pricked Aron's conscience.

Mordche returned from digging a pit for the hooves or anything unusable. He heard the grating of the knife against a rock and signaled if he could hear that, who else might? Aron stopped sharpening, showed Mordche the blade gleaming in the light of the fire they had readied. His brother-in-law nodded with understanding. The blade had to be without

168

nicks, razor sharp, to make a one-time pass on the animal's neck and through the jugular for a swift kill. "So now Yankel is going to be a *shochet* too, what a man we have here," Mordche said, a hooting owl in its dark forest home breaking tensions between the three men. The beast stood quiet, unaware of what would befall her the next moment.

Yankel drew the knife gripping the calf's upheld head and with a steady strong motion, sliced through its neck. She fell to her knees almost immediately. They waited to be sure the calf was dead before Aron made the first long cut to remove the entrails and skin the calf as best he knew, guided by the times he had accompanied his father. What fine leather it could become in the right hands he thought. Mordche dragged away what could not be used to the pit, covered it with twigs and dirt, traced over the steps he had taken with a branch and raced back to help.

Their hands and clothes covered with blood, the three looked as if they were killing one another not just with arguments but this time in earnest. They did their best to clean their hands and clothing with what the forest floor provided, ground leaves, pine needles and moss while the fresh butchered meat and entrails lay upon elevated branches to drain away the blood. They fed huge chunks of meat to the fire, turning it over and over with the shovel they had brought. The pieces sizzled and blackened over the makeshift spit. The three savored morsels of hot fat ripped from the cooling parts spread on branches later to be transferred to a blanket for hauling. Yankel reserved the hide for *Pan* Koniecny, a way to lessen possible objection to his scheme.

The sky was brightening when they made their way back. They returned the shovel and the part reserved to the Koniecny's shed. The ladder was lowered by an anxious waiting Meir, the entire group struck by the overpowering smell of meat hoisted up in the blanket. The odors of beef and smoke permeated the men's bodies and their clothing was stiff from the drying blood. The exhausted three fell onto the straw.

CHAPTER TWENTY-FIVE

Disaster

L ice sucked their flesh in the stifling heat of summer. That was supplanted by winter hunger gnawing at their bones. December came and they remembered another Chanukah. There were no candles, no sizzling *latkes* of the past, but they spun a *dreidel* carved from wood scraps and prayed for the miracle that had burned bright for the Maccabees, a hope that a miracle would find them and deliver them from Hitler.

The slaughter of the calf and its succulent meat were a distant memory, the found money cache gone. Meir tried to find favor with a past Polish trading partner. He failed to get much for a gold watch he had hidden from the others but five loaves of bread and a promise that if he were ever seen again he would be shot on the spot. His former power to forge deals was over. He never left the hayloft by his own will after that. The group was at the total mercy of the family that harbored them and the Koniecny family was under duress, their ability to feed themselves ever more a challenge, the worry over Jews hidden on their property a growing menace.

Gitel had not seen the child since the beginning of December. Each day had stretched long before her, yet 1943 was days away and it was only weeks before Devoire Ita's second birthday. Gitel slid down the iced ladder. A fine snow fell like flour she'd dusted over wood kneading boards and she tramped through the woods in the fog of a dream. The night before Aron had shaken her awake to avoid a disturbance, to quell her guttural moans and thrashing. She had whispered to Aron, her voice tremulous, "Devoire Ita came to me, the child's hands covered her eyes."

"Gitel, it's just a dream," Aron said. "You're worried. Try to sleep." He touched his lips to hers. He could not sleep.

She reached Chaszka's house, her body pulsing with anticipation. Gitel knocked. No one came and she knocked again, her knuckles raw from the cold, the image of Devoire Ita's hands covering her eyes refusing to disappear. The door opened and Gitel slipped through.

Chaszka's lips quivered. "She's not here, Guccia." The woman turned away and wrapped her sweater tight to her body. She was thinner, girlish and submissive.

"Where is my child?" Gitel put her hands on Chaszka's shoulders and drew her around. "Tell me." Her hands fell away, shaking uncontrollably.

"I don't know." Chaszka dropped to a chair. Her head fell to her lap. Sorrowful sobs muffled by her thick clothing shook her shoulders. She looked up at Gitel, a beaten look about her mouth.

"Is she alive, oh my God, please God, just let her be alive, if I never see her again, please let her be alive. I'll do anything. Do you hear me? Chaszka, anything, tell me. I'll give my life for hers this moment."

"I don't know if she's alive. My husband took her away. Three days ago he left her with them. We heard shots." She wiped at her cheeks and her eyes fell on the door as if traces of the child lingered, the last place she had seen the little girl.

"Why, why, Chaszka? How could he do this? Who can I go to? Who will tell me? Where is he? Your husband."

"He left already. For months there have been signs nailed, pasted. The Nazis hang them every place. My husband warned me. Again and again. Remember, he told you the signs say if anyone is caught hiding a Jew they'll be killed along with the Jew. He said he had to turn her in. He wasn't going to sacrifice us, for her."

Gitel was mute. Her heart pounded but she did not feel it. Her eyes saw but the images before her were frozen. Cold began to grip her mind, a numbing paralysis washed over her limbs and she stood before her friend, not knowing where she was, fighting to both accept what had been told her and hoping this was a dream. Yes, it was a dream. It would end, and she would open her eyes and it would be morning again. Devoire Ita would be on her lap, the lightness of her child's body melding into her own.

"You have to go, Guccia. And you can't ever come back. Look at me. Did you hear me? I'm a mother. I had to protect my boys. Please go, there's nothing else I can do. What am I to do?" She walked to the cupboard, took out a spoon from the drawer and dropped it on the table. It was tarnished, the little silver rose handle blackened. "I don't want to keep it." Chaszka's eyes went cold, their spark of heat and warmth extinguished, flat and impenetrable.

Gitel turned away from the woman whom she had known as friend. She released the tiny bundle of scraps she had saved for her child to the table, her words wooden. "If you still have a heart, you'll find my child and give this to her. I'm a mother, too."

Chaszka shook her head and pushed the knotted handkerchief away. Gitel grasped the spoon in her shaking fingers. She moved to the door, gave a faint nod at the crumpled handkerchief and left.

She wandered into the woods, her body in charge, an animal without reason, a thing that walked and breathed, unaware and disconnected from its mind. She wanted to cry, to scream. Her insides were lacerated, exposed to pain she had never felt, as if what was alive was gone and what was left was a purposeless, empty carcass. She fell onto her knees and began to rock, carving through the snow into the frozen ground. She could not stop crying out the child's name, begging for Devoire Ita's life until she had no strength left.

Quiet numbness overtook her limbs. A desperate cold presence invaded her soul. She fought with herself over what to do. What kind of mother was she, why did she give up the child, burrowed deep. Should she dare see Hubner? But she knew what the result would be. Aron needed her. Gitel feared for him and she stood up as though the legs that held her were no longer hers and drifted back to the hayloft.

As soon as Aron met her eyes, he knew. He pulled Gitel to their pulverized straw corner and held her. Her lips were blue and he wrapped her in the down cover. She was silent but for shallow breaths she emitted, puffs of life for which she had no desire. Her hand clutched the tiny spoon, a thing her child had held, unaware, the skin of her palm was broken.

Aron stayed next to her this way until he could no longer contain his misery. His anger turned at their families and he screamed. "Why did you make us do it, she could be here with all of us." The men clawed over to quell Aron's wrath and pleaded for him to stop before Koniecny came and threw them all out to the Nazis or Poles or to whomever was willing to slaughter them first. Aron calmed only after Gitel took his face into her hands and stroked his hair.

Family members retreated to their places, another vein of their collective body severed. Hinda slid over to Aron and Gitel. Without words, sorrow etched about her eyes, she put her gaunt hands on her daughter and son-in-law and brought still resignation to what could not be changed.

They spent day and night in whispers. Aron cried for days, crushed. Gitel swallowed her feelings as bitterness dammed her words and made grief inaccessible to her frozen heart. An ugly pall of guilt hung from the ice-crusted rafters where words were forbidden, a comforting look, a smile suppressed and shoulder shrugs of empathy all that could be offered. Aron and Gitel tried to accept sympathy but exuded recrimination. They were as raw and exposed as a limb severed from its body.

The hidden spent a second winter in frozen torpor. Meager rations occupied them and unrelenting hunger grew. Sometimes the Koniecny family's son carried out table scraps. But mostly they subsisted on dried turnips and bread, the only things the men could get when they dared to search and often came back empty-handed. By the end of February Aron and Gitel made a decision to leave when winter broke. Hinda pled with

Gitel not to go. Mordche and Yankel knew they would not change their minds. None would deny that sooner or later they could all starve. Two less, two more, what did it matter?

* * * * *

At the end of March, the promise of an early thaw signaled it was time. The night to say goodbye came. Gitel sat with Deborah and her mother the longest, the three clutching, assuring each other it was not the last time. Aron and Gitel dragged their things to the ladder. The children's faces were streaked with tears for an aunt and uncle whose forced smiles did little to veil loss. They hugged the children ensnared in a world they could not understand, imprisoned for being born. "Fools," Meir shook his head at the couple. "Fools," he hissed, "where are you going?" Aron and Gitel climbed down the ladder and left the hell of the hayloft for a dark unknown.

CHAPTER TWENTY-SIX

A Failed Sale

Wrapped in the cloak of success, bread beneath his jacket, Yankel whistled a breathless tune. He ran through the Count's sleeping orchards midst gnarled plum trees not yet adorned for spring his feet led as if he was a pigeon beating its wings back to a lost home, a rooftop coop.

"Yankel," Aron called out, trying not to startle the whistler. Dry leaves rustling, he emerged from the woven lean-to, remains of what the Matuszyński family had made long ago.

"Look what I found!" Yankel said, whirling around, his eyes wide with good fortune, his body pulsating between flight and relief.

Aron gripped his brother's shoulders. "In the light of day? You take too many chances, brother. You think you are free like a bird?"

"You found food." Gitel peeked from layers of dried boughs and took an admiring look at her brother-in-law, a man with unbridled *chutzpah*.

Yankel nodded and searched Gitel's face. She lifted herself out, an agile doe without its fawn and swallowed hard the lump from choking back the tears she was unable to shed. "We haven't found a place." She looked toward Aron and shook her head.

"I understand," Yankel said his eyes fixed on Aron. His brother's mouth hung like a fresh wound and it jerked Yankel's conscience. His face revealed remorse for the little niece full of questions, no longer among them.

"It is not your doing," Aron said reading his brother. "Are you all still with the Koniecny? Decent people."

"Where else," Yankel said. "It's worse every day. Hunger and fear change us from family into biting animals. I don't know how long I'll stand it myself. The Koniecnys have their own troubles."

Aron's head turned from side to side, a feral dog alert for danger. He pulled them under the web of boughs a sudden rush of wind warning him conversation could be carried to an enemy. The chill stirred a cache of plums, wrinkled and black, something nature had preserved and Aron had scrounged from the forest floor. They shared the shriveled banquet with childish glee, fermented fruit and bites of bread Yankel shared from what he would be taking back to the hayloft.

"Imagine, we are still under these conditions, almost two years. How much longer any of us will be able to take, only heaven knows. Not that I believe in much if this could happen to such a child."

"Aron," Gitel said, "we have to hope. This talk hurts you."

"Hurts me? Hope? Hate is what makes me live now."

"You don't know what you're saying." Gitel glanced at Yankel.

"I know what I'm saying."

A gust shook the dry tendrils above and Aron put his arm around Gitel.

"Remember, Aron?" Yankel said, "*Yidl mitn fidl Arie mitn bass?* I was humming that tune from the kino when you heard me."

Images of the fiddler and the bass player from that movie of long ago closed his eyes. "I can almost smell mother's cooking." Aron's voice trailed off in longing for a time when they were together and hardship squeezed them, yet kinship fed their souls. The blackened fruits had jarred Aron's memory as if the aroma of plum compote spit from the cooking pot and his raven- haired mother was perched prim on the chair carried from home. What today had brought them to, scattered, hiding, marked for death, every path barred, made the past poignant, and overshadowed the poverty of comforts. He shifted his eyes from his brother to his wife, barely visible. "Yankel, tell her."

"Gitel, Aron played *Arie* with the bass and pretended to bow like a maestro. Who do you think played the *fidl*? Me. Yankel. When I danced my legs kicked like a young Cossack."

Aron pursed his lips and whistled the melodic tune of their youth. He held onto his wife and his body was enlivened by what transcended hunger and fear and bitter loss. Three years ago in March they had married, the gift of fate to which they clung, their passionate threads of life entwined.

Yankel left them as stars faded into morning and dashed through the forest. He was known in the surrounding towns as a dealmaker. He had conducted business with the Poles, was respected and knew how to barter to his advantage. Yankel could embellish a story with juicy details and smooth the ruffled feathers of an adversary to make a sale. But he knew when to step away from an unprofitable scheme. He mused about the many trades he had made with the Poles, owners of the farms he passed. A rare person not steeped in judgment, decent, what his father called a *mensch* was the type of man he needed now.

The Polish farmer Vladyk Kukuryk lived in the village Swiecice. Before the war Vladyk had an active farm where he seeded barley and wheat, grew corn for the livestock and traded with other farmers for what he lacked. His village environs, with its flat plain and coniferous forests, had remained unscarred by the meanness of war ravaging the people in less remote regions. But the Nazis arrived. They plundered food supplies for themselves, leaving little for the Poles. Vladyk had bought cattle and implements from Yankel and had bartered for bushels of plums and winter apples. With Vladyk, Yankel calculated he might have a chance. His brimmed cap pulled down, he walked the ten kilometers and arrived as the sun cast an orange glow on the farmer's fallow fields.

Vladyk was by the barn having just shoveled manure from the stall of a cow whose fate became clear as each rib poked from her dull hide. The horses that had stood next to her were gone, the harnesses hung over the clean open stall doors. Vladyk shook Yankel's outstretched hand without his usual enthusiastic grip. The easy banter of the past did not flow and his eyes searched the nearby road.

Vladyk's wife Maricia stared through the window of the farmhouse. Her jaw clenched, her braids not yet tidy, she was in no mood for visitors, especially not one of Yankel's ilk. Vladyk kept an eye on her as he listened to the man whose too-cheerful tone belied the urgency of his mission. After having the baby, Maricia reminded Vladyk of her mother. His wife was becoming a truculent mean-spirited woman, her housekeeping slackened, her receptivity to his touch declining.

Vladyk listened to Yankel tell how his brother Adam was an uncommon shoemaker so skilled he employed three men in Sosnowiec. "I promise," Yankel said, "if you take them in, you won't be sorry."

"I know Adam, he's very good. What will I do with a shoemaker?" Vladyk rested a moment on his shovel. He adjusted his cap.

"What will you do with a shoemaker?" Yankel said. "Do you know the value he will bring to you and Maricia? My brother will do whatever you want, repair your neighbor's shoes and you'll have something to barter with. He will remake every pair of shoes you own, like new. I will bring you leather. Someone owes me. Instead of empty pockets, yours will be full of *zlotys*.

"Maricia will have no part of this," Vladyk said, shaking his head as if to assure the woman glowering from the window. She held their younger daughter, the child's blonde hair shimmering in the morning light. The older girl, almost four, sucked a thumb and tugged her apron.

"I own one pair of boots," Vladyk said. "Maricia has boots and church shoes. My girls, how many shoes will they need? Do you think having better shoes is worth their lives?"

"A child grows fast." Yankel ignored the reference and kept his eyes on Vladyk's, their brown warmth spurring him on. "You know my brother Adam. He will make them shoes fit for the Prince's daughters."

Vladyk smiled but his eyes spoke no. He drew his brows together in furrows of worry. He folded his hands around the shovel and inhaled the fresh clean morning air, laced with manure, a pleasant reminder that he still had an animal to tend. "Where would I put them?' Vladyk said watching his wife chew a chunk of bread with satisfaction while he had to argue with a man he knew was not one to back down. The man's eyes shifted to the potato cellar by the barn and he said, "If someone sniffs a Jew is here, we are done." He looked at his field and over to the road. This was taking too long.

"Let me put it another way, Vladyk," Yankel began.

"There is no other way, Jankiel," Vladyk said. "I am a Pole. If in the past we have been friends, if our families have traded, it is true. But now there are new rules for my life. Jews are hated everywhere. Not by me. But what does it matter? My own wife spits on the ground at the mention of one."

"Adam was captured by the German at Nowy Targ. Shoemaking saved him until he escaped," Yankel embellished. He knew well his brother had been released on a one-way transport to fulfill the plans for him, labor and death. "Vladyk, you are a fair man, a brave man too."

"I know one thing," Vladyk said lowering his voice. "Even if, and I say if, I agreed to do such a thing, Maricia would be against it. The Nazis would shoot us, sure as I stand. How can I take such a chance?"

Yankel caught Maricia, staring. Her cold eyes darted away as if honoring him with her gaze was beneath her contempt. "A nice woman like yours deserves some help, don't you think? Adam's wife is strong and works as hard as a mule, forgive such a comparison. She will treat your Maricia like a queen."

"Wait in the barn, Jankiel. Let me go to my wife." Vladyk headed to the farmhouse. "But don't think I will convince her of anything."

"I'll bring you a good cow if you agree, don't think I won't, Vladyk, I've done it." Yankel made this last ditch appeal as if to himself.

Moments later Vladyk emerged shaking his head. They stood in silence but for the courting melody of birds unaware that a life or death decision had to be made by humans.

Yankel put his hand in his jacket pocket alluding to something more. "Who would suspect you, a man so respected?"

Vladyk avoided Yankel's eyes. "I won't be able to help Adam."

Yankel bit his lips and watched Maricia leave the window. "Vladyk, you have a heart."

"Always the salesman." He shook his head. "I can't take the risk." Vladyk walked away.

CHAPTER TWENTY-SEVEN

The Bunker

Yankel raced through the woods, the sun high in the sky. He whistled the signal and crawled inside the lean-too. Defeated and spent his hands grabbed at his hair. "I failed with Vladyk Kukuryk."

"You could have waited with this news till night. I figured you'd try something. Your luck will run out, Yankel. Do we need another stone on our hearts?"

Yankel took out five folded zlotys and pushed them into Aron's hand. "It's all I have left. I was going to offer it to Vladyk even said I'd bring leather. He would have taken you in. His wife is the trouble."

"Yankel, go back to the hayloft. You did what you could. Gitel and me, we have to manage. What of your wife, your two fine boys?" Aron pushed the bills to his brother.

"You have too much pride, Aron. Learn or it will be your ruin."

"I'll take it," Gitel said, "I could use a nice pair of stockings." They burst into laughter, each clapping a hand to mouth.

"She jokes, my wife. Look at her, not just a beauty, a comedian."

Gitel scooped up the bills, folded two and handed the rest to her brother-in-law. "There are fifteen of you. Two of us," she said. "You've done plenty. Remember us to our families." They parted, the wind pinking their cheeks. Aron and Gitel had no choice but to try and sell themselves.

The next morning Vladyk spotted Aron by the side of the barn and motioned him inside. "What, all the Matuszyńskis are going to come?"

"Vladyk. You know our situation." He leaned over the empty stall and fingered the leather halter. "I could make something good for you to trade."

"Adam, your brother is a fine salesman. I can't afford a shoemaker like you."

"You buy my wife, too. You are a bit of a shoemaker yourself, who would suspect someone else does the work? I'll empty the outhouse. Whatever you ask. You are alone here. My wife, there's nothing this woman can't do. Her cooking and cheese making helped save us for a year. Guccia will scrub your house. A woman with young children has less time for her man. Believe me, I know how we men folk are."

"I can't do it."

Aron covered his face. He swallowed hard. "The Nazis shot my daughter a month ago." He dropped his hands. The moment had come to use even this. Dire need overrode dignity and pride. He was trading on his daughter's death.

Vladyk groaned, his thin face longer. "How old was this child?"

Aron faced him, shame answered. "Two years."

"Like my little one," Vladyk said. "What could a baby have done? Our priest was taken to Plazow camp. They murder us. Take our land. I hate every step the Nazis make."

"Yes, every step." Aron's head turned toward the cow's stall. He stared a moment too long.

Vladyk removed his cap, annoyed and curious. He shook his head. "Tell her if she's back there to come out."

"Guccia, you heard."

Gitel stood up by the cow's stall. Her hair was rebraided, her clothes brushed off best she could. "She's skinny, but strong. She needs to be milked, *Pan* Kukuryk." Gitel ran her palm along the cow's bony back and the animal stood calm.

"She doesn't stand so still for Maricia," Vladyk said. He watched Gitel's natural way with the cow and he nodded.

"Her father is a dairyman. Guccia knows what to do. She will work hard at anything you want." Aron stared at the man who was standing in judgment. He realized this Pole knew how desperate they were, fearful and denigrated, at his mercy.

"How many years did our fathers trade?" Vladyk said.

"Forty years the Kukuryks traded with the Matuszyñskis. Never a question of what was fair." Aron pulled the two *zlotys* from his pant pocket and held out the folded bills.

Vladyk grinned. "Adam, would I be taking such a risk for this?" But he stuffed the bills deep into his pant pocket and patted them.

It was a good sign. Aron waited. This man was unlike most and he was no fool. Gitel and he would be grateful servants: slaves. "We have a deal?" Aron said.

Vladyk wet his lips. "If there comes a time I can no longer have you here, the danger too great, you go. You agree?"

"Yes. You have my word," Aron said. His eyes met Gitel's and she answered with a decision.

She drew out the silver spoon from her blouse and held it out to Vladyk. The tarnish was rubbed away from the many times she had stroked it, feeling for Devoire Ita's last touch. "A present for your wife, Maricia." Gitel let go of the little rose handle.

"We have a deal," Vladyk said and stuck out his hand. Aron clasped the man's hand. The farmer tucked the spoon away with a glance at the woman who once again had surprised him. They were good people. Of that, Vladyk Kukuryk, the Polish farmer was pretty sure.

The arrangement cemented, Vladyk pointed to where they would hide, a shallow potato cellar covered with rough-hewn boards near the barn from where Gitel's feet would soon make fifty paces in the dark to his farmhouse and Aron would make one hundred in the opposite direction to the work shed. With Vladyk's shovel Aron began to dig. He handed Gitel the tools he had held back from those he had entrusted to the Pole in Sosnowiec; his auel and chisel to stab loose the hardened dirt walls. All night they enlarged the potato cellar. They dug what looked like a longer, deep grave and piled the potatoes to the side. Aron squared the sides with his usual perfection and Gitel argued with him to hurry until he took her into his arms and told her if they were going to be buried together, it had to be in a perfect grave. Dawn was coming and warned them the relative safety of darkness was over. They carried away the piles of dirt to the field and spread it between channels sprouting wild grasses where the crops used to flourish.

Vladyk came out of the farmhouse and stood guard by the barn, nervous there could be a visit from a neighbor. He avoided looking at Maricia. Her arms folded, she seethed from the window. "You slide away these loose boards to climb out," Vladyk instructed. Aron lowered between the boards after Gitel. He held a can to relieve themselves and a wooden crate to step on to climb out. Vladyk helped them set the old boards on top. Then he scattered dirt about as camouflage. "My signal will be three stomps on the boards. If you hear anything else, stay under." He stomped and his eyes scanned his now less tranquil homestead. Aron and Gitel understood more than he could have imagined. They had spent over a year in fear of a rustling leaf, a footstep, a distant voice, the howl of a dog and their own breathes.

"Our bunker," Aron said. It was a meter and a half deep, two meters wide and two and a half meters long. Potatoes hadn't needed floorboards and they were surrounded by dirt and sat on dirt. "Look at us, big filthy rats in a hole."

"Yes, but these rats are still alive." Her voice deadened by the airless dirt walls, Gitel held her husband's hand, raw from digging. He kissed her fingertips, felt the cracked nails with his lips and brushed back the sweat-soaked hair loosened from her braids. Gitel set about unpacking their treasures, the down quilt, the salvaged tools from Aron's workshop, two pans and spoons, a few pieces of clothing and tinted photographs, one of Gitel's uncle that looked strikingly like her bearded father and three of Aron's brothers. There had never been a picture of their child. They were down in the hole, the bunker, hidden for what they hoped would not be for so very long.

In the morning slivers of light filtered through the boards, like shadowy prison bars projected on grave-like walls that had shifted and disappeared into first night. They tensed when they heard footsteps. Vladyk tapped his foot on the loose board. "Three stomps like I'm cleaning my boots off, and you know it's me, remember," he said, his voice terse. He slid away the board, tossed down a small sack into the dark bunker and walked away. Gitel crawled over to the sack. They hadn't eaten in days and the scent of food silenced whispers and thought. She pulled open the sack. There were two cold potatoes in their skins, slices of bread and a thin piece of meat. She handed the meat to her husband.

"I can't eat it" Gitel said. "It makes me nauseous."

"I don't care if it's horse, cow or pig. When it comes to saving your life, it says we must. You have to, Gitel."

"I can't. You eat, Aron, you need it more." She had felt the same queasiness the days before and the thought added to other worries. No, it could not be. But she and Aron had been together under the boughs of the lean-to. They had forgotten time or where they were, the warmth of their bodies wrapped together in furtive bliss.

Vladyk came to fetch Gitel to work for Maricia the second night. Like a horse hitched for labor she followed behind to the dimly lit house. The woman who would be her master, Maricia, sat at the table and Vladyk excused himself with a slight, polite bow. Gitel felt the woman's eyes smoldering with anger. The bow was not deference toward a Jewess, but manners embraced by Vladyk, gleaned from custom, centuries of symbiosis with the *schlachta* classes. Maricia waved her to the table. Gitel waited to be used, nothing more. She felt the woman's eyes assessing her, staring at her girlish bosom and slim hips in contrast to her own squat body. *As long as it means Aron and I have a chance to live I'll do what I must. If she likes me or not, I don't give a hell. I'll work so she needs me.*

Gitel waited at the end of the table while Marcia pointed a finger around the room. "See what you can do. I'll be watching every move you make and don't think I won't notice. One thing, one crumb is missing from my house and I throw you and the Jew shoemaker out."

There were three rooms in disarray. The room with the oven and cupboards was the worst. Gitel scrubbed the charred food from the oven and the bricks on which it sat. Maricia watched without a word, from time to time tapping her foot. She dismissed her with one word. Go. Whatever order Gitel had restored almost disappeared by the next night. The first week Maricia's daughters slept when Gitel came to work. But as the days grew longer there had to be an explanation. "This is Guccia, your *ciotka*." And so it was. She was an aunt again.

Sabrina, the younger girl clung to *Ciotka* Guccia. Gitel bathed her once a week, fed her and combed the child's fine blonde hair between her rough fingers. She tried not to grow attached to the little one. It made her long for Devoire Ita who at the same age had spoken well, sung with Aron, fed herself and had begun to pose questions.

Four-year-old Zofia was withdrawn. Her mother gave her plenty reprimands and Gitel felt sorry for the girl with the pained eyes. Gitel found she liked stories. She told and retold Hansel and Gretel, each time Zofia taking on the part of Hansel, pretending to substitute her own finger for the chicken bone finger *Ciotka* Guccia described Hansel used to fool the wicked witch. Zofia exuded joy retelling her younger sister the story but Sabrina stayed because she wanted to sit on *Ciotka* Guccia's lap. It was not lost on Maricia that Gitel was kind to her girls. She was glad to be free from washing, hanging the frayed laundry on the rope to dry and fetching the water to boil for bathing once a week. Maricia was having less discontent over the disordered home from her husband. The windows shone, the dirt floors were scrapped tidy from spring mud, clean bowls and plates were arranged on the cupboard shelf and the permanent layers of grime on the table were gone.

"Peel the potatoes," Maricia ordered and counted them. "I'll cook them myself." Yet the woman did look tidier. It was clear no matter how she hated the *parshwha Żyd;* these dirty Jews in her midst were excellent servants. She trusted Gitel with the children, who wanted nothing better

186

than to play with *Ciotka* Guccia. She did not trust her with the food. Gitel threw most of the peels mixed with straw to thicken up the slop to the pig. But she found ways to stuff the rotting remains with their white eyes into her jacket hem. *You poor pig, not even enough time to make you fat and in my jacket I save some of your peels. I'm in competition with the pig.*

They had sat quiet in the hayloft for endless stretches of time, yet the bunker was worse. Here they were hunched and breathed the dank air. On mornings Vladyk did not sneak him out to repair shoes or do a task, Aron's mind flew to remembrance. This April day, hard rain dripping through the boards, he slid closer to Gitel. He put his arm about her. Gitel took his hand, her eyes shining in the dim light.

"When you gave away the spoon you surprised me."

"I did what had to."

"Poor Hanek. Without him maybe we wouldn't be sitting in such luxury," Aron winked. "You saw him in our doorway, chased from house to house, miserable, on a day like today."

"Three years ago, wasn't it?" Her husband needed to recant another story. The rain chilled the bunker as spring, her favorite time of the year, renewed above.

"Hanek the Hunchback pled, help me, shoemaker," Aron began. "I looked at the crooked creature that God had created and he pointed to his feet. What he wore barely resembled boots. I took the misshapen things he wore upstairs and left him barefoot in the mud. Remember? You brought him soup and then went to find leather that morning."

Aron had heard footsteps and knew it was the peddler coming for his boots. His naked feet landed on each step, a muffled, clapping sound that grew louder, the rattle of items from the pack flung over his back. Hanek knocked with bony fingers. Aron opened the door and smiled back at the peddler who showed more gum than teeth. The man's creased grimy face, crippled posture and strong odor were repulsive. Still it touched Aron, as if it was a wounded bird struggling to fly, doomed by a broken wing.

"Yes, Hanek, I have your boots ready," Aron said. He led the man to the chair last sat upon by a customer, a woman married to a member of the Judenrat, one he had been glad to be rid of.

Hanek's eyes betrayed admiration for what he saw. "They look better," he said. His pack hit the floor with a clang and he slid off a cap so stiff from the weight of accumulated years of use, it sat upright on the floor.

"They are fit for a gentleman." Aron smiled at the peddler. "Now you can sell your things to our nobles. All I ask is one *zloty*. I worked a long time."

"Matuszyński, this is not possible. A poor old man like me has a *zloty* to give for just a cobbler's job?" he wheedled.

"You insult my profession, Hanek, you know I am not just a cobbler. But I understand among my people, a shoemaker has little status." Aron's voice rose chiding but beneath it was his painful truth. He also knew it would come down to *hondling*, so he had to take the upper hand now. "How do you intend to pay for the boots? Or should I sell them to someone who will appreciate my work?"

"I am ready to offer something of the fine things I have in my pack." Hanek the Hunchback said making no move to open his wares for full view lest he expose the treasures too soon.

Aron smiled at the peddler. He sensed it was the last time those boots would be repaired, that they were a lifeline for an old man whose time on the earth was filled with sorrow, taunts, an existence of injustices. "Show me something we can use."

Hanek reached in the pack, identified an item with fingers that could see and extracted a dented pot he placed teetering on the floor. Aron chuckled at the sight of it. With a sly look of indignation the peddler threw the pot back in and this time brought out a queer-looking wood mallet that would have been of interest except the handle had been shortened too much and the head bore deep scars. Aron remained silent, working to control a smile. The next items, a dingy kerchief and a shallow chopping bowl, were of no use to him and when the peddler brought out a knife with a broken blade, Aron crossed his long arms and looked out the window. "Stars will soon twinkle, if you can't find something that is a fair trade, you'll leave the boots."

Hanek reached deep inside the pack this time rattling about until he laid two soiled fingers on something he cupped as he drew out his hand. Aron moved forward on the bench to see what the old man held. Hanek opened each finger, a routine he had used most of his life, revealing a tiny spoon, its handle detailed with an intricate rose. "Real silver this is," he said lowering his voice as if surrounded by thieves who would snatch this fortune from his palm.

"Let me take a closer look," Aron said. He felt the weight of the little silver spoon. It had substance and beauty and though it was tarnished, Aron thought Gitel would like it. He made the trade, the peddler accusing Aron of stealing his finest object, holding his boots as ransom. Hanek pulled the boots on his naked feet and walked to the door, his pack clanging on his back. "You are a good shoemaker, Matuszyński. These old feet have not felt so good in many years. May the lord bless you and your good wife. The spoon is not just a nothing, it is my last good thing."

Aron ended the story with the peddler's exact words "my last good thing." He watched Gitel's face as he finished. Something eluded him. "No more stories today," she said.

"Aron, I may be pregnant."

CHAPTER TWENTY-EIGHT

1944 More Loss

The first week of May, early in the morning Vladyk stomped on the boards. "Get out. You have to leave now."

They slept. To them it was Sabbath. They had counted the days, the months, and now the year 1944 to give a semblance of order to lives in turmoil. Friday night, Gitel had come back to the bunker. Aron waited to share scraps and be her husband. Their pleasure, his fulfillment of wanting Gitel, hers to know she was a woman and a cherished wife. A reason to be human, and go on.

Vladyk turned in all directions, his head pounded, dizzy with apprehension. The word had spread: two escaped, two missing. They searched for Jews and here he was with two under his feet. He had just had a confrontation with Maricia screaming get rid of them. Do you want us all killed? He kicked the boards again and controlled his voice. "Did you hear me? Crawl out."

Beneath, they were dumb with fear. Gitel rolled the speckled pot in the down blanket. Aron grabbed the awl and trimming knife. He threw on his tattered jacket. They climbed out squinting at unfamiliar morning brightness.

Two wretched people stood before Vladyk. "They're looking for the rest from a whole group that was shot."

"Who?" Aron said.

"Jews. I don't know who and I don't care. If they find you here...."
Vladyk listened for sounds of danger. "Leave and don't come back for two
weeks." He looked toward the house. "I shouldn't let you back."

"Vladyk, you'll be all right." *Before Vladyk changes his mind and throws
us out for good let me try to save what's left of us.* He took Gitel's hand and
they disappeared.

They ran deep into the pine woods, moss cushioning frantic quick
steps. "Where can we go? Who are they searching for?" Aron caught his
breath. "Come we'll try for the lean-to."

"Who could they be hunting? I'm not going to think anything," Gitel
said.

The couple ran steadily and rested among low brush until afternoon
when they reached the lean-to, the orchard's plum and apple trees heavy
with rose hued blossoms. Aron lifted the dry, tangle of branches and Gitel
slid in. They fell asleep after hours of vigilance, the signs of the next day
about to dawn with dense black clouds.

Gitel had foraged in forests and meadows. She had gathered tart
blueberries from fat bushes and plucked raspberries from thorny thin
branches. She knew which mushrooms grew in damp, shaded places. She
had stuffed cakes with berries that oozed purple syrup, eaten them with
fresh cream in her father's dairy, and filled herself with their sweetness.
But it was mid-spring and the earth offered little. Her only choice was to
search among the curled lacy ferns that poked from the ground. Exposed
in the orchard, they crawled to find anything to stay alive. On her hands
and knees Gitel picked as far as she dared, filling the pot with tiny
strawberries and wild parsnips, thin young roots Aron dug from the earth,
each second aware someone might spot them. They ran back to the lean-to
drenched and waited for the speckled pot to catch water.

The brittle boughs above did little to keep them from being soaked
and they hoped the pelting rain would slow down trackers. But wind,
hushing through the trees to dry the saturated forest floor after days of
rain, and returning songbirds were a comfort. At the end of the two weeks,

in the middle of the night, frantic with hunger, Aron and Gitel sneaked back to the Kukuryk farm.

Days later, the last of the light seeping through the boards overhead they heard determined scratching. Vladyk stomped his signals. This could not be him.

"That's it, it's over," Aron mouthed. "We're found." He reached for the awl, the needle-like tool for stabbing stitches and clutched Gitel's tensed arm.

"If we are finished, then I want to at least stick that thing right in their eyes," Gitel mouthed back adrenaline coursing through her.

"Be still." Aron's heart beat out of control, his eyes wild.

The scraping ceased. A hoarse, frenetic voice spoke. "It's me, Gitel. Aron, it's Mordche. Don't be afraid, I'm alone. Are you down there?"

"Mordche!" she gasped.

"Yes, it's me, Gitel."

Aron slid back a board, his hands unsure. But the face he met was his bother-in-law's. "Hurry. The hole's not deep," he whispered.

Mordche gripped the boards with his huge hands and dropped down. His eyes emitted a menacing glow to the thick blackness. His head fell to his bare knees. Aron shoved the boards into place and sank next to him.

"You're safe, Mordche," Gitel whispered. "I didn't know if we'd ever see you again." She crawled toward her brother and touched his bare arms unsure he was real.

"Safe," Aron shook his head, "no one is safe. Mordche, they search."

Mordche stared at the boards above his head. "No one saw me, Aron." There was nothing he could do to spare them the ugly truth. He braced against the dirt wall. Barefoot, his chest heaved in a body covered by shreds. He was prey, hunted, unable to let its guard down lest it pay with its life.

"Keep your voice low," Aron whispered. "Vladyk made us leave this hole two weeks ago. He didn't know who was caught. I found out from him the Armia Krajowa is searching for Jews. Our people, Mordche?"

Footsteps approached. The three froze. "It's Vladyk," Gitel said, motioning to Mordche to stay calm, her brother's fright and self-protecting malice engulfing her. A foot stomped three times on the board. She pushed in front of Mordche. Aron shoved away the board and caught the small sack.

"Thank you, Vladyk," Gitel said, the words sticking in her throat.

"Maricia wants you in the house. Come when you're done. And look out well before you get out. Adam, stay down there."

Aron waited until the footsteps faded. "I don't know what he'll do if he finds you. Yes, you'll see the big meal Maricia sent. What we live on."

"What happened? How did you find us?" Gitel said.

Mordche leaned forward. "How I found you is a miracle. Yankel told me about a potato cellar near the barn when he tried to convince Vladyk to take you in last year. I swear that's all Yankel said. I knew this farm in Swiecie from years ago. I hid in the woods, stealing what food I could. Over two weeks." He stared at Aron. "I think Yankel got away. But I don't know what happened to him."

"You don't know what happened to my brother." Aron's whisper was frosted with accusation.

"Got away, Mordche?" Gitel clasped her hands. "What of the others, my dear brother?"

"Dead." Mordche unable to control a cry, blurted, "only the two of us ran."

"No." Gitel repeated over and over. "How much can we take?" *Let my heart feel nothing.* She inhaled the stagnant air. The image of Devoire Ita covering her eyes swept over her. The omen. The dream she had the night before she learned her child had been given up to the Gestapo.

"Gitel, nothing will be left of us." Aron said.

Numb, eyes grown visible with tears, their dark shadows grabbed onto each other. They sat laboring with sorrow.

Aron smashed a fist into his hand. "You haven't told what happened to them, Mordche. Who were the sons of bitches happy to do this?"

"We heard them from the hayloft. A squad from the Armia Krajowa came. There was no way out. They got hold of the young Koniecny and beat him with a pistol until he said how many we were and where. They dragged us down. One of the killers shot the Koniecny boy dead anyway. There were horrible screams from Koniecny's wife and daughter. The bastards threw her husband to the ground. They kicked him until his blood ran. We had to watch and wait for our turn, the children terrified. My God, it was awful."

"*Pan* Koniecny," Aron said. "What those poor people did for us and this is their payment."

Mordche nodded his face a dispassionate disguise. "Three shoved us into their wagon with a mounted machine gun and drove to the Adama Village forest. The horses stopped in a clearing. They made the women, all of us, take off our shoes, everything and throw it in the wagon. Mother begged them to spare the children. The tall one took down the machine gun."

"Mother," Gitel sobbed, her fury rising. "Aron's family, my sister, Deborah, all of them?"

"Their bastard faces. They said nothing but *Żyd*." Mordche spat releasing hatred at the dirt wall. "The tall one lifted the machine gun across his arm. He started firing. Our people fell, flesh ripping, screaming. It felt like bullets tore into me. Something made me start to run. They'll kill me anyway I thought, what is left to lose? Yankel took the other way."

"They should rot in hell," Aron hissed.

"I wasn't sure, was I hit or not. The rattle of the gun stopped and started again. And it was quiet. I kept running."

Gitel covered her ears as if to shield her soul from the death screams.

"The screams," Mordche sobbed and covered his face, "they won't leave me. What could I do? Oh, God, what did I do?"

Gitel's body trembled and she tightened her arms about her bony frame.

"When the machine gun stopped, I didn't know in what direction I was running. They chased me, fired after me with pistols. I ran my heart pounding like it would bust open. All I could think was I had to get away. My legs kept running."

"How did you escape?" Aron said.

"I don't know. Believe me. They yelled, kill. Kill him. I felt their boots hitting the ground, one boot scraping like he had a limp. Remember Gitel, when the thieves came to rob Father? We were young, the one who dragged his leg? Just in front of me was a low bridge. Like something was showing me a place to go, I saw a hole under it. I jumped off. And crawled inside. Moments later they ran over the bridge. Every boot banged over me. I was sure they could hear my heart pounding. After, I got out and hid in the woods. All night I hid and for days."

"They'll find us," Aron said. "If there's enough time and the Americans don't smash the Nazis. Vladyk hears they were pushed back by the Ruskies. They're moving west fast. If not, we save them the trouble and starve to death."

Mordche's eyes squeezed shut. "May fifth. Thirteen bodies they counted. The butchers are searching for us. The Armia Krajowa is the Polish underground, the Home Army. They fight against the Nazis. Why hunt us?"

If they search for two who escaped, maybe my brother is still alive. But Aron did not dare reveal this hope. "Why? To some, we're all communists," he said. "And most of the Poles hate us. You think the Home Army is going to welcome the Russians? Think again."

Mordche nodded but his troubled thoughts flew elsewhere. "I didn't want to add to your *tsuris* from losing Devoire Ita. We missed her so. I didn't know where else to even try."

Gitel stiffened hearing the child's name. Her face contorted into a hideous mannequin's mien. Her little girl's terrible end, the bitter guilt, and now, all of them were gone. It was unbearable. Gitel tried to stop it, sound a luxury forbidden here. But a deep, crazed scream ripped forth and pierced the boards, an unprotected pain that filled the grave-like hiding place with fresh grief.

"Gitel," Aron said, "please, my love, what's the use? He'll throw us out." He took her hand and it lay limp in his. *All I have left is my wife.* He pulled her to him as if he could draw in her entire shattered being.

They shared stale morsels of bread, the odor of rotting potatoes wafting from the sack. Gitel eyed molding potatoes peels they had thrown in a corner. Aron followed her eyes and knew they would be forced to eat that too. Not a word was said between them. What was there to say? They were starving. Their Polish keepers had little themselves and now with three, there would be less.

Smells made Gitel nauseous and hunger made it worse. She put a hand to her mouth. The sense of crushing loss worsened by the fear of what was growing inside her. "Aron, I have to go. If I don't leave soon Vladyk will be suspicious. And how will I explain to Maricia if she heard my scream?" Gitel's voice faded into the walls of the bunker.

Mordche watched his sister climb out. He was safe for now but the horror he had escaped tormented him. Who was he to be alive? That he was not lying among the dead broke any peace he could find. And yet there must have been a reason. Was it nothing but the will to live and luck that had spared him? Mordche's fingers tore into the dirt. He relived the rattle of the bullets and his mother falling to the forest floor until he could no longer resist sleep.

Maricia quizzed Gitel about the scream and why her face was swollen. "Aron beat me," she said. *What can I say, that the twisted bodies of our families rot in their own blood in the Adama woods? That my heart screams it no longer wants to feel?* But the woman shook her head, eyed Gitel's belly and told her she was a liar. Gitel had to use the excuse she had left. How else could she cover for her brother and the news that had cracked her iron will? They had returned to the bunker themselves only days before and would be thrown out and caught.

"I'm pregnant," she said unable to look at the smirk she thought Maricia wore. "It was a bad pain." Gitel promised it would never happen again. She started scrubbing the plates Maricia had left in the bucket. It was no longer a secret. But she would give the woman no reason to doubt she was a valued slave. She would give her last strength. She would work until the end. *Please, God give me strength.* Gitel walked to the table and wiped the day's mess into her hands.

CHAPTER TWENTY-NINE

A Price for Passion

V ladyk found out the night Mordche dared to hitch the plow to his boney broad shoulders and pulled it through the furrows.

"I recognize you," he yelled. "What the hell do you think you're doing? Get off my land. Take the other two with you."

"You see what I'm doing, Vladyk," Mordche gave a guarded chuckle to hide desperation. "You know a full moon is best for planting potatoes. In October you'll harvest."

"Why am I the lucky one with the crazy Jews who won't leave me alone? Harvest what? We have nothing to plant," Vladyk said disgusted from the trouble he had brought upon himself.

Mordche stuck his hands into a burlap sack wrapped about his waist and legs meant as pants. "My sister, Gitel, saved the eyes of some of the potatoes she peeled and now look. Even if a quarter sprout, you'll have a few bushels." He dropped shriveled potato eyes in a furrow and stomped hard with the shoes Aron had pieced together. Mordche looked at the Pole and nodded, the two of them shadows in a fallow field, a full moon glinting. "I stacked every branch I could find behind the barn for your kindling last night. Adam told me you traded for a little flour for his work in the shed. That means a little bread. You'll see, Vladyk. If you let me stay, all of us, for the rest of our lives we'll owe you. We'll pay what we can. I swear on my life. We will honor this promise. From the first zlotys we make."

In the end, Vladyk relented. He believed a human was a human. He was not so much of a believer and left the church business to others. But for as long as he could he kept the news from his wife that he had allowed another Jew to hide.

August stifled the three in the bunker. Hunger occupied every thought. As their guts shrank, their stomachs swelled. They could not stop scratching the red scabs from the blood-sucking lice. It was impossible to sleep. Gitel, on the verge of giving birth, did her best to accept what she feared would happen. That she would die in childbirth terrified Aron. Gitel sat, her arms braced for support on the dirt. Sweat dripped down her face. *Where can I hide this shame? What kind of woman can I be to bring another life into hell?*

"Gitel, do you remember when the thieves came and how Bialek warned father? Can you imagine, it's more than ten years," Mordche said, trying to distract his sister. Her face revealed too much, this sibling who had been most like him from his earliest memories, as if they were born twins.

"Mordche, I have no patience for any more stories." Gitel shifted her body but found no comfort. She had lost more weight yet what was inside her had found a way to grow. Her teeth were loose, her hair straw and the once pearl white skin was a sickly pallor.

Pity fractured Aron's voice. "You have something better to do, Gitel?" *I'm responsible for this. It's because of me she suffers.* It throbbed in his head. *Me, who can never get enough.*

The only way Mordche could take them out of this hole was in their thoughts. So he tried again. "Aron, did Gitel say your father-in-law Wolf had a revolver?"

"She told me, Mordche. But you know what? You tell it this time and we'll see who tells a better story."

Mordche leaned into the space, the walls dripping sweat. If for a little while they could remember they had been allowed to live, if not problem-free, able to defend what belonged to them, maybe it would let them keep a grip on their sanity. Mordche began in soft Yiddish, a wistful prayer filled with longing that transported them to another time and place.

In 1929, in the early hours of a summer night Wolf was awakened by whining and throaty growls from Bialek, alert by the bed. Uncustomary as it was for dogs to sleep indoors, Bialek had earned his master's respect as a worthy judge of character, and as an exceptional protector. His thick white coat was testament to the care lavished on him. Wolf touched Bialek and signaled him to stop. With one more threatening growl, the dog obeyed. Wolf reached under the bed and laid his hand on the revolver. He had used it another time to defend his family. The news of a gunshot fired on his land had piqued Count Dzianat's curiosity. He had ridden down on his favorite Arabian and demanded his tenant give up the gun. Wolf explained how robbers had stolen a week's worth of his farmer's cheese and butter. That if he had not taken action his storeroom would become a target. The Count, aware authorities looked away when crimes were committed against Jews, still warned Wolf to do away with the gun. With a pull on his elegant whiskers the Count, *Hrabia* Dzianat rode away, his saddlebags bulging with blocks of Wolf's finest farmer's cheese.

Wolf's head swerved to the tapping on a window. Perhaps Bialek had warned him in time. Whoever, they were not interested in the dairy. It was the Herszkowicz home this time.

"Brazen thieves," Wolf snarled, pulling on his boots by the bed.

Mordche awoke and signaled to his father. The noise was coming from the back where the girls slept.

"I'll give what for," Wolf said under his breath. "You'll get a bullet from me." He waved his son back and his heated whisper commanded, "Stay with the rest." With that Wolf thrust open the door Bialek at his heel. Mordche crept behind Wolf into the darkness. Struck by the sound of his father's fury, Mordche crouched down. Wolf charged back to the house and confronted two men, one smashing the rear window with a crowbar.

"Stop, you miserable thieves!" Wolf yelled and signaled Bialek into action. "I have a revolver and it's loaded. I'm going to use it," no hint of fear in his booming voice.

The shorter of the two sneered at Wolf. "You coward Jew, you'll do nothing."

"Nothing?" Wolf echoed as the taller man made a swift approach toward him. "Nothing but this." He lifted the revolver and pointed at the man's head. He cocked the hammer back.

"He means to shoot," the shorter of the thieves screamed. Bialek smelled the fear, and jumped at the man's pant leg. The dog snapped his jaws shut.

The whole family was now aware that something terrible was happening, that Wolf and Mordche were in danger. They scrambled together and Hinda took control of the panicked children. "I don't need to sit *shiva* for you, boy, stay put," she implored her youngest. With that, Hinda wrapped around her the only thing within reach, Wolf's prayer shawl and ran to the door. "Let them have what they want, Wolf. Be careful!"

He ignored his wife's pleas and held steady, ready to shoot. The larger man, recognizing Wolf's intent, turned and ran. "Enough," Wolf commanded. Bialek released the smaller man's pant leg. He staggered off shaking a fist. "Next time we'll kill you."

Mordche seized the opportunity to pursue but the twelve-year-old was no match for the strangers fleeing his father's wrath. Yet he heard as one man ran, an unusual cadence, a foot scraping, maybe from a limp. Unable to follow any further, Mordche started back, the sound of that gait seared into his memory.

"Go in the house," Wolf said to Mordche taking the winded boy by his nightshirt. "You disobeyed me. One of the Polacks could have killed you. Say your morning prayers and thank God he spared you."

Lost in the past, Mordche finished the story and fell against the sweating wall. *I was spared again, just like Father told me I had been so long ago.* Night was changing into day and the first light revealed their features.

Gitel had fallen asleep. "Good," Aron said. "Let her rest. I don't have to tell you what she's made of but Gitel will need every bit of her strength. Since she can't hear me, Mordche, I have to say, you told it better. But then it is your story. Yours and Wolf's. Who knows where he is, my father-in-law, a lion of a man, a *mensch*."

"Maybe father is…" Mordche sighed unwilling to speculate aloud. "Do you think the one with the limp had a hand in the murders? He would be the kind. In the AK with a band of Jew haters."

"We have few friends, Mordche. The one with the limp, who knows?"

"I'm almost sure. That sound never left me." Mordche began to sway, the *Kaddish* prayer for their dead loved ones spilling from his lips and Aron joined him.

* * * * *

Being pregnant was endless discomfort for Gitel. The work got harder but being trapped in the hole with two men who no longer knew where to look as her misshapen body distended, was worse. She numbed her mind to hope about the outcome as months passed but could not find release from the dread of what might happen. Whispers of escape, how to keep an infant alive when they were reduced to eating mold from urine-covered potato peels reduced Gitel to her primal imperative, remaining alive. At the end of August, the baking sun rising on another miserable day, her labor began. She was frightened, yet as the pain intensified she was relieved the wait would be over. She sat on the damp down cover easing pressure from the hardened dirt. The cherished quilt stuffed with fluff which she imagined was alive was so soiled, Gitel felt sorry for it. But now what was certainly alive was beginning to rip through her. She doubled over. Aron did the unspeakable when her moans became cries. He had no choice. He slid through the opening, broad daylight blinding him and ran to a place he had never been, the house.

"Bring her," Maricia said. "If someone comes and hears, it will be more trouble." She chased Vladyk and the girls from the house. Aron ran back to the bunker but Mordche had already lifted his sister out. Aron held Gitel's hand and guided her steps. *If anything happens to her* raged through him *I'll do away with myself.* She dropped his hand and he watched Gitel enter the house. Mordche peeked from the bunker and slid the boards shut as Aron dropped into the hole.

Maricia had given birth twice with her mother's help and attended many births around the countryside. She extended her arm and helped Gitel onto a chair. She brought a wet rag to the woman whose eyes shown with pain and dread. Gitel tried to focus on the room where the day before she had swept the floor and managed to help Maricia with some mending.

"You're good at everything, Guccia," Maricia said, "except sewing."

"Sewing and not being pregnant," Gitel said. "I think it's coming, Maricia." She let out a long, deep cry. Shaking on the chair, Gitel clutched the table.

"You have to get on your knees, Guccia." Maricia helped Gitel down to the floor.

For the first time in the almost two years she had known Maricia, Gitel felt something different from the woman. It was more than pity. "The girls like you, Guccia," she said. "You are good to them." But Gitel could no longer hear anything. She squatted on the floor and made her trembling legs hold her.

"Yes, good, push down," Maricia encouraged and put a hand on Gitel's shoulder. Gitel yelled. She felt her insides tearing, unrelenting, sharp intense pain. Moments later her breathes slowed. She puffed out her cheeks with relief as the contraction subsided.

"I envy men," Maricia said. "It's always us who God makes go through this." She dipped the rag into the bucket of water, rung it and wiped Gitel's face.

"Me too," Gitel said. The pain came again, too much to control screams and she bore down, the baby's head pushing out. Gitel moaned for it to be over soon, grateful this birth was different. With the next spasms, the baby slid into Maricia's hands.

Gitel squatted over the blood pooled on the floor. Maricia used her foot to shove the last of the rags to Gitel. She fell to the floor groaning and gripped the rags between her legs. With what strength was left she lifted her face to see Maricia's hands covered with blood. The woman held the poor little thing, crying in fits. Gitel turned away, an empty broken animal. It was Vladyk who came and took it away. Gitel did not ask where. She knew she would never see her baby again.

CHAPTER THIRTY

1945 Swiecice in the Past

Snow crunched under Vladyk's feet. The steps grew louder and he stomped with urgency. "What is he doing here now?" Aron whispered to Gitel. She shrugged her shoulders. Soft light snowflakes fell and sunlight cleansed white the morning above as if in anticipation of good news.

Aron nodded at Mordche and they both sat up on their knees, Mordche's head almost touching the boards. Their hands pressed the cold dirt floor ready for whatever action might be required. "He's alone," Gitel whispered, bringing raw cracked fingers tips to a heart that still raced. Splotches of light forced through the boards glinted.

Vladyk stomped on the boards again. "You're free!" he yelled. He pushed away the snow with his boots and tossed one of the boards aside. Shimmering crystals drifted down the hole, their bunker.

The three brought rag-covered hands to their eyes. The brilliant morning sun illuminated the place that never saw light, their eyes experts in the darkness. It was too much for exposed rats with keen night vision used to shades of gloom. Almost two years before, Gitel and Aron had dug with Vladyk's shovel and two small shoemaker's tools. They had lowered themselves underground and covered the hole with the boards. That first Spring night they could not imagine it would be for so long. They had wondered if they had dug their own grave thirty meters from the farmhouse. As starved as they were then, two years later they were bone covered by thin skin in desensitized bodies. This last year, the three of them had faced reality. It was unlikely they would survive another winter.

"Don't you hear?" Vladek shouted. "I said you are free! The Ruskies liberated the whole area down to Krakow. January 15. I'll remember this day forever. They're pushing west to smash the Nazi pigs. The Americans and the British, they'll finish them soon."

"Vladyk?" Aron peered up shielding one eye. In a hoarse whisper, "Is it true? No trick?"

Vladyk reached an arm into the hole and kicked the other boards aside. Even in the winter, when smells were muted by the freeze, the stench wafting up to the fresh clean air made him cover his nose. "Look what I have in my hand." He waved a bottle and a thick shot glass. "Would I bring my vodka to you if it was not so?" he laughed.

Mordche pulled himself up from the crouch, his chest at the edge of the bunker wall. Vladyk put his empty hand out and Mordche with strength surging from will hoisted himself up. He reached his forearm down into the hole that had been his home.

Aron braced against an iced wall to steady. "Gitel, grab your brother's arm, it's time." Mordche reached for her and Aron's mind flashed with images of the trench he had climbed out of long ago. Nazis eyes had pierced his with conquest. He pulled his skeleton out of its prison.

The three stood stooped, limbs shaking. They stood impervious to winter, their eyes squinting at the light, their minds trying to believe. Fear of being exposed, the dark walls removed, what they had prayed for, to be released from captivity filled each with joy, confusion, doubt and wonder. And fear.

"So, let's have a drink of this good vodka," Vladyk said, "before Maricia finds the bottle missing from the cupboard."

Vladyk poured a glass for Aron first. Aron put the glass to his lips, lifted his head and gulped back the clear liquid, his tongue scavenging for drops. "*Na zdrowie*, to your health," Aron said to Vladyk. He wobbled toward Gitel shaking his head in disbelief.

"Your mustache is red," she said to her husband whom she had not seen in such a blaze of sunlight for far too long.

"And you are still beautiful," he said to his wife. He touched the matted hair once a shining crown. He did see that fresh beauty had been replaced with indelible suffering. Her green eyes, their refusal to be extinguished shone up at Aron. Mordche and Aron clasped hands wordless and exhaled white puffs of pure air.

Vladyk poured a glass for Mordche. He drank back the vodka with a loud, "Ah! *Do dna*, to the bottom."

He extended a full glass to Gitel and she shook her head, no. Vladyk drained it. He stared at the three shadows covered with rags. "It is time for you to go. Put your things together." Vladyk peered down into what had been his potato cellar. There lay Gitel's soiled down quilt, a few tools, a rusty pot and something wrapped in a stiff cloth.

"You have to leave now," he said his eyes scouring the white fields. "I don't want my neighbors to ever know."

They were mute. Three stooped skeletal figures unsure of how to behave at the moment of liberation. What kind of man would have risked such a thing? Vladyk had agreed to harbor hunted Jews. They turned over in their minds this mystery of humanity, bits of goodness amongst swirling evil. They had understood they would be creatures of the night, only coming out of the hole when they hoped no one would find them and even in the dark of the night the terror of being caught had never left. And still their eyes darted about unsure of where to look and rested upon this man. Vladyk Kukyrk.

"Can I say goodbye to the children and Maricia?" Gitel said looking toward the farmhouse where she had worked for two years, almost every night.

"Go. Tell Maricia to give you something to eat. Then leave." Liberated or not, Jews were pariahs. Even factions of the Armia Krajowa, their Home Army, hadn't they slaughtered the families of these Jews in his midst? There could be reprisal against him and his wife. His girls might pay the price if anyone suspected he had sympathized with Jews. It was true in the past, democratization of rights had been bestowed but things had begun to change when Vladyk was a young man. In any case, the hatred and carnage the Nazis had wrought on Poles was his concern. Many had been made slaves for this supposed master race. His own people had been starved, stripped of their rights, forced from their land and murdered. He would soon learn the educated and the *schlacta* had been decimated. His duty now was for his family and for Poland in ruin. He felt overwhelmed as he contemplated his own freedom. He had done enough.

Gitel shuffled to the house, a frayed kerchief pulled tight beneath an emaciated face. She handed Maricia the small empty sack and waited outside. Maricia brought it back and what Gitel weighed in her hand was very little. "Maybe the girls shouldn't see you leave like this," Maricia said.

"No," Gitel said straightening up best she could. "I wouldn't want them to see their *ciotka* like this. The light tells too much. They are good children, your daughters."

"I wish you well, Guccia. It was not easy. For any of us."

"We will never forget. As soon as we are able, we'll begin to repay you in any way can. It is because of you and Vladyk we are alive."

Maricia held out her hand and Gitel took it.

CHAPTER THIRTY-ONE

Back to Ksiaz Wielki

They left the Kukuryks and believed it was their last hiding place. Crouching for so long in the bunker had been deleterious. What would have taken an hour to walk the five kilometers to Ksiaz Wielki took far longer. Each step, each stop, made them wary they would encounter trouble. Strangers to freedom, they were filled with doubt and afraid to even gaze at the trees laden with glittering snow.

Like nocturnal moles thrust out of a winter borough and exposed to sudden light, they were overwhelmed. Forced into an unnatural state, they had grown unaccustomed to being humans. Their own voices sounded foreign and they spoke in excited whispers. Aron, Gitel and Mordche walked through open white fields and tried to find routes among the trees. They feared meeting an enemy who did not know or care Jews were also among the liberated. There were few tracks in the snow on the road so they ventured out to shorten travel time. Once so familiar, the smoke rising from chimneys in the distance appeared threatening. Houses loomed large after an eternity in a place with barely enough room to turn or air to breathe.

A stream they passed was frozen so washing themselves was impossible. But they rubbed snow between their hands to refresh and sucked melted snow from their palms to quench thirst. Hunger had gripped them, twisted and starved them. Each day had taken them closer to death. Their minds had focused on two things, how to get anything to eat and how to keep secret their hiding place by making themselves useful, invisible slaves. This moment hunger receded and the newness of the sudden release from agony filled them with gratitude. Tears of joy reflected in each other's eyes.

Later they sat in silence among snow-encased shrubs, a natural frozen fortress for rest and marveled at the sun they had prayed to see. They prayed to be free then ate bits of food Maricia had given Gitel. The two wrinkled potatoes, shriveled turnips and crusts of dry bread tasted better than any sumptuous meal they could ever have conjured.

"I see Maricia's cooking did not improve with your lessons, Gitel," Aron said.

She brushed her hands over the tatters left of the once-elegant suit tailored in Bedzin years before the world went mad. "She was a slow learner," Gitel smiled, showing brown stained teeth. "But neither did my sewing improve."

Mordche laughed, his whole body vibrating. Aron and Gitel hesitated then joined him. Laughter had been denied. But the moment was over and merriment was overridden by longer shadows and the knowledge their weak bodies had kilometers before them.

It was late afternoon when they saw the hill rising to Ksiaz Wielki, the town they thought they would never see again. Once an easy stroll, the gradual incline was difficult. But more difficult was the reception from the people, the Poles who had remained. The good news of liberation did not seem to pertain to the three of them. Everyone they recognized averted their eyes.

"Look at this," Aron said shaking his head in mock consternation, "our friends don't recognize us."

"I don't recognize myself," Mordche said feeling his face with a rag-covered hand. "Well, what are we going to do? We can't stand in the middle of the street like ghosts."

They trudged along the length of Dembrowska, the once vibrant main street. The houses populated with Jewish owned tailor shops had lost their purpose. The bakery that had belonged to the family of the young man with the story of Balzac was boarded. The groceries that had been taken over by Poles were shut. The liquor store was empty. Its wood sign with the hand-drawn bottle with the word *wodka* swayed, the wind gaining strength. There was no visible commerce. Another Pole they knew raised his eyebrows as he passed and crossed the street. Gitel wanted to see the stone synagogue. They hobbled down the street and stared at its windows holding shards of broken glass.

"Let's walk to our old apartment. Perhaps we can find someone with a heart," Gitel said. They stood dwarfed by the neglected church behind them and peered across the street at the house where Devoire Ita had been born.

"Beggars covered in rags," Aron said catching his image in the window of what was once the bakery on the street level. He knocked on the door with frozen exposed knuckles. A man opened the door wide enough to show his hostile eyes. Aron recognized a former customer.

"Get away," he spat. "We're free from you filthy thieves."

"*Pan*," Aron said, "I don't want to take your place. You know us. We mean no harm. We lived in the attic of this house." The man's eyes disappeared. He bolted the door with finality before Aron could ask for temporary shelter.

This is worse than we thought scraped beneath each dejected step. They slid along the iced street to Balcha's house. Gitel's sister had lived and prospered there along with her husband and children. Seven months before they were among those taken from the hayloft by wagon into the Adama Woods. "Maybe there is no point going to my sister's house. Whoever lives there may give us the same treatment. But I'm going to try," Gitel said. She climbed the steps to her sister's apartment. A family of Volkesdeutche who lived there made it clear that no help would be coming from them and that Jews had no rights to what was now their property. She stepped from the front door and her eyes told Aron and Mordche what they expected. The house stood but what belonged to family was a monument to what no longer existed.

"I'm going to see if Dr. Yoblonski is still in his house," Aron said. "You stay with Mordche. If there is any one left in this town with decency, with a soul, it will be him."

Gitel and her brother watched Aron shuffle up the street, fighting to balance against the wind. It was the same main street that had connected their small rural town to centers of Polish culture and what only years before had been a mecca for Jewish intelligencia, merchants, scholars, manufacturers, musicians, doctors, and tradesman, a people, a culture. They had no idea this had almost been obliterated. Mordche and Gitel stood under the eaves of what had been their sister's doorway and watched Aron duck into the Polish doctor's house.

Dr. Yoblonski drew back when he saw Aron before him, a man dressed in rags, unkempt with sunken wounded eyes. "It's Adam Matuszyński, Dr. Yoblonski. I know what I must look like to you, a thing that has crawled out of a grave. In a way I just have, me, my wife and my brother-in-law."

The doctor extended his hand and Aron hesitated to touch him, but the handshake was genuine. "None of your people are here, no one has returned to Ksiaz Wielki," he said.

The doctor's face revealed pity and Aron tried to stand as straight as his body allowed. "We have to start over and make something of ourselves again. We have our two hands. Now that we are free, we want to regain our strength and lives," Aron said. "I came to ask you, Dr. Yoblonski, if you might lend me some clothes. You see what's become of me. I will repay you from my first pair of shoes."

"Let me see what I have that may fit," he said assessing the stooped man with the hunger carved, sunken cheeks.

Aron was exhausted from the hours of walking, but would not dare sit on a chair, nor had he been invited to do so. He listened to the clock chime quarter after five, the light in the room softening, shadows hugging the graceful legs of the doctor's desk.

"This is what I can give you, Adam," Dr. Yoblonski said, handing Aron pants, a shirt and socks. In his hand he held out a few *zlotys* and a few *grochen*. The doctor, tall and thin, stood enormous next to the shriveled man who had always been fastidious even with tools and glue surrounding him. The doctor peered at the almost unrecognizable shoemaker.

"Doctor Yoblonski," Aron said, "it is impossible to tell what in this world people must endure. It cannot be described. But among us are men who still have quality. We are alive because of one. I know you are also such a man. I thank you with whatever is left of me."

"Adam, you will learn what the situation is in our town. The war is officially over here, yet the hatred continues. The Russians liberated the Krakow-Plazow Concentration Camp today. I heard on my crystal radio what is being discovered. But Russian soldiers are everywhere with their propaganda, urging our people to celebrate their great victory. I wonder if we exchange one oppressor, the Germans, for another, the Russians. We Poles want neither of them. What do you intend to do now, Adam?"

"We want nothing but to live here, to work, the same as all people," Aron said. "To have time without fear. What is left of my people, I don't even know. What I sense from you, Dr. Yoblonski, is not many."

"Adam, you must face the truth. The rest of the Jews from here were herded into the Miechow ghetto. From there they were sent to Belzec. Many Poles in our town are gone as well, replaced by the Volkesdsutche like Hubner. The whole war has been a terrible business for us Poles."

"Belzec." Aron's head dropped further from the weight of the word. He remembered the young man who had escaped and brought them the news of what they had refused to believe, the first of the gas chambers the Nazis were perfecting into killing factories. He stood stooped and motionless, ashamed that such a thing had befallen his people.

"I had no idea what happened to you. I only knew you were gone and I heard nothing else. Before you left you witnessed your family and Jews taken away or killed on the street, in the cemetery. Many of my friends were happy to see all of you gone. And I can tell you that they will not welcome your people back. Among the few Jews returning to their towns, I hear some have already been killed."

Aron stared at the doctor, his body and mind unable to absorb more.

"I help you now, but it will not be possible to be seen with you or any of your people in the future. You understand."

"I understand," Aron said. The sunken blue eyes spoke thanks to this Polish man. What, Aron wondered, had he come back for? What lie ahead?

They searched the street for a place to rest for the night. With the sun setting the cold bit into their bodies. Gitel's shoulders and hands were wrapped in the down cover. Aron had put on the clothes the doctor had given him. Standing next to Mordche he appeared well dressed in comparison, though the pants hung on his bones. Mordche took what was left of Aron's rags and stuffed them into his shirt and pants. The men rubbed their hands and shifted from foot to foot.

"A nice dance," Gitel said, smiling at her husband and brother hovering in a doorway.

Aron had the few *zlotys* the doctor had given him in his pocket. "What do you think I can get for us with some of this?" he said, feeling for the *zlotys* as someone approached.

"Money is money," Mordche said.

A man with a scarf covering his face and a package under his arm was walking towards them. Aron stepped forward. "*Pan*," he said, holding out a few grochen from the money the doctor had given him. "We have traveled all day, is there a place where we could sleep for the night and get some bread?"

He waved Aron away.

"Please, *Pan*, you see my wife, she is not well. We need bread. We have no food." The man lowered the scarf from his face. He looked at Aron, at Gitel wrapped in the blanket, and at Mordche doing his best to straighten.

"What are you looking for here?" he said. "There is no work and no place for people like you."

"*Pan*," Gitel said, pulling the blanket tight against the wind and the thickening falling snow. She recognized his Polish accent. It belonged to a Volksdeutche. "We want nothing here, just a place to rest. Tomorrow I will feel better and we will leave early."

"Go to the end of the town, that way," he pointed, "like you are leaving for Krakow. You will come to a small shack near what was the forge. It may be open. Use it tonight and tomorrow it's best you leave."

"Can you sell us some bread?" Mordche said, smelling what was under the man's arm, like a starving mongrel ready to pounce.

"Who are you people?" the man said eying Mordche. "I've never seen you in my town." He shifted the package to the other arm.

"Who are we? Who are you?" Mordche said.

"*Pan,*" Aron said shaking his head at Mordche. "You are very kind. My friend is hungry and too tired. He meant well. Thank you, we will find the shack. But if you are willing to sell your bread for a good price, I can pay." Aron took out two *zlotys*.

"Three." The man fixed the scarf about his face, and walked away three *zlotys* richer.

"Mordche," Aron said, "you have nerve. I told you what Yoblonski said. You see yourself our welcome."

"You want to throw out the few *zlotys* we have?" Mordche said.

"If you have a better plan," Aron said, "show me. We have bread and I don't care about anything else."

"Let's go," Gitel said. "More than a year squeezed together in the bunker and the two of you still have so much to argue over."

Snow added to the urgency. They had to find shelter. The road was rutted and slippery for weary weak legs. Finally, they came to where the row of houses ended. There stood the shack just beyond the forge. It hung together like a patched pair of old shoes, crooked bits and pieces thrown together, and Aron thought of Hanek the Hunchback. Mordche pushed the knob on the narrow door. It creaked open.

Gitel stepped inside first. Aron and Mordche followed. "She thinks we have a bargain," Aron said. "Can't you wait? It's probably got rats."

"Good. They'll have company. Maybe they'll share secrets where to find food," Gitel said. "It smells like kerosene. More fit for the devil. No, rats would have more sense than to move in, even for the winter."

215

The floor was littered with broken tools once used in the forge. The Slomynsk family who owned the forge were hard-working Poles. It was uncharacteristic to discard tools. Everything was of value, repaired and reused.

"It looks like the Germans may have commandeered the forge for themselves," Aron said. "The Slomynsks would never leave so much to rot and waste."

"Maybe the Nazis were smelting at their forge for another purpose," Mordche said.

"They're finished," Aron said. "Whatever was going on is over."

Straw covered the frozen dirt floor beneath Gitel's feet. A small window on the side facing the forge was opaque with clinging snow but its whiteness drew light into the shack. Her eyes, accustomed to blackness, saw the tasks before them here. The walls were smeared with pitch, uneven streaks covering most of the interior. A few burlap sacks were thrown against the rear wall where three drums stood. An anvil leaned beneath the small window. A wide tin pipe hung down from the ceiling in the back. Snow floated through the pipe to the floor. The space was small and the ceiling slanted lower toward the doorway where Gitel stood. "Compared to that bunker grave," she smiled, "we have a palace."

"The kerosene stink may be coming from the drums over there," Aron said brushing the snow off his borrowed clothes.

"We have work in front of us." Gitel took Aron's arm and leaned her head against his shoulder. Work was nothing new and she placed her hands on bony hips, grateful she would be doing it for her family.

"For a bread and three *zlotys* it's a bargain," he said showing Gitel the remaining *zloty* before stuffing it deep inside his pocket.

"For sure they used this shack for something to do with the war," Mordche said coming back in. "I just took a good look in the back. Nothing is there. Whoever it was, they stole everything else."

Aron and Mordche cleared a small space by the door. Gitel rolled up the down quilt warming her body and dropped her sack, ready to work.

216

It was after seven and the moon had risen. Its full face would be gracing them with light.

"Men, come here," Gitel said. "I fooled you. I saved bits of potatoes. And with the bread, we can manage easy a few days. Now figure out how to use that chimney pipe or we keep freezing."

Aron marveled at the woman in rags. She was ravaged by starvation, emotional torment, and yet she had thought ahead. That spirit she exuded much of her life, stripped from her womanhood loss by loss, he believed would return. He never doubted what she meant to him. Everything. "How long do you think we can stay here?" he said, filled with adoration for Gitel.

"Until they chase us out," said Mordche. "No one has been in this shack for who knows how long. Why would they bother now?"

"Does it belong to you?" Aron said.

"Listen," Gitel said. "This is a discussion for tomorrow."

"And what happens if tomorrow morning a Slomynsk tells us to get out or worse?" Aron said.

"Then you can remind him about Meir and the hundreds of *zlotys* he made for them," Mordche said, his eyes searching the effect of his words on Aron, now barely visible inside the darkened shack. The mention of Meir had turned Aron away and Mordche was sorry he had baited him.

"Not hundreds, thousands of *zlotys*. Meir put me through hell when I was a boy. But he had a business head. The Poles liked doing deals with him and he made them plenty money. He could have done other things, too," Aron said. He knew Meir should have helped their parents more when he still had means. The family was hungry and suffering. His brother had been obligated to do much more. The bitterness escaped from Aron and he felt it was perceived by Gitel. She remained silent. Everything would take time, they were broken people in need of healing. And the ugliness of what they had just left resided in them. In different ways but in all of them, it had eaten away parts of their humanity.

"You see the pitch on the walls," Aron said, feeling with his hand, eager for the present. "They meant to keep the shed dry to protect something. They must have stored kerosene in here."

"You're right," Mordche said. "This is could be luck." There was no further mention of Aron's brother as they began the enormous task before them. It was dark and snow fell without stop. The moon's reflection on the whiteness, the first taste of air from an open sky held them in joyful disbelief.

The men dragged the debris behind the shack. The anvil stayed. In their weak state, they rolled the cans of kerosene beyond the shack and buried them beneath snow-laden branches. Freedom was foreign. But work was not. They had worked very hard, almost without stop and now for the first time in years, they were doing it for themselves. Snow covered what they had cleared, and camouflaged what might look suspicious to anyone poking about in daylight. Gitel stuffed the pipe hanging from the ceiling with a torn burlap sack they found. She put whatever straw she could harvest from the floor in the better sacks to bed down on. Then she pulled them to the corner furthest from the window.

"A good thing it's freezing or the lice would be jumping in the straw," Gitel smiled when the men came in.

"The whole town will be buried under snow. We won't have to worry about lice or being discovered here yet. Not tomorrow," Mordche said looking at Aron, who was also covered white.

"Enough for tonight," Gitel said. "How we are still standing I don't know. Let's clear the rest tomorrow."

"Tomorrow I go into the kerosene business," Mordche said.

"I'm going to get my tools back from the Pole who has beeen holding them for me," Aron said. He looked at the anvil and thought it might be very handy indeed.

Aron took the first watch. He leaned against the pitch-covered shack wall. The breathing of his wife and Mordche melded with his own, reminiscent of the months they had huddled together in the bunker. Not to keep their guard up would be foolish. *How did we live through that*

218

hell? Was it more the mind or the body that made it possible? Aron remained absorbed by the question. There was luck, too. But he believed his mind had grabbed the passion for a woman who like him, had refused to let go of the bond.

It was over. But was it over? He had lost much of his faith. He had lost his precious girl. They both suffered the loss. Gitel had a life taken from her like a piece of worthless spoiled meat. He dared not imagine it. There were things a wife could not share. He sat on the floor unsure what he should be hoping. For freedom from being hunted? For a time when he could eat his fill? For a place where he could be next to his wife, hold her and live. It always came down to existence. He listened to their breathing and could not stop thinking about when their breaths were alarmed with fright, or when an unrecognized voice made him think it was the end. Aron watched over them.

In the days that followed, regaining strength, Aron went to the Sosnowiec and found the Pole to whom he had entrusted his tools. Now Aron would repay him with work favors. Though a few tools were missing, there was plenty to restart his workshop. The Pole had kept his word. Aron carried the pack to the abandoned shack by the old forge. He had little space but compared to the bunker, it was paradise.

As they slowly straightened their spines, they did the same with their lives. Mordche began to trade the kerosene. Aron had work. Those returning, most of them Poles, a few Jews, were desperate to have something done about repairing their shoes, at times the one item that had meant the difference between life and death. Gitel worked with gusto the entire day to find leather, food and small items to make small comforts. Her strength was returning. The spirit and resourcefulness that had helped her survive, she now used to rebuild their lives.

CHAPTER THIRTY-TWO

Remnants Return

They began to relearn how to live as humans. Yet freedom was in question. Who they had lost haunted each and filled them with guilt. There was unrelenting anger against the Poles. Hatred festered against the Nazis for the ruination of all they had loved.

Daily discoveries of another family member or friend's death stung. Tensions rose with the Poles and there were fights over confiscated property. News of the killings of Jews returning to towns and cities reached them. Killings in Lodz, Sosnowiec, Krakow and Warsaw added more corpses to what they could not fathom, the whispered millions. It continued and life in Poland remained insecure.

Halina, the daughter of the bakery owner from whom Gitel and Aron had rented the attic apartment, returned to Ksiaz Wielki. Her family had lived in peace with their Polish neighbors. Jews and gentiles alike had come daily for the breads, rolls and sweets her father and his two helpers had baked. In November 1942 the Jews in Ksiaz Wielki had been in the final stage of liquidation. Halina's mother and young brothers were separated and taken to one camp, Halina and her father to another. Her father, aware of the plan to kill inmates, found Halina on the morning of the selection. He gave her the silver candlesticks he had hidden in his coat and made her promise to escape. Luck found her and she did.

Until liberation she posed as a Polish orphaned maiden, and worked for a German couple in a border town between Germany and Poland. She had found the Matuszyński name on a list of survivors posted in Miechow, the first town she had come to after being freed to go home to her family. None of them were alive. Halina was eighteen and alone. Aron and Gitel were the only people left alive she knew. Finding them, she begged for sanctuary with the same perfect features that had enabled her to survive. Aron and Gitel took her in.

The shack near the forge served as Aron's workroom. There he labored for hours each day, keeping the door open for light and air. That morning he finished a pair of shoes. He stood them next to the pair of tall brown boots he had completed. He was happy the two pairs were bringing a good price. With this first money he and Mordche planned to visit Vladyk and begin to make good on their promises. Aron would repay the doctor and then they would leave quietly for Swiecice. Aron set down the upper part of a shoe he was stitching, pushing the waxed twine though the holes with the same awl he had held in captivity, the tool, an amulet.

Sometimes, Mordche took Halina with him to sell or trade. A romance was flourishing. "Your brother and Halina won't be back for hours," Aron said, rubbing his hand on Gitel's thigh. "Nice material, your skirt, but let's feel the goods beneath." Aron was thrilled to have some time alone with Gitel. He reached for her hand and pulled her into his lap. He wanted to caress her, kiss the skin regenerating its softness. He was starved for their lovemaking. Her figure was beginning to fill out. She regained her desire to look attractive, had bits of time to tend to herself. New growth of her hair starting to wave was held in place by combs Mordche had gotten as part of a trade for the kerosene. Gitel smelled not of perfume, but of the strong naphtelene soap she used to wash and boil their few items of clothing on the contraption the men had hooked up to the chimney pipe, the first item they had bartered for in order to make the shack livable.

Gitel touched his lips. He kissed her palm and motioned to the bed, the burlap pallets of straw covered by the washed and aired down cover. They lay embracing, echoing the excitement of pleasure. Fear, grief, lack of privacy and the horror of the unspoken birth had quashed intimacy. They satisfied this hunger for one another, a hunger that had fed their survival.

By May, Gitel held another secret.

Summer wild flowers flashed red, blue and yellow in the meadows. The four lifted their faces to the sun, felt its warmth and gave thanks for what they had prayed to see. Gitel had remade an abandoned shack into a livable place. Aron had made boots for one of the Slomynsk brothers, a tribute for the use of the shack. The Pole insisted on bringing heads of cabbage and a small amount of sugar, something none of them had tasted in five years. There was an understanding they could remain and there was a hint of security with a few Polish neighbors.

In June, their industry was constant. Mordche carved a niche for himself. He had found a source for kerosene and continued to trade. He carried a large metal can of kerosene on his broad back like he had once done with cans of milk and he traveled by foot from town to town. He wanted to give up the heavy kegs for more transportable items on the slow route to accumulate money. He began to buy tobacco, salt, and anything obtainable. Mordche was aware that he was a Jew among hostiles and he had to be prudent. The little that was available - flour, eggs, potatoes, even beets and cabbages were expensive and the competition fierce. Mordche took risks and traded with the Poles that were willing. A handful of Jews had come back to Ksiaz Wielki and Aron found more customers. All hours of the day and sometimes into the night he was absorbed in buying leather, working and selling. It was slow progress, but Aron was starting to make a living again. They were accumulating zlotys. He and Mordche had made a quick trip to visit Vladyk and Maricia. The Kukuryks were glad to see them thriving and thanked them again and again for this first step. Before they left, Vladyk warned Aron and Mordche to be careful. He had heard about more attacks against Jews.

* * * * *

At the end of the month, Yankel appeared. Was this a ghost? "It's me," he sang, kissing Gitel and showing off his handsome jacket. "I found you." The reunion lifted Aron's spirit. His brother's return was a great joy. Until that moment, he did not know if any of his family had survived. The three Aron, Yankel and Mordche sat in the shack and traded stories.

"A blessing," Gitel said, her eyes unable to leave her brother-in-law's face. "Yankel, to have you with us is a great blessing." She put a metal cup with steamed chamomile buds she had foraged and slices of bread she had baked on the table while Halina helped, a shy smile on her full lips. Gitel was becoming mother, sister and friend to the young woman who had no one else left.

"You know about my dear ones," Yankel said running his hand through still bountiful hair. "Ginendal, my precious wife, my two beautiful boys are gone."

"Yankel, you don't have to say another word," Gitel said. Halina wiped tears from her azure eyes, the striking ones that had enabled her to pass, and had witnessed too much.

Yankel looked up at his sister-in-law's face. Gitel had let him make the choice of what to reveal and at the same time given him cover. "Yes, I need to," he said. "Many times I sneaked out to find food for all the children. My son Berel was five years old and Itzyk was seven. The children were starving, their eyes sunk into their little faces. Did they have to fast every day and night like it was Yom Kippur?"

"We fasted enough days and nights. I don't need Yom Kippur anymore," Aron said.

Gitel flashed a look at him and entwined her fingers.

"I was in the Adama Forest when those shots stopped everything. The machine gun blasted as they fell. I ran." Yankel shook his head, heavy and mournful. "Later, I sneaked back to the Koniecny. I didn't know where to go. They hated my face. I understood. I hated it myself. A shoe was left from my little son and I hugged it, my sanity leaving me. I became insane with rage. I started to howl and cry, and they chased me off like a mad dog. My heart was torn into pieces. I came to in the morning, out in the open, and I no longer cared whether I should live or not."

"It's enough, Yankel," Aron said, pity for his brother, pity for the loss he read on all the stone faces.

"No. It will never be enough. I wandered in a trance in hope of getting anything I could steal or lay my hands on. From Charsznica to Miechow I walked. Why there, I don't know. I was pulled by a string, my feet followed. I hid there, in the cellar of what was once an apothecary, not that anything was left but empty bottles. But I loaded my pockets and used them to trade for small things just after the liberation. Then one morning Sara and I crossed paths. She had been in Dachau, lived through her own hell and had come back to her hometown. No one was left from her family."

"A very pretty girl, I remember her," Aron said a smile turning into a knowing nod. "She's our second cousin from our father's side."

"We were both alone. I heard that in Sosnowiec some Jews had returned and maybe there was opportunity to find work in a bigger city. I had always liked her and asked if she wanted to come with me. It turned into love, my friends," Yankel's shoulders rose in a plea of forgiveness. "What choice do we have but to go on? All of us are shattered inside and we get thrown together with others who are broken and looking. We are but human and a man needs a woman to live." Yankel looked at Aron and at his sister-in-law, Gitel.

Mordche glanced at Halina. She met his gaze.

They had all become master communicators without words.

"So, Yankel," Gitel said, "you are not coming back to Ksiaz again."

"No. I'm finished with this place. When I saw the Matuszyński name on the list in Miechow, it was the first happy moment in years. I came to see who was left of my family. And to make preparations for our wedding. I know many of the farmers in Giebultow. I want to buy chickens and down for my Sara."

"I'll go with you," said Mordche. "It's not so safe to travel alone. I know every pebble in Giebultow."

"I don't like the whole business," Aron said. "We have few friends here, but at least I have a better idea who my enemies are."

"Aron, you've been a worrier since you sprang out of our Mother's womb. I'll have the lion with me." Yankel appraised Mordche regaining his fierce body.

"You'll see. There'll be a chicken for you too Gitel," Yankel said taking a dancing step, humming a polka tune.

"Never mind the chicken." Gitel winked but dropped her tone. "Bring yourself back to Sara and send my brother back alive."

Yankel and Mordche left early the next morning, relishing the warmth of day, the wonder of walking like free men surrounded by open countryside. They were discarded remnants from a homeland that had not welcomed them back. But they were alive. And on a mission for the future.

When they got to Giebultow, Mordche wanted to pass his old house. The narrow wood bridge leading to the other side of the stream was just as he remembered. Water flowed faster here where the banks narrowed. Big-faced yellow sun flowers hung their heads as they had from the time he was a boy. But his people were gone. Only memories were left. No more scent of dairy products, no voices of his family.

They inquired. Yankel and Mordche found farmers willing to sell down and chickens. Stars blinked in the heavens by the time a deal had been struck. There was a sleeping arrangement made in an empty cow barn.

"You go find another place to sleep, Mordche," Yankel said, when the farmers had left. "I didn't like the way they looked at us after I paid. I don't trust them. It's always better to separate, anyway."

"Yankel, I didn't trust them either. Did you have to remind one of them he owed you a debt from beef you delivered? I don't have a good feeling about this. We should leave now."

"Go. Find another place to bed down. There are few hours before morning. Taking a train to Sosnowiec with three chickens squawking will make for a good story. I don't want to leave Sara alone too long. Another second cousin, Willie from Miechow, you've met him, he's there with her. He said he came to find shelter with us. He's a nervous little toad, always hopping around Sara. I don't want him to get any big ideas. Sleep fast," Yankel said with his impish grin.

Mordche ran for the corncrib behind the barn. He covered himself with the dry husks just as shouts began. Pistol shots cracked and screams were cut short. Mordche lay frozen. The horrid screams reverberated in his skull. He heard one of the Pole's say they should get the shotgun from the house to finish the big one. Mordche slid out of the corncrib on his belly and crawled into the woods. He knew every tree from boyhood and he scooted among them without stop until he was back to the shack.

He pushed open the door. Aron was awake. Gitel, startled, sat up. Halina slept in a corner they had made up for the women. "It's bad," he said. His arms hung, his face seared by guilt.

"Where's Yankel?" Aron stood. His eyes tore into Mordche.

"They killed him." Mordche turned away. "When will God show his mercy on us?"

"Enough!" Aron shouted. "I don't want to hear anymore. There is no God. What God would let happen what has happened here. God has no mercy on us. Dead? Everything about him is about life. He made it through all this hell to be killed by murdering Poles. Isn't it enough that I picture my daughter's face every night when I close my eyes? All their faces come to me asking why. Yankel, Yankel where did you go? For what?"

"I'll find another place for myself," Mordche said. "I know you can't even look at me."

Aron opened the door of the shack and stepped onto the road. All was quiet. The stars extinguished overhead. A warm day was beginning. Another piece of his flesh and blood, his last brother from the family he was still mourning. Yankel had appeared as if in a dream, a hope. Aron whirled around and stared at the shadows in the room. Mordche's head was between his knees. Gitel sat near Halina. She was awake and crying like a little girl. Aron's hands gripped the doorframe and Gitel caught his forlorn eyes. She felt his hurt and he saw this in her eyes. Lost, he walked back into the place where they had dared to remain.

"Gitel," Aron shouted, "if I had a gun, this minute, I would find whoever did this to my brother and I swear I would drive a bullet into his head."

They sat together. The birds sang while the day lost hours.

Aron broke the silence. "There're going to kill all of us." His eyes spilled tears. "If we don't get out of Poland none of us will stay alive. We have to go and soon. You had *mazel*, Mordche. This time, Yankel didn't."

"We're going together," Gitel said.

"Where will we go?" Halina asked. "Are they ever going to stop?"

"Tomorrow we're going to see about a wagon to Miechow," Gitel said.

"Yes," Aron said, "from there we'll take the train to Sosnowiec. They have some kind of Jewish organization there. Maybe they'll help us find a safe place. There is no choice. We have to run from here."

The next days' grief stoked action. Mordche feared the men who had murdered Yankel would look to do away with him. The three made him stay in the shack to avoid reprisal and keep away the evil eye. They had to plan a route to Sosnowiec, hire a driver with a horse and wagon to get to Miechow and follow in the same footsteps as Yankel would have. The route spooked their thoughts. None of them had identification papers. They would travel as Poles returning home from dislocation during the war. There were plenty of Poles returning from the work camps, wandering and homeless.

Mordche took his chances and began to sell as much of his trading goods as he could. Aron worked faster than ever to finish contracted shoes. Halina shadowed Gitel wherever she went. "How can you walk so fast?" Halina asked her. "You are pregnant."

"I'm not sick. Don't believe those silly tales about being weak when you're pregnant. I have plenty energy. We have to buy food wherever we find it and put together as much as we can. Who knows what lies in front of us?" But the pregnancy was a great worry, one that she and Aron both carried and spoke of it in sharp whispers.

"I remember the night you had Devoire Ita," Halina said. "I was twelve and had already been with my mother when both my little brothers were born." The memory filled Halina with dispair. She sucked in her lower lip and became pensive. "Mother chased me away from your apartment. But it didn't matter, I heard you even when I went down to our bakery on the first floor."

"Your mother tried to calm Aron down. When I began yelling, she sent him to get my sister," Gitel said. "Then my sister sent him for the doctor. We knew there was trouble. I'm sorry I scared you."

"She was the prettiest child, Gitel. Her golden hair shone and she learned so fast. I wished for a little sister like her. It was as if every part of her spoke, even her skin."

"She had everything, my little girl, but *mazel.*"

Halina stopped, sure that asking anything else about the child or her whereabouts would be hurtful. Gitel lost in reverie stared past the young woman. This time had to be different she prayed. The one thing she knew she could do was move and take action. Whatever they could to be free had to be done. *There is no other way to save this child.* "Let's go," she said, "we have work to do."

They walked to the center of the town and Gitel slowed her pace. "That's the place I heard the Nazis shoved your family and the others who were left," Gitel said. She pointed to the market square where the last of the Jews in Ksiaz Wielki had been assembled that early November morning.

"Yes," Halina said. "You and your people had already left. But Father refused to believe how terrible our trouble was until we got to Belzec."

"Hubner told Aron Devoire Ita was brought to that spot the morning the savages shot her. If that woman didn't wanted to keep her, why did she take her in the first place he told Aron. He's still here, Hubner, that monster. A fine citizen of Poland again."

Halina covered her mouth. "I don't know how we are able to accept such things. I wonder who am I now? There are parts of me that I don't recognize or feel."

"A big piece of me is buried with my little girl."

"If I'm alive," Halina said, "why me and not my brothers?"

"We live from one moment to another, child. I try to make myself think only of what lies ahead and how to move in that direction. But sometimes I need to relive the pain because with it, there is also the memory of the joy I once felt. Come, Halina, we need to find a horse and wagon and a driver so we can get to Miechow."

"You know I how got here from Miechow? I gave the driver one of the two candlesticks I had hidden. My *bubbe* used those candlesticks every Friday night. Father shoved them into my hands before he told me to get out if I could. That was the last time I saw him. I have one candle stick and the spice box left, both good silver."

"You'll need those for your dowry," Gitel winked at her.

Halina blushed, but both women knew the man who had caused the rich pink glow.

CHAPTER THIRTY-THREE

Miechow to Sosnowiec

Getting to Miechow was the first step to severing tethers from a homeland soaked with their blood. Though the decision to leave Ksiaz Wielki and Poland was agreed upon, they had to execute the plan. Leaving was filled with risk, devouring stability they had worked to recreate. At least the summer months ahead would not be as difficult for travel. Aron, Gitel and Mordche had lived in the woods and if they were forced to do so again, as long as they had food, some money and could pass as Poles, their chances improved. Mordche's first lucky endeavor, the kerosene, had been profitable. The fuel scarcity had led to many sales. Then he had begun trading with salt and cigarettes. They would carry items like cigarette papers that appealed to men, but the best was *zlotys* in their pockets. The plan would be to trade, as needed, and hold back the currency as long as possible.

Transportation to Miechow fell upon Gitel and Halina, the group reasoning it might be advantageous for the women to negotiate. It had not rained for weeks and they walked along the Krakow-Warsaw Highway dust clouds rising beneath their feet. They were passed by wagons, and from time to time a car bumped by. Men hammered fence posts along a field planted with rows of corn. Bursts of delicate silks signaled the harvest was near. A scarred landscape softened with forgiving meadow grasses offered a vision reminiscent of any dry summer's end.

The message of hunger gurgled and Gitel knew the call for food was not hers alone. She faced the future not fearful for herself but with the life she was entrusted. The loss of Devoire Ita was as raw as the moment she learned it. *We have to find a way. Nothing will ever be the same, yet if this child does not survive I may not be able to bear the loss.*

Gitel carried bread and pieces of river carp she had saved from their last Sabbath. They left the road, the shade of trees heavy with pinecones promising relief. Repetitive waves of locust song strafed the air and enveloped them with invisible musicians. Halina made a fan of ferns and opened the buttons of her checked blouse. She settled next to Gitel.

Fallen needles blanketed the forest floor beneath the green canopy. They leaned against the trunk of a large pine, "I love this," she said. Gitel rubbed the pine needles between her fingers and inhaled the invigorating scent. "It reminds me of Giebultow. The woods around our house were thick with trees. We saved the cones to burn in the winter."

"You made use of everything," Halina said. "It was different in Ksiaz Wielki where I grew up, more like a city. My parents and I…" She stopped and sat reconstructing her own world.

"My mother liked how the house smelled and I liked seeing the chimney puff when I ran through the snow to the dairy."

On the road, they stopped near a wagon and watched a man load sacks. He swayed another onto the wagon bed and arched his eyebrows at the two women approaching. He pulled a limp handkerchief from a pant pocket and his rolled up sleeves revealed strong browned arms covered with matted hair.

"Hot day," he said smiling. He wiped sweat from the back of his leathery neck.

"In August, we have days like this," Gitel said smoothing back moist hairs about her face, "but in January we miss it. My father always said he wished there was a way to save the summer heat for the bitter months of cold."

"A good trick if it could be done," the man said. He picked up another sack and tossed it on top of the others.

"I see you are busy with this work," Gitel said, "but my sister and I are looking to hire a driver with a horse and wagon."

Halina's eyes widened with appreciation. Gitel was wasting no time and took command as she often did. She smiled at her protector and stepped closer when she heard Gitel utter the word sister.

"I have to drive these sacks of fresh hay back. You see all this land?" he said his voice elevated in deference. "He used to own farther than you could see. I work all my life for him, Count Dzianat. His horses wait for me. They get better care than my children."

Gitel imagined the Count and the son who had refused to acknowledge a mere Jewess. She did not reveal that her father had been dependent upon the same nobleman, and she wondered how far the Count's holdings had extended or how many lives he had impacted. "He must be rich and powerful," Gitel said.

"Yes, but with the war over and the Russians in power again, he's worried what he has left will soon be taken. Most of his horses got stolen by the Germans," the man said. "He's lucky he was able to come back. Most of the nobles fled for good or were killed. He has little land and the big house left. I myself am worried about the future. At least we're rid of the Nazis and the whole lot of the vermin."

"Of course, there are always benefits we can be thankful for," Gitel said reaching her arm around Halina. What vermin she could imagine. She would be extra cautious.

"Our parents were driven from their home in Miechow," Halina said.

"Yes," Gitel said, "we've been searching everywhere for them. With heavy hearts my young sister and I give up our search. We have to go back without them."

He patted the horse and swiped at his face with the rag. "I've heard of plenty good Polish girls who lost their homes and families like you. The times are bad for us. Still too hard," he said lifting the last sack onto the wagon, its contents opening up spilling out fresh hay. "*Spzak kref,*" he cursed under his breath. "For the right number of *zlotys*, I could be persuaded to be your driver."

Gitel seeing an opportunity began gathering the loose hay to stuff back in the open bag. "Maybe your horse would like a handful," she said looking at the mare, rivulets of sweat running down her muscled flanks.

"Go ahead give her some. It's the special kind he grows for the horses he has left. He checks everything. I don't think he'll miss a handful of hay. His Arabians don't eat so much. They say the Count's eyes are everywhere. The rich are more tight with their fists than the poor," he said squeezing a palm over his hand.

Gitel knew it was time to make the deal for the horse and wagon. "I want to make a fair price with you but I have no experience to figure such things. I'm a plain country girl. What do you think to charge us for a ride to Miechow?" She stepped in front of the horse and held out the hay. Nibbling hay from Gitel's hand, the mare chewed, saliva foaming about her gentle purple lips.

"Let me see," he said, squinting at the haze as if he calculated a complicated mathematical formula. "It is more than ten kilometers from here. Ten *zlotys*."

"Oh." Gitel picked remaining hay stuck to her fingers. "So much," she exhaled. "We have to go back to Ksiaz which is even closer to Miechow than where we stand now. We found a place to rest there for the night and left our few belongings, too exhausted to carry our things as even today we searched for our family." She paused to stroke the horse's mane and added, "and consider, you are taking us only one way."

"So what do you think," the man said, "if we say seven *zlotys*? I don't go until I finish with the Count. Getting on his wrong side is bad but his sons are worse. I can tell you the older one is no good to any of us. We do the work and he complains. In two days, I can take you. Thursday morning."

Knowing that she would have to contend with the revelation there were two additional passengers, Gitel knew not to jeopardize her good fortune. "Well, if that is what you think is fair then we have no choice but to accept," she said. Can you come early in the morning so the heat will not be too much on your horse?"

"Early is better," the man said, satisfied that he had bested two countrywomen. He had held back that he had business in Miechow, the county seat, for his employer. "Where do I meet you?" He added, "I am Franz. What are your names?"

"Please pardon us, *Pan*. It is so hard to trust these days. I am Guccia and my sister is Halinka," Gitel said.

"I think a good place to meet us is by the old forge," Halina said. "It will be easy for you, *Pan*. You know Ksiaz Wielki if you work for the Count. That way we will be near the highway and closer for you." Halina gave him a big smile and he stared at her young, pretty face with obvious interest even if he was married.

"A good idea," Gitel said nodding at Halina. "So much more convenient for *Pan* Franz."

"I know the forge. I took wagons to Slomynsk, a good craftsman. He made shoes for the Count's horses himself. How do I know you will be there, at the forge, as you say, and not waste my time?"

How do I know you will come? "I will give you the only money I carry. Two sisters alone cannot be too careful," Gitel said, taking out a *zloty* from her pocket and handing it to the man, whose canny, sweaty face creased into a smile.

"The rest you'll pay when we get to Miechow, yes?" he said, not taking his eyes from Halina.

The two women nodded and smiled at Franz, the hard working Pole still under the thumb of a *shlachta*.

"Now I know we have a deal," he lifted his leg over the bridge of the wagon and settled into the seat. The horse looked back at him. The man released the pole brake, picked up the reins, and the wagon moved into the middle of the road.

"Thursday," Gitel said waving at the man.

"Thank you, *Pan, dzień dobry*," Halina said sighing with relief.

With two days before the departure, they worked together almost without sleep. Gitel traded for eggs and flour and spent the days and most of the nights baking bread and cooking. August heat made it impossible for them to keep milk and so with the last of it she made buttermilk, a luxury they all insisted was for her alone, for the teeth tightening in her mouth and of the new life they were all taking ownership. It was unlike Gitel to obsess. But she was plagued with worry over this pregnancy.

"How many breads are you making?" Aron said. "Are you starting a bakery, Gitel? I thought that was Halina's business."

"Aron, those three are for trading and eating," she said pointing to elongated breads. The ones I have marked on the bottoms, you see the marks? Into those I baked our money. With them we have to be very careful." But unlike the Poles, who revered bread so much they marked the bottoms with crosses, Gitel made little half moons on three so when the time came, she could identify the ones baked with the money.

"Where you get those ideas, I don't know. But I kiss you a thousand times," Aron said grabbing Gitel and pressing his lips to her forehead powdered with coarse rye flour.

"I must tell Mordche when he gets back," Halina said.

"He knows, Halina. I baked some of his money already."

"So that's why you asked for my money." Aron winked. "I thought it was for the silk stockings you never got."

Gitel shook her head and mouthed the word men. "All of us must know which breads to use first. I baked forty zlotys into each marked one. This way if anyone tries to rob us, maybe we can still get away with the money breads."

"We'll have to eat them sometime," Aron said. "But until we do, I think the best place for the money will be in your sack, Gitel. You are worth ten thousand *zlotys*."

"Is that all?" Gitel wiped the last of the flour from her beaming face.

Wednesday they sat together late into the night their bundles by the door. They were leaving the few things they had accumulated without offering them to anyone, just as they had done before they had gone into hiding. The departure was a secret. Eventually someone would discover the shelter they had fashioned. Perhaps Slomynsk might view what they had done as an improvement. A makeshift oven was connected, the dirt floor even, the window clean, a piece of burlap material nailed over it for privacy. The straw beds would remain, along with the crude chairs Aron and Mordche had nailed from discards.

A pale horizon lifted the night sky and early morning dew cooled the air. It was eight months since Vladyk had stomped on the boards over the bunker and yelled you are free. Again there was uncertainty but they wished this to be the last of Ksiaz Wielki. Aron and Mordche stepped out of the shack each holding a bucket. Mordche took the night waste bucket to the woods. There no longer would be a reason to retrieve it. With an empty bucket in his hand Aron headed in the same direction as the early risers.

He passed the old synagogue. There were no pigeons pecking at the cobblestones. The birds used to wait for those fortifying their souls each morning before beginning a new day. Afterwards the men threw a few breadcrumbs. The pigeons bobbed up and down. The dominant ones fluffed neck feathers to win their prizes and pushed the weaker to wait, sometimes for nothing. Aron slowed down near the alleyway where his parents had lived and emptiness invaded his core. How would he be able to reconcile all the loss? His small flock of pigeons had lived on the roof of the ramshackle house and their coos had given him happiness. The church, prominent in the square overlooking the town, knotted his mind into strands of discordant thought. *It was religion that caused so much trouble. Was it worth the misery? Maybe there should be just one religion or maybe none.* But what he had been born into resonated. It held him up and still defined his life. So much of what he had experienced as a youth, culminated with the last years of desperation - because of what he was. Why were beliefs so confounding that it made him and his people into the other, rejected, something to be shunned, feared or reviled? He struggled over the existence of a God who seemed impotent against evil.

Those who had no running water in their houses continued this primitive but necessary task of filling their vessels at the town well. There was as little conversation this day as in the past few months. Aron waited to fill his bucket. A woman wearing a bright flowered kerchief peered at

Aron with open distaste. Each filled buckets, turned away and left. But this Thursday Aron's steps were lighter. He headed back toward the shack carrying water to refresh and fill bottles for the ride. Whether these Poles talked or not no longer made a difference. He wanted to say farewell to Doctor Yoblosnski. But knew it would be unwise and so he headed home. Home, he mused. This land had not been a welcome home for many years. He would be happy not to face eyes that shot contempt.

Gitel and Halina stood by the door when he returned. Gitel's arms were folded under her chest and Aron noticed more fullness, her shape softening. "Where is Mordche?" he said. "Is he hiding?"

"It's not a joke, Aron," Gitel said. "The driver is not here yet and we haven't agreed on what to tell him when he sees the two of you."

"If he gets here," Aron said putting the bucket inside. "Oh, there is our nobleman. Your brother relaxes in his castle." He began filling small bottles with water.

"You're in a very fine mood this morning, my husband," Gitel said. "But when the driver sees you it may not be so funny."

Mordche stood staggering in drunken mockery. "I say we tell him you found us last night, two handsome men and you can't live without us."

"What do you think of that?" Aron said putting his arms around Gitel.

"I think you're both a couple of fools," Gitel said pretending to slap her husband's hands. "You think the man would be so stupid to believe such a thing?"

Halina watched Mordche perform his antics. "He's a man, why not?" She giggled, her trill filling the shack.

"I think we should say you were looking for work, finding nothing, you were leaving and saw us by chance waiting with our things. We told you of our plans to go to Miechow and since it is a big town you want to go and try your luck there," Gitel said.

"What if he argues the wagon is too small?" Aron asked.

"We watched him load one sack after another of hay into the wagon, full up to the top. If the horse could pull such a load then I'll remind him. Mordche, you'll *hondle* with him if he argues," Gitel said.

"Mordche, let's move away from the shack after we wash up. It's almost half-past six. If he shows up it will be soon," Aron said.

With a last look inside the shack they had called home, they closed the door and moved their bundles out. The two couples stood together rehearsing and then the men moved their things away to support the story. Halina stared up the street to where her parents' house stood. She could not see it from this end of the road but the thought stung. "It's my house," she said angered over all the unfairness. "What right do they have to it? My honorable parents worked hard. They earned it. It should be mine now."

Soon a horse's rhythmic clopping could be heard on the compacted dirt road. Through a brown haze a man sitting atop the wagon seat, reins in hands came into view. The mare slowed her pace, her tan hide moist.

"It's him," Gitel said picking up a bundle with the money breads. "Don't forget our story. Halina, please stop crying." Beads of sweat formed on Gitel's upper lip.

"You just get her under control," Aron said, standing like a ready soldier, his bag of tools by his feet, a symbol of what had enabled him to defend his life and his wife's. "Mordche and I know what to say."

Franz stopped the wagon and jumped down his boots encrusted from work in the barn.

"What is going on here?" he said looking at Halina but pointing to the men. "What are they doing here? Are they making her cry?" He stuck out an accusatory finger at the men.

"No and yes," Gitel said. "The tall one reminded her of her husband. He was killed fighting for our Home Army. So tall and brave. He was my favorite brother-in-law, may he rest in peace." She crossed herself the way she had seen her Polish girlfriends do. "Left a widow and at such a young age."

238

Halina wiped tears, her shoulders shaking not from the sorrow and anger she had felt moments before, but from mirth over Gitel's telling. "*Pan* Franz, they are fine men, only looking for work. They saw us with our things and want to leave this place for better opportunity. Guccia told them of our arrangement." She wiped her cheeks and turned away trying to regain composure.

"You don't mean they want to come to Miechow in my wagon?" Franz said. "No, that is not possible."

As they had agreed, it would be Mordche who would negotiate if need be, he stepped forward, shaking his head. "I can understand why you would be unsure about what to do. The nice ladies told my friend and me they were waiting for you, a good man."

"Don't try that good man business with me," Franz said.

"The younger one is still mourning her man, her husband who resembled me. I mourn for my homeland. We two were soldiers. My friend here was captured by the Germans and escaped. He shot plenty of the sons of bitches. Please, pardon my rough talk, ladies," he said with a face that could not have been more earnest.

Franz looked at Aron. He had been a soldier too. Most men had been. He got into the seat and sat behind the horse without a word.

"We met them less than half an hour ago," Gitel said. She released the bundle between her legs and Aron got in front of it. "They risked their lives for us, for our Polish people, may we grow strong again. Come, Halinka, let me help you up. Everything will be better in Miechow. Stop crying."

Mordche watched as Halina climbed into the back of the wagon and settled herself next to the burlap sack she carried. "What can I offer you to take us? My friend and I have made so little," he said.

"One odd job after the other around here," Aron said. "We have no wagon, no fine horse like yours."

"What do you have?" Franz said leaning toward the horse to inspect her fine qualities.

239

Gitel had no intention of getting in until she was sure Aron and Mordche were coming. She stepped back to where the bundle sat and straddled it aware she was protecting most of their fortune. "You, the tall one," she said, nodding to Mordche, "what can you offer this good man, Franz, who has kept his word?"

Mordche dug deep into his pocket and took out cigarette papers. Aron reached into his boot and removed five zlotys. He slapped the money into Mordche's palm. "It's all I have," Aron said. "I almost give my life for my countrymen and this is all I'm worth."

Franz, seeing his deal enhanced from his original quote, said without further hesitation, "For our beloved Poland."

The ride to Miechow took longer than they imagined. Franz let the horse go at her own pace, slow. Mordche sat next to Franz. "Why should you waste your time?" he said. "Wake up that horse." Aron was in the back with access to his tools should the unforeseen happen. But Franz was master, held the reins loose and did what he wished. Quite enamored of Halina, her looks the epitome of fresh Polish beauty, the news she was a widow made him even less anxious to part from her.

They encountered wagons and were passed by trucks en route south to Miechow. There were long stretches of road between towns where it was more barren, dry and hot, the trees stricken motionless. There was no conversation amongst them as silence was the best protector against misspoken words. Franz warned as they neared the town they would find Jews had returned to Miechow. By late morning they arrived to a scene they were not expecting. Franz dropped them near the railroad station and the couples watched the wagon drive away.

There was visible commerce. The shop doors were flung open against the heat to entice passersby with luxuries most had not seen or touched in almost a decade. Everything from fruit to pieces of fine furniture could be bought for a price. Though Polish was predominant, a Yiddish word escaped here and there.

Jews owned a shop or two and though Mordche eyed possible opportunity here, he knew full well it would not be viable. Halina held his arm, her heart opening. Aron did not waver in his thinking. Nor could he distance himself from the recent murder of his brother. Yankel danced before his eyes, pulsating with life. Gitel had lived the beauty of motherhood and the unspoken horror of the birth in Swiecie. If she lost this child the part of her that could yet feel was in danger of being eradicated.

They melded into the chattering crowd, moving toward the station platform and milled about. "Excuse me, sir," Aron said to a man passing, "where do we buy train tickets?'

"No one buys. No one sells tickets. If you can get on the train, you go," he said, the abundant clothing he wore on this hot day appeared not to affect him.

"You mean people just get on and no one checks?" Gitel said. "What about documents?"

"Who has documents?" He hurried away to board. They counted twenty cars, all of which looked packed; windows open, some faces peering out with blank expressions, others with eyes closed perhaps dreaming of reunions with loved ones.

"Please *Pan*, which train goes to Sosnowiec?" Mordche asked another traveler holding a crate of hens, his weight unsteady on the metal steps of a car blocked by passengers pushing.

"They all go," he called out, his voice straining against clucking, imprisoned fowl. The load and he were shoved into the car.

A shrill whistle blew and blasts of steam concealed the locomotive at the front of the platform. Those who had not gotten on began scattering in all directions. There were arguments over seats through the open windows. A conductor cursed as he tried to close a door and shouted at passengers standing on the steps unable to board.

Aron grabbed Gitel's arm. She was already running through the throng of people searching for cars where steps were not blocked, her arms securing the bundle. She maneuvered her body to avoid the crush against her most precious load.

"Here," shouted Mordche. "Aron, Gitel, here!"

Up ahead they spotted him, his head above the crowds. They forced their way through. Halina clutched Mordche's sleeve, doing her best to stay with him. Mordche shoved past four more cars packed with people. He jumped on the stairs of the next, dragging Halina behind him and lifted her into the packed car. "Hurry," he yelled back to Aron and Gitel. He blocked the entrance to the car and the locomotive bellowed a huge steam blast into the air. The train whistled and jerked forward, couplings banging, sparks flying. It inched out of the squalid station. The train was leaving behind those too weak to outwit the more aggressive.

Aron ran to stay with the moving cars, the tool bag crushed against his side. He grabbed Gitel's hand, a step behind him. He pulled her forward. The bread bundle tight under her arm, she reached up to Mordche. He hoisted her onto the steps. "You're more solid than I thought," he said his arm around his sister.

"Aron, faster," Mordche yelled. Aron struggled to keep his balance, fifty kilos of tools weighing him down. With a quick glance at Gitel's anxious face he grasped the step rail and jumped on the train gaining speed. Aron fell over the tool bag as Mordche pulled him into the car. They were on, breathless and unsure how they had all made it. With no place to sit they held on to one another, eyes wide with relief they were together.

They were one step further. To what was the question?

CHAPTER THIRTY-FOUR

The Opera Hall

The conductor, a scrawny Pole with a permanent look of surprise, shouted at the rowdy passengers and pushed through the impassible aisles. A soggy navy uniform clung to his body and beneath the matching wilted cap his unshaven his cheeks huffed. He would eject anyone who stood between cars he threatened. "Rabble without tickets, leeches," he seethed and excoriated. "Let him kiss our Polish asses," a passenger shouted. The wheels spun and continued on their mission to return Poles to their hometowns or Jews to wherever they could find safety.

The train moved at a steady pace through towns too insignificant to warrant a stop. Until it broke down. Inadequate repairs had been made on the bombed tracks. There was no way to judge how long they could remain stuck.

"Look how packed the train is, Gitel. We're not the only ones trying to figure a way out. Maybe I should beg someone seated to give up a seat so you can rest?" Aron pled.

"Never mind, I'm better off than some of those around me. I feel sorry for them."

"Do you always have to play the strong one?" Aron said, exasperated at his wife's refusal to at least try to take advantage of her condition.

"Because." She said in a voice only meant for Aron. "Sitting will not help." To Mordche and Halina she pantomimed with her fingers, who wants a piece of bread, a smile lifting cheekbones, defining what were becoming good looks.

"You know what I want," Aron said his lips tightening, "I want a wife who has a little mercy on herself. There has to be a limit, Gitel."

"Here," she said, tearing pieces of bread, aware of the loaves hidden beneath the down cover. "You'll be better off with something in your mouth."

Aron said nothing more as he chewed. Gitel passed bread to Mordche and Halina. Since she was seven years old she'd been kicking up her heels like the spirited runaway calf Aron had once seen his father-in-law to be trying to corral. What a moment it had been, Wolf, his *tzitzit*, the ritual tassels flying about his waist, stamping his feet pretending fury as the calf slipped through his big stride and powerful grip, the geese in the yard honking and beating their wings.

Finally the train moved. Aron would make sure Gitel got some rest. It was not her judgment he doubted or that she showed bravado. But they both knew what was at stake. Wolf 'Giebultow's daughter had learned how vulnerable and uncertain the world could be. Aron trusted she would fight with her last strength and profound faith even if his had been damaged.

They dared to speak hushed Yiddish in a public place. For the first time in years Yiddish, their mother tongue repressed and whispered, was flowing from passengers like the waters of a gentle lake licking a shallow protected cove. Yiddish, the vernacular of a people in tiny villages or the grand cities of Europe, with its color and plaintive expressions, the language that bound Jews to their own culture. It was a root that grew beneath a dispersed people always considered the other. It flourished as if it grew on a massive ancient oak, the fresh shoots of words sprouting and absorbing the dominant cultures into the trunk that supported their lives.

The train traveled due west and made its first stop in Wolbrum. Confusion ensued as the passengers pushed to get off, the remaining, jockeying for better positions before the crush of the next wave. The four held onto their territory in the car. It was close to the door, which remained open despite warnings and provided some air circulation. As new passengers shoved aboard Mordche was an immovable boulder, buffering Halina and Gitel from bags and elbows fighting to infringe. Aron stood like a soldier, his heavy bag of tools a natural defensive border. Once again the train conductor yelled out commands. The train left the station, smoke from the locomotive billowing from the stack, the steam bathing them with sweat. They glimpsed the last of Wolbrum, a flat plain of unending wheat fields on one side, a once busy town with a white church steeple vanishing on the other.

Just before six in the evening the train stopped at the Sosnowiec railroad station. The riders pushed off the train onto the platform. Minutes later the station was packed with crumpled people and twined packages. The train belched the last of its steam, the din dissipated and the service ended for the night. Mordche, who had travelled to Sosnowiec by wagon on many Thursdays, knew the town. Aron had lived in Sosnowiec for several years while he became a master shoemaker and his business began to flourish. He hoped it would be like coming home to an old friend. The crowds pushed into the nearby streets and scattered. The four stood on the street, spent.

"Sir, do you know where we can find a Jewish refugee organization, the American Joint I think they call it?" Aron asked a man, who had disembarked along with them. He had lifted the brim of his dark fedora as he rushed from the platform. Aron spied the skullcap beneath. It had marked the man as a religious Jew.

"You looked like one of them, a Polack. I saw you on the train and thought, already his woman is having another little anti-Semite. I'm going there myself," he said. "She's a Jew, your woman?"

What have I gotten into? Aron smiled. "I worked here. If you know the name of the street, we'll be able to find it. Even give you directions if you need. Yes, she's the real item."

"You must know the market square then," he said, impatient to be on his way. "I'm told it's in a fancy concert building behind the police station.

They give temporary housing. Let's hope the Polish police don't bother protecting us, you understand what I'm saying?"

Aron nodded his thanks. "Let's hope," he said. "You can follow us. I know the way." *What a sour little man. Maybe he was deranged by his horror. So my wife looks like a shiksa...*

"Lead, Aron," Mordche said. "We better move fast. From what I see a hundred of our people will be searching for the same place." He took Halina's arm.

They went to the market square. Even late in the day men and women still strolled about. Life was returning. Children's voices added a pitched lightness and rapid Polish rang in the heart of the city. Aron knew that three years before Sosnowiec had more than twenty thousand Jews among its one hundred thousand inhabitants. The city was known for heavy industry, mining and numerous businesses but he would soon learn that less than two hundred of its Jews had survived. Sosnowiec was a hub for the remnants like him, Gitel, Mordche and Halina. Once its railroad was a mecca for trade. Now it was a transit stop, a way out of Poland to anywhere else.

"This is Guiezdna Street, the main market square," Mordche said to Halina. My father brought our wagon to that end, where you see the empty stables. We stopped there to give water to the horse, give him oats. We carried the sacks with cheeses on our backs almost to the same spot we stand on, each week. Imagine my father carrying a huge sack like a bag of feathers."

Aron was tired and impatient. One thing was on his mind. And it was not to reminisce about Sosnowiec. "You were in a hurry, Mordche. Are we going or are we gossiping? We'll talk later. Gitel, is your brother turning into a *yenta*?"

They found where the Jewish Joint Distribution Committee was headquartered. A long line of people waited to mount the steps of the former concert hall, a structure that yet retained some of its former grandeur.

"Right here, Jan Kiepura the 'Lad from Sosnowiec' performed," someone was saying.

"His magnificent tenor soared in the best opera house of Vienna," another refuge added. "His mother was a Jew, a violinist, his father was a Polish baker."

"Did you hear that?" Gitel whispered to Halina. "His father was a baker." Gitel had no knowledge about this famous Pole. Halina thought about her own father, a devout man. A baker. Aron had never stepped into an opera house in his life but had listened to opera music on a radio or at a movie. He stood and hummed a tune he had heard the great Caruso sing. He had no idea from what opera only that he liked the music and never had forgotten the melody. Massive carved wood doors were propped open with cinder blocks, the odor of humans packed together pungent in the heated night air. They inched up the steps, each one damaged or missing a marble saddle altogether.

An administrator sat at a table near the door, the constant buzz an overcrowded hive in disarray with angry worker bees amassing. He explained to those within earshot that first they would have to register as refugees. He would search his lists for their names. If he could find their names, he droned on, they would have priority to stay. He made clear this housing was temporary.

"Please sir," Aron said when it was his turn. "I don't have to tell you what we went through. I'm sure you hear plenty. Those of us who were able to hold on to our lives, we each have ten stories. But my wife is pregnant. Do you know what that means?"

"I can only do what I can do. I don't see you on any concentration camp lists. You'll have to wait." He shuffled papers. He pushed up a soggy shirtsleeve. He looked around the hall at the mass of mislaid humanity amid hundreds of bundles strewn across the buckled wood floor, cots wedged together in the provisional barracks of the once famous concert hall. His mind did not want to absorb more.

After giving the administrator the required information, Aron repeated with intensity. "Sir, do you know what that means?"

247

"Yes." He stared at Aron. Then he focused on Gitel's belly. A hint of color rose on the pasty complexion in need of revival. "No woman has come here pregnant so far. You are an unusual case. I'll make room for the two of you. Bring your things to this block." He crossed out two spaces on the diagram and pointed Aron to the tall windows on the right side.

"We are a family," Gitel said. "This is my brother and we've been together during this whole hell. That's his wife." She pointed to Halina. "You'll find her on a list. I won't be separated from them now. When we have our place, I'll remember your help, sir. Would you accept a piece of our good, fresh bread?"

Smiling, he found Halina's name and threw an admiring but dubious look at Mordche.

"If bread doesn't interest you, maybe something else?" Mordche added to sweeten the pot.

The man smiled. "You will have to find cots from another block and move them. You all say you're married." He shook his head, doubt stretching his lips again. "Don't come back to me if you can't find any cots. You'll have to negotiate with them." He pointed a stub of a pencil at men and women with clothes in tatters and faces to match.

Halina waited with Gitel in the block they were assigned. The men made their way around the room disturbing disgruntled remnants. They found cots, spares stacked beneath others, the hoarders did not want to part with. Mordche and Aron were persuasive, as two cigarettes were all that was needed to free the cots.

"So, when was the wedding?" Mordche asked Gitel.

"Listen, did it help us stay together? For now I have nothing else to say," she said. Halina smiled at her best advocate.

"My darling, it was your beautiful belly that did it," Aron grinned.

They squeezed together four cots and began bedding down for the night. The plumbing was far from adequate for the hundreds. Lines for the latrines snaked from the big doors back out to the street, the odor reminding Aron of his apprenticeship with Lech. A few bare bulbs swung from long chains and projected shadows on the walls. Myriad heads inched forward in slow motion, surreal images on broken plaster.

To her surprise, in the light of the swaying bare bulbs, Gitel spotted Max, a man from their town. He was bobbing about securing his territory for the night. Their eyes met, magnets for the familiar. Here in this place of bedraggled strangers there was a pull to what had once been home. But Max was from an opposite pole; one that Gitel sensed might repulse Aron.

Max stood, straightened his rumpled suit jacket and left the far side of the hall. He sidestepped over cots, shoved bundles, and ignited a few tempers before he got to Gitel. The men shook hands. They stood together as if reunited, warmer currents amid turbulent chill waters.

"Gitel, I knew it was you. We were on the same train," Max said. "Manya and I left early this morning. We too had a man drive us in a wagon to Miechow to catch the train to Sosnowiec. Look at this place. From one *gehenna*, to another."

"This is heaven, not hell, Max," Aron said. "Take in a good long breath, these are your people."

"My people need a bath." He gave a little laugh, amused with his cleverness. "In Ksiaz we watched you the last days, scurrying around. Manya noticed first and told me you were up to something. We plan to get married as soon as we can."

"This is good news, Max," Gitel said.

"Sit, sit, all of you," Max said. "A man, a woman alone. My wife was killed in Auschwitz. We all knew Manya's family. She doesn't know yet who has survived. Each day we discover something else we don't want to learn. We are a couple now. She's over there watching our things. A little nervous bird. You can't be too careful." He raised his two fingers and tried to get the attention of his woman, the little bird waiting on the other side in a temporary nest.

The reunited from Ksiaz Wielki continued their conversations.

The same story will be repeated a thousand times. Aron's mind fled elsewhere. *Wasn't that what had led to my brother to his death? If it hadn't been that would it have been something else. Who could blame this man for wanting warmth, a new life?* He looked at his Gitel. She carried their new life and he would watch over her. This time he vowed nothing would wrench away their future. And the thoughts led to Devoire Ita. She flashed before him and he could not stop. Scene, one after the other flickered and his leg jerked with his racing mind.

"What do you mean, scurrying around?" Aron said. "We were careful not to draw suspicion." Max stared at him and Aron felt the other eyes on him too. Had he missed some of their conversation? He had to calm down.

"To the others," Max said, "there were no hints. But to us, the tormented, the eyes tell a different story. Every movement of the body tells a different tale. We watched. Manya told me she thought Gitel was pregnant. Who knows how women sense these things. That's when we figured you were leaving. Believe me, we were afraid of the Poles every moment, just like you. And after what happened to Yankel, we had no choice but to follow what you were doing."

"Yankel," Aron said. "Who told you? We didn't say a word."

"We heard. Don't you think killing Yankel was a prize for them?"

Aron had never liked Max. He heard he had been connected with the Judenrat in Ksiaz Wielki, always wheedling to find advantages. Of all the good people he missed from his hometown this man, with his inflated self-worth because he had come from parents who owned the mill, was before him. Aron was sure he wanted something.

"Could this be Halina? I recognize you now. Your father bought flour from us. Such a fine man," Max said.

Halina shook her head. Her lips began to tremble.

"He's not among us anymore. Let's talk of other things, Max," Gitel said her hand on Halina's. "Manya knew what day we were leaving?"

"No, no," Max said. "This is a happy coincidence. Gitel, I know it's very late and I am embarrassed to ask such a thing but Manya is in pain with hunger. Even a little bird has to peck at something. She begged me to speak to you. She's not strong and practical like you."

Gitel reached for the bag. She was afraid to betray anything that would make Max think there was more than just bread she was protecting. She pretended to fumble about. She removed one of the plain breads, tore off a good size piece and handed it to Max. *Hunger is hunger. May I never have to be under someone's mercy or have to beg for food again.*

"We won't forget your kindness," he said to Gitel. "There are few people like you." He nodded to the others, tucked the bread into his jacket and stepped through the maze across to Manya. Gitel watched Max as she stowed her bag under the cot. The heat was unbearable and the noise in the open hall was filled with occasional laughter, arguments, and the low hum. A deep, hacking cough came from a man close by.

"I know how generous you are, my wife," Aron said with a gentle touch to her cheek. "But please remember, we don't have a fortune. You just learned a lesson, people are always watching. Sleep. You need rest for two."

Halina slept. Mordche turned his head away and drifted off.

They had made it to Sosnowiec. The day, filled with unknowns, had ended better than expected. They needed rest to fortify for what was next. No one knew what lie ahead only that they had to stay together. A family.

Gitel whispered to Aron before closing her eyes to the day, "You're right. We have to watch every step we take." She placed her hand on her belly and once again felt the kick of life beneath her palm.

CHAPTER THIRTY-FIVE

The Price of Information

Morning lit the chipped plaster and peeled away hopes their problems were over. The refugees lay on the cots and stared at the ceiling. Their voices began to fill the hall. They picked through bundles for whatever they had to ease the lack of comforts. Lines of them assembled to leave through the doors flung open to the street. The administrator sat at his desk in the same shirt, creases on his face in concert with the worried ones waiting to be admitted.

"Where are you pushing?" A woman in line snarled, accustomed to commands and orders from uniformed guards eager to inflict pain for any perceived infraction.

"Each morning I tell you the same thing," the administrator said. He shuffled the lists on his desk with tobacco-stained fingers. "You have to wait your turn." The pay for this trouble barely fed his tobacco habit and he was desperate for a smoke.

"How many outhouses do you think there are in Sosnowiec?" Another waiting to leave said, losing her patience. "Go behind the building and walk to where the farmers used to leave their wagons. Find the woods."

A man nearby Gitel could not stop coughing. His frail body shuddered as he gasped for air. He held a rag over his mouth to contain the hacking. A young woman stood over him. Her hollow eyes spoke of sleepless nights, her shoulders bent with resignation. "He doesn't have long to wait till the next world," she wailed.

Halina volunteered to stay, the breads secure under her cot. Aron got up to join the line and Mordche followed. Gitel was glad she would leave the coughing. She dreaded the thought the sick man might have typhus. She had to protect her health. Strong, she smiled to herself. *Max said I was strong. Do I have a choice?*

Halina combed her long brown hair. "Mordche gave me a present." She turned the tortoise shell comb over in her hand and felt its sharp teeth.

"Watch over our things, Halina. I know you are a clever girl." Gitel squeezed by the sick man and stood behind Aron. *Presents. Presents can have many meanings.*

Two rows away, the hacking man was doubled over. "There is no such thing as dying in peace," Aron said rubbing the grime accumulated on his cheeks. "If only we had a little water to splash on our faces."

"Let's think of life," she said. Gitel scanned the hall with the array of misery. "You are handsome, dirt or no dirt. I better look out for all the women hunting for husbands here. There are plenty who are."

They moved closer to the door. In the light of day, the lost souls hanging on were a terrible realization. Only months before, most of the refugees packed into the hall, had been prisoners in concentration camps. They were the ones who by luck, circumstance or will had found a way. Weak from imprisonment and the loss of family, damaged in body and mind, they were here. They could not yet speak of what had happened to them in Treblinka, Dachau and Sobibor, Mauthausen or Auschwitz. Or Chelmo or Buchenwald, all death factories. Their bared arms revealed blue tattoos. Actuarial tables had been designed by diabolical minds, proud of what they planned to achieve. Selves obliterated, they had been more machine than man. They were numbers, placeholders with calculated life spans based on minimum calories to achieve maximum labor until…

A woman reeled near the door, her hair wild, thick torn stockings twisted about her ankles. She cried again and again, "Why me? I lived for this? Where is my sister? She was the smart one, the pretty one. Look what's left. Look at you all. Who wants us?"

"Shut up!" A man on a nearby cot with skin so thin his bones poked through rose. "You rotted potato. You stink up the whole cellar and spoil what's left. March back to Birkenau. The Nazis will take care of you."

Silence fell over the wretched hall. Eyes shifted to the grand windows hooded by the heavy velvet drapes. Their rich maroon folds were hidden beneath layers of dust and held in place by frayed gold tassels. Outside birds fluttered free from debate, free to perch on maple trees and be off again.

"We have to find a way out of here fast," Mordche said stepping onto the street, searching for something familiar to regain his bearings. "The conditions in there are very bad."

"In the meantime, I'm hungry. My belly is not that big yet, but the women are staring." Is *it out of pity or envy?* Gitel pulled out the bread she had hidden beneath her blouse.

"Take a little extra for yourself, you need it," Aron said, pushing back the larger piece of bread she held out to him.

"Look at you," she laughed, "so fat we may have to let your pants out. I left Halina a nice piece and told her to watch over the things. I'll talk to the administrator as soon as we get back. Bread may buy us information. Let's hurry. The poor girl has to go, too."

"Now I see where we are," Mordche said his aquiline nose taking in the fresh air. They walked back toward the town square, passing early market shoppers searching for goods. Poles manned the remaining stalls. The Yiddish jargon absent, there were rents in the market cloth of the once vibrant patchwork stitched together for commerce.

"The air. This is what I needed," Aron said. "I was choking in that room. There's a stream nearby. We can wash and get water."

"I know the place. That's where we watered the horse," Mordche said. "He was smart. The horse knew the best water. Good, I see you brought the *sloyikahs* to fill."

They encountered others who like themselves could not tolerate the crowds waiting to use the latrines in the morning or the fights over rations in the evening. Chatter came from congregating groups. Camaraderie was a balm for the remnants.

"Let's cut into the forest over here," Aron said. "Come, we'll beat the crowd."

The thick woods offered both shade and privacy. Aron led them to the stream. He sat on the forest floor, removed his shoes and socks, and motioned to Gitel to do the same. "If I could go into the river for a swim, I'd be a happy man," he said, throwing back his head of dark waves.

"So stay and go in," Gitel said. "You have something better to do?"

"Gitel," Aron said, "you are an angel. It's Friday, we'll pretend it's your *mikvah*."

"A *mikvah* is not a conversation for me," Mordche said looking away. "It's for married men."

"You have to hurry back to Halina anyway, Mordche. Not that I think you need convincing," Gitel said. "The girl will be relieved to see you."

The world of married women and the ritual *mikvah* for the Sabbath or any other purpose was not a topic Mordche wished to pursue. Perhaps his sister was going to weave Halina and her plan to marry him off into the *mikvah* conversation. He more than liked the young woman. If his sister was pushing him into being responsible, maybe he would let her. He waved to the two people with whom he had shared almost anything a human being was capable of or could withstand. Mordche turned and left. His big steps tramped over parched undergrowth and soon he was hidden among the trees.

"I think we scared Mordche. Men are shy when it comes to these things. I'll have to explain it to Halina," Gitel said. "She probably knows very little about what a *mikvah* means to a woman. When the time comes, I'll be like a mother." *For my dear child, I failed.*

"Never mind. Mordche doesn't act so anxious to get married. Let's see about my woman," Aron said beckoning Gitel to join him in the clear soothing stream.

"Come in the water. Are you scared, Gitel?" he said softly. *We don't know what will be, where it's safe. I mustn't fail.*

She did not answer. She remembered moments when nothing frightened her, when she was unaware of what cruelty lie ahead.

Aron removed his pants and shirt. Gitel hung his clothes on low-lying branches. She removed her skirt and pulled her blouse down to cover her belly. She waded into the water almost to her knees, splashing her face and arms, rubbing her pale skin.

"Come closer, Gitel," Aron said taking her hand. "I won't let you fall."

Aron put his arm around her shoulders. The stream was not deep but meandered, the end out of sight. He submerged then splashed about revived. As always, he could not take his eyes from her face. He waded to Gitel and embraced her to his bare, wet chest. Gitel pushed back his dripping wet curls and kissed him.

Up ahead they heard voices.

"We are not the only ones who need this," Aron said, leading Gitel to the bank of the stream. "I feel better. You're beginning to shine again. It's time to go back."

They had bathed, a brief pleasure to be treasured. "Tonight is Sabbath. There will be no place for us to be together."

"Hush Gitel. I just need you near me."

The man with the wretched cough died and the diseased body was removed. His clothing and valise were burned in the street before a relieved group of onlookers. They were afraid to go near the keening woman who was with him to the end. This older man had saved her life in Buchenwald. Now she was alone. Those around him were fearful of being infected by what had killed him and the woman was banished to a far corner of the hall. In the aftermath, Max and Manya moved closer to their hometown friends.

The beginning of September was so hot the people staggered about as if being tossed in a vessel on turbulent seas. Like the close quarters of a crowded hold, the air was laced with sickening sourness.

"How many more can the organization push into this place? A few people leave, even more come to replace them," Halina said wiping at the sweat on her upturned nose. She received an admiring glance from a young man waiting as she made her way past to the women's line.

"I really have to go," Gitel said one hand under her abdomen, a step in front of Halina. "The baby is running around this morning. Did you notice the man in the black vest, the way he looked at you?"

Halina's cheeks reddened. She averted her eyes. "Do you think it is a boy then?" Halina whispered to Gitel as they approached the open doors, flattered by the stares of the fine looking man in the vest.

"I don't know, Halina, I just pray to God it's a healthy child with a better life." Her mind went to the place Devoire Ita lived. The child's inquiring eyes searched Gitel's face for answers. "Let's be quick," Gitel said. She negotiated the broken marble steps. "I hope I can hold it all the way to the woods."

The sky thick with clouds promised relief. Pigeons sat on the red slate roof across the street. Anticipating the summer shower, their wings drooped at their sides and they were motionless. The men and women dragged their feet, the cobblestones grabbing at the soles of their shoes. Gitel and Halina blended into the street scene distancing themselves from the refugee hall like two Polish women in a hurry to get to whatever work they had been lucky to find.

"I wonder if I could buy leather for Aron," Gitel said. "Max is right. Aron has made it pretty good. Maybe I should look in the market. Most of them have shoes that are falling apart and after the first pair he fixed three weeks ago, he has a dozen waiting. If the opportunity comes to buy I will. It doesn't spoil. Oh, here it comes. The rain feels so good."

They hurried to the place near the stream the four of them had staked out as their own, the trees in full leaf giving shelter from the rain. Gitel and Halina filled two bottles with water from the stream. Rain pelted over the rocks by the bank and thunder cracked. Lightning slashed through the darkening sky. Halina grabbed Gitel's arm.

"I'm so frightened of lightning," Halina said. Her hands covered her face. She had many fears from years of being alone. Resourceful, but young, there was no one to rely on but herself. She had feared being exposed every moment she worked as a Polish servant girl. Halina had told Gitel she was terrified a Yiddish word escaping while she slept would be her end. She had told the German couple who agreed to let her work for them she was a farm girl whose parents had been killed. When they quizzed her about why her hands were so smooth, she lied and said her father had seen great promise in her, unlike her dull siblings. That he had insisted she be schooled and to prove it, she recited long poems in Polish she had memorized and showed them her exquisite penmanship on scraps of paper. Halina's hands were no longer as they once were, girl smooth.

Gitel gathered the bottles and stashed them in a sack. She grabbed Halina's hand. They started to run. "I'm not afraid of lightning, but I've seen enough trees blackened to know we have to get out of the forest as fast as we can."

"Gitel," Halina struggled, "you run faster than me." She ran alongside her protector, the woman who she was beginning to love. When they got to the road it was pouring, but safer. Cooled by warm summer rain they walked back arm in arm sloshing through the mud. Gitel had lost her sisters. Halina was becoming one.

* * * * *

Gitel spoke to the refugee administrator and parted with food. Nothing came of it. Aron suggested Mordche part with cigarette papers and that did not help. The weeks turned into the coming of Rosh Hashanah and then October's cooler weather began. They broke open one of the three breads with the money. In Sosnowiec food was available for a price as was information. Yet every tip led to a dead end. They agreed to invest the money they had earned in Ksiaz Wielki to sustain them and get out of Poland. What if they ran out of money? The Jewish organization was underfunded and on top of that the hall was more crowded as more streamed in from threatening hometowns. They learned there were camps for the displaced being set up in Germany by the Allies. These places were for the homeless war refugees, most of them Jews. But finding a way to get to the camps was up to them. Ten Jews had been shot and thirty stoned to death in Kielce. There was panic in the concert hall. The unfortunates had lived through their tortures and in the end lay murdered in the streets. It could happen in Sosnowiec.

The first week of November, Max said he overheard talk that would get them out. "I have news," he said, untying a shoe and taking a critical look at the sole.

"Let me see," Aron said reaching for the shoe.

"Is this one of your stories, Max?" Mordche said, in no mood for another piece of frustrating information.

"No, this news gets us out of here. All we need is money." Max raised an eyebrow for effect.

"Where is the money coming from?" Mordche said.

"Will you let him talk?" Gitel said.

"Good," said Aron. "After I fix your shoe, you can give me some of your money."

"Look, you've made plenty in this hell hole with your shoe business," Max said, chestnut eyes narrowing on Aron.

"Is it my fault you have no talent?" Aron said. He turned over Max's shoe. "When winter comes your feet will pay for this hole. Might as well pay me. And what, I made forty *zlotys* in two months from the rich *schlachta* here? A fortune, right?"

"Stop," Gitel said. "Max, tell me the news if they don't want to hear it." She and Aron exchanged imperceptible smiles in recognition of his industry.

"Didn't I tell you she's a smart woman, Manya," Max said squeezing Manya's hand. "First we have to get to Prague."

"And then?" Aron said, opening up his tool bag.

"Then we have to hire a guide and walk into Germany."

"Just like that. We walk into Germany. How far is it, Max? Did you ask? Maybe I'll make us *lederhosen*," Aron said.

"My husband has a mouth," Gitel said.

"My darling," Aron grinned. "Let him talk. Go on, Max."

"There are guides, reliable Czechs we can hire who will take us from Czechoslovakia into Germany. It's where the DP camps are. It's a long way."

Halina leaned forward. "I don't want to set foot in a camp. The word alone scares me. And what's DP?"

Max steamed. He had real facts and these people did not even have appreciation. "Look, DP is 'displaced persons'. That's what we are. You, and you." He jabbed his finger at each of them. "All of us. Me. What country wants us? Didn't the damn Poles just murder more Jews? What the Nazis didn't finish, they will."

"What's the distance, Max? I'll ask again," Aron said.

"It's about a hundred fifty kilometers." Max looked down at his bare foot, his face a map of uncertainty.

"What about Russia? Why not go there?" Mordche said.

Aron dropped the shoe and threw up his hands. "Their propaganda machine accuses us of being disloyal. You think the communists will let us in!" It's like the business with the Polish AK, loyal fighters and won't let go of the lies. They killed thirteen of our families in one shot. What do you think the Russians are going to do to the Poles? Love them? Just another reason to get out of Poland now while the Russian Bear gives the Poles a nice big hug. Not that they don't deserve it."

"Who does want us? The Russians liberated us. This whole business stinks," Mordche said. "Maybe we'll go to Palestine."

"Not so fast," Aron said. "We're still sitting on cots in Poland. Look, I've been nosing around too. Max has the right idea. I heard the best DPs are the American ones. The allies broke up Germany and Austria into zones. They say the British and French camps are bad and the Russians, you can imagine. The Russians treat us the worst. The longer we stay here, the more the American zones will fill up. We have no choice." He looked around the packed room. "These people aren't stupid. It's going to be a race."

They sat and tried to measure in their minds a hundred fifty kilometers and the number of foes they could encounter.

"All I know is I'm in my seventh month," Gitel said, matter of fact. But inside she churned. The great distance was daunting. And the longer they stayed in Poland the worse it could become.

"Oh, my God," Manya said. "Maybe you should stay here. How can you risk going pregnant?"

"She's going," Aron said.

"Manya, whatever, she'll have an easier time than you," Max said, wishing he could swallow it back.

"Let's get serious," Mordche said. "Can we trust the guides? How much and how soon can we get to Prague?"

"They're talking three hundred twenty zlotys. I figure if we take a few families with us it will cost us each less. They say we have to walk two, maybe even three days, through mountains, forests, who knows what. Don't forget, winter is coming."

"Max, stop," Aron said. "I'm not forgetting anything. Do you have money?"

"Right," Mordche said. "Where is all this money coming from? The more of us, the riskier. A big group will attract attention and slow us down. And Gitel—what about her condition?"

"Gitel is her father's daughter," Aron said. The woman he knew could run rings around most. But Mordche was right; his wife was in jeopardy no matter how brave she was willing to play. He nodded at his brother-in-law and covered for his wife. "Of anyone here, you know better."

"We each get busy and find out more. Don't worry. I'll get the money. I say if we can, we leave by the end of this week." Max got up. "I have to go for a smoke." His hands shook as he pulled Manya to her birdlike feet.

CHAPTER THIRTY-SIX

Another Wrinkle

Irst it was dry as sandpaper and now the deluge would not let up. Aron and Mordche waited for the women. What did women do that it took twice as long? As refreshing as the air was outside, the effect inside was the opposite. The floor was soaked and the hall was a stew of bodies and vapors.

Finally, there they were. Gitel and Halina returned from their morning toilet and dried themselves off with rag cloths that served as towels. They sat on a cot to eat with the men.

"Az mir est broit, veren de bachen roit," Aron said. "If one eats bread, one's cheeks glow red," enjoying the singsong Yiddish ditty.

Gitel reached into the bag. "I'm surprised you helped yourself to eat. Where's the other bread?"

"What do you mean, Gitel?" Mordche said. "We're waiting for you and Halina."

"What's wrong, Gitel? Are you all right?" Aron said. His wife's face had lost its color.

"A bread is missing. There were two left with the money. We agreed not to break those until we paid our share for the guide and bought food for the trip," she said in hushed tones. Her hands probed the bag. She was as pale as the milk in the buckets she had carried as a girl in Giebultow.

"Let me look." Mordche reached toward his sister.

262

"Look." Gitel shoved the bag to her brother.

Mordche searched the bag. He felt the bread at the bottom of the bag and ran his finger over the half-moon inscribed on it. There was only one left. They sat in disbelief. The constant din around them was unabated by this sudden terrible turn of events.

"I have a pretty good idea about who took the bread. Who's always hungry around here?" Aron said glaring at the empty nearby cots of Max and Manya. "Where is he?"

"Aron, you have no idea who took the bread. Even if it was Max, how would he know there was money baked into it?" Gitel said.

"Who watched our every move in Ksiaz Wielki? Who figured out you were pregnant? Maybe Manya knew before you knew, Gitel," Aron said, his jaw twitching.

"It won't do any good to point fingers. Maybe yes, maybe no. There are plenty hungry people here. You didn't steal when you were starving, Aron, Mordche?" Gitel stopped. "I stole for my child."

Aron jumped up enraged, shouting, "You think there has been a day, a night she's not in my heart? I'm breaking my fingers to get us out!" Burning acid reached his throat. The bitterness choked him. His shouts brought a beat of silence. Then the expression of angst was swallowed almost as fast as it had been spewed. Nerves had been stretched to their limits. Now this once operatic theater played live dramas. The arias were discordant, short bursts, fading until the next.

Aron sat. He looked straight ahead. Gitel moved to his cot and put her head on his stiff shoulder.

"So what are we going to do?" Halina said. She slid close to Mordche, her eyes wide on Aron.

"We're going to open the bread, hide the money, eat and live. That's what we're going to do," Gitel said. She passed around generous chunks in defiance of the discovery.

"Here comes Max now with a big smile on his face," Mordche said. "I bet he has more good news."

"Sure," Aron said. "Look at that son of a bitch." He ripped off a piece of bread, but it remained in his clammy palm, a lump of bad luck.

"Nobody has a word to say to him," Gitel said. "If he did it, one way or another the truth will spill out. In the meantime, let's listen. This should be the worst that happens to us from now on." Her stomach was in knots. She had to maintain composure. Everything she carried depended upon it. *Please, God, help me. Help us. I'm only human. I beg for your help.*

"I'll be alright," Aron said. "It passed." He stared at his wife and she met his gaze with a steadiness he needed.

Max walked toward them. Manya next to him seemed to melt away in the sweltering room. His smile revealed good news.

"Victyr is his name and we meet him near the railroad station as soon as we get to Prague." Max's lips glistened.

"Right, and how is he going to know when we arrive? One of my prized pigeons from when I was a boy will fly there with the news? Tell us again, Max. How much does he want?" Aron said, clenching his fists for control. His eyes bore into the man.

"He's excited." Max grinned and thrust his chin at Aron.

"Never mind, Max," Aron said. He took a step toward him. "You look pretty excited yourself. We agreed to take the train to Prague. So Mordche has been asking around. No one is checking. Poland is still a mess. They let us Jews go for free. Anything to get rid of us."

"Yup," said Mordche, "free as birds. Special payment for serving in the army and because they like us so much."

"You two are full of jokes today," Max said. "Papers, what about that? I want to make papers for Manya and me. What's making you so cheerful?"

Aron ignored the comment. Cheerful. *Look at him, he wants papers too.* That cost money and he was pretty sure Max hadn't come with much. But Gitel was right. They had to move forward. It was time to go and this was their best opportunity. A theft was not going to prevent them from trying to get free. "If we are sneaking over the Czech border to Germany, we can't worry about papers. We don't have the time or the money to make decent looking documents. Do you?"

Max shook his head. "We don't have the time."

"So if we increase the size of the group, like we discussed a few days ago, it will cost much less. You find a way to get word to this Victyr in Prague, Max," Mordche said.

"I thought you didn't want a big group because it was riskier?" Max said.

"We changed our minds," Gitel said. "Right, men?"

"Right," Aron and Mordche said as one.

"We looked at the train schedules. They're not exact. Nothing is. But an agent told us we go from Sosnowiec to Krakow and from Krakow to Prague. It's the only way," Aron said. "Our first chance is the day after tomorrow, if we catch a break."

Max tapped his foot. "I'm going to the train station. The telegraph office is there and I'll let my contact know. So when should I say?"

"Say the day after tomorrow," Aron said his hands in fists behind his back.

It was a crisp fall day, the pure air one of the glories Poland offered in early November. What they had come with was what they were leaving with minus the food and the money that had disappeared. The group expanded from the six of them to six more and they all boarded the train at Sosnowiec Station. Even more refugees crowded the train cars. This time Yiddish was heard from every compartment. The Poles returning from the East were coming home and the happiness of being on their soil shown from their thin faces.

In the afternoon the train stopped in Krakow Station. The enormous ivory brick buildings and alabaster columns stood untouched by Nazi bombs, the way they had remembered. They stood on the platform and waited for the transfer to Prague. Unimaginable. They were going to a foreign country and had no idea how they would be received, no knowledge of the language. How could they have agreed to such a thing? Were they insane to risk sneaking into Germany of all places? The word alone filled them with fright and hatred so deep it smothered them in poisonous rage. And the answers were always the same. They wanted the chance to live.

"This is it," Aron said. "When we board the next train it will the last of Poland for us."

"Good riddance," said one of the six who had joined them.

Halina stood next to Mordche, a reverie consuming her. Poland had been cruel to her entire family. "No, I never want to be in Poland again," she said, locking arms with Mordche, her man. He stood straight and tall, stoic. He stared at the track.

A train moved toward them to take them away. "We have come to this point. There's no turning back," Gitel said.

CHAPTER THIRTY-SEVEN

The Trek

While Victyr worked to expand the group so the travelers from Sosnowiec could satisfy their financial agreement, he sent another guide to the station. For a price, this man also smuggled refugees across the Czech border. He spoke Polish well enough to calm their worries over safety and asked if they were hungry. It was difficult for them to fathom this kind reception. Poland had offered hostility and death.

The man led them to Josefov, the ancient Jewish ghetto where the group was to be divided for the stay in Prague. Aron and Gitel moved through the streets entranced by red-tiled roofs, gilded stonework and soaring buildings. Prague had been fortunate unlike many European cities lying in rubble. The few kilometers they walked marked them as desperate asylum seekers – the displaced in flight. Still, they breathed the air of openness and it filled them with possibility, the sweet taste of freedom on their tongues.

Once in Josefov he turned onto Parizska Street, a stiff breeze kicking up from the river. He wound through alleyways, one building crushed against the next most that had housed centuries of their people. Until the Nazis. The man dropped Max and Manya, and the others at the arranged places. The last were the two inseparable couples, Aron and Gitel and Mordche and Halina. He halted at the Josefov Cemetery, a tangle of overgrowth. Dense with terracotta and ashen tombstones, the carved Hebraic letters were polished by time. The stones stood quiet, a hush of coolness emanating from a petrified world. With an impish smile, the guide pointed at tombstones leaning as if locked in debate and uttered the word 'golem'. They had heard stories of a wondrous rabbi who had created this creature. Here they stood, imagining which stone jutted forth and testified that it belonged to him. Centuries ago, the rabbi had fashioned the Golem from fire, water, air, and earth. It had sprung to life. The rabbi had meant for the Golem to do good. But the Golem had turned to evil destruction. Disbelieving and questioning, the four held onto each other. Was it the myth about the Golem of Prague or their own reality that was most difficult to believe, their feet touching this very ground.

The guide left them with a woman who lived in one of the ancient houses, a worn sign picturing book spines swaying beneath high arched windows. She was from a network of volunteers who had offered to feed the refugees. The woman covered her table with bread, Cheeses and *tredelnik*, fragrant Czech cinnamon buns. Food was what Aron, Gitel, Mordche and Halina had dreamed of. Its abundance and meaning filled their eyes with thankfulness. Jana was not a Jew nor did she speak Polish. But there were enough similarities with her Czech as they reached for words. They learned the woman had lost her husband and human-to-human their eyes met the pain that resided there. She saw they were embarrassed by their neediness and she encouraged them with her soothing voice and expressive hands. But when Jana's eleven-year-old son came home from school, he brought friendship. Kuba showed them his collection of badges, prizes he had earned for his special drawing talents. As a schoolboy, Mordche had excelled in map drawing. He and the boy became good friends.

A Josefov charity provided cots in a dormitory. But for Gitel they offered a high wood bed with carved posts. She had never slept in such luxury. She and Aron had not been in a bed since they had fled the attic in Ksiaz Wielki on a moonless November night. Aron brought her close and told her she was everything. That her face shone with the life she carried for them. Gitel closed her eyes, nestled her head on Aron's shoulder and felt the flutters of life. "If there is a Golem," she whispered in her husband's ear, "it should stay far away." *Not yet. When the time is right, when you will be safe.*

Days later, in the early morning hours, Jana brought them back to her home for the last time. After a quick meal, the woman with the open face whose actions told them more than words, put her hands together in a gesture of prayer then packed foods into Gitel's and Halina's bundles.

"I would not mind living in such a place, Aron told her. "This is how human beings can treat each other. I wish I could tell you in Czech, we will remember you and the people of *Praha*."

Gitel put in Jana's hand a little billfold Aron had stitched from the last leather pieces in his tool bag. It held a *zloty* and several *grochen*. "For your boy, Kuba." She hoped the words were recognizable. "Your son is smart and good like his mother. His father would be proud." They left the ancient house permeated with the spirits of a world they longed to know.

It was time to meet Victyr on the west side of the Vlata River, the exit point closest to the once Jewish ghetto. All sixteen refugees, their faces mirroring excitement and anxiety assembled by the Manesuv Most Bridge. Victyr's Polish was not good and the guide who had first greeted them had come along to help. But two men, Hungarians, spoke Polish and Czech. They became the translators. The guides collected the money. With this task done, Victyr gave the three hundred twenty zlotys to his partner and the deal was sealed.

First light shimmered on the river and they left in groups of four to avoid suspicion. The refugees reached the edge of the city and reassembled in the Kravoska Zahrada, the once beautiful gardens torched and destroyed. Victyr, wiry and strong from the missions he had undertaken, pulled a brown woolen cap snug over his ears to camouflage in the woods and on the mountain terrain. He surveyed the large group of ill-equipped refugees and his coal-black eyes stopped. Victyr pointed at Gitel.

"No one told me about a pregnant woman. She stays in Prague." One of the Hungarians came forward, hesitated for an instant, looked at Aron, and translated.

"She has to go," Aron said. "We paid."

Gitel stood quiet. *Isn't this what a wise woman must do?* Her heart began to throb with dread she would be left behind, Aron trapped with her.

Victyr shook his head with an emphatic no. "In the hurry to get off the bridge still dark, I didn't see. It will take us three days if we're lucky with such a big group. I've never taken a pregnant women." The Hungarian made the rapid translation, though the guide's meaning had been clear.

They all stared at Gitel.

One of the men in the group said, "I say they should have told you. I paid my money and I want to get to Germany. From there, is the only chance I have to get to a country that may let me immigrate. She's not going to stand in my way. What do you say to that?" The man slung his bundle onto his back and motioned forward with closed fingers. There were murmurs of agreement.

Aron said, "I vouch for my wife. If she has trouble, we'll see it right away. And if that's the case we'll track back to Prague. The rest of you can go on."

Victyr shook his head. The shorter of the two Hungarians echoed next to him. "Last trip we were robbed. The spirit was with us. No one was killed. I have one pistol with me and I'm not the best shot."

"I am," Aron said. 'And I'm not shy about it.'

The men faced one another. Aron's eyes, pools of angst and determination met Victyr's, sure and dominant. He stomped the heel of his thick boot. "I must be a crazy Czech," he said under his breath. "Tell him," and the Hungarian started almost in concert, "we make fifty kilometers a day. If his wife has any troubles, we leave them."

Victyr turned to the group and lowered his voice, the Hungarian echoing. "If we get stopped for any reason, I do the talking. Yes?" Sixteen pairs of eyes blinked acquiescence. He began to arrange them for the trek. The two Hungarian were behind him, the three emaciated men next. He motioned to Manya and Max and placed them behind Halina and Mordche. His eyes avoided Gitel and Aron as he moved the three women behind them. The last two men, who he sized up as fit enough, he instructed to take up the rear. "We're going to move fast. Stay together." The sun in bloom, Victyr led due south, away from the protection of Prague.

Hours later they were in the Sumava Czech forest. Still fresh from their days of rest in Prague, they trampled underbrush with enthusiasm, lulled by the rustling of stubborn golden leaves clinging to old growth oaks and silver beeches, the last of the trees to relinquish what sustained them.

"We stop here for food. No food, no energy. And if you have to go, don't wander. We must reach the Sumava Mountains, thirty kilometers from this point by dark."

The group sat, relieved. Gitel had to go more often now and Aron walked her behind clumps of fire-red bushes. "I see you're doing pretty good. But don't get too many fancy ideas."

"So far, not bad. This forest reminds me of when Vladyk made us leave the bunker."

"Come." He kissed her forehead, wanting to linger. "We don't want to give Victyr any more reason to think we're trouble."

They took off, woodpeckers hammering on towering tree trunks. As the terrain rose toward the mountains Victyr heard the beginnings of complaints. Not by voice but by the slower feet, the expected signs of fatigue. One of three women behind Aron and Gitel stopped short and sat. The men behind began to shout. Victyr ran back, his arms flying warnings for quiet. "Do you want to bring an enemy to us?" His black eyes popped with anger.

"My feet, I can't feel them," one of the three women cried. "Were you on a death march from Dachau? With filthy rags for shoes, in the bitter cold. You have no mercy."

The three emaciated men had suffered this torture. "It's true, what she tells," one of them said. "The Nazis were chased by Soviets from the East and Allies from the west. They ran like rats from their death camps. Those murderers. They tried to march us to Germany. By the thousands.

Walking skeletons. The ones too sick, the dead, they left in the fields and on the roads of Poland."

"Hush! All of you." Victyr pulled the pistol from his rucksack. He waved at them to drop.

Gitel kneeled next to the woman. "No one will hurt you here," she whispered. "It's not easy for any of us." She put her hand on the unyielding shoulder of the woman from Dachau. "We won't leave you."

The Hungarians took their positions behind the guide. More than pity emanated from their intelligent faces.

Victyr pulled off his cap, dropped to his knees and put an ear to the ground. "I don't know what it was, I hope an elk." He stood. "The more we stop with this kind of talk, I warn you, the more chance we'll get in trouble." The taller Hungarian translated the guide's admonitions. He threw pitying looks at the woman who must have been exquisite. Her refined bearing trying to hide the trouble she had caused. His eyes fell to the patched shoes.

"Get up," Victyr ordered. "Do you want to get there or not? If it rains, we go. If it hails or snows we don't stop. I don't care about your feet," he said to the woman. "Any of your feet. My job is to get you into Germany. Alive. Do you all understand?" He shoved the pistol back in his bag, reassembled the sixteen and forced a quick pace. In silence, they made the thirty kilometers the guide demanded of them and reached the Regen River to replenish water and bed down them for the night. Though it was cold, to make a fire was too risky. The trees reached their bare limbs to a black sky flecked with crystal jewels.

"Is there really a Golem?" Halina said sliding closer to Mordche.

"When you're young you believe such nonsense," Mordche said. "To me it's a *bubbe maisse*. I don't believe in a grandmother's fairy tales."

"Never mind the *bubbe maisse*," Gitel said to her brother, "just don't keep Halina too warm until a few things are settled." There was laughter from those still awake. She and Aron wrapped themselves in the goose down, this thing that seemed both warm and alive. How proud her mother had been to give it. *Mother, my dear mother if only you were here.*

Victyr woke them as the last stars extinguished. They stood stiff from sleep on the forest floor. He pointed ahead to the Sumava Mountains. A Hungarian began simultaneously. "The paths are narrow and you'll walk in single file. It's a steep climb but not too bad, and the shortest way. Put your things together."

Aron fell in behind Gitel to keep an eye on her. In front of them, Halina stumbled. She had never climbed a tree, nor run after a goose to stuff its gullet or raced through the meadows. Mordche steadied Halina when he saw her tentative, unsure steps. She had no choice but to climb.

On the descent, the trail twisted and dipped and was much steeper. Far off, ravens soared over what appeared a sea of greens and blues. A brisk wind flapped Gitel's scarf. She smiled and picked up speed. "Slow," Aron warned as she distanced herself. Misjudging her bulk, she sped down the trail. Instinctively she threw out her hands before she fell.

"Wild, you're just wild, are you ever going to learn?" Aron ran down. He pulled Gitel up and let out a worried sigh. "Where were you running? My God, are you alright?"

Gitel winced unsure.

The commotion stopped the group again. Victyr ran up like a stealthy cat. He shoved members against the mountain wall, and scooted between them "Is it your knee? I see your stocking is torn," he said.

"Lucky me," she said, "my big stomach saved me from falling on both." Gitel hid her scraped hands behind her. Her concern was neither for her hands or her knee. She knew she would be in turmoil until the moment she felt the next kick, if there was one.

"Can you make it down?" Victyr said pointing to where the trail widened. It's about a hundred meters."

"Don't worry, I'll help my wife." Aron gave Victyr a rueful look as the guide ran down. "What do you think you're hiding, Gitel? Show me what you did to your hands. I know you too well."

"Oh no," Halina said, her eyes on Gitel's heaving belly.

"Mordche," Aron said, "take Halina and keep going. That's the best you can do for us."

The guide concerned about the position of the other fourteen in his charge jockeyed between them and led the group to a natural clearing. The fourteen watched Aron and Gitel pick their way down.

"We'll rest here for food and water," Victyr said, scanning for signs of changing weather. The group slumped to the ground. "Not for long," he added. A wind picked up from the east but at least it would be behind them until they made camp for the night.

"You're a tough lady," Victyr said, smiling at the pregnant woman tending to herself. The women were gathered around.

"Didn't I tell you to stay in Sosnowiec?" Manya chirped.

Halina glared at her. Manya had depended on Gitel's generosity.

"Don't worry about me," Gitel said picking pebbles from her knee. She felt the sudden sharp kicks. Maybe she was freed her from what she feared most – that she had already failed.

"Leave her alone," the woman from Dachau said, her stunning slate eyes on Manya. "She does better than you and most of us women." She nodded toward the men engrossed with the guide. "Some of them, too."

They walked until night released their exhausted bodies. It had been eight more hours of grueling pace with breaks for food and water. The group of sixteen had made almost a hundred kilometers in two days. They sat close to the guide, breathing hard, rubbing aching legs, the heat from their bodies still providing warmth. Victyr settled them in the spot where he had camped with other groups. It was close to a small lake and a waning moon revealed the tight silver ripples.

"We're still in the Bohemian Forest, the Czech side, but only for a short time. Tomorrow, we go to the *Schwarzwald,* the Black Forest," the Hungarian translated. "Rest well. We start again in a few hours." There were moans and complaints. "We need the early start or you won't reach the DP camp till dark."

Streaks of orange light and the swaying treetops greeted them. Victyr stamped his feet and smacked his hands to warm from the cold night. They all followed suit. There was little conversation. Crossing the German border shook each mind with visions of what they had endured. Victyr flipped open his compass from habit and led them around the lake to fill water containers. They dipped their hands and splashed their faces, surprised to find the lake water was warmer than the fierce wind battling their clothing. The guide marshaled one group on the heels of the next and within an hour they were in the *Schwarzwald*.

Shadows from the walls of trees cast an impenetrable darkness. The canopy of fir, pine, spruce, oak and beech, even in November, conspired against the sun. Finally in Germany they moved as fast as the labyrinth of trees allowed. Aron's feet met the Black Forest floor and he was overwhelmed by thoughts of his time as a prisoner-of-war. He was on German soil. The war was over and Freiburg stalag in the past. Yet they were still in peril of being apprehended as Jews without papers, rights, or a country that wanted them. Always it had been Gitel, his passion for her that had lifted him up. His eyes rested on her roundness and Devoire Ita's face appeared. His spirit was lacerated and he doubted it would ever heal. Aron watched Gitel and felt both her strength and vulnerability. She was the keeper of their future. He sensed the weight of it in each of his resolute steps.

Before them was the peat bog, a vast, soggy open meadow of shallow rivulets in endless patterns flowing through shrubs, matted ferns, layers upon layers of plant life. They had never seen such a thing. Manya was in a twitter and Max steamed over her inadequacies. "I can't go any further," she whined. "I won't step into that slime."

There was panic over falling into the spongy matter. No one wanted to set a foot in, but there was no choice other than adding great distance and more time. Victyr paired the stronger men with the women and Max coaxed Manya along, threatening he would leave her to rot among the shrubbery if she did not shut her mouth. Reluctant, the group of sixteen started across the open bog.

They were in the swath of blue and green, the sea-like field they had seen the day before, high above from the Somava Mountains. Each dragged through, suddenly knee-deep in places, their shoes sucked by thick muck, their clothing saturated. Aron's heavy bag of tools banged at his side and he wondered how his wife in her seventh month had the strength. Her raw knee had to pain her yet she not had complained. Gitel's breathing intensified and Aron took the bundle from her shoulder. She laughed it was light as feathers. But the sweat on her brow told a different story. Aron gripped her hand and together, they dragged through the primordial mud.

Victyr bobbed among the taller shrubs as if his legs were iron springs. "It's almost over," he murmured to each. "Hold on," he encouraged, "we're almost at the end." Behind them the Black Forest receded. He had previously encountered trouble from marauders near the German town they were approaching. These wanton groups could be bribed but not always and from the size of this one, Victyr doubted they had enough money in the first place. The closer they got the more he was concerned. This was when the refugees he had escorted were totally exhausted and easy prey. This was the moment they had to be as unobtrusive as possible.

They were not.

Manya began to scream. Something had caught her. She was sure an animal was tearing her apart. Her hysteria rose. The group froze. Victyr growled at Manya to stop screaming and she began to whimper, a wounded dog whose master was about to put an end to it. Mordche ran up from behind, pulled Manya from the muck and threw her over his shoulder. Her shoe was gone. Victyr saw the advantage Mordche had given him to get out of their exposed position and he shoved the group into motion. "We're in danger," he yelled. He began to run. They followed, the houses and smoking chimneys in sight. The bog was melding into drier uplands, far easier on their footing. The terror of being caught now, after they could almost touch safety, charged them with bursts of strength.

Aron pulled as Gitel struggled through the last of the bog. They were side by side, the smile on her face telling him she was going to make it. With all her might Gitel strained forward hoping no harm would come to what she carried. Mordche, weary from the woman on his shoulder, birdlike or not, held a moment until Max caught up. "She's yours," he said righting Manya to her feet. What a prize, he thought as he ran back to catch hold of Halina. The young woman, her cheeks blowing out with relief took his hand and did her best to match his strides. The last of the group, the woman from Dachau and the three men in desperate condition were shepherded by the tall Hungarian. Victyr ran back to the laggards and released the Hungarian to run on his own. The four were doubled over barely able to catch their breaths. Victyr stayed with them, muscles tense, senses on alert for marauders who might still swoop in and derail his good fortune. They faltered as Victyr coaxed them out of the open meadow.

Finally his band of sixteen mud-covered, spent people stood together in the German border town. They stood mute in a place they had struggled to reach, their shoulders pulled inward. They took guarded steps, sniffing the air for danger. What would be their reception in this place, the incubator of horror? Germany.

The burghers used to seeing the disenfranchised and displaced passed the latest group of discarded humanity with unenthusiastic glances.

Victyr had done well. He had kept them moving and safe, guided them away from places he had encountered thieves, and encouraged them to brave the daunting distance. Now that they had reached the German state of Bavaria, he reiterated the directions to find the nearby DP camp. Each thanked the Czech again and again. Victyr gave Gitel a respectful nod, told Aron he was glad not to have seen his prowess with a pistol and slapped the backs of the Hungarian translators with whom he'd forged a kinship. To Mordche, he gave his broadest smile and winked toward the woman who stood with one shoe.

It was time for the group melded by the temporary bond to disburse, each to find his future. The guide turned east and left the bedraggled troop of refugees.

CHAPTER THIRTY-EIGHT

A False Beginning

Pocking Displaced Persons Camp was not far from where their guide had left them. Each hoped it would be a safe place where death did not hover. They spoke of freedom. For Aron and Gitel, it was where a child could begin to thrive. Filled with the dreams of a future, six from Ksiaz Wielki and two Hungarians followed a road traversing the cool meadows. A few horses communed on gentle rolling hills dotted with majestic pines.

Their minds commanded anesthetized feet and they refused to stop until the enormous yellow masonry church spire of Waldstaff Pine City came into view. They walked through the town, fooled by clean sidewalks and neatly attired burghers eager to get home before dark. On the outskirts of Waldstaff the muffled roar and ugliness of Pocking DP was revealed.

Rows and rows of low barracks with rusted roofs sat on a rutted road, a massive warren that once held worker slaves for the Nazis and now housed seven thousand abandoned people. Many were ill, angry, and unhinged. Most were disheartened. A few had reunited with family. A man in blue, a camp policeman waved them into the filth-strewn yard, the maw of the beast. There were hundreds milling, a low roar of voices pitched with the urgency of securing rations from carts, wheel barrows, or from the back of a tarped truck. From center of the confusion, a woman limped toward Gitel.

She shook her head and flailed her arms at the darkening sky. "Don't step into this hell. Babies were killed, here. By a German, may she burn in hell, like they burned my people." The woman brought her fists to her breasts and pounded what lay inert. Her voice gravel, she said, "Run as fast as you can."

"Chaya, you *meshugganah*," the camp policeman screamed. "You go to hell." He turned to the eight of them. "This is what I must deal with. The crazy, night and day."

Gitel and Aron's eyes met. Chaya. Her name had different meanings. The word could mean animal. Or the word could mean life.

"I tell the truth. I swear on the ashes of my little ones." She reached a purple tattooed arm to Gitel.

"I warn you, one more word from you, Chaya. You'll get nothing to put in your ugly, toothless mouth."

"There's nothing here," she spat. "He's a big shot. Ask him what he did in our death camp. Look at him. He has, we starve. Save your baby." She moved to put a shriveled hand on Gitel's.

"Please," Aron said, fear for his wife, pity for this creature. "Please don't touch her."

Gitel took the woman's hand and laid it on her belly. Her eyes filled with tears for the woman, for herself, for all the babies who were no more. The woman looked at Gitel's protruding belly and limped away. The eight stood hungry, depleted. They followed the DP policeman across the yard to the induction hut. There were five refugees in front of them. The eight of them sat on their bundles carried from Poland to Czechoslovakia to Germany.

Chaya had not made up her story. It had happened six months before Pocking was converted to a refuge camp. A hundred babies were born to inmates of the concentration camp. Most with deformities, a German midwife smothered the babies. Mercy, she had said when she was caught. She had performed mercy. Aron and Gitel were shaken.

When their turn came Aron said, "We learned there's no hospital here. My wife has had troubles giving birth and we've lost a child. There's a short time left to find a place where she has a chance. If I had money, I would give it all away. I'm a shoemaker. I will give you my tools."

"Keep your tools. Should I treat you better than all of them?" He pointed to the yard, the angry din, the putrid smells unhidden by the darkness.

"She carries our future and for our people," Aron implored.

The Hungarians stepped away but the others from Ksiaz Wielki made a wall around the man at the table. Max pulled four stained bills from his jacket and laid them on the table. He avoided the eyes glaring at his hand, breaths audible from those whom he had known since childhood.

"What am I supposed to do with worthless Polish *zlotys*?" the man grimaced and shoved the bills back at Max.

Mordche leaned over the table. "There are men roaming your yard who will find uses. That's my sister. The last I know alive of my family."

The man took the crumpled *zlotys* from the table and promised to see what could be done. They stared at Max. None said a word. The group left to find the assigned barracks.

Gitel could not sleep. Chaya's story fed her superstitions. Her senses searched the heatless room for anything that moved. She shivered with dread that someone would once again kill what she bore. Her body demanded rest and when she could no longer resist, she fell into a fretful sleep. The Golem, disguised as a barren woman, crawled on its haunches searching to fill an empty womb, the mouth agape in soundless sorrow. Gitel called out garbled sobs from her sleep. Was Chaya an angel sent to protect? Or was she the foreboding omen of a disaster to unfold?

The next day, Friday morning, the six were told to load their things into a truck bound for Foehrenwald Displaced Persons Camp, near the town Wolfratshausen. The truck was on the weekly run to pick up any supplies Foehrenwald DP could spare for its poor sister, Pocking. The driver stood to the side and relished a cigarette. From behind the barracks the two Hungarian men appeared. One spoke to the driver in Polish. "We learned you are taking our friends to a better camp."

"I don't care what you learned," the driver said. "If some of the others begging to get out of this shit place see, I'll have a revolution on my hands."

The Hungarians jumped into the truck.

"Get out of there, you bastards," the driver hissed.

"What's the difference?" Aron said. "The truck is empty. They were with us the whole time from Prague. Without them we would have had bigger problems."

"I'm sick of all of you and your problems. I'm a Jew, too. But it never stops. We do a favor and what happens? It's not enough."

"We're not Jews," the shorter of the two Hungarians said. His hand fanned out currencies to the driver. Hungarian pengos, Polish *zlotys* and German Reich marks. "Take them," he said from the shelter of the truck.

"Money talks in every language," Mordche said to the driver. "You'll buy a lot of cigarettes with that. He lifted Halina into the truck.

Lots of surprises. Gitel glanced at Max hidden in the shadows of the tarp. Manya carped. *I'll bet Max parted with our money last night.* Gitel mulled this over in her mind and waited for Aron to help her into the cab of the truck.

Aron smiled at her. "I hope you bake again soon. This time with just extra sugar." He jumped into the back of the truck with the others.

The driver flicked the last of his cigarette, stuffed the fanned bills from the outstretched hand into his coat pocket and said, "Let's go."

CHAPTER THIRTY-NINE

Foehrenwald

Gitel sat in the cab, one arm tight around her middle, the other braced against the metal door. The driver lit cigarette after cigarette, each stub igniting the next and ground the stubborn gears, cursing. The truck banged over the barely passable roads, but made the hundred eighty kilometers in five hours. They arrived in Wolfratshausen, Gitel green with motion sickness, dizzy from the cigarette smoke.

"This is where I stop," the driver said. The eight of them stood away from the truck happy to smell air free of exhaust. "From here you follow the road for three kilometers. My truck has a drop of petrol left. It's a miracle we made it."

Gitel thought it was a miracle she was in one piece.

They walked again. Aron and Gitel had been promised there was a hospital in the Foehrenwald DP. Was that true? Would this refuge camp be any different? Competition was fierce for the better camps. Would they be allowed to stay, was on each mind. The trek that had begun on a Monday before the sun rose in Prague was now in its fifth day. Aron knew they had to stop running. His face was pinched from worry. The truck ride had been hard. That on top of the enormous undertaking his wife had managed. Gitel did not want to alarm Aron further. She walked in silence with Halina on one side, Manya on the other. She fought the nausea and moved her swollen legs with trepidation.

The men walked and listened to the Hungarians. A decade before they were young lawyers employed by a well-respected law firm. They had been removed from their homes in Budapest in 1944 for joining an anti-Soviet party. The Soviets, in the throes of taking power from the retreating Nazis, eliminated Hungarians opposing them. Caught in the middle by the sympathizing Horthy regime, the two had escaped to Pest. They were swept up with Jews and dissidents and ended up as slave labor in Auschwitz-Birkenau. The war over or not, they feared retribution from the Soviets in power. The Hungarians had to find a country that would grant them political asylum.

The day was bleak and the north wind blew a stinging drizzle as they approached Foehrenwald DP Camp. The eight sojourners stopped in an open yard. Numerous pitched roofed double story buildings radiated on streets and formed a small village. Rain did not hamper the hundreds wandering, animatedly talking in the central area. Numerous lines snaked in front of various buildings. People jostled for positions. Aron asked a couple where to register and if there was a hospital, hoping they were not too late on the race for space.

The woman pointed to a building that had been designated as a hospital. They stared at Gitel, a pregnant anomaly among the thousands of women in the camp. "Don't expect a palace," the man smiled, scanning pleasant looking buildings. "Appearances can be deceiving. They squeezed six thousand in here, more than double the capacity. We live in hope to take the next step out of this place," he said. Not with anger but optimism he explained they would find a way.

The man wants out. I need to get my wife and me in were Aron's urgent thoughts.

Aron's eyes lighted on straggly evergreens demarcating streets. He asked what was this place, Foerhenwald. The man explained that I.B. Farben, a giant German company had been one of the most powerful in the world. They built this complex to house twenty-nine hundred workers secretly making munitions and chemicals for the German war machine. Without them, the Nazi war effort would not have been possible he emphasized. The man was a chemist before the war he seemed pleased to add and was aware I.B. Farben still had powerful tentacles gripping the world.

"Men." Gitel interrupted, "They say women can talk."

Aron looked at her, mortified. "I'm so sorry, Gitel. Forgive me."

"I only hope when the time comes, the conversation won't be about politics." She took Aron's arm and he felt her full weight, Gitel unable to make light of her worries.

They were assessed for Foehrenwald intake. This was one of the three largest among the network of camps hastily set up in the American Zone by a Jewish group, the American Joint Distribution Committee and the United Nations Relief and Rehabilitation. The camp was overwhelmed with mostly Jewish refugees. They needed shelter, food and medicine to restore their damaged bodies. They needed clothing, a way to make a living again, relief from the demons plaguing their minds and most of all, to be accepted by a country that would allow them to immigrate.

A soft-spoken man asked Aron questions and wrote answers on triplicate forms. From which country do you hail? Where were you born? What is your level of education? Where were you during the war? Do you have a profession? Are you suffering from a disease? Are you aware of surviving family? Have you anything of value?

The room full of people looked at Gitel. It was clear she was carrying something of great value.

They were admitted as wind cleaned the clouds away. The three couples were sent to a building on Ohio Street. It was one of the houses in the sparsely wooded complex subdivided to hold more than was possible. In the tumult of a room shared by twenty, they dropped their bundles on the assigned single beds. Many served two people. Halina giggled when she saw Gitel shaking a finger at Mordche.

It was Friday. The sun was setting and a few women prepared to light Sabbath candles. In the years Gitel had been hiding or on the run, when there were no candles, her mind lit with tradition and she always remembered. The women saw her condition and brought a plate of candle stumps and a box of matches.

Gitel stood. Her head was covered with a kerchief and she raised her hands to cover her face. Aron was by her side. Tears fell on her cheeks. She recited the Hebrew words.

Baruch atoh Adonai Eloheinu melech ha'olam asher kidishanu b'mitz'vosov v'tzivanu l'had'lik neir shel Shabbos.

The steam from a radiator whistled softly and ten women repeated the blessing with Gitel. In room after room in the buildings set in the refugee camp it was recited, this most basic of all Jewish rituals almost obliterated.

Blessed are you, Lord, our God, sovereign of the universe who has sanctified us with His commandments and commanded us to light the lights of Sabbath.

Foehrenwald Displaced Persons Camp did not have all they had needed yet when complaints arose Aron and Gitel remembered the hayloft, the woods, the bunker and Aron's captivity. They could not stop thinking of the hunger that had eaten their bodies and will. They could not stop mourning the family and the child they had lost. But they had managed to be together. Aron and Gitel learned what needed to be done to live in Foehrenwald. There were rules. When to line up for rations, where to line up for concerns about health, how to register for job training classes, how to request accommodation with only six to eight in a room, when an emigration counselor could advise them, where to check for family members listed alive or dead. There were crowds and waits for everything. The most important questions were about how they were going to make a home for the child. God willing, Gitel added, to ward off the evil eye and concerns about the hospital for when the time came.

The streets in the complex were named after American states. Manya and Max moved to another building on Ohio Street. The time had come to separate. There had always been an uneasy peace. Aron never asked Max about the money. Though it no longer mattered, his mistrust had not changed from the first time he had seen Max in Sosnowiec and long before in the town they would never see again, Ksiaz Wielki. Just a week later Aron, Gitel, Mordche and Halina were transferred to Indiana Street. They shared a room with only four others, a great improvement. Khaki army blankets divided the room for a bit of privacy and they had the luxury of two toilets and two sinks in their building section, housing fifty-four people.

At the end of December Gitel was in her thirtieth year and in the ninth month of pregnancy. In their dingy, cramped room, she found ways to make them comfortable. She cooked on a communal stove and delighted her neighbors with the scents that brought reveries of lost family and a once home life. Halina, a willing student at her side, kept Gitel from dwelling about how Devoire Ita had been born. There was no Dr. Yoblonski here. Gitel's worries grew as the baby kicked with vigor.

Winter came fierce and blanketed the camp in Bavarian whiteness. They acclimated and began dreaming about a country where they would be accepted to live in freedom. The four practiced saying the American street names, breaking their tongues on Missouri, Kentucky, Florida, Illinois, pronunciations that made them laugh with the challenge. Maybe, maybe America would accept them. And they dreamed of Palestine. Maybe. Maybe there.

Aron formed a partnership with a young apprentice and word spread that the Indiana shoemakers were the best in Foehrenwald. Mordche sized up the situation and made trips to Wolfratshausen. Halina tagged along. They planned to get married in the spring and she walked as a proud woman beside her husband to be. Trading was in Mordche's blood and he was driven to find a commodity. He came back excited, with news he was making contacts with jewelry merchants. Aron wondered if 'trading' meant the black market. Mordche smiled and explained. He shook his head at his brother-in-law with the perfect shot, straight as an arrow and winked, "Gray, the gray market."

CHAPTER FORTY

1946 The Shoemaker's Daughter

In January, Gitel had nightmares. She kept the others in the room awake, the strung blankets inadequate to muffle her restless moans. When he was not hunched over the shoes and boots, Aron ran to stand in long lines for extra rations of canned milk. Gitel needed to stay as strong as she could for what they feared, another breech birth. Or the unthinkable. No one had given birth in the camp thus far. Their hospital only served the very sick. Though Gitel never thought of her condition as a sickness.

She had become a celebrity. Eyes followed her bigness wherever she went. Gitel was careful. She walked the yard and left long strides in the deep snow. "Soon," she'd say when women in the camp stopped her. Some would place a hand on her belly, wishing for new life. And from all the bellies Gitel saw growing around the camp perhaps she had magic. Perhaps pregnancy was contagious.

Then it began. She was in labor again. Gitel recognized the feelings as the same ones she had experienced years before when Dr. Yoblonksi had attended her. "It's time," she said to Aron. Now everyone in the room was aware, a tiny bulb from the ceiling, illuminating the event.

She gripped Aron's hand. "We have to go." Snow fell on the American named streets and few people wandered on them.

"Mordche," Aron said, "hurry to the hospital and tell them Gitel is coming."

Mordche returned with the news that the night doctor had not yet arrived.

It was late in the evening. Aron walked beside Gitel, his arm tense, intertwined with hers. He was taking the woman who meant more to him than his own life to an unproven hospital. His heart pounded with every slip on the ice- covered streets until finally they were in front of the hospital building. He let go of Gitel's hand into one of a nurse's not knowing what else he could do. Aron had let go of her hand once before, never to see what she had bore. There was no trusted Doctor Yablonski, the Pole in Ksiaz Wielki they had so admired.

Aron waited, listening to his wife's cries behind a closed door. No, it was not going to be an easy birth. His head was in his hands and his thoughts collided. This new life, would they be blessed with it? Did he deserve this? What was his purpose and how had he survived when there were so many who had not. Perhaps he was spared to be a witness, to tell of the suffering that had befallen his family, his people. It would be his obligation to tell the truth. He had learned too much about humanity, the evils, the ugliness, as well as the good, and the mercies. Gitel. She was a believer. And he believed in her. He did not know what else to do. He bowed his head and began to pray for his wife and his unborn child.

One of the nurses on duty tended to Gitel. They waited for the doctor. Maybe it was just the snow. But it had happened before. The night doctor had just not appeared. Gitel's contractions came more frequently. The nurse did her best to help her, the only woman so far to test the camp hospital for birth.

And still a doctor did not arrive.

"I know you're trying to help me," Gitel cried. "I feel the baby coming. I think feet first." The nurse knew with a breech birth once the labor became intense, there was danger the baby would become asphyxiated. This woman's contractions were perilously close.

The nurse squeezed Gitel's shaking hands. "I hear a doctor! You will be helped. I know he hears you. Please, try to be calm."

From the outer room, the other nurse on duty assisted the doctor. She gathered what he commanded as he scrubbed. He was the German doctor assigned to Foehrenwald from the better-equipped hospital in Wolfratshausen. "Of all nights," he said. "I waited for my relief to show up. He's late. Or he's not coming. I was about to leave for home. Something pulled me back."

Aron sat and waited. He prayed for forgiveness and for help.

"She has to be the one who came to me last week," the doctor said. "She told me she was worried. That she had troubles giving birth. All women are worried, I assured her."

"This baby and I have been running for months," she said.

"You are lucky, I told her, that you have held on this long. She looked straight into my eyes. You'll be my luck she said. This time, you'll be my good doctor."

Awful cries came from the room where Gitel lay.

"Let's take a look at her," the doctor said.

Gitel recognized the German doctor and implored him with her eyes. The baby was ready to emerge feet first.

January 15, 1946, exactly one year to the day after Aron and Gitel were liberated from their imprisonment in the bunker, the first child was born in Foehrenwald Displaced Persons Camp. The birth record stated Aron and Gitel were the parents of an infant girl. The child was healthy. A miracle. Conceived in a town from where her parents had fled. The child had survived an implausible journey and was born with the help of a German doctor. She bore the legacy of two people who had a passion for one another and the luck and the will to live. They were a family again. Aron and Gitel longed for freedom and were going to fight for a country and their child Hinda Ruchel Matuszyńska, the shoemaker's daughter.

GLOSSARY

a mensch tracht un gut lacht 'man plans and God laughs' Yiddish

bahnshutz 'dog handler' German

beshefinish 'newly created life' Yiddish

bubbe maisse 'old wives' tale' Yiddish

cheder 'school for youngsters' Yiddish

chuppah 'wedding canopy' Yiddish

ciotka 'aunt' Polish

Commandant 'Commander' German

da bude 'go to your shack' (dog house) Polish

danka 'thank you' German

daven 'pray' Yiddish

dorf 'rural village' Yiddish

dreidel 'small spinning toy' Yiddish

du bist ah yid 'You are a Jew' Yiddish

Dzień dobry 'good day' Polish

Einsatzgrupen 'Nazi mobile killing units' German

gehenna 'hell' Yiddish

gewehr 'weapons' German

goyim 'non-Jews' Yiddish

grochen 'small denomination of coins' Yiddish

havdalah 'Jewish ceremony that marks the end of the Sabbath' Yiddish

heil 'hail' German

Herr 'Sir' German

Hrabia 'a nobleman, Count or Lord' Polish

hondle 'negotiate back and forth' Yiddish

hund 'dog' German

Judes 'Jews' German

kapota 'long black coat' Yiddish

kapusta 'cabbage soup' Polish

kara 'tax/fine' Polish

kino 'movie or movie house' Yiddish

kiddush 'prayer with bread and wine for the Sabbath' Yiddish

kovid 'honor' Yiddish

kreig 'war' German

kugel 'pudding' Yiddish

kubelwagen 'jeep-like vehicle' German

Kristallnacht 'Night of the Broken Glass' German

latkes 'potato pancakes' Yiddish

l'chaim 'to life' Yiddish

linxt 'left' German

mazel 'luck' Yiddish

mazel tov 'good luck' Yiddish

mensch 'upstanding human being' Yiddish

meshugge "crazy' Yiddish

mezuzah 'small, metal encased prayer holder on door frames' Yiddish

mitug 'midday dinner' Yiddish

negidestes 'wealthy lady' Yiddish

offizierslagers 'officer prisoner of war camp' German

Pan 'sir' Polish

Porets 'Landowner' Yiddish

Prosze Panie 'Please, Sir (the respectful, formal use of sir)' Polish

rechts 'right' German

Reichsfuhrer 'Reich leader' German

schlachta 'noble classes' Polish

schnell 'fast' German

shaitel 'wig' Yiddish

shiksa 'gentile woman' Yiddish

shiva 'seven day, ritual wake for the dead' Yiddish

shochet 'ritual kosher slaughterer' Yiddish

shteibel 'small prayer house' Yiddish

shweine 'pig' German

siddur 'daily prayer book' Yiddish

slivovitz 'plum whiskey' Yiddish

sloyikahs 'jars' Yiddish

soldaten 'soldiers' German

tanta 'aunt' Yiddish

tehillim 'psalms' Yiddish

tot 'dead' German

tsuris 'life troubles' Yiddish

untermenschen 'undesirable humans' German

verboten 'forbidden' German

vinkl 'little corner' Yiddish

warschtadt 'workroom and the array of tools' German

wurst 'sausage' German

yenta 'gossipy woman' Yiddish

Yidl mitn fidl, Arie mitn bass 'Julius with his fiddle, Arie with his bass' Yiddish song the 1936 movie *Yidl Mitn Fidl*

zlotys 'currency, paper money' Polish

zug 'train' German

Żyd 'Jew' Polish

Made in the USA
Lexington, KY
18 March 2017